A Union Not Blessed

A Union Not Blessed.

James Green

Chapter One

Philadelphia

Library Hall, home of the American Philosophical Society

10.30 a m Wednesday March 13th 1805

'Treason, sir. An ugly word and a dangerous one.'

'Would you prefer me to dissemble, sir, an outright lie perhaps?'

Anthony Merry, Envoy Extraordinary to the United States of His Britannic Majesty, King George III, shifted uneasily in his chair. His blunt companion was Aaron Burr, lately Vice President to Thomas Jefferson.

Merry sat back and tried to look at his ease.

'Let it be called treason then, Mr Burr, as it will be your neck in the noose if you fail.'

The room in which they sat was liberally supplied with comfortable chairs and writing desks, the walls lined with books and the high ceiling decorated with ornate plaster-work. The venue had been well chosen by Burr, their presence in such a place would arouse no particular comment nor any surprise, and the time of day gave them the room to themselves. If two men of consequence happened to cross paths while in Philadelphia, what more natural than that they should meet and talk and if both were of a philosophical turn of mind then what better place than the home of the Philosophical Society?

'Come, sir, an answer if you please. Will London support me?'

'My dear Mr Burr, you are a person intimately familiar with the workings of governments so you of all people must know

1

that I cannot give you any such assurance.'

'Mr Merry, today I am no more than a private citizen. But as you say, I do indeed know intimately how governments work, so my question to you again is, will the British support me?'

'Do you ask me as Envoy from the Court of St. James or do you ask it, keeping in mind where we are meeting, as a philosophical question?'

'I ask it as a blunt question and expect an equally blunt answer.'

'Oh dear, American directness. Tell me, Mr Burr, why are bad manners considered a virtue in this country of yours?'

'Take care, sir. Envoy or no I'll not sit and be insulted by you or anyone else.'

'But my dear sir, I do not refer to you. My comment was drawn from my experiences of your illustrious President Mr Jefferson.'

'To hell with Jefferson and to hell with your experiences. Answer my question or bid me good day.'

'Well then. If, and I stress the if, His Majesty's Government decided to offer you some support for your venture what would you expect?'

'Three frigates and as many support craft as necessary to hold open New Orleans.'

'No forces on the ground?'

'No. The troops needed are already arranged.'

'Indeed! You have a private army somewhere?'

Burr ignored the question.

'And five hundred thousand dollars.'

'You say the sum lightly, sir, as if it were mere small change.'

'So it is to the British Crown.'

'No, sir. It is a great deal of money, a very great deal.'

'A pittance to get the Louisiana Territories. Two years ago Jefferson paid almost four million dollars to the French for them. Or don't you think they are worth it? I dare say I could go to the Spanish if your war with Napoleon has so emptied your treasury.'

Envoy Merry edged towards an answer.

'And if I was to recommend the support of your venture, what assurances could you give me that our money and ships will be a sound investment?'

Aaron Burr gave Merry a somewhat pitying smile.

'Your father was a successful London wine merchant, was he not? I therefore presume you are a person intimately familiar with the workings of business so you must know that I cannot give you any such assurance. Or do you, keeping in mind where we are, ask the question merely as a philosophical speculation?'

Anthony Merry, justly rebuked, returned the smile.

'Touché, sir.'

Aaron Burr leaned forward.

'Merry, you do not know me well, but you know me well enough to understand that I do not waste my own time nor that of others. I can deliver the Louisiana Territories. The military resources are already available to carry it out. What I need is money and sufficient sea power to ensure that America cannot blockade the mouth of the Mississippi. That is all I will tell you at this time. Now, sir, there are other people I must see and places I must go. You agreed to come here to Philadelphia to this meeting so I assume you take my offer seriously. Well then, will the British support me?'

Anthony Merry felt uncomfortable. This man, lawyer, soldier, politician, co-founder of the American nation and until so very recently Vice President, was a formidable man, a serious man. And he would not be put off any longer. Merry doubted very much whether he would go to the Spanish, but he might, he just might. The Louisiana Territories were vast and opening up rapidly. Merry couldn't even begin to calculate their economic potential. But in Burr's ambitious venture he saw something far more important than commercial gain; he saw the possibility of recovering Britain's lost colonies. Added to which he had a strong personal reason to support the venture, his intense loathing of President Thomas Jefferson. Ever since Merry had arrived in Washington Jefferson had been at pains to insult and belittle Britain through him.

'And if I recommended support, Mr Burr, what exactly are you offering?'

'I can take the Territories but I couldn't hold them, not without naval support and more troops. When I become master of the Louisiana Territories …'

'And, of course, take a suitable title. King perhaps? Emperor?'

Aaron Burr ignored Merry's facetious question.

'When I will control the Territories I am prepared to allow Britain to station troops there and give full facilities to the Royal Navy in New Orleans. I will also grant full and free passage for British trade on the Mississippi River. That would give King George a highway to ship goods from Lower Canada through the Territories all the way to the Caribbean.'

'You would trust us that far?'

'No, not trust. As you said, I am intimately familiar with the workings of governments and from my recent experience at the hands of my own government I would say that my days of trusting anyone, anyone at all, are well behind me. I have been a soldier, sir, you have not. I understand warfare. Believe me when I tell you that this thing is done in all but name, if your government supports me.'

And Anthony Merry found that he did indeed believe him and, although he could never like the man, decided he would recommend to London that they support him in his venture to become master of the Louisiana Territories. Merry's only regret was that by the time the thing was done Thomas Jefferson might have served out his second term and would no longer be President when British troops were once again garrisoned on American soil and the Union Flag flew from His Majesty's warships in the mouth of the Mississippi.

'Well then, Mr Burr, I will make my recommendation and if London accepts it you will have your ships and your money. But the decision rests with London. All I can do is recommend.'

Aaron Burr stood up.

'I ask no more. Good day, sir.'

And without offering his hand he turned and left.

Several days later, from Washington, Anthony Merry despatched a letter to Lord Mulgrave, Secretary of State for Foreign Affairs ...

I am encouraged to report to your Lordship the substance of some secret communications which Mr Aaron Burr has sought to make to me since he has been out of office. Mr Burr has mentioned to me that the inhabitants of Louisiana, the lands recently purchased from France, seem determined to render themselves independent of the United States and the execution of their design is only delayed by the difficulty of obtaining previously an assurance of protection and assistance from some foreign power. It is clear that Mr Burr means to endeavour to be the instrument for effecting such a connection. He pointed out the great commercial advantage which His Majesty's dominions in general would derive from furnishing almost exclusively, as they might through Canada and New Orleans, the inhabitants of so extensive a territory. Mr Burr observed it would be too dangerous and even premature to disclose to me at present the full extent and detail of the plan he had formed. In regard to military aid, he said two or three frigates and the same number of smaller vessels to be stationed at the mouth of the Mississippi to prevent its being blockaded by such force as the United States could send and to keep open the communications with the sea would be the whole that would be wanted; and in respect to money the loan of about one hundred thousand pounds would, he conceived, be sufficient for the immediate purposes of the enterprise.

Aaron Burr, after his secret meeting with Anthony Merry, continued his clandestine journey. He left Philadelphia for Pittsburgh where he had arranged to meet an old army colleague with whom he had served in the late war and who had subsequently prospered considerably in his military career, not least from Burr's quiet but insistent support when Vice President. It was this colleague who would now return those favours and provide him with the army he needed. After that he would take boat down the Ohio River to meet a man who had already created for himself his own small kingdom, albeit only an island one, but whom he felt sure would be both able and willing to provide funds and other necessary support for his venture.

It was perhaps not altogether true that the thing was done in all but name. But that had been, at Merry's own suggestion, more a philosophical answer to a philosophical question. He almost had his army, soon he would have funds and now, he felt sure, he had the support of the British.

Aaron Burr was well pleased with his progress and he allowed himself to consider whether his answer to Ambassador Merry had been so very philosophical after all. For once the thing was done in name then it would be done in fact and he would be a private citizen no more. Nor would he have to serve as second-in-command to some vain, weak ingrate. As for titles, others may have joy of that false grandeur and welcome. King he was happy to leave to Mad Farmer George and Emperor to the likes of Napoleon.

No, they were tyrants all and he had fought long and hard to throw off the yoke of such ancient tyranny. The title he wanted was the only one worth having. What Congress had denied him he would take for himself. He would be acknowledged at last by Jefferson, Adams, Clinton and all the others as President, President of a free nation made up of free men. President Aaron Burr.

Chapter Two

The Gallows Tree Club, Boston, Massachusetts.

3.30pm Friday March 15th 1805

'Gentlemen, I think I speak for all right-minded men of business and patriotism when I say that this is an age of golden promise …'

A loud snort interrupted.

'Dammit, sir, if I hear one more jackanapes tell me that this is an age of golden promise, then hang me if I won't call him out. Call him out, sir, and damn well shoot him down.'

There was an uneasy stirring. Lunch had been taken and the best business brains of Boston had foregathered, as was their custom, to smoke, take wine or coffee and set America and the world to rights.

But things were not going well, no one in that gilded room of powerful minds and high morals was truly comfortable. Peace there might be, but the times were unsettled and tensions rose too quickly even among friends.

Having gained the floor with his outburst the Angry Man pressed his advantage.

'Damn and blast any golden promise. What we have, gentlemen, is a mess, a political porridge of incompetence, corruption and damned self-serving.'

An ally took up the theme.

'And porridge of any sort, as we all know, is poor food for business to work well on. Gentlemen, I run merchantmen, and trade must …'

An opposition sniper, keen to disrupt this new advance, chanced a shot at the Angry Man.

'Corruption you say?'

The Angry Man glared at his questioner.

'Corruption I said and corruption I meant.'

But the sniper had aimed well for other than glowering at his assailant the Angry Man failed to take his accusation any further and the leader of the Golden Promise faction re-took the field.

'If our government's all you say it is, sir, and if you say it is I must defer to your superior knowledge of such things …' and here he smiled, paused and looked about him to let the slower minds take up his satirical intent. 'If it is indeed as you say, then how do you account for the Louisiana Territories?'

There were murmurs of assent and support. Golden Promise had, without doubt, made a significant advance.

But the Angry Man, though he had suffered a setback, was not ready to admit defeat.

'And why do we have the Louisiana Territories? Money, sir, money. Those territories were bought and paid for with solid American dollars made by honest men, men of business not damned politicians.' The tide of battle swayed once again. Golden Promise was forced to give up his gained ground. To attack the Angry Man's point meant attacking money and business, always a bridge too far. The Angry Man pressed his advantage. 'Jefferson sits in the clouds in that new capital Washington while honest business is hedged about with laws and taxes. Honest men make the money and damned politicians …'

But he paused. It was all very well to damn politicians but you had to have something to actually damn them with.

Another ally stepped into the breach and eyed the sniper.

'You asked earlier about corruption, sir. Well, my friend here is a man of sentiment and discretion, and being such a man he declined to name names. But I'm given to plain speaking so I'll give you a name, sir. Yes indeed, I'll give you a name'. He paused, looked about him at the expectant faces, then exploded his mine. 'New York.' He sat back and looked with ample satisfaction at his handiwork. Heads nodded and looks were exchanged, words of agreement were spoken and muttered. Seeing that it had been a masterstroke, the ally pressed on. 'New York is left free to gather to itself the scum of the earth, to fill itself with Jews, Irish and God knows what else. It hauls in the polyglot sweepings of Europe by the boatload and uses them to steal the bread out of the mouths of true-born Protestant Americans. And who runs New York? Is it men of business, honest men of sweat and toil like ourselves? No, gentlemen, it is not. New York is run by idle, self-serving jacks-in-office, damned politicians.'

The Angry Man looked around enjoying his ally's victorious assault. Attack New York and Boston fell in line to a man. The defeat was turning into a rout. He drove home his ally's success

'Look to New York and you'll soon see exactly what I mean about politicians, gentlemen, exactly what I mean.'

The feeling took the room.

'Damned porridge, couldn't have put it better myself.'

'Scum of the earth.'

'Jews.'

'Irish.'

'What the hell does polyglot mean?'

'New York.'

'Then why not damn well say so?'

The Angry Man and his allies sat back well satisfied. The field was theirs, Golden Promise was in the basement with no takers. With no more need of anger he took undisputed possession of the field and continued. 'Look at the place, gentlemen, could anyone here breathe its air and not feel tainted?'

His ally shared the victory.

'And look at the men who run the place, villains all.'

It was a mistake.

New York, in the abstract, as a name and a rival, was fair game. But men were individuals and were far from abstract. Republican Democrats and Federalists in the room readied themselves to defend their own.

Yes, indeed, a mistake had been made, a strategic blunder in the very moment of victory and it was quickly taken up.

'What's that? Put names to these villains, sir. Do you mean Clinton?'

'No, sir, no. Not Clinton of course.'

A retreat.

'Then who? Schuyler, perhaps.'

Neutrals began to stir and take an interest.

'Dammit, I served with Schuyler.'

'Damn fine officer, good-looking wife as I remember.'

'Burr? Do you say Aaron Burr's a villain?'

The ally realised too late his error and knew that without relief he was doomed. He turned to his Captain who looked at him as if to say, fear not, I shall not fail you, and the Angry Man took to the field once more.

'Aye, gentlemen, the names you speak are all ones we can honour as Americans. But mark me, gentlemen, what did the foul air of New York do to two of the best of those men. Brought them down, sirs, brought them low. Hamilton dead at the hand of Burr just last summer. Two of our best men down by a single shot –'

'How two? Burr didn't die.'

'No, sir, Aaron Burr lives, if by living you mean no more than breathing, but in every sense that matters to this country Burr is as dead as Hamilton.'

The mood changed as they reflected on the fatal meeting of the two men just outside New Jersey the previous year.

'Pity it was Hamilton that went down. Not a man I could agree with but a true American. Now Burr, well Aaron Burr's another kettle of fish.'

'A pity then that Hamilton wasn't a better shot. But none of the Hamiltons could hit a barn even from the inside. It's only three years ago that his son was dropped in a duel.'

'Good shot or bad shot, Hamilton was called out by Burr. What could a man of honour do but accept the challenge?'

Several heads nodded in agreement when Golden Promise, though only a moment ago so down, returned to the field revived.

'Wrong, sir, wrong. Burr was finished before the duel. Jefferson had dropped him as Vice President and he lost out as Governor of New York, and in my opinion, gentlemen, that is all to the good. The country is better off without Aaron Burr. It wasn't New York air that did the damage it was –'

A somewhat diffident voice as yet unheard insinuated itself firmly into the talk.

'I sometimes wonder, gentlemen, whether New York isn't in the right, and a rigorous suppression of duelling might not be in the best interests of the common good in these more enlightened times.'

Heads turned and looked at the speaker of this double blasphemy. There was a second of strained silence. Then someone laughed loudly.

'Ha, ha. Damned good, Macleod. Damned good.'

The tension passed and the room was full of laughter. Lawyer Macleod had made a joke, although from the look on his face he seemed unaware of having said anything amusing.

'Truly, gentlemen, I think that in this day and age there should be no place for honour killings.'

There was more laughter and one man remarked quietly to his neighbour that Lawyer Macleod had a very dry manner in his wit but it was somehow all the funnier for it. The neighbour nodded and spoke loudly the thoughts of the room.

'Aye, Macleod, we all know your feelings in the matter of honour killings, and there's two men in a cemetery near here, each with a pistol ball in his head, who know it as well.'

There was more laughter and even the Angry Man seemed willing to forget his earlier manner and concede that his previous conflict with Golden Promise was now finished.

'I see married life agrees with you, Macleod. There was a time, and not too long ago either, when you wouldn't have been here in this club taking lunch, never mind making jokes at your own expense.' He turned and offered an olive branch to his erstwhile opponent. 'I agree with you, sir, up to point. There's one man among us who has a future of golden promise now that he has a handsome young wife by his side.' He turned back to

11

Lawyer Macleod and raised his glass. 'You're a lucky man, Macleod, I drink to your good fortune and to your charming wife.'

He drank and others joined in his salute which, if it did anything for the lawyer, seemed to cause him embarrassment more than pleasure. He rose.

'Thank you, gentlemen.'

'Not going so soon, Macleod?'

'There's work to do, I must return to my office. My compliments, gentlemen, and good-day.

And Lawyer Macleod was gone.

The supporter of Golden Promise used the silence after this sudden and abrupt exit for a friendly sally.

'Well, sir, I wonder if you'd have been quite so emphatic about shooting people down if it had been Lawyer Macleod who had suggested this was an age of golden promise?'

His remark was greeted with gentle laughter and the man, his anger well passed, took the barb well and smiled.

'Perhaps I might have phrased my words differently.'

Another offered an opinion.

'A funny stick, our lawyer, and still a degree too touchy for my taste.'

'But still not a man anyone would want looking at them down the wrong end of a pistol.'

There was thoughtful laughter of agreement.

'Strange man, Macleod, and much changed in my opinion. I can't say I can make him out since he flitted away and then flitted back.'

'Aye, a bit of a mystery our lawyer ever since he took to wandering.'

'I'd wager there's an interesting story behind it all if he'd care to tell it.'

'Or if that pretty wife of his would.'

'But they neither of them *do* care to tell it, in fact they're both damned tight-lipped on the subject.'

'Hell's teeth, why doesn't someone have the gumption to come straight out and ask him?'

Heads turned to the questioner.

'Aye, sir, you ask him, and if he calls you out for prying into his private life –'

'Which he takes a deal of care to keep private.

'– just tell us where you want the body sent.'

There was laughter and the questioner's look showed the assembly that he had withdrawn his suggestion.

But Lawyer Macleod's skill with a pistol was not a serious topic, not the stuff on which these powerful minds chewed after their lunch. There was a warm blaze in the big fireplace and the early spring weather outside remained as it had been all day, uninviting. The gathering settled down deeper into their chairs, refreshed their cups and glasses, drew on their pipes and once again returned to business. There could be neither respite nor triviality for these men and the call of duty always found them ready. There was a world to set to rights and the place to begin, as always, was with America.

Chapter Three

Outside the warmth and comfort of the club a bitter wind blew and the March sky threatened late snow. Macleod walked through the busy Boston streets wrapped in his thick coat, one gloved hand plunged deep in his pocket while the other held the brim of his tall hat securing it against the wind. He was not headed back to his office. He was going home. The small lie told to his companions caused him no pang of conscience. His private life was exactly that, private.

If anyone had told Lawyer Macleod that he was considered something of a mystery to Boston society he would have been amazed. In his own eyes he was a commonplace man of business who chose to keep himself to himself, nothing more. But the Boston that lunched, dined and gossiped thought otherwise. Until three years ago he was known as the city's best business and contracts lawyer. He was also known as a bitter, middle-aged widower with no family and no friends, a man who lived little better than a miser, shut away in a few rooms of the big town-house left to him by his father and served by one ancient, crotchety maid-of-all-work. So the years had passed until, suddenly, he had shut up his office, left Boston and disappeared, only to return some months later with a beautiful young woman twenty years his junior.

Boston morality was shocked, nay, stunned. Lawyer Macleod may have been that *rara avis*; a wealthy Boston Catholic, but even a Papist must have realised that the young woman's position in his home was at best highly ambiguous and at worst downright scandalous. But before Boston could suitably express its perfectly justified moral outrage both Macleod and the young woman had suddenly disappeared again! After several months they returned and moral Boston breathed a sigh of relief for on the third finger of her left hand the young woman wore a ring. She was now Mrs Macleod.

The new young wife, Marie, was beautiful, Catholic and came from New Orleans. That much soon became common knowledge, but, as both Marie and Macleod were strangely reticent to provide any further information, society drew its own conclusions.

Macleod had been ensnared!

It was the old, old story. The young woman had sold her considerable good looks to gain his considerable gold – and Boston society honoured her for it.

Worldly-wise tongues wagged out their version of the story as if they'd had it direct from the Macleods themselves.

Somewhere on his travels he had encountered this beauty and she, realising he was a prize, had snapped him up. But once she had seen Boston the young woman showed she had brains as well as looks and, with eminent good sense, had insisted that in Protestant Boston it had to be marriage or nothing and, so it seemed to Mr and Mrs Worldly-wise, she had got her way.

But if society cast Marie as a clever adventuress she stubbornly refused to play the part for them. Once she and Macleod were settled as husband and wife both were satisfied to live simply, happy in each other's company. They hired a housekeeper who also served Marie as maid and a serving man who doubled as Macleod's valet and also acted as coachman. As their weeks of married life grew into months neither Macleod not Marie saw any reason to increase their household.

Boston observed all this and agreed that marriage had, after all, not totally eradicated Macleod's miserly inclinations. On further consideration of the situation, having nothing but themselves as models on which to build their theories, they came to the conclusion that the new Mrs Macleod was not sorry to see so little of her husband's wealth spent. The more would come to her on that unhappy day when her much older husband finally shuffled off this mortal coil. Heads nodded knowingly and sly looks were exchanged. A deep game and a long one, but considering the rewards, a most excellent game.

In the Macleod home French was spoken. Macleod's mother had been French and he had been brought up to speak the language fluently. Their housekeeper-maid had been employed because she spoke the language well enough. Without the stimulus of necessity Marie's progress in English was, understandably, slow and laborious. She understood most of what she heard but only spoke enough English to be able to go out and exchange simple greetings and pleasantries and, having no need at home to improve, she went out less and less. Marie shopped in the company of her maid and sometimes lunched with a few ladies who spoke French well enough to make conversation enjoyable. But it was, for the most part, a lonely existence and, worse, it was pointless.

Boston did not know it and, she hoped, would never know it, but when she met Macleod in New Orleans she had been a woman very much in the forefront of fashion and society. But, despite all the gaiety and gushing that her position had involved, she had been no more than a thing for show, a necessary social adornment to a wealthy, aristocratic fop of a husband who preferred to share his private life and his bed with another man. Macleod had taken her from that misery and shame and given her a place in his heart and his home and she loved him deeply for that. But as time slipped past Marie felt that she was in danger of drifting into a life which, although less humiliating, was equally without a purpose. She sought comfort in her Catholic faith and confided her concerns to the priest who at once diagnosed her problem. The answer was simple, she needed a child. She was a wife, and a good Catholic woman was never truly a wife until she was a mother, God willing, a mother many times over.

She took away his advice and thought about it, and the more she thought about it the more it seemed to be the answer to all her anxiety.

For a time she brought a frequency and passion to their love-making which surprised Macleod. He did not object, rather the reverse, but he *was* surprised. By night Marie used passion and by day prayer. Her heart ached to be able to give her husband a

16

new life and to have herself a child whom she could watch grow and flourish. A child whom she could love and care for. Their child.

Months passed but the cycle of her body stubbornly refused to vary. They slept together often but into her passion Macleod seemed to sense a kind of desperation which he could not understand. Nights of love-making came and went, days of candles lit and prayers offered passed, but no new life came into her.

Finally a year of marriage was celebrated but Macleod noticed that the joy of their anniversary was somewhat muted in his wife. He did not know it but a fear had crept into Marie. What if she was barren! That the fault might lie with her husband never crossed her mind. If there was a failure then it must be hers, a punishment for past sins. God's judgment. That was the way her Catholic mind worked.

Macleod increasingly noticed her moods and restlessness and it slowly stole over him that she might not be altogether happy. He thought about it. He brought his dry lawyer's mind to bear on the problem. It wasn't money. Whatever she asked he gave, although she asked for little. He offered to hire a proper lady's maid to be a companion. She refused. She did not want or need any more servants. He asked if she would like to open more rooms, perhaps redecorate some of the house? She did not. Finally he offered to give a ball and invite society into their home. She burst into tears and fled the room.

After some days of slow deliberation he found he was left with but one solution. She was bored. She needed younger, brighter company. He was twenty years her senior and a lawyer. Her love for him had begun to fade in the prosaic routine of domesticity. He had been a fool to think it might be otherwise. But Macleod had one last hope. She needed a child. His heart ached to be able to give her new life and to have himself a child whom he could watch grow and flourish. A child whom he could love and care for. Their child.

But a fear had crept into him. What if he could not father a child! That the fault might lie with his wife never crossed his mind. If there was a failure then it must be his, a punishment for past sins. God's judgment. That was the way his Catholic mind worked.

And so their lives settled down for another year. They lay together at night and came together still, but less often and with less passion. A fear had crept into their lives and each noticed it in the other. Each assumed the fault where there was none, and each bore in silence that which neither needed to bear at all.

The cold March wind blew strongly as Macleod headed homeward heedless of the bitter weather. His thoughts were elsewhere as they had been so often lately. It could not go on as it had. They had grown apart, he was losing her, and it cut his heart like a knife. Although his was a slow and deliberate mind he saw that the time had come when he must make some sort of decision. It could not, nay, it would not, go on.

He found he had reached his front door and stood for a moment, then made his decision. No. It would *not* go on. He would confront the problem head on, he would bring it out in the open and lay it bare whatever the consequences. As he opened the door of his house he was a man of iron, a man resolved, a man impatient for action.

He would ask a friend for advice!

Chapter Four

In his decision to seek out a friend for advice Macleod was a man not blessed with an abundance of choice. The number of people in Boston he could count as true friends was really quite small, in fact there were none. But it had not always been thus. The Macleod who joined Washington's army early in 1779 had been a happy and gregarious young man with a wife and baby daughter. It was from those far off times that Macleod dredged from his memory the friend to whom he would go, a military surgeon, Gideon Hood. They had met when he had been wounded for the first time at the battle of Stony Point. The wound was in the lower abdomen, not too serious, and Macleod was back campaigning four weeks later. But while convalescing he and Hood became friends and Macleod suggested that they spend some leave time together if it could be arranged. Some months later they were able to set off together to the small, quiet town where Macleod had arranged for his wife and daughter to stay in case a British attack was made on Boston.

On arriving Macleod had been told that British artillery had bombarded the town in the mistaken belief it held Revolutionary troops. The house in which his wife and child lived had received two direct hits and both were killed, his daughter instantly, his wife dying one week later of wounds. Hood had accompanied him to the cemetery and stood with him at the graveside where mother and daughter lay together in the cold ground of eternity.

Macleod and Hood had immediately returned to duty and Macleod became a grim, silent man who, in action, was brave to the point of recklessness. It was Hood who had taken him aside one day after a particularly bloody and quite unnecessary skirmish and told him in no uncertain terms that if he wished to die then he should put a ball in his own head at once and not waste any more good American lives which were needed to bring the war to a satisfactory conclusion, and, if he wasn't man enough to blow his own brains out, Hood offered to do it for him there and then.

It was the action of a true friend, kindly meant and left Macleod in no doubt that Hood would indeed put a ball in his brain if he should lose, by the rashness of his own behaviour, just one more life placed under his command. So it was that Macleod once again become a steady and dependable young officer though cheerfulness never returned.

After the war Hood set up medical practice in Boston and was one of the very few men who might have been reckoned a friend of Lawyer Macleod. But after two years Hood married a widow from New York, moved away and Macleod became the lonely, wealthy miser that Boston knew for so many years.

But now Macleod had need of Gideon Hood once more. He needed him as a friend and as a surgeon for, though a man of little or no imagination, Macleod had convinced himself that the wound he had received at Stony Point had in some way impaired his ability to father a child. Needless to say he was unwilling to establish the truth or otherwise of this self-diagnosis by using one of the many doctors in Boston. If he was right it would soon become common knowledge and make a life, already difficult, utterly unbearable.

Macleod told his clerk that he would be gone for about two or three weeks, the time he calculated he would need for travel to New York and to locate his old friend. His excuse for suddenly leaving was that an old fellow-officer now living in New York, Gideon Hood, had asked him to pay a visit both as friend and lawyer. He had used a similar story once before and either hadn't the imagination to make up a new one or thought, mistakenly, that what had served once might serve again. No one had believed the story the first time and, even though some few remembered Gideon Hood, no one believed the story now, especially Marie. But Macleod took ship for New York with high hopes and a brave heart thinking that he left his wife and

20

Boston satisfied.

While Macleod sailed happily towards New York, Marie stayed miserably at home. Her husband had gone away. He had grown tired of her because she was young and foolish, could not easily speak his native tongue, could not even take an interest in his work because she was too stupid to understand it. Worst of all, she was a wife who could not give him a child. He had gone away from her, not able to bear her presence any more. How could it be otherwise? He had told her a story so weak that he could not mean her to believe it. It was his way of letting her know that he needed to be away from her, to seek another who might give him all that she could not. If Macleod lacked imagination then the sad fancies that filled Marie's mind for many days after her husband's departure more than restored the family average.

Macleod arrived in New York and was pleasantly surprised. He, like other Bostonians, regarded New York with some degree of scorn as cheap and second-rate. A pushy, upstart place, out for what it could get, any way it could get it. Yet he was welcomed at The Tontine Coffee House with genuine enthusiasm and, what is more, given a fine room at what seemed to him a more than reasonable price. The Tontine Coffee House was one of the very few places in New York Macleod knew by name, several of his most prosperous clients had stayed there when on business in New York and spoke highly of it. It was centrally located on the corner of Wall Street and Water Street, opposite the Merchant's Coffee House which it had supplanted in importance. He was glad to find that, though only some thirteen years old, it was an elegant, four-storey building of sober design as befitted a place where brokers and other serious businessmen congregated. He was also pleased to find that its public rooms were not at all brash and noisy. In fact it was, for what he had been led to believe was a centre of commerce and a hub of activity, rather quiet. But that suited him as he was not here in his capacity as a commercial lawyer. He reserved judgement of course, but this first impression of New York was most reassuring.

The following day, after an excellent night's sleep and a good breakfast, he set out into the great city and at once began his search. How hard could it be to find one particular doctor in New York? Macleod soon found out. There was no shortage of medical men but none that was Hood or knew of Hood or wanted to know of Hood. By the end of the day it was clear to Macleod that the medical profession of New York was not in the least bit interested in his enquiries.

The fact was, Macleod had been unfortunate in the timing of his visit. New York was yet again in the grip of an outbreak of Yellow Fever, but this time more virulent that ever before. His good fortune in the matter of accommodation was due entirely to the fact that each day thousands of those citizens who could afford it fled from the city to avoid the pestilence. The Tontine Coffee House catered particularly to such a class of citizen and, as visitors more informed than Macleod had wisely postponed any business in New York, he had been made especially welcome. It was not until he returned to the Tontine tired and dispirited that he had learnt the truth of his situation. At dinner that evening he asked the waiter if the dining room was always so sparsely populated with guests. The waiter, a sad-looking fellow, looked around at the ten or so people eating.

'Oh no, sir. Usually we're busy, often full. But it's the fever you see.'

But Macleod didn't see.

'What fever?'

'Yellow Fever, sir. The city's riddled with it and it's worse this time than ever before. Most of our gentlemen have left and won't return until the worst is over. Didn't you know, sir?'

'No, I didn't.'

'Ah, that would account for it then.'

'Account for what?'

'Being here, sir. We was all wondering why you'd come. You'll be leaving tomorrow I suppose, now that you know?'

And the question, Macleod realised, was an interesting one. Stay in a city awash with Yellow Fever and look for Hood, or leave the next day and perhaps save his life.

'Will you be wanting a pudding, sir?'

'No.'

'Cheese perhaps?'

'No.'

'Fruit, nuts?'

'No. Nothing more.'

'Very well, sir.'

The waiter left and Macleod retired to his room to think about his situation. The question posed by the waiter was an interesting one, a most interesting one indeed.

Next morning, after a sound night's sleep, Macleod came down to breakfast with his mind made up. The same waiter as the previous evening came to his table.

'Shall I ask them to make up your bill, sir. I assume you'll be leaving us after you've breakfasted.'

'No, no bill. I will be staying.'

'No bill?'

'No.'

'You'll be staying?'

'I will.'

The waiter, a married man with three young children who lived in a poor part of the city where the fever was thriving, was stunned. He, himself, had tried to get away with his family. He had even considered getting away without his family but his wife, knowing him, kept a close eye on his movements. That a man with money, a man who could leave any time he wanted, should of his own will choose to stay! He pulled himself together with a visible effort.

'Just as you say, sir. I'll get your coffee and breakfast.'

Macleod busied himself for all of that day and the next with his search but after these two fruitless days he retired to his room and thought the matter over once more. Should he go or stay? Obviously finding Hood would take a little longer than he had allowed for and the Yellow Fever was a damned nuisance, complicating an already difficult situation. It was all very vexing. To leave might save him his life, but it also left him exactly where he had been before his departure from Boston.

Intolerable. For Marie's sake he had to know the truth. Was he incapable of fathering a child? He made up his mind, he would stay and continue his search even if it killed him.

Chapter Five

He did not know if Hood still practised as a doctor. He did not know if Hood still lived in New York. He did not even know if Hood was still alive. But if he was in the city and alive Macleod was determined to find him. And finally he did. He had started his search in neighbourhoods around the Tontine Coffee House. These neighbourhoods were affluent, the ones least affected by the fever. At the end of the second day his search had widened sufficiently to include neighbourhoods less affluent where there was no shortage of evidence of the virulence of the disease. Several front doors had wreaths tied with black ribbon and Macleod passed two carts on which were cheap, pine coffins – one obviously that of a small child. Following this cart as it made its way through the shabby street were a man and a woman. He had two young children by him and she a babe in her arms. Macleod stopped, stood and removed his hat as the poor cortege passed. Others on the street, and there were many, ignored the procession. It was obviously too common a spectacle to attract attention or sympathy. It was here, among the homes of the labouring classes that Macleod found a doctor who knew the name.

'Hood, Gideon Hood? Well I can tell you where to find him but I don't recommend you try to make an appointment with him.'

'And why not, sir? Is your opinion of his skill as a doctor –'

'Oh no. I have a high regard for Hood's skill and also for his dedication. It's just that he has a long list of patients at the moment, a very long list, and getting longer by the day. Still, if only Hood will do, I'll write down where you should go. Go down to the ferry that crosses to Staten Island. Hood is in charge at the Marine Hospital. Anyone will tell you how to get there.'

Macleod took the address, thanked the doctor and left in high spirits. He had found his man and nothing, certainly not something as trivial as a long patient list, was going to get in the way of speaking to him. It was as the doctor said, everyone from whom he asked directions to the Marine Hospital, Staten Island, was indeed quick to speed him on his way.

It was dark by the time Macleod arrived at the ferry, which turned out to be no more than a large barge tied up at a newly-built wharf and attended by shadowy figures who flitted around in lamplight. Macleod accosted one of the figures.

'I want to go across to the Marine Hospital.'

The figure, a bearded man with an ill-looking countenance and grimy clothes looked at him. 'Go on then, I'm not stopping you.' He shook Macleod's hand off his arm and hurried away.

Macleod went to the barge. A man was untying a mooring rope at the front.

'Are you going across to Staten Island?'

'I am.'

'May I cross with you?'

'Are you a doctor?'

'No.'

'Ill?'

'No.'

'Then why do you want to cross?'

Macleod was puzzled by the question but answered as best he could. 'I am a friend of Doctor Gideon Hood and I –'

'Oh, you should have said so straight away. Jump in, sir, we're about to shove off. They have a full load for us to bring back and as you see we're empty going out so there's plenty of room.'

Macleod boarded the barge which the man and three others pushed away from the wharf and began to row out into the darkness. In the distance across the water Macleod could see lights.

'Is that Staten Island?'

'It is, sir.'

Macleod left the men to their work and the barge slowly moved towards the lights.

On landing Macleod stepped out of the boat on to another wharf, also in darkness, with figures moving about by lamplight. Beyond the lamps he glimpsed stacks of what looked like packing cases but his interest in these was nil so he asked the way to the Marine Hospital which, it turned out, was close by. He was thankful that the roads were well lit as if people and traffic used them long after sunset, yet at the moment he was alone on the road.

The Marine Hospital was a several-storey building which loomed up in the night, massive and forbidding. He was stopped at its imposing front doors and asked his business but at the mention of the name Gideon Hood he was at once given directions and sent on his way.

After walking through several dimly lit corridors he finally saw an open door from which light spilled out into the gloom. Macleod headed for the light and stood in the doorway of an office. Inside was his old comrade-in-arms.

'Gideon, it's good to see you after so much time.' Hood looked up and stared blankly at the figure in the doorway. 'Do you not know me, then, Gideon? Am I changed so much?'

Gideon Hood was wearing a soiled white coat over his crumpled clothes and looked worn out and weary. He was a balding man, a few years older than Macleod, short and plump and looked past the lamp on his desk with tired eyes. It was late, the corridor was dark and empty. Suddenly Hood's eyes focussed and he came to life.

'No, sir, I do *not* damn know you. Who the hell let you in?'

'I told them I had urgent business with Gideon Hood and they told me to come here.'

'Well, you've found me. Now state your business or go to hell. I don't give a curse either way.'

'I'm Macleod, we served together in the late war. You came to Boston for a time after the war. It was before you married and came to New York. We were friends.'

A vague recollection seemed to dawn in Hood's eyes.

'Macleod? I remember the name, I served with a man of that name. He became a lawyer in Boston. What do you want with him?'

'I am him. I am Macleod.'

But Gideon Hood's attention was already elsewhere.

'Then dammit, why come to me? I'm a doctor not a lawyer.'

And Hood turned his eyes back to the desk littered with papers and stared at them for a moment. Macleod walked across the office and stood at the desk. Hood picked up a pen and a sheet of paper covered in figures, looked at it hopelessly and then looked up at Macleod as if seeing him for the first time.

'Yes?'

'I need your help.'

Hood waved his pen to a chair and Macleod sat down.

'I thought they said the last load for the day had come. Oh well, how many do you want to send me this time and which district are they from?'

Macleod was confused by the question.

'I don't understand.'

'How many cases?'

'Cases?'

'Fever cases, dammit, what else would you be sending to a quarantine hospital?' He threw down his pen and wagged a finger at Macleod. 'I warn you I won't take dead ones, they're your problem. That's been tried too often. If they die in transit you'll get them back on the same boat that brought them.'

Hood picked up his pen again and stared at the paper. Macleod tried again.

'I haven't come about the Yellow Fever. I have come on another matter, a personal matter.'

'Personal?' Hood threw down the pen again and looked angrily at Macleod. 'Who the hell are you and who let you in?'

Macleod saw that he would be fighting a losing battle unless he put his business before Hood immediately.

'Well then, the fact is … the reason I came, sought you out … my being here is, how shall I put it?'

'Confound you, put it plainly, put it any way you like but get it out.'

'Can I have a child?'

The question seemed to rock Hood back in his chair.

'What!'

'Did the wound you tended damage my,' Macleod searched for the right words, 'did that wound cause any …'

'What wound?'

'The one you tended when we first met. Battle of Stony Point, July of seventy-nine. Lower body, musket ball. Nothing serious but still it may have …'

A voice came from the doorway.

'We've got rid of the corpses, they're being loaded now. We've swilled down the beds with the solution. Are we still to burn the bedding as you directed? I call it pure waste, why washing wouldn't do …'

Hood looked past Macleod at the voice and responded fiercely to the new arrival.

'No it wouldn't damn well do. Burn the lot and get fresh, d'you hear? Fresh bedding to every bed or I'll have you burying bodies yourself until you drop dead and then I'll gladly bury you myself.' The man left the doorway and Hood turned back to Macleod. 'What was it your were babbling about? A wound wasn't it?'

'Yes, in the late war, lower body, a musket …'

'Great heavens man, do you have any idea how many wounds I tended in the war?'

'No, I suppose not. A great many I dare say.'

'Aye, sir, you could call it a great many. Too damn many. And do you know how long ago it all was?'

'Yes, a few years now, a good few years.'

Hood ran his fingers feverishly over his few straggling hairs then seemed to suddenly to sag, as if all force had gone out of him.'

'Yes, and too many to remember one wound even if I wanted to and I assure you I don't want to. Is that why you came? God's teeth, man, if the thing's troubling you why not go to your own doctor? Why seek me out?'

'No, no, it's not troubling me, at least not in the sense that I think you mean.'

Suddenly Hood became animated again. He waved a hand past Macleod.

'Do you know how many cases there are out there?' Macleod shook his head. 'Or how many of them will live?' Another shake. 'Or the chances that me and everyone else working on this blasted hell-hole of an island will end up as fever-cases ourselves?'

But Macleod pressed on.

'No, I … I can see you're busy. If you could just tell me …'

Hood gave up, overcome by a great weariness from incessant work and almost no rest. He could no longer oppose the man opposite him. He surrendered unconditionally.

'What is it, exactly, that you want?'

'I sought you out for help in a personal matter. A matter of some delicacy. We were friends once and I find myself in need of a friend. I came to you because I could think of no one else to turn to. I need to know if I can give my wife a child.'

There, it was out.

Macleod waited and looked at Hood who in his turn looked at Macleod with a kind of despair. Then, with a half-sigh, he sat forward. 'Tell me about your wound.'

'Lower body, ball went in about here and lodged inside. Must have been pretty much spent or maybe a ricochet because it didn't go in too far. As I said, not a serious wound but it may have, well, inside, might it have done something that would prevent me from becoming a father? You removed the ball so I thought you would know if it had.'

Hood's voice was resigned and his manner like some automaton as he asked the necessary questions.

'Does your member stand to attention when called on?'

Macleod nodded.

'And does it fire when ready?'

Again a nod.

'It pretty much does all that your wife expects of it?'

Another nod.

30

'Then if it can do that the wound you spoke of did no harm. If your wife hasn't conceived, well, there might be many reasons or none. Some couples can't help having children whether they want them or not, others try everything under the sun and get nothing for their trouble. It's a mystery to me, still, there you are.'

And he sat back.

Macleod was somewhat nonplussed.

'You mean you can't help me?'

'If you both know what goes where and why, then it's just a matter of sticking at it. Now, sir, if you don't mind we'll end your little private consultation. I have one or two other patients to attend to with rather more serious problems.'

Clearly their conversation was ended.

Macleod paused a moment then held out his hand.

'Thank you, Gideon. I'm staying at the Tontine Coffee House on the corner of Wall Street. Perhaps we could dine together before I return to Boston?'

Hood ignored the outstretched hand so Macleod let it drop back to his side.

'Tell me, Macleod, always assuming I had the free time to go out and dine, would the Tontine Coffee House welcome a visit from the Superintendent of New York's Fever Quarantine Hospital? And if they did, do you think the Superintendent sets his fellow workers a good example by flitting off to the centre of New York to mix with the general public? Why the hell do you think they went to the trouble of putting us on this island in the first place and calling it a damned Quarantine Hospital?'

'Yes, I'm sorry, I didn't think. All I meant was …'

But Hood had picked up his pen and was again working on one of the sheets of paper that littered his desk. Macleod realised that his meeting with his old friend and comrade-in-arms was now definitely over so he quietly left.

The boat was loaded when he arrived at the wharf and almost ready to go but Macleod paused before asking to board. In the lamplight of the boat the packing cases were now revealed for what they were, coffins. To take this boat back

31

meant keeping company with deceased fever patients.

The man on the boat whom he had first spoken to recognised him.

'Finished already, sir? Coming back with us are you?' Macleod paused in answering. 'It's the last run tonight, sir. It's this one or wait till morning. Come, sir, we must be off. Our passengers are getting restless, ain't they lads?'

This sally brought happy laughter from the rest of the crew and Macleod, not wanting to stay on Staten Island until morning, stepped aboard. If these fellows could so cheerfully carry their gruesome cargo why should he hold back?'

On the return journey he reflected on what Hood had told him, which was not much and nothing that helped him at all. Yet that, it seemed, was all his trip to New York would achieve.

At dinner that evening he sat in the dining room toying with his food. He had no appetite, but he went through the motions because he could think of nothing else to do. The dining room was sparsely attended and Macleod sat alone deep in thought when suddenly someone sat down uninvited at his table, leaned across and looked across at him closely.

'It is. Great heavens it is. By all that's holy, Macleod. Where in God's name did you spring from, Jean Marie?' Macleod looked at the stranger who addressed him so enthusiastically. He was a man of middle age with thick black eyebrows but silver hair which hung down over the back of his high collar. He had a handsome, striking face but it was a face that meant absolutely nothing to Macleod. The man obviously knew him, however, and knew him well enough to use his Christian names. The new arrival sat back as Macleod looked at him blankly. 'Ah, I am forgotten. You do not remember your old friend.' He pushed back his chair and stood up. 'Allow me to re-introduce myself. Sebastián Francisco de Miranda Rodríguez at your service.'

And he gave a small, stiff bow, laughed loudly and sat down again.

Chapter Six

'My God, Miranda, is it really you?' Sebastián Miranda tapped himself on the chest with the flat of his hand and assured Macleod that it was indeed he and no other. 'But what are you doing here in New York?'

'Business, the same old business of freedom.'

'Are your family with you?'

'No, they are still in London.'

'Well, whatever your business I'm heartily glad to see you.'

'And I you.'

'And what brings you back to America? When you left Boston in '84 you told me you were going to England to try to get European support for your mad South American ideas.'

'What mad ideas, old friend? Is it mad to want independence for your country? Is it mad to want freedom? If it is, then America must be a veritable Bedlam. But let us not talk yet about my ideas, mad or otherwise.' He waved a hand to the sad-looking waiter who stood idle by a wall. The waiter came to the table. 'A bottle of champagne and a dozen oysters.' Miranda looked back at Macleod. 'We must celebrate.'

'I'm sorry, sir.'

Miranda turned back to the waiter. 'And what is it that you are sorry for, my friend?'

'Champagne, sir? Is it a wine?'

'Is it a wine? Of course it is a wine. It is *the* wine. Bring us champagne.'

The waiter's air of gloom deepened. Things were slow and he knew why. Death surrounded them. He felt warm, too warm. If death waited on every street corner might it even now be nibbling at his collar? In such circumstances he couldn't bring himself to be politely urbane. 'We don't have the wine you ask for.'

'No champagne!'

'I do not know the wine, sir. I can do you the oysters and we have some very good Marsala.'

'My dear sir, I appreciate your recommendation, I know the wine and in other circumstances it would be an excellent suggestion but I asked for champagne.'

The waiter gave an apologetic shrug. 'I'm sorry, sir.'

Miranda stood up. 'Come, Jean Marie, we will leave this place and go where I know there is champagne. As for oysters, well, we will see what we can do.' He gave the waiter a look of scorn, took Macleod's arm and led him from the dining room talking loudly. 'I admire America, I have always admired America. In many ways it is a shining symbol of our present Age of Enlightenment, our Age of Reason.' He paused in the doorway and turned. The sad waiter was still standing by their vacated table staring at nothing in particular, no doubt contemplating last things. 'But in some aspects it is still a place bordering on savagery.' He directed a final, withering look of contempt at the waiter on whom, it has to be said, it was wasted. 'I do not know the wine indeed!' He then led Macleod out into the lobby of the hotel. 'Well, I promised you champagne, my friend, and yes, oysters. The occasion deserves no less.'

In the lobby they stopped. Macleod's mind was slowly working, though to no great purpose.

'What is this champagne you're so intent upon?'

Miranda looked at him with raised eyebrows.

'You do not know champagne? Is that possible? Boston was not a frontier town as I remember, but then again, nor is New York. No matter, after tonight, to celebrate our reunion you will remember champagne even if, once again, you forget your old friend. Now, go to your room and get your coat and hat and I will get us a carriage and wait here for you.'

Macleod set off to his room in a strangely uplifted mood. The unexpected meeting with his old friend had promoted his cause not one jot that he could see, but he was still cheered by it. As for this wine, this champagne, well, one wine was very much like another. It was probably some new European fad, a fashion in drinking that had come, would go, and would be forgotten, as fashions did in everything.

He went up to his room and got his coat and hat then closed the door behind him and walked down the dimly lit corridor towards the staircase. He had almost reached the stairs when he thought he heard a noise behind him and suddenly the building fell on his head and everything exploded in a roar of inchoate noise.

Chapter Seven

It was black, deepest black. Far away there were voices. They were coming closer but it was too dark to see anything. The voices had difficulty in penetrating the searing pain in his head. He wanted to put his hand to it but he couldn't move his arms. He was lost in some awful empty place.

Then, despite the pain, his mind cleared and he was conscious. He opened his eyes.

He was sitting in a hard, upright chair in what appeared to be a large cellar. His arms were tied behind his back and a rope round his body held him fast to the chair. A lamp hung on a wall and two men stood by the only door, talking.

'Now we've got him, what do we do with him?'

'We find out who he is and what he wants.'

'What if he's nobody, just somebody Miranda sat down to talk to?'

'Don't be a fool. Miranda's not the sort to sit at a table with a total stranger. It was an arranged meeting. They were about to leave together. He has to be somebody.'

The speaker looked across at Macleod and saw that his eyes were open. He walked across, looked down at him closely then stood up and slapped him hard across the face. The blow was so unexpected that Macleod nearly toppled sideways.

'That's to let you know we mean business.' Then he slapped Macleod hard again with his other hand and looked at him with a nasty smile. 'And that's for nothing in particular except to show you I intend to enjoy my work.'

Macleod felt the taste of blood in his mouth and the pain in his head became worse, a thing only a second before he would have said wasn't possible.

The man doing the slapping was young, in his early

twenties, fair-haired and solid but obviously, from the cut and style of his clothes, no common thug. Macleod spat out some blood.

'Where am I? And who the hell are you?'

'No no. I ask the questions and you confine yourself to answers. Now, let's have your name.' He turned to his companion. 'Always begin with introductions, I say, it's only polite.' The man at the door, mousey-haired, short and slim, was also young and well-dressed but, unlike his fair-haired companion, looked acutely uncomfortable. The man turned his attention back to Macleod. So, your name, my friend?'

'It will mean nothing to you.'

The man leaned forward and caught Macleod's hair in his fist and yanked his head back. The pain performed yet another miracle of increase and forced a cry from Macleod's lips.

'Your name?'

'Macleod.'

The man let go of Macleod's hair and stood back. The nasty smile was there again.

'See, that wasn't too hard.' He looked around the room. 'Welcome to my parlour, Mr Macleod. It's a cosy place as you see, and quiet. You can scream and holler all you like here. No one will take any notice because no one except ourselves will hear you. Now, Mr Macleod, who are you and what's your business with our mutual friend Miranda?' The man looked down at him and Macleod examined his face. He had no idea who he was, what he was doing or why. To the best of his knowledge he had never seen him before in his life. 'Come along, Mr Macleod, if that really is your name, all I want is answers to my questions.' He gripped Macleod's hair again. 'Let's not make it difficult shall we?'

The other young man stepped forward. 'I think I heard something, Steuben. In fact I'm sure I …'

He sounded worried, but Macleod's questioner dismissed the interruption angrily. 'Nothing, you heard nothing. No one knows we're here.'

But the next second proved him wrong, for the door burst

open and a man came in carrying a lantern. The fair young man, the one who was apparently called Steuben, let go of Macleod's hair. The new arrival glanced at Macleod then at the tall young man.

'Damn you, sir, damn you for a fool and a blunderer. What's the meaning of this? Explain yourself, sir, if you can.'

The new arrival was a big man of middle age with a mane of grey hair and a military look to the way he carried himself. Behind him another smaller man had crept into the room and stood to the rear of the speaker as if sheltering. He was plump and bald with eyeglasses pinched on his nose and glanced timidly round the room from his cover as he spoke. 'I thought it best to tell you, Colonel. It didn't seem a sensible thing, no, nor helpful, to have unconscious men bundled into the house through the back door by night and taken down to the cellars. It didn't seem at all the thing we wanted so I thought you should know.'

He let the eyeglasses drop from his nose and dangle on their cord as he retreated back into his cover. He did not like the way the tall young man was looking at him.

The man he had addressed as Colonel turned slightly. 'Thank'ee, Ogden, you did right.' Then turned his attention back to the tall young man. 'Who the hell is he, sir, and what's he doing here trussed up like a damn fowl? Explain yourself, sir, damn well explain yourself.'

But there was no explanation because at that moment the door again slammed open and another man crashed into the room. The four men already in the room cleared a way for the newcomer who stood and glared at them all then turned and looked at Macleod.

It was Miranda.

'By God, someone shall pay for this.' He looked at the four men then settled on Macleod's questioner. 'This is your work, Steuben, it has to be. Only a half-witted poltroon like you could do this.' Miranda crossed to Macleod and began to untie the ropes that held him. 'My friend, how can I begin to apologise? For all the world I would not have had such a thing happen.'

Macleod stood up and massaged his wrists where the ropes had held him then put a hand to his head. When he looked it was smeared with blood.

Miranda turned and stepped across to the man called Steuben and slapped him hard across the face.

'I will give you satisfaction as and where you wish when it will be my great pleasure to shoot you down as you so richly deserve.'

The young man looked at Miranda with pure hate in his eyes but he said nothing. It was the military man with the lantern who spoke. 'Now, now, Miranda, this won't do. We're all on the same side. My son, I admit, may have been hasty, he may have …'

Miranda turned on him. 'Your son is an imbecile, sir, and a blackguard and, if he will not answer me, then he is also a craven and a coward and can be of no use to me nor my cause.'

The young man finally spoke up for himself. 'Name your time and place, Miranda.'

'Now, now, gentlemen, now, now. Is this wise, is this helpful?' It was the man who had taken shelter behind the Colonel who spoke these words in a pacific manner. 'I ask you all, is this suitable?' The small, plump figure slowly edged forward from cover like a cautious snail emerging from its shell after a thunderstorm. 'We are all men charged with a mission, are we not? And are we not comrades bound together by a common purpose? Do harsh words and violent actions among ourselves further that purpose? Are they at all helpful to our mission? I ask you as a friend and colleague, is this right, gentlemen, is it all that it should be? Is it at all what we would want it to be?' His words so gently spoken, his movements so small and tentative, his eyes, once more sheltering behind the rimless eyeglasses, held them. The tension eased slightly. The little man removed his eyeglasses and looked at them all one at a time. 'Come now. Let us go upstairs and behave like friends and comrades.' He looked at Macleod. 'This gentleman has been roughly handled and brought among us whether we like it or no, and it must be decided what is to be done about him.' For a second Miranda seemed about to flare up again but the little man put his eyeglasses back and continued looking at Macleod. 'You seem to have been ill-used, sir. No doubt you would like to, er, to –' he looked for a suitably pacific phrase '– to repair yourself.' He smiled and took off the eyeglasses and smiled a conciliatory smile. 'Yes, to repair yourself.'

There was a momentary pause, Miranda seemed unsure and glared at Steuben who returned the look in kind.

Macleod had no idea what was going on but he agreed wholeheartedly with this small man. He wanted to be out of this cellar and, as had been suggested, to repair himself. If Miranda and this Steuben character began again there was no telling what might happen, so he said the first thing that came into his mind.

'I was promised champagne.' All eyes turned to him. 'A wine I believe. I can't say what sort because I've never had any. But I was promised champagne.' He paused and looked at them. 'And oysters.'

The room exploded into sound as Miranda gave out a great laugh, stepped over to him and clapped him on the back.

'So you were, Jean Marie, so you were, and promised by me,' and he looked ferociously round the room, 'and you shall have them if I have to spill blood to get them for you. Come, you shall have them at once.' He moved to the door holding on to Macleod's arm and stopped in the doorway. He turned to the men in the room and spoke as if throwing down a challenge. 'Champagne and oysters, by God. Champagne and oysters or you have my sacred word that blood will be spilt.'

Then he laughed once more and led Macleod from the cellar and up the steps.

The small man took off his eyeglasses and wiped them with his handkerchief.

'Have you champagne and oysters, Colonel?'

'I have champagne,' he gave the young man Steuben a look which no father should give to a son but, alas, so often find they must, 'and my son and his friend here can go out and damn well get the oysters.'

The small man put his eyeglasses back on his nose and with his handkerchief mopped his brow.

'Thank God for that.'

Chapter Eight

Macleod was sitting in the middle of a New York street, stark naked. Someone whom he could not see was drilling a hole in the back of his head with a red-hot augur. What was odd was that many of the people who walked past him were from Boston and knew him well, yet none tried to help. He felt deeply saddened that he should sit there, unclothed, being treated in such a way and be ignored. Then the unseen hand stopped drilling and started banging, driving spikes into his head.

The knocking finally penetrated Macleod's disturbed sleep and he opened his eyes.

His head hurt, his eyes hurt, his mouth felt like he had a piece of saddle blanket stuck in it and his stomach was strongly registering its own angry protest among the clamour.

The knocking grew louder. Macleod threw back the bedclothes, sat up on the side of the bed and tried to stand. He was successful at the second attempt, and immediately regretted his success by discovering that, bad as it had been lying down, standing was much worse.

A voice joined the knocks.

'Open up in there, open up.'

Macleod shuffled to the door holding his head and noticing that he still wore his shirt from the previous day. Scattered across the floor were the rest of his clothes. He opened the door which immediately pushed against him knocking him back, and a man walked into the room, turned and stared at him. He was a slim, youngish man who carried a stick, not as an affectation, but because he walked with a limp. He had dark hair, dark eyes and wore a well-cut overcoat. He regarded Macleod for a second.

'My God, Macleod, what on earth do you think you look

like?' He took a watch out of his waistcoat. 'It's almost eleven, man.' Macleod slowly closed the door and turned to his visitor who grinned at him. 'It must have been some night.'

Macleod slowly went back to the bed where he sat down heavily. 'What midden did you crawl out from, Jones?'

The man laughed amiably. 'Come now, Macleod, no need for harsh words among old friends.'

'We were never friends and we never will be. I don't know what you want and I don't care. Go to hell, Jones, and have the goodness to close the door quietly after you.'

'Dear, dear, such words to someone who once saved your life.'

Macleod glared at his visitor. 'And who was it who put my life at risk in the first place?' But he quickly let his anger subside as he found the consequences to his fragile state were too severe. Anger was not a defensible position. 'What is it you want?'

'That's better. It's a small thing, hardly anything at all.' He patted the left side of his chest with his hand. 'It's just that I have here in my coat a warrant for your arrest duly sworn and signed.'

This information jerked Macleod's attention away from his bodily ills. He looked at Jones who was still smiling amiably as if he'd said he had tickets for a concert. Macleod knew Jones and who it was he worked for and, knowing these things, did not doubt for one second that he was telling no more than the truth. If he said he had an arrest warrant in his coat he certainly had one.

'Arrest? On what charge?'

'Treason. Penalty, if convicted, death, hanging probably or maybe a firing squad. That you will be convicted is, I'm afraid, beyond question. Unfortunately for you the evidence is complete and overwhelming.'

Macleod had now done what a few moments ago he would have thought impossible, lost interest in the way he felt. He was even able to stand.

'Treason! Are you mad, man? I have never committed any

treason.'

'No? You think not? Hmm, I fear I must disagree. We both know, do we not, that you acted as an agent for a gentleman who conspired with others including a foreign power to overthrow the government of the Union. You can't have forgotten your old friend the General?'

'But you know all about that. That was all Bentley's work. I was a mere pawn in one of his damned intrigues. Good God, man, Bentley planned it all.'

'Yes, it's a defence perhaps, but I don't think a very good one. You see it stands or falls on whether Bentley will back your story and I rather think he won't. These days he has the full weight of high office on his shoulders and he must think of the greater good.'

'High office? What high office?'

'Comptroller of the Contingent Fund of Foreign Intercourse.'

'Never heard of it.'

'No, very few have. It's by way of being, how shall I put it …?'

'Plainly, damn you.'

'Well then, enough to say that, despite its considerable influence and powers, it enjoys its anonymity. By the way, there is another name on the warrant, Marie Macleod also known as Marie de Valois, late of New Orleans now resident in Boston.'

Macleod sat down again. 'I don't understand.'

'Then all will be explained, but first I suggest you dress. I can hardly take you in charge in nothing but your shirt.' Using the end of his stick he picked up Macleod's trousers from the floor and tossed them to him. 'No time for hot water to wash and shave I'm afraid, just make yourself as decent as you can.' Jones limped to the door and pulled it open. 'I'll wait downstairs. I know you won't do anything foolish. Try to be quick about it, I've a carriage waiting and it costs money.'

The door closed. Macleod looked at it blankly for a second then slowly got up, gathered the trousers from the bed and began to dress.

44

The carriage stopped outside a house in a depressingly respectable area, a place where senior clerks lived alongside minor professional men whose modest talent had assured them of only modest progress.

Jones descended from the carriage and led Macleod up the steps to the front door which opened before he had knocked. They went into a gloomy, narrow hall and were led by a woman servant to another door. She pushed it open then stood to one side. The room they entered should have been a living room but was, in fact, a well-equipped office dominated by a large desk behind which a man sat smiling at them.

'God's blood, Jeremiah, you brought him, and what's more brought him on his own legs. From the report I got of him last night I would have said the thing couldn't have been done.' The man turned his attention to Macleod who stood sullenly glowering at him. 'Well, Macleod, considering the condition you were in when Miranda put you back into your room I thought you might have to be brought to me on a stretcher,' he turned once again to Jeremiah Jones, 'or that you might be able to do no more than bring the remains so I could view the body.'

Jones laughed.

'He looked as if it was a close-run thing, sir, I assure you.'

The man stood up, came round from the desk and held out his hand. 'Good to see you again, Macleod, can't say you're looking well because you're not, but good to see you anyway.'

Macleod ignored the outstretched hand and the man, Cedric Bentley, let it fall to his side but he retained his smile. 'What's all this about a warrant for my arrest, Bentley? You know I never committed any treason. You know it better than anyone.'

'Do I? Well, perhaps I do.' Bentley returned to his desk and sat down. Jeremiah Jones stepped forward and handed over a folded document which he had taken from inside his coat. Bentley opened the document and read it. 'I'm afraid there's very little I can do, Macleod, it's just as Jeremiah told you. You're arrested on a charge of treason.' He dropped the document onto the desk. 'Trial almost certainly to be held "in camera" given the nature of the evidence. Guilty verdict inevitable then –' and he drew an outstretched finger across his throat, '– you and Marie, both. Pretty woman, your wife, clever too. Very sad. Still, can't have people going about trying to steal our country from under our noses, can we? You must see that.'

And Bentley looked at Macleod, still smiling, and waited for Macleod to be reasonable and agree that he did indeed see that.

Bentley was a man of similar age to Macleod but dressed very much in the fashion of the day, tight trousers, polished black riding boots, high neck-cloth, florid waistcoat, and cutaway coat. But there was nothing of the dandy in his look or speech. Despite the smile he had a hard-looking face and eyes that gave no hint as to his thoughts or feelings.

But Macleod was neither impressed nor intimidated by his looks or his words. He knew Bentley, knew him well enough to stay silent and wait for him to say out loud why he had done what he had done and what it was that he wanted.

Bentley reduced the calibre of his smile but did not switch it off altogether. 'Still stubborn, I see. Well, no harm in that. I wondered if marriage might have softened you, but if it had then you would be of no use to me.'

Bentley waited but Macleod still stood, silent and waiting. Jeremiah Jones stepped forward. 'Would you like him taken away and persuaded to be more co-operative, sir?'

Bentley laughed. 'Good God, you're quick on the violence, Jeremiah. No, Macleod will sit and talk when he's ready and I want him willing not forced. You can go now and leave us to yarn over the good old days.'

'Very well, sir.' Jones left the room and Bentley pointed to a chair in front of the desk.

'Come, Macleod, stop looking at me like that and sit down. You had a heavy night with your new friends and if you keep up with your present attitude you'll only make yourself feel a damn sight worse than you need to.' Macleod did not speak or move. 'Well then, let's see if I can do something practical to persuade you to unbend a little.' Bentley got up and crossed to a

46

walnut cabinet. He opened it took out a glass and mixed something in it then brought it back and held the glass out to Macleod. 'Drink it down.' Macleod looked at the glass but didn't take it. 'Come on, man, it isn't poison. If I'd wanted you dead then you'd be dead already, you know that.' Macleod took the glass and held it. 'Down in one for the best results.'

Bentley went back to his chair and sat down. Macleod stood, waited a moment as if still unsure then quickly drank down the liquid.

He felt a burning sensation in his mouth and throat and had a feeling that liquid fire was running down into his stomach. It took his breath away and he lurched forward and put the glass heavily on the desk and almost fell into the chair. For a second he sat fighting to regain his breath in between coughing uncontrollably. Bentley sat calmly watching his convulsions. Then everything became calm. The fire gave out a gentle warmth, the coughing stopped and his breath came normally.

Macleod looked at Bentley who was smiling broadly, obviously amused by the effects of his potion. 'Worked, did it? It usually does.'

Macleod found speech difficult, but he forced out the words, 'What the hell is it?'

'Something I keep by me. You're not the only one who has heavy nights with dubious characters and finds himself up and doing the next morning with the need for a clear head. It's a mixture guaranteed to raise a corpse so long as it hasn't been in the water above a week.'

Macleod found himself changed enough to give a small, grudging laugh. 'I felt exactly like such a corpse when Jones came calling.'

'I know you did. I was told the state you were in when Miranda took you back to your room. I wasn't joking when I said I doubted if Jeremiah could get you here on your own two legs.'

'I don't remember much about last night except that we drank a wine called champagne, must have drunk it by the bucket. Seemed harmless stuff, fizzy, more like a ladies' drink, but it must have carried a kick.'

'It does. Do you remember meeting Miranda in the dining room of your hotel?'

'Yes, I remember that and I remember going to get my coat and hat. After that I remember coming-to in a cellar with my head cracked and trussed like a turkey.'

'That was courtesy of Steuben Smith and his friend Boseley Caulk. The one's a hot-head and the other's his lapdog. After the cellar what do you remember?'

'We had champagne and oysters.'

'And?'

'We talked, at least Miranda talked, I wasn't in the mood and didn't particularly like the company. There was a military man –'

'Colonel Smith, the hot-head's father, it was his house. A man of some consequence and influence. Go on.'

'And a small, round, mouse of a fellow called Ogden.'

'A merchant in a substantial way of business and as for being a mouse … well, never mind that. What then?'

'I'd already been hit on the head and it mustn't have taken long for the champagne to do the rest because after a short while it all sort of blurs.'

'Yes, I bet it does. Miranda brought you back to your hotel shortly after midnight and dumped you into your room. How do you know Miranda?'

'I met him in Boston in the winter of '84. The war was over and I was trying to put my life back together and making a thoroughly bad job of it when Miranda was introduced to me by a surgeon friend, Gideon Hood. I'd known Hood in the army, he'd set up practice in Boston and somehow he knew Miranda. Miranda simply took over my life, such as it was. Once he knew that I'd lost my wife and child he became my constant companion. We ate and drank together, more drinking than eating as I remember, and he told me of his plans. He was part fanatic, part dreamer and wholly mad. He had some sort of crazy plan to create a new country which would stretch from Cape Horn up to the Mississippi, everything the Spanish and

Portuguese held in the Americas. He even had a name for it, Colombia, after Columbus, and it was to have an hereditary Emperor, the Inca he called him. I remember so well because when he talked about it with such passion you could almost believe it made some sort of sense. But it was all fantasy, of course.'

'If you say so.'

'And he kept on pounding away about the future, about how it was every man's highest duty in life to create a better world, a freer world, that humanity had to do away with injustice. As I said, he was mad. All that high-flown nonsense was probably the drink talking more than anything else but some of it must have stuck because when he left for Europe, to England he said he was bound, I found I could actually face the future. I felt for the first time since the end of the war that I might be of some use, that there might be a higher purpose for me. So I set my hand to the task.'

'Higher purpose? What do you mean, be of some use? Help Miranda in his schemes for South America?'

'Good God, no, they were dreams, all hot air and empty gestures. What I set out to achieve was to become the best business and contracts lawyer in Boston. And I damn well did it.'

Bentley sat back looking at Macleod in an odd, pensive way as if trying to weigh what he had heard. 'Miranda never told you why he was back here in America?'

'He may have done, I don't remember. As I said, he did the talking while I did the drinking. He always had a head like stone, I remember that. In Boston I would often wake up in my chair the next morning feeling like death and in he would breeze about mid morning as fresh as a spring sunrise. God knows how he managed, but I'll tell you this …'

'What would you say if I told you that before he arrived in Boston and took over your life Miranda had met with both Washington and Jefferson?'

Macleod gave a derisive laugh. 'I'd say you were as mad as him. Why would Washington or Jefferson meet with a man so full of crackpot ideas?'

'For the same reason Andrew Hamilton, Tom Paine, and Henry Knox chose to meet with him.'

The names silenced any further laughter. They were the men who had founded his country.

'But why? Why would men like that waste their time on someone like Miranda? He drank like a fish and talked madness.'

'Madness? Those whose names I've mentioned thought not. Of course if you think you know better about such things than they, then so be it.'

Macleod considered what Bentley had told him. 'So Miranda really is important?' Bentley nodded. Macleod resumed his thinking and Bentley waited patiently. 'And arresting me is something to do with Miranda?' Bentley nodded again. Silenced reigned yet again for a few minutes. 'You want me to do something for you that involves Miranda?'

Bentley stood up angrily. 'God's blood, Macleod, does your brain still only work in baby steps? If we go on at this speed we'll both die of old age before you get there. Miranda knows you, you are his friend. As far as he's aware you have no connection with our government and your meeting was entirely fortuitous. That being so I want you to re-establish your friendship. Why do you think I knew where you were?' Macleod pressed his brain for the answer. But, apart from the fact that his head was still suffering, he was a lawyer, a business and contracts lawyer, and had a slow step-by-step way of thinking even when at his best. Bentley did not wait for Macleod's answer to surface. He rounded the desk and stood over Macleod. 'We were watching him, you ninny! Him, Smith, Ogden, and others. We were watching him and we found you. Now do you understand?'

'No, no I can't say I do. Why were you watching them?'

'Heaven give me strength. What do I do, Macleod? What would you say my line of work was? It hasn't changed since we last met, so why do you think I was watching them?'

Macleod cast his mind back to his last encounter with

50

Bentley. What had he been doing? Working for the government. What was going on if Bentley was involved? Then it crashed upon him. 'My God, Bentley, they're going to steal the country! It's happening all over again.'

Bentley nodded slowly as if encouraging a slow, backward child. 'Close enough. For the moment let's just say they're up to no good and it's my job to keep an eye on them. And you're going to help me, Macleod, just like before.'

Macleod thought about before, and didn't at all like the thoughts that came to him. 'Dammit, no, Bentley. I was no good then and I'll be no good now. I was an unwitting pawn, you know that yourself.'

Bentley went back round the desk and sat down. 'Well this time you'll be a witting pawn,' he picked up the document, 'or you and your wife will hang for treason.' He dropped the document back onto the desk. 'It's for you to decide, Macleod. As I told Jeremiah, I want you willing. The choice is a very simple one. Do as I ask or die and take your pretty wife with you. Take your time,' he pulled his watch from his waistcoat pocket, 'you have a full two minutes to decide.'

Bentley slipped his watch away, folded his hands and sat back smiling once again while Macleod made up his mind.

Chapter Nine

My Darling Marie,

First, I must beg you not to worry, but the truth is we must be parted for a while. I am in New York and there is an outbreak of Yellow Fever. Again I beg you not to worry, for though I am not well I am in no danger.

I am in a hospital and by great good fortune it is superintended by my old comrade in arms, Gideon Hood. He assures me that mine is not a serious case and I will make a full recovery. However, so long as I might carry the vile infection and pass it on, isolation is the only course. Gideon has found me comfortable quarters, though how I will pass the time I do not know.

My main thoughts are with you, my darling, being apart must be as difficult for you as it is for me, but dearly though I wish to be at your side once more, it cannot be countenanced whilst there is the slightest chance that the evil that I carry may harm you. We must be strong and brave and let our great love, even at a distance and under such circumstances, carry us through this difficult time. I know you will think of me as I think constantly of you. You are in my thoughts and prayers each day and God will reward our faith and patience I am sure.

Again, my dearest love, do not worry. I will not write from this place again for even paper and ink, so Gideon says, might be touched by the contagion. But as soon as I am free of any possible taint I will write, although any letter to tell you of my return will travel slowly compared to the winged feet that will carry me back to you, my own, my dearest, my one true love.

Your adoring husband.

Marie recognised the hand and the signature. There could be no possible doubt about the writer of the letter she held. It was indeed her husband, Jean Marie Macleod.

'It's a very pretty letter, Madame.'

Marie looked up from the page to Kitty, her maid. 'Tell me, Kitty, did you ever hear my husband talk in such a way?'

'No, Madame, but such words as these are usually spoken when the parties are alone. Does the master never speak so to you in moments of tenderness?'

Marie threw the letter onto the living room table and stood up. Kitty rose dutifully. Marie walked around the room in an agitated fashion then came back to the table and sat down. Kitty dutifully sat.

'It is intolerable. First he grows cold to me. Then he leaves telling me a story an infant wouldn't believe. Then this.' She made a scornful gesture to the page lying on the table.

'But it's in his hand, Madame.'

'His hand, yes, but not his words. He held the pen but some woman told him what to write. My husband could no more compose a letter like that than hop across the stars.' The anger passed and tears came. 'He has left me, Kitty, he has found someone new. He blames me because I cannot give him a child, because I am weak and foolish.'

'No, Madame, I'm sure there's some sort of explanation.'

But Marie turned her head away to hide her tears and waved a hand for Kitty to leave. Kitty left the room closing the door quietly behind her.

In the kitchen Lemuel Trott, the manservant, valet and coachman, was sitting at the big pine table. There was a flask in front of him and a mug in his hand. He paused from sipping his drink when Kitty came in.

'How is she, storming or blubbing? It'll be one or the other, or maybe both. Silly cow.'

Kitty walked to the table, deftly picked up the flask and took it to a solid oak cupboard. Lem put his mug down and shouted to her back. 'Hi, what d'you think you're doing? Give me back my grog.' Kitty ignored the demand, put the flask into the cupboard and turned a key in the lock then walked back to the table. Lem held out his hand. 'I'll have that key and look quick about it.' Kitty gave a half smile and her hand swooped under his outstretched arm and quickly picked up the mug before Lem could get his hand back to it. Lem stood up angrily, knocking over the chair he'd been sitting in. 'Give me that drink or, by God, I'll –'

But the threat died on his lips as Kitty stood facing him.

'Or you'll what?' Lem hesitated then turned and looked down at the table avoiding her eyes. 'No answer? Then I'll answer for you. You'll get a blade in your belly that's what. Lay so much as a finger on me and you're a corpse. Not that there's so much life in you as you stand.' Lem almost winced as she gave a nasty laugh. 'Dangerous fellow, are you? Big, bad bully-boy, are you? My God, look at you. Why, I've trodden in turds that had more life in them than you.' She went to a large tub that was full of cold water and dirty dishes; the accumulation of days, and dropped the mug into the scummy water. 'No more until I say so.'

Lem bent down, picked up the chair and sat down heavily. His bravado, such as it was, had come from the flask and, like the flask, was now locked away. 'You're a hard woman, Kitty, that's what you are, hard as brass. There's not a tender bone in your body.'

Kitty came back to the table and stood over him. 'No, nor a stupid one. I've a good crib here and it ain't going to be queered by you. Master's off gallivanting, is he? Found himself a bit of something tasty and means to enjoy it for a while, does he? The wind being in that direction you've decided to lay up and take it easy, have you?'

'It's not my fault if there's damn all for me to do.'

'And me? What is there for me to do? Fetch, carry and cook. And if that wasn't enough I have to listen to Madame la Muck moaning on each day, as if not having some sweaty brute about the place to bounce on your belly morning, noon and night is the greatest tragedy since the slaughter of the innocents.'

'The slaughter of who?'

'Never mind who. What I'm saying is this, if I have to work you'll have to stay sober.'

'Why? She don't go out in the carriage and there's damn all for me to do if she stays in. You're her maid and you're the housekeeper. She eats in her room when she eats at all so I'm not even needed for serving at table. Why not have a little tot now and then?'

'Cos they're not so little and it won't be now and then. Let you have your way and you'll be drunk as a priest from morning to night. From now on you'll do as I say and like it. And you can start by getting upstairs and seeing to the fires. They need more logs.'

'That's maid's work, not manservant's.'

'From now on it's your work and so is anything else I say you'll do, or you'll be out on your arse in military time, at the double.'

Lem tried to re-assert himself.

'And who'll throw me out with master gone?'

'I will, and by God I'll make sure that you bounce, you sorry piece of used-up shit. Now get going.'

Lem looked at Kitty and didn't like what he saw. She was by no means a big woman, more what you might call neat, and with her plentiful red hair could have passed for pretty if she'd made the effort. But in the first few days of taking up his duties he'd found that she neither wanted nor would tolerate any attentions he might have wished to bestow on her. Lem wasn't a particularly bright individual but his few years at sea had taught him to spot a fellow seaman whom it was best not to cross, the sort who needed and got a wide berth. Kitty, despite her trim figure and pretty face, was such a one. Lem stood up and sullenly left the room.

Kitty went and opened the oak cupboard, took out the flask of rum and a clean mug, and went to the table. She wanted to think and the rum would help things along. Despite what she'd told Lem she didn't believe that her master was off dallying any more than she believed he'd composed the letter, nor did she believe what was in it. What was he up to?

She poured out some rum and drank it down at one go then poured another and sipped it thoughtfully. What sort are you, Macleod, a fool who appears sharp or a sharp 'un who chooses to look a fool? Molly could never decide about you and she had brains, aye brains enough to spare. She sipped again. And no more can I decide what you are for all that I've slipped myself alongside you and your empty-headed doll of a wife.

If asked, which of course they never had been, Marie and Macleod would both have said that they had never met Kitty Mullen before she entered their service. But they would have been wrong. They had met, more than once, and Kitty knew them both, knew them well. Some years previously she had played maid to a lady who styled herself Madame de Metz when in good society and Mrs Dashwood when out of it, but whose real name was Molly O'Hara, sometime prostitute, sometime thief, sometime agent for the British Crown. Kitty had worked with her for a man in London, Jasper Trent. Trent performed some vague and ill-defined role for the British government but whatever it was he did for King and Country it gave him the power of life and death over the likes of Kitty Mullen and Molly O'Hara and anyone else who lived by their wits outside the law.

What the business was in which Macleod and Marie had been involved, Kitty had never properly understood, but it had been a dirty game involving high politics coming out of London and Paris. Molly had told her it was all to do with getting America back for King George. But Jasper Trent was far too cunning a fox to let the likes of Molly O'Hara know anything near the truth. Whatever it had been about, it had resulted in four deaths, and those were only the ones she knew of. Her role had been to follow Macleod, carefully and unseen, from the door of this very house in Boston. She had tailed him down to the docks where Molly had set it up to finish him and snatch his wife, Marie. She'd stood in touching distance behind him on the dockside, ready to put her blade into his ribs when someone cracked her head and put her down and out. My God he was

56

slippery when he wanted to be. And yet …

Kitty surfaced from her memories to take another drink. That was Macleod all over, he'd let you walk up behind him as if he was a simpleton, a ninny, then, when the knife was all but in, he slipped away from you, free and clear.

Now he was up to something again and was in New York. Why? What's your game, Lawyer Macleod? What are you up to? Your letter's clever enough, Yellow Fever, isolation in hospital. You've made damn sure your pretty doll-wife wouldn't come looking for you and it leaves you free to roam as you please. But roam to do what? That's the question. There's intrigue in this and my guess is it's Government work again, like last time, I can smell it. But more than intrigue I can smell money and it's alongside you, somewhere in New York. That's where you're berthed and buying time so you can stay. Her thoughts turned to her old friend and comrade-in-arms. Ah, Molly, where are you when a girl needs you and there's money to be made?

Lem returned and looked around the kitchen.

'Who are you talking to?'

Kitty realised that she might have let her mouth wander as well as her thoughts so she turned her head and nodded to the side of the kitchen.

'That tub of dirty dishes. I was telling it how you would sort it out as soon as you got back and it was thanking me kindly.'

Lem looked at the flask and then at the tub.

'I can't make you out, Kitty, first you lock away the rum then it's out again. Then you say you're talking to a tub. I sometimes wonder –' But he stopped short of finishing what it was he wondered. Kitty sat forward, looking at him with a coquettish smile and her head slightly to one side.

'What? What do you wonder? Come on, Lemuel, no secrets between sweethearts is there?' And she laughed, finished off her drink, poured another and set it on the table. 'There you are, a drink for your thoughts.'

Lem shuffled. 'No, it was nothing.'

Kitty picked up the mug and swallowed the dark liquid.

'You're a fool, Lemuel Trott, you passed up a drink for no good reason. Reckon I don't know what you were going to say? The day I can't read you like a Dame-school primer I'll give up working, take the veil and go into a convent. You were going to say you sometimes wonder if I'm right in the head. That was it, wasn't it?'

Lem gave her a frightened look. 'I wouldn't say that, not about you, Kitty.'

'No, you wouldn't. Because you wouldn't dare. You're a weak man, Lemuel Trott, and a coward. But you have one virtue, you can do as you're told. So set to and do them dishes.'

Lem looked at the tub. 'But the water's cold.'

'And dirty. So bring some wood, set a fire, and get some hot and keep your trap shut while you're about it. I've thinking to do.'

Lem paused for a moment and looked on with half-hopeful eyes as Kitty poured another drink. But as soon as it was poured she raised it to her own lips and he turned away leaving Kitty to her thinking and his rum.

Chapter Ten

It was no more than a step across Wall Street to the Merchant's Coffee House and Macleod found, waiting there, the mousey man he knew from his night at Colonel Smith's house as Mr Samuel Ogden. On seeing Macleod enter Samuel Ogden rose. Macleod came to the table and threw down on it a note. 'Well, sir, I received your note. You have asked me to come and here I am. State your business.'

Mr Ogden took off his spectacles, took out a large white kerchief and gave them a polish. 'I will be glad to, sir, glad to, if you will sit.'

Macleod sat and Ogden followed suit, putting away his kerchief and replacing his spectacles on his nose.

'Well, Mr Ogden, why this meeting?'

Samuel Ogden picked up the coffee pot which was on the table together with two small cups. 'Will you take coffee, Mr Macleod?' Macleod nodded and Ogden poured. 'Cream?' Macleod nodded again. 'Sugar?' Another nod. These polite pourparlers completed and the coffee cup pushed before his guest, Samuel Ogden moved on. 'Well then, as to my reason for asking for this meeting. You'll excuse my boldness if I say that we are new acquaintances, sir, and barely that. Our meeting the other night was chosen on neither side but was, how shall I say?'

'Forced? Why not say forced, for that's what it was?'

'Well, a little strong perhaps,' and he smiled a conciliatory smile, 'but I think, under the circumstances, we can allow forced.'

Macleod found himself impatient with this circumlocution. 'Come, sir, why this meeting?'

'Very well. As to this meeting, Señor Miranda may know

you, Mr Macleod, but I don't and neither does my good friend Colonel Smith. One night's drinking under what you choose to call forced circumstances,' here he gave Macleod a deprecatory smile to show how accommodating he was trying to be, 'isn't, how shall I put it? Isn't a solid foundation for establishing bonds of friendship. I'm sure you agree?'

Mr Ogden's eyes behind the rimless glasses on his nose were all eagerness, so Macleod condescended to oblige him. 'I agree.'

Samuel G. Ogden sat back and beamed. 'I knew it, I positively knew it, sir.'

'Knew what?'

'That you were a man of sound reason, solid sense and calm disposition.' He leaned forward and lowered his voice although the coffee house was almost empty. 'I will confide, sir. I will be so bold as to become confidential. Señor Miranda cannot be relied upon to maintain a calm disposition. He is of a hot-blooded race and is liable to, how shall I put it?'

'Boil?'

Samuel Ogden, seeing a joke had been made sat back and dutifully laughed. 'Ha ha, well said, sir, most apposite. I see I am talking to a man who knows how to talk, sir. Well then, that being so, let's talk, talk to some purpose.'

Macleod looked at his untouched coffee cup. He hadn't wanted it in the first place. He had only agreed to this meeting because Bentley had told him to get close to Miranda, to observe him, to see what he did and who he met. This man Ogden was a friend or associate of Miranda so, on receiving a note from him requesting a meeting, he had come. And what had he found? This timid, fussy, little round mouse of a man who was now sitting opposite him and who had finally, it seemed, got himself ready to come to the point.

'Not before time, Mr Ogden. What purpose?'

Samuel Ogden gave a small, preparatory cough. 'Is Señor Miranda an old friend of yours, Mr Macleod?'

Macleod decided he disliked this man, disliked his looks, his manners, his fussy affectations and his infuriating refusal to get

60

to any point.

'Old? He's a few years older than me, so old enough I suppose.'

Ogden ignored the heavy sarcasm of Macleod's reply. 'Ha ha, witty, sir. Old enough. Very whimsical. But is he a friend of long standing?'

'No, we mostly sit when we talk.'

This time there was no forced laughter and the eyes behind the pince-nez were no longer eager but had become hard and, although the fixed smile remained, it seemed to have changed as, indeed, had the man. This was no longer a timid mouse of a man but something quite different and the tone in his voice became almost threatening. 'I see you are a careful man, Mr Macleod, not quick to give out information of a private kind. Are you by nature a close-mouthed man, sir, or is it by choice?'

Macleod noticed the change and, despite himself, was a little impressed. 'Neither, I like to talk, if I have the right man to talk to and anything to say.'

Ogden's friendly smile returned and with it his amiability. 'Good, better and better. I dislike close-mouthed men. When they choose to speak it's usually the wrong time. Well then, I'll be frank. The Colonel and I are not minded for anyone, not even a friend of Señor Miranda, to become familiar with us or our business. As Señor Miranda is intimately engaged in that business we would prefer that you take leave of your friend and go about whatever it is that brought you to New York. There, sir, that's frank enough, I think you'll agree?'

Macleod nodded. He agreed. He was also surprised. He was being warned off by this little, balding, man who was looking at him across the table like some favourite uncle who had just stood him a treat.

'Frank enough, Mr Ogden, so I'll return the favour. You and Colonel Smith and that dolt of a son of his, Steuben, can all go to the devil.' He stood up. 'Good-day, sir.'

Macleod strode out on to the street, crossed over to the Tontine Coffee House and disappeared inside. Ogden sat at the table and watched him all the way.

Samuel Ogden did not move or speak nor appear to react to Macleod's abrupt departure, but anyone looking at him now would certainly not have seen any resemblance to a favourite uncle. What they would have seen was the face of a man capable of doing great harm, a dangerous man. It was in the eyes mostly, but also in the set of the mouth. Yes, a man capable of great harm indeed.

Chapter Eleven

Macleod received another note later that morning from the limping man, Jeremiah Jones, who was downstairs in the hotel waiting for him. The note was curt. "Come at once. Bentley wants to see you again."

Macleod resented this peremptory summons but also knew that any attempt to resist Cedric Bentley's orders was futile so he left his room, went down and met Jones who dispensed with any greeting and led him to a waiting carriage.

Macleod considered, as he and Jones travelled silently together, whether he should mention his recent meeting with Samuel Ogden and decided he would not. Quite why he came to this decision he was not sure but in part at least it was because it gave him some small satisfaction to withhold from Bentley for a time something which he wanted.

On their arrival the front door was again opened before Jones knocked and once more they were led into Bentley's office. Bentley, behind his desk working on some papers, looked up and began speaking at once without offering Macleod a seat. 'If I'm to keep you here in New York in the government's service I suppose I must provide you with lodgings at the government's expense. But nothing so fancy as that place you're in. I have to answer for my outgoings and the purse I draw from is a damnably tight one.'

'It is immaterial to me where I stay.'

'To you it might be but not to me. You'll move at once. Jones will take you there now.'

'But my clothes and the –'

'At once, Macleod. Someone will see to your belongings and settle your bill. Now get out.'

Bentley resumed his work and Jeremiah Jones opened the

door. Macleod stood for a moment but then turned and he and Jones left the house and re-entered the carriage.

'I'm sorry about that, Macleod. He's a little snappy today, I'm afraid. Something must have happened.'

Macleod, thoroughly annoyed at being summoned on so trivial a matter and then dismissed so abruptly, was about to vent his anger on Jones, but then decided that it wasn't worth the effort. 'I'm sure it must.'

The carriage took them to Broad Street in a district on the eastern shore of lower Manhattan, not so very far from Wall Street but definitely lower in the social scale, although nonetheless bustling. From Broad Street they turned into Pearl Street and stopped outside a three-storey building which had the look of a small warehouse but proved to be Macleod's new hotel. Jeremiah led the way in.

'Here you are, Macleod. They're expecting you and all the necessaries have been dealt with. I'm sure you'll find it comfortable, if a little less extravagant than the Tontine.'

Macleod looked around. The place was dull, solid, and dingy, but he supposed, and indeed hoped in a city in the grip of Yellow Fever, clean.

'Do I sign in?'

'No, as I said, everything is taken care of. Settle in and then write up a report of your meeting this morning.'

Macleod turned to Jones.

'What meeting?'

'The one you had not long before I came to you.' Jones smiled at the surprised look on Macleod's face. 'We trust you, Macleod. We know we can trust you, but that doesn't mean that from time to time we won't be watching you. By the way, why didn't you tell Bentley about the meeting?'

Macleod now felt grateful for Bentley's manner as it gave him a ready excuse. 'I didn't get much of a chance, did I?'

'No, I suppose not. Anyway, as I say, settle in, write the report and get it to Bentley.'

'How?'

'Just hand it in at the desk.'

Macleod looked at the reception desk. A man in a black suit, with a dingy look like his surroundings, was standing there looking at them. 'Him?'

'Anyone behind the desk. Anything handed in there will get directly and safely to Bentley.'

Macleod looked at the dingy man once more. 'Are you sure about this?'

'Oh yes. This hotel, although it does actually cater to genuine customers, also serves as a sort of discreet safe haven for certain associates of ours, like yourself for instance. Now I must be on my way. There's writing materials in your room but if you need anything else just ask at reception.' He called to the man at the desk who came across to them. 'See that Mr Macleod is taken to his room.'

'Yes, sir.' The man turned to Macleod. 'Be so good as to follow me, sir.'

'Good bye, Macleod. I know I leave you in safe hands.' Jones turned and limped away.

'If you would be so good, sir.' And the dingy man in black led Macleod away to his room and his writing materials.

Macleod sat at the desk in his room and wrote out a short report about his meeting with Samuel Ogden which he folded, sealed, addressed, and took down to the reception desk.

Macleod was about to return upstairs to his room when he heard a voice call his name across the lobby. He turned and coming towards him was Miranda.

'Jean Marie, are you occupied for lunch?'

'Good God, Miranda. How did you find me so soon? I only just got here.'

'Your note, of course, telling me you were moving hotels.' Miranda looked around. 'Though why the change to this place I cannot imagine.'

'My note?'

'Yes. To my rooms. Do you not remember? You did send the note, did you not? It was not signed but I assumed it was from you. Who else would send it?'

'Oh, ah, that note.' Macleod gathered himself together. The

note had obviously emanated from Bentley. If he was to do the work Bentley required of him it would, of course, help if Miranda knew where he was staying now he had suddenly disappeared from the Tontine. 'Yes, that was my note. Of course it was. Who else would have sent it?'

'Well, no matter. As I said, are you occupied at the moment?'

'No.'

'Then I insist that you lunch with me and a friend.'

A sudden thought struck Macleod. 'Not Ogden. I left him not so long ago and he warned me to stay away from you. Told me to go about my business and have no more to do with you.'

'Pah! Ogden is an interfering old woman, ignore him. But the friend with whom we shall lunch is not an old woman, no indeed, she is a young woman.' And Miranda gave Macleod a broad wink and took his arm. 'A woman of great charm and also great talent. A woman who –'

'Is not your wife.'

Miranda pushed Macleod's arm from him and stood looking offended.

'Why do you say that?'

'Because it's true. You told me yourself that your wife and child are in London.'

'So they are. But what has that to do with my friend with whom we shall lunch?'

'Nothing, unless it is more than lunch you intend which, from your manner, I suspect it is.'

Miranda once more took Macleod's arm and walked him slowly towards the hotel entrance.

'You are correct, of course, but what is a man to do? My wife, as you say, is in London and I am here. I am a man of passion, I need the society of –'

'Someone who is not your wife.'

Miranda laughed and Macleod, strangely cheered by his old friend's companionship, laughed as well.

'Well then, I see you are determined to undermine my little escapade. So be it. You will join me for lunch with the young lady and you will do your best to see that my designs on her are frustrated. But we must agree that it is for the lady herself to decide.'

'Agreed.'

Chapter Twelve

The restaurant to which Miranda led Macleod was set out in booths so that those dining there could do so in comparative privacy. On arrival Miranda was warmly greeted and they were led to a booth at the rear of the room. Almost immediately a bottle of wine arrived which Macleod recognised from its shape and corking to be champagne. Three glasses were put onto the table beside the bottle.

Miranda smiled across at Macleod.

'They know me here so they make sure there is always champagne chilled and ready when I arrive.'

Macleod looked at the bottle.

'Hmmm. What few memories I retain of that particular wine are not happy ones.'

'That is because you were a little injudicious in your drinking and, seeing as how you drank so soon after that cretin Steuben Smith parted your hair with his cudgel, I'm surprised you have any memories of it at all. However, today we will drink in great moderation, no more than two bottles.' Suddenly Miranda was on his feet and Macleod realised a lady had arrived at the table. He rose.

'Mr Macleod, I have the honour and privilege to present to you Miss Dolly Bawtry, a lady as talented as she is beautiful.'

Macleod and the lady looked at each other. Neither spoke and from their manner it was immediately clear that they were anything but strangers. Miranda looked from one to the other somewhat at a loss that his introduction had produced such an unexpected result. As always in such situations the lady was the first to recover her poise. She gave a slight bow to Macleod and then turned to Miranda.

'My dear Francisco, what a one you are for surprises, I'm

sure. First, that we have company at all for our lunch and second that the company is an old and very dear friend.' The slight Irish brogue of her voice changed to fluent French as she turned to Macleod. 'M'sieur Macleod, how very interesting and unexpected that we should meet again.'

She offered her hand which Macleod took but did not kiss.

'Madame de Metz.'

The lady, Dolly Bawtry to Miranda but apparently Madame de Metz to Macleod, turned a radiant smile on the two gentlemen and her English returned.

'A new friend and an old friend,' she sat down, 'what could be more charming? Pray gentlemen, be seated.'

Macleod sat down in a stiff manner which he hoped made it quite clear to this young woman that he reserved judgement about the situation in which he found himself. Miranda sat looking frankly bemused.

'Dolly, it appears you know my friend Jean Marie?'

'Know him? Why my dear Francisco, I've been within a whisker of having someone stick a knife in him.'

And she laughed.

Miranda laughed loudly at her joke but the laughter died quickly when he caught sight of Macleod's set face and realised it was no joke. 'There is a mystery here. Explain it to me, Dolly, and explain who is this Madame de Metz?'

But it was Macleod who answered. 'No mystery, Miranda. Madame de Metz was the name this lady used when she and I became acquainted in New Orleans. We found ourselves on opposite sides in a business venture. The matter of the knife is the lady's way of saying that she played what I would call a strenuous game.'

'But not strenuous enough for, as I remember it, you bested me and my friends.'

'No, not I, others were involved. I was nothing but a mere pawn.'

'Oh come now, no false humility. A pawn perhaps, but never mere.'

Miranda interrupted the exchange. 'Come, I demand it,

explain to me.'

Madame de Metz, or Dolly Bawtry, took charge of the situation and let her imagination take flight. 'My husband, whom I married as a very young girl, was French, of the nobility, Count Justin Claude Thierry de Metz. He died on the guillotine. I fled to London and made my way as best I could. I was still Madame de Metz when Mr Macleod and I met in New Orleans and found ourselves rivals in business. Now I am in New York and I am Dolly Bawtry. The Countess Justin Claude Thierry de Metz would hardly have done for the theatre so I changed it to something more suitable. There, Francisco, you have your mystery solved.'

Miranda clapped. 'Bravo, Dolly. A name and a title are one's own to do with as one chooses. I myself was once Count Miranda all over Europe.'

Dolly turned back to Macleod. 'And how is the pretty Marie Christine de Valois? You seemed to have completely captivated my sometime friend when we last met in Boston.'

Macleod's voice was stiff with formality. 'The lady of whom you speak is now my wife.'

It was Dolly's turn to clap her hands. 'How wonderful. You seemed to have taken all the tricks from our encounter. I hope you are both truly happy.'

Miranda leaned forward took up the bottle and, with a flourish, twisted the cork which flew out of the neck with a loud retort. Miranda poured three glasses of the foaming wine, put down the bottle and held up his glass. 'To friendships old and new, and to love, life, and happiness.'

Dolly took up her glass. 'Come, Mr Macleod, we're not on opposite sides now, we're all friends round this table. No knives needed nor wanted.' She held up her glass. 'Old times forgotten and new horizons welcomed. Love and happiness for all.'

But Macleod did not respond and his glass lay untouched.

'Come, Jean Marie, don't be sullen, be a jolly fellow and let the dead past bury its dead. Once you and this lady were opponents, now you will be friends, my friends.'

Miranda drained his glass and poured another. Dolly did the

same and held out her glass. Macleod slowly picked up his glass. 'To duty and America.'

And he sipped his champagne.

'Well, old friend, it is somewhat sombre but we will let it pass.' Miranda held up his second glass. 'To duty and to country.'

As he drank Dolly raised her glass to Macleod. 'No knives needed nor wanted?' She held her glass and waited.

Macleod gave a small bow of his head in acknowledgement. 'Let us hope so.'

They both drank and Miranda poured them all another glass and called loudly for another bottle.

Chapter Thirteen

As befitted a doyen of the New York stage, Dolly Bawtry had comfortable rooms in a comfortable, but not altogether respectable, hotel. It was the sort of place that theatre folk and others of the more gypsy professions used when in funds. Dolly was naked and sitting up in bed with a pillow at her back and beside her, lying down and looking up at her, was Miranda.

'What sort of business were you both in?'

Dolly adjusted her pillow. 'Land. We were both after the same piece of land.'

'Ah, development?'

'You could call it that.'

'A big development?'

'Big enough. I worked for a party based in London, Macleod worked for an American interest.'

'A lot of money involved?'

'A lot of everything. Even Paris was in on it. Ever heard of a man called Fouché?'

Miranda nodded. 'Yes, I have indeed heard of Monsieur Fouché, Napoleon's Chief of Police.'

'Then that'll give you some idea. It was a big thing. I never understood all of it. The American interest won in the end so I went back to London, but there was nothing there for me so I came over here and finished up on the stage as New York's darling, Dolly Bawtry. There, now you know my life story, so get out of bed, get dressed and clear off. I have a show to do this evening and I need to get down to the theatre.'

Miranda pulled back the bedclothes, got out of the bed and began to gather his clothes which were scattered across the floor of the room. 'Was it true?'

'Was what true?'

'Madame de Metz. The aristocratic husband who went to the guillotine?'

Dolly thought about it, about the legion of aristocratic men who had been, at one time or another, in her bed. 'True enough, up to a point. As true as you being Count Miranda.'

Miranda laughed from inside his shirt as he pulled it on over his head. 'We are what we make of ourselves, are we not?'

Dolly agreed. 'We are. And we all have to use what comes to hand wherever you start from.'

Dolly leaned out of bed to a table at her bedside and poured herself a glass of flat champagne. Miranda watched her and the lower part of his shirt moved, revealing his continued interest. Dolly lay back on the pillow with the glass in her hand and noticed the obvious evidence of passion. 'And you can put him away, he's had all he's going to get so standing to attention and saluting is just wasting time and effort.'

Miranda shrugged. 'Some things are beyond a man's control.'

'Well pull on your breeches and button them up, that'll control it.'

Miranda bent down and pulled on his breeches. 'Was Macleod ever your lover?'

Dolly spat out the mouthful of champagne she had just taken as an involuntary laugh shook her. She brushed the wine from her breasts and licked her fingers. 'Lover! Macleod? Not him, he was about as horny as a eunuch in a harem. Anyway, he fancied another lady, Marie de Valois. Now she was a proper lady, married to a real aristocrat, youngest son of the Duke of Toulouse.'

Miranda was sitting on the edge of the bed pulling on his riding boots. 'And now she is Macleod's wife? Did he steal her away from her husband?'

'He shot the husband.'

Miranda turned, surprised. 'In a duel?'

'In de Valois's bed where he lay with his boyfriend. He shot them both,' she paused and then gave a shrug, 'or had it done. I could never make out Mr Macleod. As soon as I had him marked as a simpleton he'd pull something that made him look as sharp as a needle.'

Miranda was dressed now except for his coat and neckerchief. He picked up his coat, pulled out a wallet and put some notes on a table by the bed. 'Your business in New Orleans was more than just business, I think.'

'Think what you like, but I'll tell you this, go careful with our Mr Macleod. Fool or a fox, he knows people who can make things happen.'

'Things?'

'Things like de Valois and his lover. Just before I left New Orleans they fished a maid-servant out of the docks. She'd had her throat cut.'

'Macleod did that?'

'Or had it done. I told you, he's a strange one. Oh so plain and oh so honest. But things happen, things go his way. So take my advice and if you've any business that's at all delicate, keep Macleod well clear of it.'

'I will remember your advice, Dolly, and I thank you for it.'

She raised her glass to him and gestured to the notes lying on the table. 'That's all right, Francisco, my love. It all comes in the price.'

Miranda smiled at her as he tied his neckerchief and took one last regretful look at her breasts as she raised the glass to her lips and drank.

Once Miranda had left, Dolly gave herself up to thought. Why was Macleod in New York and what was he up to? That he was indeed 'up to something' she did not for a moment doubt. Then she switched her thoughts to the man who had just left her bed. Miranda was a great talker who said very little of consequence but he was also 'up to something'. Dolly's certainty of this was not based on any pillow-talk from Miranda, her source was Colonel Smith's son Steuben. That young hot-headed cavalier had cast himself in the role of rival to Miranda for Dolly's favours. In doing so he had sought to impress her and talked freely of the important and dangerous business he, his father, and the merchant Samuel Ogden were brewing with Miranda. Up to now Dolly had not been interested in his bravura ramblings of foreign conquest. She couldn't see how his business, important or not, could bring her any profit. But now things had changed.

If Macleod was sniffing about it meant intrigue and almost certainly on an impressive scale, and intrigue like that meant money. There was always a buyer for such information. Her erstwhile employer, Jasper Trent, in London for one. He would pay well if the project interested him. But she was alone in New York. To get anywhere she needed help, someone by her who had brains and experience. Someone like Kitty Mullen. But where was Kitty now? She had chosen to stay on in Boston when Dolly, as Madame de Metz, had returned to London to report her failed mission to Mr Trent.

Her thoughts, though she could not know it, echoed exactly Kitty Mullen's own sentiments. Where are you when a girl needs you, Kitty? Where are you when there's money to be made?

Dolly threw back the bedclothes and got out of bed. Never one to pass up even the slightest chance of picking up any loose money lying about, with Kitty or without Kitty, she needed to push this thing along and see where it would lead her. Once up she dressed but not, as she had told Miranda, to get to any rehearsal. She wished to make enquiries about Mr Macleod and then, tomorrow perhaps, as Miranda had kindly supplied the name of his hotel, she would pay him a visit.

The next morning at around ten Macleod answered a knock on his door. He had been writing a report to Bentley telling him that Madame de Metz, now Dolly Bawtry, was in New York and had been introduced to him by Miranda.

He went to the door. It was the dingy man in black from reception. 'Lady below, Mr Macleod, begs your leave and asks if you'd spare her a moment of your time.'

'Name?'

'Dolly Bawtry.' The man smiled a knowing, rather lecherous smile. He was impressed. 'Seen her myself, several times at the

75

Theatre House. Very talented lady with wonderful, er, wonderful …'

'I'm sure she has. Tell her I'll be with her in a moment.'

'Certainly, sir.' And the man withdrew.

Macleod went back to his report, folded it, locked it in a drawer and put the key into his waistcoat pocket. He had no intention of inviting Dolly Bawtry to his room but while he was with her his room would be unoccupied and he did not put it past her to have his room searched while she held him in conversation. Whether the name was Dolly Bawtry or Madame de Metz, caution was always the watchword.

Dolly was waiting in the foyer and she did not, this time, hold out her hand when Macleod stood in front of her.

'You wished to speak to me, Madame?'

'I do.'

'What is it you want?'

Dolly looked around.

'Won't you invite me up to your room? It's all a little too public here.'

'I won't invite you anywhere, I assure you.'

Dolly smiled. 'Well then, let's walk. You don't object to being seen with me in public?'

'Why should I walk with you? We have nothing to say to each other.'

'No?'

'No.'

'Come, Mr Macleod, don't be unkind. I need to talk to you. Let the past be behind us.'

'You may say anything you wish to say here.'

'Ah, now there you're wrong. Here isn't a good place for my kind of talk. I don't doubt it's a very good hotel and respectable enough but I've asked friends about it and some say they think it might leak.'

'Leak?'

'Not the roof, the walls. It's my opinion what these walls hear gets passed on. My friends and I may be wrong of course and you would know more about it than me, I'm sure, but it's a

76

feeling I get, so I'd rather walk.' She saw Macleod's hesitation. 'I assure you, Mr Macleod, you've nothing to fear from me. I'm a stage actress now, any knife in my hands would be wood not steel. I'm no danger to anyone except the poor souls who write the words I mangle. Come, walk with me for a short while. What harm can it do?'

A great deal, thought Macleod, though how that harm might manifest itself he couldn't imagine. But as she had entered his life again and as Bentley had told him to be alert to what Miranda did and with whom he met, Macleod decided that he would indeed walk with Miss Dolly Bawtry. But nothing would induce him to give her his arm. On that he was firm.

'Very well.'

'Come then.'

They left the hotel and turned into the street. They had not gone more than a few paces when Dolly slipped her arm through his and held it fast. Macleod pulled but Dolly held him. Macleod realised that to free himself he would have to struggle and make a public display of himself. That, alas, he found he could not bring himself to do.

'Behave yourself, Mr Macleod, don't wriggle so.' A man passing them smiled and raised his hat to them. 'See, there's more than one gentleman on this street as would be happy to have me on his arm.'

'As indeed I would, Madame.' Dolly smiled at him. 'More than happy to have you on some other man's arm.'

Dolly gave a light laugh and tapped his arm with her free hand.

'Still the gay charmer, I see. But putting that to one side I want to tell you something. Something about your friend Sebastián Francisco Miranda, something you ought to know.'

Chapter Fourteen

Marie was crying again. As the days passed her situation became more and more one of despair. Nor was it helped by the words of comfort offered by her constant companion, her maid Kitty.

'Don't take on so, Ma'am, he might not have the Yellow Fever. Maybe it is some other fever not quite so fatal.' Marie wailed and put her face in her hands. 'Or if he has the Yellow Fever maybe he'll get over it. A few of the strong ones do, I'm told.'

Marie took her hands from her tear-stained face. 'He is dead. I am already a widow, a widow for the second time.'

'Never say it, Ma'am. Why, not so long ago you thought the letter nothing but a pack of lies, the words of another woman meant to deceive you.' Kitty continued brightly. 'And if that's the case then your husband might not have any fever at all but be alive and well, happy somewhere.'

Marie gave another wail and waved Kitty away.

Kitty went down to the kitchen where Lem Trott sat at the table, slowly polishing a boot.

'Why do you do it? Why do you twist the knife in her? Can't she make enough noise blubbing without you going and making her feel worse?'

'Me? I'm giving her comfort I am. I'm being balm to that poor woman's tortured soul in her hour of suffering.' Kitty sat down. 'And how do you know what I say to her?'

'I listen. I've passed the door when you're a-comforting of her and what you say even makes my back-hair tingle. You're driving her out of her wits is what you're doing, though why you do it is more than I can see.'

'Then stop looking or listening and get on with your work.

We'll be needing the carriage in a day or so and I don't want to be seen out with a driver who's scruffy as well as the worse for drink.'

Lem bent his head to his boot once more.

'Each time you say you comfort her you make it worse. What are you up to, Kitty? You're up to something, I know.'

'The poor woman's distraught, she has all sorts of horrible imaginings. What she needs is a friend to advise her.'

Lem allowed himself a small satirical laugh. 'And you're that friend are you?'

'Why not? There's no one else. She doesn't go out at all any more and no one comes to call.'

'Because if they do, you send them away. I've heard you do it. I know.'

Kitty laughed. 'You know. Oh yes, you know all right. If you know what pot to piss in that's all you know or ever will know. In a day or two the Madame and I will need the carriage to take us to the docks and we'll be gone for some time, so she'll be closing up the house and you'll not be needed. If you can keep your gob shut, stay sober and turn out respectable when we want to leave, you'll get a month's wages in place of notice. If not you'll get nothing.' She gave him a sneering look. 'Lemuel Trott knows all right. Knows what's good for him if he's any sense.' She pulled a small key from somewhere in her dress and tossed it onto the table. Lem looked at it. 'Go and get the grog out.'

Lem put his boot aside and picked up the key and made a tentative enquiry. 'One mug or two, Kitty?'

Kitty looked at him for a second then smiled. 'Two. I don't mind you having a spot now and then. You're not a bad sort when you know your place.'

Lem quickly brought the flask and mugs, put them on the table, sat down and watched as Kitty poured and pushed a mug towards him. He took it and held it while Kitty poured one for herself.

'Where is it you'll be going, Kitty, you and the missus?'

'Timbuktoo. If anyone asks, we've gone to see the Grand

Mogul and buy a big black stallion of a husband for Milady Muck.' Lem laughed cautiously, it might be a joke but then again, it might not. You never knew with Kitty. Kitty drank her rum and poured another. Lem nursed his as he guessed another was not likely to be forthcoming. 'I've got a bit of advice for you, Lem, and I give it free because of my great esteem for your honesty and good sense. When we leave, the house will need to be closed up. Now, if you're a sensible chap, then I'll see to it that you get the keys to do the job.'

'Good of you, Kitty. I appreciate it.'

From the tone of his thanks Kitty correctly assumed he had no idea what it was she was offering.

'And when the house is all closed up I warrant it won't be opened again for some little time. So if, when it is opened, certain dainty things, things that are portable and would fetch a good price, are found to be missing, nobody would be able to do much about it. Especially if the man who did the closing had left and gone away no one knew where.' She pushed the flask across to Lem who took it, slightly stunned at both what she had said and her allowing him another drink. 'Take what you can carry, flit to where you're not known then you can sell up and drink yourself to perdition in style. And if that ain't putting out the hand of friendship and deservin' eternal gratefulness then may your shrivelled soul rot in hell. Which it probably will anyway.' And she raised her mug. 'Fair shares for all and a quiet death.'

Lem grinned as he held up his mug. His was not a nimble mind but even he could see that Kitty was offering him a neat thing. 'Here's to you, Kitty, a true friend.'

Kitty stood up, picked up the flask and went to the cupboard and locked it in. She then went to the door. 'Now finish that grog and back to work. There's wood needs chopping and there's washing to do and after that, well, I'll think of something. I've got to go up and give some more comfort upstairs.'

Lem laughed. 'Much more of your sort of comfort and she'll croak herself.'

But he saw from the look Kitty gave him that his wit had fallen on stony ground, so he threw back what was left of his drink, picked up his brush and boot and got back to work.

Kitty gave him one last satisfied look and left to go back to her mistress and give her comfort in this, her dark hour of need.

The following morning Marie sat with Kitty and for once, instead of crying at what her maid had been saying, she was thinking about it and wondering if what she had suggested was sense or nonsense. It would not be putting it too strongly to say that her mind was torn in two irreconcilable directions.

'But there is Yellow Fever in New York.'

'What if there is, Ma'am? You're withering away here from sorrow. Yellow Fever, nor fever of any sort, can do you any more harm than what you're doing to yourself here. It breaks my heart to see you so. You don't eat, you don't go out, you see no one.'

Marie looked down at her hands in her lap. 'No one comes. I am abandoned. Everyone knows my shame.'

'Very true, Ma'am.'

'Oh, don't agree so readily, Kitty.'

'But what else can I do? You're fading away before me. Why not do as I ask? Let us both go to New York and find your husband. He said he was going to see an old friend and in the letter he said he'd found this man called Gideon Hood so ...'

'No. It was all a lie. He was going to New York to meet some woman.'

'But Gideon Hood is real enough, I've made enquiries. He was a surgeon who served with your husband and set up doctoring here in Boston for a while after the war. Then he married a widow from New York and moved down there. Your husband may well have contacted him. It's a chance, maybe even a good chance. Let us settle this thing once and for all. I know I'm being bold, Ma'am, but it's only out of love for you. As you say, yourself, what is there for you here except loneliness and shame? You can't stay locked up for ever.'

Marie was coming round to the idea of leaving Boston. Kitty

could see it in her looks and manner, but then her manner changed.

'But what if he was to return while we are away looking for him? What if he found me gone and the house shut up?'

Kitty wanted to scream but she forced out the words as gently as she could manage.

'There's that of course, Madame. Or he might already be dead.'

'Oh, no, don't say it.'

'You said it yourself, a widow twice over.'

'But I was distracted, unwell.'

'Or if not dead then maybe warming the bed of some jolly little companion.'

Marie's hands went to her face. 'No, no more for pity's sake.'

Kitty pressed on. She wanted to be on the move and days, precious days, were passing to no purpose. 'I only say it to help, Ma'am. Whatever your husband is up to it must be faced and, to be faced, it must be known, and the only way to know is to go to New York and discover the truth.'

The hands came down and Kitty gave a silent sigh of satisfaction. The silly cow had finally made up what there was of her mind.

'You are right, Kitty, I must be brave, brave and strong. You must pack and make all arrangements. We will go to New York and face what must be faced.'

'I'm sure you've made the right decision, the right and wise decision. Never fear, dear lady, I shall stand by you come what may. I shall be at your side every minute of every hour. We shall find your husband, never fear, and then we shall know the truth.'

Marie gave her a sad smile and laid a hand on her shoulder.

'You are kind and good, Kitty. Without you I don't know if I would have had the strength to come to this decision.'

I bloody well know you wouldn't, thought Kitty, and it's been too much like hard work to get you there.

But she kept her thoughts to herself and smiled angelically at her mistress. As for packing and arrangements, the trunk was downstairs ready packed and their passages booked for the day after tomorrow.

It had indeed been hard work, damned hard work, but it was Kitty's firm conviction that when Macleod was found it would be well worth it, well worth it indeed.

Chapter Fifteen

Bentley looked up from the paperwork scattered across his desk and scowled.

Macleod had written him a note insisting on a meeting and the ever-present dingy man from reception had delivered it. Now, once more, Macleod stood in front of the desk in the same anonymous house where he had been taken twice before by Jeremiah Jones.

'It had better be important.'

'I don't know whether it is or it isn't. This is not my line of work but yours. You're the intriguer, Bentley, not I. I didn't ask to be drawn into your foul –'

'For God's sake stop your maundering and get on with why you came.'

'Do you remember meeting a woman at my house in Boston during that Fouché business, a woman who falsely styled herself Madame de Metz? She was in the company of an Englishman who styled himself Lord Melford.'

'He styled himself so, as you put it, because he *was* Lord Melford. Yes, I remember them. They declared themselves British agents. That would make them pretty memorable I'd say. What about them?'

'The woman, Madame de Metz, is here in New York. She now goes under the name of Dolly Bawtry and is an actress,' Macleod paused, 'on the stage.'

Bentley seemed unimpressed by this sensational revelation. 'Where the hell else would she be an actress?'

Macleod pressed on. 'Quite. But she is also the friend, I would guess the *intimate* friend, of Miranda. He asked me to lunch and introduced me to her.'

Bentley stood up and began to slowly pace the floor.

Macleod stood and waited. On arrival Bentley had not invited him to take a seat and it pleased him that his news seemed to have given Bentley something to think about.

'Hmm. Not good, Macleod, not good. I wanted you to be at Miranda's side but, damn it all, I didn't want you to bring every one of your past friends and acquaintances to bear you company.'

'I didn't bring her, she just turned up. How was I to know that Miranda was –'

'Was what?'

'Her friend.'

'Her *intimate* friend?'

'I cannot know for sure, it is purely conjecture on my part.'

'And your conjecture is correct, he's been in and out of her bed a couple of times. But as he's a man of healthy appetites and she's an actress I took it for no more than it seemed. Now you tell me Dolly Bawtry is Madame de Metz. You're sure I suppose, no chance of a mistake?'

'She came to my hotel and we walked together.'

'Why?'

'Why did she come to my hotel or why did we walk together?'

'Either, both! God's breath, man, what did she want? What did she say? Does she know you're working for me? Does she know what Miranda's up to?' Bentley paused but Macleod did not respond. 'Well, man, answer can't you? What are you, struck dumb suddenly?'

Macleod gave Bentley an aggrieved look. His was an orderly, lawyer's mind which took and dealt with one question at a time and Bentley had asked, in rapid succession, no less than four separate questions.

Macleod made a supreme effort. He had given his word to work for this man, under duress it was true, and more to save Marie than himself, but his word had been given nonetheless. 'Nothing. Not much. No. And, I don't think so.'

'What! What is this gibbering? Answer my question, curse you.'

85

'I have.'

'No you damn well haven't. You've just –'

But Macleod cut across Bentley's words.

'What did she want? Nothing. What did she say? Not much. Does she know I'm working for you? No. Does she know what Miranda's up to? I don't think so.'

Bentley, with an effort, choked back his angry words, went back to his desk and sat down. 'What exactly did she say, as best as you can remember?'

'That she was having an affair with Miranda, that he was an adventurer and had captivated her with tales of his exploits. She said that he was something of a buccaneer and that while she knew marriage was impossible, she loved him dearly. She also hinted that close association with him and those he was doing business with, Smith and Ogden, could be dangerous. She believes they are conspiring to take control of a country somewhere.'

'She said that?'

'Yes.'

'Very well. What else did she say?'

'That our meeting came as a complete surprise to her. She had no idea that I was in New York nor that I knew Miranda. Naturally I thought she was lying and said so. She assured me that she was no longer in any way connected to the British government, that she had never wanted to work for them in the first place but a man named Trent in London had forced her into going to New Orleans. It was a case of work for him or go to the gallows for some crime she was involved in. Naturally I assumed she was lying and said so. She asked me what I was doing in New York. I, rather cleverly, told her I was paying a visit to an old army comrade; a doctor named Hood.'

'Naturally she assumed you were lying and said so?'

Macleod looked surprised and offended. 'Not at all. She accepted my story completely.' He allowed himself a somewhat self-satisfied smirk. 'There really *is* an old army comrade in New York and his name *is* Hood, Gideon Hood, and I did visit him on, well, on a private matter that needn't concern you, so if she checks on my story she'll find it true.'

'If you say so. Go on.'

'She asked me not to tell Miranda about her having worked for this man Trent. She swore that was all behind her but she felt he might take against her if he knew she had once been a British spy.'

'And that was all?'

'Yes. I told her I could promise nothing but that I would not mention her past to Miranda unless circumstances arose which required it. I thought I did rather well with her. I felt that I should report her presence and what she said to you as quickly as possible and insisted on this appointment so as to make my report verbally. That way it would be more complete and accurate.'

'You thought you did well with her, did you?'

'Don't you?'

Bentley appeared to give the question some thought.

'Well, you told her you had chosen the middle of the worst outbreak of Yellow Fever New York's ever had to pay a social visit to an old army friend. In addition you told her that circumstances might arise which would make it necessary for you to reveal her past to Miranda, indicating that you were not a free agent in the matter but answerable to some higher authority. I'd say that, brief though my acquaintance with the lady was in Boston, she seemed to me be sufficiently intelligent to work out pretty well that you were involved in something and the something was Miranda. If, since your conversation with her, she watched you or has had you watched then by demanding a meeting with me you would have brought her to this place and by now she will know that I am the higher authority you are working for. Other than that I suppose you could say that you did well. But if you did, I would naturally assume you were lying and say so.'

Macleod shuffled uneasily. 'Dammit, Bentley, I did my best. As I said, you're the intriguer, not I. This must show you that I can be of no good service to you. Why not let me leave and get out of this? Why not get Jones or some other who has talent or experience in your kind of work to keep an eye on what Miranda and his friends get up to?'

'No, no, Macleod. Firstly, Miranda trusts you because he knows you. Secondly, you have no known current connection to any agency of our government and thirdly, and most importantly, you're lucky. You were lucky last time out and you've already been lucky this time.'

'Lucky, how?'

'You've flushed out Madame de Metz, or Dolly Bawtry as she now calls herself. She was under our noses and we missed her but you're not here five minutes and you've got her to break cover and come running to you. God knows how you do it, Macleod, but you do, and so long as you do, you'll work for me,' the smile was not at all welcoming, 'or you and your wife can do the other thing. I still have the warrant.'

'Very well, but I warn you, luck is a fickle friend and without it I think I'll prove pretty poor material as a deceiver.'

'I'll take my chances on that. Now get back to your hotel and wait until you hear from me.'

Macleod went to the door with as much dignity as he could muster, which was not much, and left.

Almost as soon as he had left Jeremiah Jones came into the room.

'You heard it all, Jeremiah?'

'Yes. How did we miss her? I thought we had all of them well covered.'

'We did, and having them well covered we grew sloppy. She was up there on the stage plainly for us to see so we didn't bother to look too closely. That's how we missed her. Now, thanks to Macleod, we know about her but the question is, what shall we do about her?'

'Have her fished out of the river?'

'Still as bloodthirsty as ever, Jeremiah? What good would killing her do?'

'It would take her out of the game.'

'And Jasper Trent would have another in as soon as he found out and he would make sure that we would not know the

88

replacement.'

'You think Trent sent her?'

'Don't you?'

'I suppose so, who else is there?'

'But why did Trent send her? He must have known there was a chance of her being recognised. If he took that chance it must be because it had to be her, no one else would do.'

There was silence for a moment as they both considered the point. Jones was the first to offer an opinion.

'It has to be Macleod. Any pretty face with a willing nature could get close to Miranda and the same goes for Steuben Smith. We can rule out the Colonel and Ogden as her employers and that only leaves Macleod. She was chosen by Trent because he knew Macleod would get involved.'

Bentley gave the matter a moment's thought.

'Poppycock!'

'Why so?'

'If what you're saying is true, and I don't believe it for a moment, then it means that Macleod came here with the intention of meeting Miranda.'

'Well they met, didn't they? And, other than Macleod's version, we have no way of knowing how that meeting was engineered.'

Bentley gave a dissatisfied grunt acknowledging the truth of Jones's point. 'And if Macleod somehow engineered the meeting, what then?'

'Then Macleod is part of some plot originating in London and involving Macleod teaming up with the de Metz woman.'

Bentley didn't have to think about it for long before deciding it didn't work.

'No.'

'Why not?'

'Because Macleod isn't part of our game and nor is he part of anyone else's.'

'You used him once and you're using him again. I'd say he was a player, willing or otherwise.'

'I know the man.'

'We both do.'

'You've seen him. There's no way he's an agent. He never was and he never will be.'

Jones saw that on this subject argument was pointless. 'Very well, if not what I say, then how do you account for the de Metz woman and her meeting with Macleod?'

'I don't. I don't take your version on board but I'm damned if I've got a better of my own.' Bentley sat back and looked at Jones. 'Perhaps we take all this too seriously.'

'Can it be taken too seriously?'

'Oh I don't mean the burthen of the thing, we can't take that too seriously, I mean the detail. We missed the woman because we were sloppy and took our eyes off the detail. Maybe now we're in danger of letting the pendulum swing too far in the opposite direction and inventing details that don't exist.'

'There is no doubt that Jasper Trent exists. Macleod and the de Metz woman exist. Miranda and his friends Smith and Ogden exist and so does their little plot. And, most importantly, ex-Vice President Aaron Burr exists.'

'Yes, true enough, Aaron Burr certainly exists. So?'

'My point is that we must take all details into account whether we know them to be true or not.'

'So, we assume some connection between Macleod and the de Metz woman. We also assume the woman is working for Trent which means that Trent knows about Miranda's business with Smith and Ogden.'

'And also about the Burr business?'

The question caused Bentley to think hard for a moment.

'No, on balance I think not. I think Miranda has to be Trent's target. It makes sense. We know the British intend to use the Maitland Plan in South America and use it damn soon.'

'We know that for certain?'

'A force is already being planned and a commander chosen, General Arthur Wellesley. It will sail in the spring of next year. The Maitland Plan gives them a foothold in South America. If they're to capitalise on that foothold they'll need the support of men like Miranda, Bolívar and O'Higgins. Smith and Ogden

90

plan to take the Province of Venezuela and if they're successful before the British can mount the Maitland Plan His Majesty King George can kiss goodbye to any ambitions in South America.' Bentley nodded to himself. He was right, he knew it. 'No, Miranda is Trent's target, I'm sure of it. Trent wants this Venezuelan venture stopped or delayed but without antagonising Miranda.'

'A neat trick if he can pull it off.'

'Neat indeed.' Bentley thought for a moment. 'No, London can't know the extent of Burr's plans yet.'

'I wouldn't want that to be an error of judgement, sir. President Jefferson wouldn't be in a forgiving mood if you proved wrong.'

'No, he wouldn't. Still, we could both reflect on that as we swung together at the end of our ropes, couldn't we?' He turned his smile on Jones. 'If it turns out that I am wrong.'

Jones was not slow in taking the point. They were very much in this together. 'In that case, sir, I suppose we must make a judgement and stick to it. Speculation is all very well but it has to lead to action at some point. What action do you propose?'

'We can allow that Macleod is either an agent or an accident, one or the other. Either way he wrote the letter to his wife that I dictated and agreed to work for us on Miranda. Very well. We'll go ahead with my original plan but keep in mind that he might have other interests and, if he has, they almost certainly come out of London. No such doubts need apply to the de Metz woman. We must assume she is working on Miranda for Trent. Very well, let's get Miranda away from her and break any link she might have with Macleod.'

'How? It would take a considerable engine to get Miranda to move at this juncture in his affairs.'

'Then let us use a considerable engine, let us use the most considerable engine available to us.'

A horrible suspicion entered Jeremiah Jones's mind. 'You don't mean?'

'Yes, Jeremiah, I do mean.'

And for a fraction of a second Jeremiah Jones could have sworn he felt a thick, coarse rope slip around his neck.

Chapter Sixteen

'Washington!'

'Washington indeed.'

Samuel Ogden looked first at Miranda then at Colonel Smith. Both men were puzzled and concerned while Steuben Smith, standing to one side scowling, offered them his opinion of Miranda's announcement.

'It's some sort of trick.'

Miranda gave Steuben a look of scorn. 'Steuben, only a nature as mean-spirited as your own would say that. It is a summons to the capital, Washington, to meet with President Jefferson and with Secretary of State Madison. It is a triumph.'

Miranda's scorn was returned with interest.

'And why would they summon *you* to Washington? To explain what we have been doing? To let them know that we've been recruiting an army, buying weapons and providing transport ships?' He gave a derisive laugh. 'It must be known already and probably has been for some time, and they haven't bothered us so far, so why would they summon you now? And why you? Why not my father? He's the moving spirit in all of this, not you, for all your false bravado and high-flown talk of ideals.'

The verbal assault only caused Miranda to smile gently.

'You are right, Steuben. Your father, ably assisted by his good friend Samuel Ogden,' and he gave them a small bow, 'are indeed the moving spirits behind our little venture. What you fail to grasp and have always failed to grasp is that to me this is only a small part of a much greater adventure. You cannot see further than gaining Venezuela because your horizon is as limited as your intelligence. For me this will only be a beginning, the beginning of freedom and independence for South America from Cape Horn to the Mississippi, the creation of –'

Colonel Smith interrupted this flow of eloquence. 'Hold hard, Miranda.'

Miranda turned his attention from the younger Smith to the elder. 'Colonel?'

'Ogden and I are backing you and Steuben to take Venezuela from the Spanish. That's our business together and that's all of our business. We're not part of any great adventure or scheme and as for any ambitions on the Mississippi, the Louisiana Territories and New Orleans are American soil now. Ambitions in that direction would be treason and I'm no traitor.'

Samuel Ogden, concerned at the rising tensions, immediately poured the oil of his words on waters that were getting too troubled for his taste. 'Now, now, gentlemen, friends all, and comrades. Señor Miranda has been invited, suddenly and unexpectedly we all admit, to Washington to meet the President and the Secretary of State. Well then, let's say it's an honour that reflects on us all no matter whose name is on the invitation.' He turned quickly noting that Steuben was about to speak. 'And let's say we'll know what it's all about, trick or triumph, when it's over, and not until then. Let's agree there *is* an invitation and only the one named in it can go and, the invitation being from the President himself, that one *must* go. Well then, the thing's done and we must abide by it.' And he bestowed a hard look on Steuben Smith to drive his point home. 'Now, gentlemen, life goes on. Señor Miranda must make ready to travel and the Colonel and I have more mundane things to see to. Yours, Señor Miranda, is the high part, the part of consequence. But the low part, the humble part of fetching and moving, the quiet part of buying and getting, must also be seen to. So, Señor Miranda, we bid you good-day and God's speed. You, Steuben, must go to the docks and see to our latest shipment.' The oiliness of the tone gave way to the sharpness of command. 'There were too many problems with the last one.

94

Some of the weapons were rusty and the flints of very poor quality. See that they understand that we don't want the same problems again.' Steuben hesitated, but the look and the tone of Samuel Ogden persuaded him to leave, which he did without farewells.

Miranda watched him go then turned to the two men. 'I leave you both knowing that our venture could not be in safer hands.' Miranda gave a formal bow and also left.

The two men left in the big living room stood in silence for a moment. Then Ogden took his spectacles from his nose and gave them a thoughtful polish. 'Well, Colonel, what do you make of our friend's sudden invitation?'

'Sudden indeed. Too damn sudden.'

'And to what purpose? That's what puzzles me. The government, you assured me at the outset, were well aware of our project.'

'I would not have entered into it were they not.'

'And, as one can hardly keep the raising of a small army and provisioning it with weapons a secret, we haven't been overly cautious in that direction. If the government wanted to close us down we'd have been arrested months ago.'

'This invitation to Miranda can have nothing to do with the government wanting to close down what we're doing. I haven't said this out loud to you before, Ogden, but you're a man of experience and intelligence so I imagine you've already guessed, this project not only has the blessing of the government it has support at the very highest level, the very highest.'

'And all totally deniable at whatever level. Yes, I had guessed that was how things stood. Had it not been the case I would never have come into the matter. I'm as much a patriot as the next man but even when a man is a patriot he must eat, and to eat must turn a profit, and without government support, even their unofficial and totally deniable support, our business would never make a cent.'

'You're a merchant, a man of business, I know that you must see things in the light of profit and loss. But I'm a soldier, I

95

march to an altogether different tune. You want a profit, well and good if it can be made, but I want to serve my country, no more, no less.'

'And your son, Colonel, don't forget Steuben. However he styles himself when he has Venezuela; King, Emperor, President, he'll have his own little country and be as well settled and safe as he's ever likely to be.'

'Perhaps so, but my first motive in this was and is to serve America. Do you know why the men of consequence in Washington leave us alone, even grease our wheels in ways no one can trace back to them?'

'A friendly country ruled by an American ally would be very much in their interests.'

'True enough but there's more to it than that. If we don't take Venezuela from the Spanish the British will, and damn soon too. I have been told of a thing called the Maitland Plan.'

'The Maitland Plan. What is that?'

'A plan by which the British, if successful, intend to gain the whole of South America.'

Samuel Ogden, who prided himself on his own capacity for spacious thinking, was impressed.

'By God, all of it?'

'Aye, and if we don't get into Venezuela and take it before the British get their plan into action then all of South America will fall under that damn Union Flag of theirs and they won't stop there. They'll march up into Mexico and when that happens they'll march down from their northern colonies in Canada and America will be caught in a British vice.'

'Does Miranda know of this Maitland Plan?'

'Oh yes, in fact he worked on the plan himself. I first met him in London when I was secretary to John Adams's legation. Miranda used the Nootka Crisis of '90 to get the British to listen to his ideas for an independent South America. They liked what they heard and saw at once it was their best way of recovering their lost colonies, but the way things played out in Europe they couldn't act. Three years ago they took up the idea again and Sir Thomas Maitland put it all into a military plan. If

96

we don't take Venezuela this year or early next the British will invade and my guess is they'll have South America under their boot inside a year.'

'So soon and so quickly? Could they do it?'

'They can and they will because they won't be alone. They'll get all the South American hot-heads who've been shouting independence on their side by false promises. The likes of Miranda, San Martín and Bolívar would follow any flag that looked like it might help them kick out the Spanish. After that I wouldn't like to think what would happen.'

This Maitland Plan and British intentions in South America were all news to Samuel Ogden, and bad news at that. 'I see. But why summon Miranda to Washington?' His face brightened. 'Unless, of course something has changed with the British and their plan or something changed in South America.'

Smith took up the idea. 'Aye, that would account for it. Who better placed to advise Jefferson and Madison if there have been developments we know nothing about. Miranda's hand-in-glove with the likes of O'Higgins, Bolívar and San Martín and the Maitland Plan was all based on his ideas.'

'They may want his advice, no more.'

'Just so, Ogden. His advice, no more.' The two men were pleased. They had talked themselves out of bad news into good news and could now enjoy it. Colonel Smith gave a spacious sweep with his hand. 'It has to be that or something like. Why, Miranda's got connections all across the globe.'

Samuel Ogden gave an encouraging nod.

'Of course he has. He's a Mason, in fact all these South American hot-heads are Masons.'

Smith gave his friend a conspiratorial wink. 'And so are Jefferson and Madison.'

Ogden let out a satisfied 'Ah!' This was good news indeed.

Colonel Smith went to a table and took up a bottle and held it to Ogden.

'Well then, Colonel, why not? Just a small one to celebrate our friend Miranda's meeting in Washington.' Colonel Smith poured two glasses and brought them across. Ogden raised his glass. 'To fortune, success and profit.'

Colonel Smith raised his. 'To America, duty and service.'

And the two men drank, well pleased with the way the day had gone.

Chapter Seventeen

Macleod had used no real plan in his search for Gideon Hood and consequently had wasted much time, but Kitty Mullen was different. She was very much a woman of purpose and method. She settled Marie and herself at a hotel and, the morning after their arrival, went straight to the Office of Law Enforcement. Having gained an interview with a senior City Constable she had told him what amounted to more or less the truth.

Her mistress's husband, name of Macleod, an important lawyer from Boston, had come to New York on business. He had not returned and not communicated and, knowing that there was a Yellow Fever outbreak and fearing the worst, her mistress had come to find him. His business in New York was with a doctor, Gideon Hood.

The constable to whom she spoke was, as she had anticipated, not in the least bit interested in any lost lawyer from Boston, important or otherwise. But he did inform her that Doctor Gideon Hood held the position of Superintendent at the Isolation Hospital on Staten Island and, that information gained, Kitty returned to the hotel.

'I have found Gideon Hood, Madame. It is as Mr Macleod wrote in his letter. He is the Superintendent of the Isolation Hospital on Staten Island.'

The horror showed clearly in Marie's face. 'But an Isolation Hospital would be full of fever patients. If we go there we shall surely die. Coming here at all was a great risk. To go to this island will mean certain death.'

'Don't you worry, Ma'am. I wouldn't risk your dear life. I'll go and see this Doctor Hood. You stay here and wait. Don't go out, don't see anybody. Keep to the hotel and you'll be safe, I promise.'

So Marie dutifully kept to the hotel, took her lunch in her room and saw nobody, which was just as Kitty intended it should be.

Kitty went to Staten Island where she did not seek an interview with Dr Hood but spent her time confirming that there was no patient at the hospital by the name of Jean Marie Macleod, from Boston or anywhere else, and there never had been.

Thus armed she returned to the hotel and continued her enquiries at the hotel's reception desk where once again she stuck, for the most part, to the truth.

'He's an important contracts lawyer from Boston, well off, he would stay at some place businessmen of his class would use.'

The man behind the reception desk was quite young and, from his manner with her, Kitty suspected that he might fancy himself as rather a ladies' man so was as flirtatious as the subject under discussion would allow. The young man leaned forward casually on the reception desk and gave her a knowing smile.

'Doesn't sound a very sharp lawyer, your mistress's husband.'

'Why so?'

'Chose a bad time for coming here, business or no. Yellow Fever don't make distinctions between folks from New York or anywhere else. Why it might even be so bold as to force its attentions on a contracts lawyer from Boston.' He gave her a bold smile. 'Very forward, New Yorkers are. Maybe you've noticed it?'

Kitty smiled, leaned forward and tapped the young man's shoulder. 'You're a wicked fellow. I can see I shall have to keep a close eye on you.'

'Close as you like. Can't be too close for me.'

And the young man leaned fractionally further as his smile widened.

Kitty pulled back and lost her smile. 'Well, maybe later. For now I need to know where to look for Mr Macleod.'

The young man took his cue. The flirting was over, if only for the time being he hoped, and addressed her initial question.

'Now, you asked where a man of position and substance from Boston might take a room here in New York. My best guess would be the Tontine Coffee House, corner of Wall Street and Water Street. That's where most of the business big-wigs meet or those from out of town choose to stay.'

He went on to name two more possibilities at which point Kitty, satisfied she had enough to be going on with and, knowing where she could put her hand on the bold young man again if he was needed, bid him good-day with a charming smile which hinted at promises of things to come, and left the hotel.

At the Tontine Coffee House, which Kitty visited first as the most likely of the hotels, the man on reception remembered Mr Macleod. The reason he remembered was because the gentleman had left without taking any of his belongings. They had been collected by someone else and taken to another hotel, a very inferior place to their own, on Pearl Street. His bill had been settled in full but not by the gentleman himself. The man at the reception desk said he thought at the time it had all been very mysterious.

'If you ask me –'

'Which I do, you being a knowing and observant man.'

The man gave an appreciative smile. 'Then it's my opinion that the fever took him and the management wanted it kept quiet.'

'The management?'

The man nodded his head to a door behind him. 'The high-ups here. Didn't want it to get around that a guest in their hotel had died while staying here. Things are bad enough without your guests dying on you. I think they took the body away quiet-like then made it look like he'd left.'

'Well, dear me, is that what you think?'

'Stands to reason. He was a well set-up man, not short of money and had a good room at a better than fair price. Why move? I ask you, why move, especially to a very inferior

101

hotel?'

'Why indeed? What's this other place called?'

For the first time in their conversation the man exhibited some caution. 'Why are you asking?'

Kitty smiled winningly. He wouldn't take much jollying along, she was sure, but the day was passing and she was in a hurry.

'I'll need to check if he ever turned up there and if he didn't, well, enquiries, formal enquiries, can be instituted.'

The man looked doubtful. 'Formal enquiries?'

Kitty nodded and then leaned forward and became confidential. 'I represent the family. He's not come home and they asked me to find out what's happened. He's quite important in Boston, one of the nibs.'

'Is he?'

'Oh yes, and between you and me, if it turns out you're right, and I think you are, I wouldn't be surprised if there might not be a little money in it for you, seeing as it would have been you that put me on the right track. The family would treat you fair if I told them it was you who helped me find out the truth.'

'Oh well, in that case, it's on Pearl Street. Here, I'll write it down for you.'

And so it was that at around seven in the evening, after a long and arduous day, Kitty arrived at the hotel where Macleod had been billeted by Bentley. But the dingy man in black was not at all as accommodating as had been the young man at her own hotel or the older, but no wiser, man at The Tontine Coffee House.

'Macleod? Can't say I remember the name. I can ask, of course.'

'What about your register?'

'Ah, I'm afraid that's private information, not available to just anyone who asks. Why are you asking, by the way?'

But Kitty was as cautious as the dingy man about giving any information. 'I'll leave it for the time being.'

'If I can find out anything from any of the other staff I could send it to you.' He picked up a pen and dipped it in the inkwell.

'Where should I send it?'

'Timbuktoo, care of the Grand Mogul.'

And Kitty left.

When she arrived back at her own hotel she was not in the best of moods so it was perhaps regrettable that Marie was somewhat petulant in her welcome. 'Kitty, what a time you've been, you've been gone all day. I was so worried.'

'You had no visitors?'

'No.'

'And you didn't go out?'

'No.'

'Where did you eat lunch?'

'Here in my room. I had a tray sent up. Why so many questions, Kitty? You seem angry about something or upset. Did you find out anything? You must have found something to have stayed away for so long.'

Kitty sat down. She was tired, foot-sore and had little inclination to play her part of the loyal maid-servant, but play it she must. She needed Marie.

'Your husband did visit Gideon Hood at the Isolation Hospital. I forced them to let me see him but he refused to tell me anything. I told him I had come from you, that you were distraught with worry, but he wouldn't budge. I even showed him the letter Mr Macleod had written. But you know what men are, thick as thieves and always ready to cover for each other.'

'So you found out nothing?'

'Not quite nothing. He did let slip which hotel your husband used when he arrived.'

Marie stood up, excited. 'Then we must go there.'

'Sit down, Ma'am, I've been there but he's moved on. Moved on some time ago.'

Marie sat down. 'Oh.'

'But don't fret, I know the hotel he's gone to.'

'And have you been there?'

'No, Ma'am, it would be no use me going. They'd tell me nothing, after all, who am I? But if you were to go –'

Marie was up again. 'Then get my bonnet and my cape and

103

we must –'

'No, Ma'am, not tonight, it's too late.' She forced out a concerned smile while in her head she said; and I'm too bloody tired and what I want is a spot of something to revive me, not running around nurse-maiding you. 'Early tomorrow I shall take you there and we shall see what we can discover. Now, you must eat again and then rest. I will go down and order a dinner sent up.'

Marie sat down again. 'You are right, of course, it has been a terrible day for me, one of worry and care but it has ended in hope. I will do as you say. I will dine and rest.'

Kitty's concerned smile deepened but her thoughts were of a different hue; aye, you'll rest if I have to lay you out with a bloody chair leg. I'm for a bottle of something strong and a meal in my belly. But, with an effort, she found words of comfort and encouragement.

'That's right, milady, rest and be strong for tomorrow.'

'You are kind, Kitty, you have a great heart. I will not forget your kindness whatever the outcome of our search.'

She leaned forward and took Kitty in her arms and kissed her cheek.

'No, Madame, it is you who are too kind. But now I must go and get you your dinner.' Kitty stood up and went to the door. 'Eat then rest and leave tomorrow in God's good hands.'

Marie smiled a saintly smile. 'I will, Kitty.'

Kitty left the room and let her thoughts run freely on.

And while God's got his hands full with tomorrow we'll see what I can screw out of today's work. You're up to something lawyer Macleod, sure as God made little apples. Done a disappearing act, have you?

Well, I've found people before who thought they could give me the slip. I'll find you and I'll find what you're up and when I do I'll not need that doll of a wife alongside me any more and it will give me considerable pleasure to cut her pretty throat from ear to ear, considerable pleasure indeed.

Chapter Eighteen

Spring in London was being kind and all that was best and brightest in Society, from the simplest gentleman to the greatest lady, looked forward eagerly to the coming summer. Great things were expected, momentous things. Things that would stagger the nation!

And what was it that London Society looked forward to with such heightened anticipation? New and startling developments in the war with France? A breakthrough in the bitter political struggle between the Tories and the Whigs? A solution to the Irish Problem?

Come now, be sensible.

Well, what *was* London Society so agog about?

Dahlias.

Dahlias!

Yes, Dahlias.

Last year the miracle had finally occurred. Lady Holland's gardener had finally cultivated the first dahlia to be grown in England. Holland House in Kensington had become the Mecca of London. The newly-formed Royal Horticultural Society had declared it an unqualified triumph. Christian ladies of a pronounced evangelical turn of mind had, for a moment, forgotten the foundation of the new British and Foreign Bible Society and basked in the splendour of the famous red flower from Mexico. In the coming months, everyone asked themselves, how many more gardens in London and in the Great Houses up and down the country might not soon be adorned by this latest manifestation of the staggering variety of beauty that made up God's wonderful and infinite creation?

Yet one man in London walked with a leaden step, Lord Melford, second son of the Earl of Glentrool. His trouble? He had just left a difficult interview with his father. True, all interviews between Lord Melford and his autocratic father, the Earl, were difficult, but this latest had proved the most trying to date. Lord Melford passed through the busy crowds of the Strand, turned into a side street and entered the doorway of a substantial but anonymous government building and ascended the stairs to his office on the first floor.

Aristocrat though he was, Lord Melford was also a toiler. No society drone he, but one of the world's workers and this small office was his place of work. He put his hat, stick, and gloves on the rack inside the door and crossed to another door where he knocked. A voice bade him enter.

Jasper Trent was sitting at his desk which, rather surprisingly, was clear of any papers. In his early thirties, he could not be considered good-looking, being thick-set with short, grizzled hair and a style of dress chosen for comfort rather than fashion, and at some point in his career some enterprising artiste had rearranged his nose. His manner on welcoming his assistant was cheerful.

'Well, Melford, how did your meeting with your father go?' Lord Melford was a complete contrast to the man at the desk. Elegant from his neck-cloth to his skin-tight breeches, he was clearly a slave to the latest fashion. He sat down heavily, looked down at his knees and seemed to be having difficulty in formulating a suitable answer to the question, so Jasper Trent provided his own. 'That badly, eh?'

Melford looked up at him.

'Worse. He wanted to see me about Hector.'

'Your brother? He's in London, I know, convalescing.'

'Convalescing? Is that what they're calling it? The poor chap's slowly dying. Oh it may take a couple of years, but the mark of death is on him.'

'Come, come, Melford, having your leg shot off is bad, I'll admit, but if the field surgeons didn't finish him off he's likely to make a full recovery now he's back here in London. He'll have no right leg of course so not full in that sense but ...'

'Oh he'll live, for a while. But Hector only had one real

interest in life and that was soldiering. I believe he was never truly happy unless he was involved in the general slaughter, in the thick of it, on his way to it, or talking about it when away from it. Now what's left to him? He'll sit in a chair in that great mausoleum of a house of ours and damn well fade away. God's teeth, Trent, if it was in my power I'd do the brotherly thing and put a pistol to his head. We were never close, in fact we never liked each other but, dammit, one has one's family feelings. He never did me a harm that I remember and I hate to see him as he is. What's more our father has made up his mind that Hector will now probably never father a child.'

'Isn't that rather for your brother and his wife to decide?'

'I may as well tell you, Trent, that Hector was never one for the ladies. His inclinations, such as they were, were more towards … Well, never mind what they were. Let us say that he would probably have got round to doing his duty by his wife at some point, but it would have been an act of duty and nothing else. And from what the surgeons have told Father it wasn't just his leg he lost. I don't see any heir coming from Hector's loins and neither does my father. There, now you know what he wanted to tell me.'

Trent pondered this piece of news. 'I see.'

'Do you, Trent, do you indeed? I doubt it. What it means is that if my father is to have a grandson to continue the line it must be provided by me. Unless, of course, the old devil marries again and sires another son himself.'

'Unlikely I would have thought. Even if the old gentleman were willing to try and if he could find a young lady of suitable family could he, as it were, come up to scratch?'

'He might. He's always been a horny old goat and I don't doubt I've brothers and sisters enough from the wrong side of the bed-sheet scattered around here and there but he knows it would be a doubtful outcome at best and he's made it clear he wants the job done by me and done damn quick. That means marriage and family life until I can show him at least two bonny baby boys.'

'I see.'

Lord Melford rose angrily from his chair. 'Curse you, Trent, no you don't see. He's told me that until my duty is done I'm to take the utmost care not to put myself in the way of any danger. He's learned his lesson with Hector.' He paused remembering his father's manner of expression and his choice of words. 'Made it clear, damnably clear I can tell you.'

'I see, yes, I do see now. He was referring, no doubt, to your work for me?'

'Of course. He knows what it is we do here and he knows, up to a point, my part in it. Somehow he got to hear about that business in Egypt.'

Trent let his surprise show. 'Did he indeed?'

Melford flopped back into his chair.

'Don't underestimate him. He's an out-and-out self-centred bastard but he's in as thick as thieves with all that's rotten in our politics, which is most of it. He's been cosying up to some of Pitt's people since Addington was ousted last year. And he doesn't like you, Trent, and he'll break you if he can.'

'I know and, for what it's worth, I don't like him and I, in my turn, will break him if I can. But that's for another time.' Trent leaned back in his chair and put the tips of his fingers together. 'I don't like him knowing about our part in the Mehmet Ali business. The Ottoman Empire is falling apart but it has a long way to drop before anyone starts composing its funeral oration. It wouldn't do for our occasional help in its fall to become too obvious. That it *is* becoming too obvious is clear if your father knows about it. Mehmet Ali will be made Wali of Egypt soon and Sultan Selim won't oppose it. When that happens Napoleon will be finished in that part of the Mediterranean and Egypt, Palestine, and Syria will all be closed to him. You did well with Selim, Melford, and did better to get out alive.'

'I wouldn't discount the French too much. Selim will go whichever way the wind blows best for him.'

'Perhaps you're right, but you did well whatever the eventual outcome. However, back to this business of you becoming a husband and father. Do you have any lucky girl in

108

mind or will you let the Earl choose one?'

'For God's sake don't mock me, Trent. I'm some little use to you now I think. I may have started out as an empty-headed coxcomb but I've done my best to –'

Trent raised a pacific hand.

'So you have, Melford, so you have. You're an able and trusted assistant and I do wrong to laugh at your expense. I apologise.'

'Then what's to be done? Even if I tie myself to a desk here in London that won't suit my father. He made it clear he wanted me to cut all ties with you. It's my opinion he is getting ready to hang, draw, and quarter you and he doesn't want me anywhere near you when it happens. He wants me to father children all right but he's also using this Hector business to put clear water between you and me.'

'Yes, I think you're right. Still, it had to come one day so let it come now. As for you, you must choose. Your father's wishes or your work here? It is obvious it can no longer be both. Go and consider your position and let me know your answer by tomorrow morning.'

Melford rose slowly, stood for a moment then sat down again. 'Tomorrow? That's damn little time. I suppose you know what you're asking? If I oppose the Earl, God alone knows what he'll do, cut me off without a penny probably.' Then a thought occurred to him. He had not worked for Jasper Trent without picking up a sense of their trade. 'Look here, Trent, if you need an answer that quickly then I would say there's something pressing you, something other than my father. Could this something involve me?'

Trent grinned. 'Well done, Melford, you've come a long way in a short time. Yes, something's pressing me and yes, it could involve you. I think we may have a way to get the American colonies back or, if not all of them, a worthwhile portion. If you decide to stay on here and defy your father then it might involve you. But it would mean going to America and it would certainly involve danger, perhaps even considerable danger. The choice is yours,' Trent waved his hand, 'now go and make it.'

But Melford didn't move. 'By God, if it's as you say it is, then you can have my answer now. If Hector can't and I won't, then the old bastard must fire his own pistol wherever he can get a shot in and hope for the best. If there's any chance of getting even a small part of the colonies back then I want to be part of it.' Lord Melford sat forward eagerly. 'Come now, Trent, what is it you have up your sleeve?'

'Among others it concerns President Jefferson's late Vice President, that worthy gentleman, Mr Aaron Burr.' He opened a drawer and took out a letter which he put on the desk and pushed across to Melford. 'Read that, it's from our Envoy in Washington to Lord Mulgrave.'

Trent sat in silence while Melford read.

'And can he do it? With our help can Burr take the Louisiana Territories?'

Trent shrugged. 'The Foreign Office seem to think so.'

'Will they support him then?'

'Mulgrave will, but politicians come and go. Our thinking must be beyond the tenure of any Government, especially one with such a slender hold on power as the present one.'

'What is it you want me to do?'

'I need someone to go to New Orleans and talk to Burr, someone whose judgement I trust. If Burr can take the Territories, well and good, but I need more than Envoy Merry's assessment or that of Lord Mulgrave. To bring it off he'll need an army and he's enough of a soldier to know it will have to be a damn good one.'

'Has he got one?'

'He must think he has. But I need to be sure.

'And if he has?'

'We'll support him.'

'And he'll owe his conquest to us. We'll have an ally on America's western flank.'

Trent gave a dismissive snort. 'Gratitude? You think I'd allow the support he asks for no more than his gratitude?'

'Then what?'

'To let him be our cat's paw. If Burr can win the Territories, well and good, for then we will step in and take them back from him.'

Melford laughed. 'By heavens, Trent, it's majestic, wonderful. So I'm to go and meet with Burr and find out if he's got his army?'

'Yes. Go to New Orleans. I've arranged a meeting there. But first go to Washington. Merry sent me an urgent despatch concerning Sebastián Miranda and I replied I would send someone. See what it's about and then go on to New Orleans.'

Melford rose.

'When do I leave?'

'At once as always. Remember, your prime concern is this Burr business but see that nothing untoward happens to Miranda. Merry was damned vague but Miranda is important to us and will become more so. Do whatever you can.'

'I will, Trent, you may rely on me.'

'I am, Melford, I am indeed.'

Chapter Nineteen

Marie entered the hotel on Pearl Street and walked across to the reception desk. She was so obviously a lady that the dingy man in black at the desk greeted her with deference.

'Good morning, Madame, how can I be of service?'

'I understand my husband is staying here; Mr Macleod of Boston.'

The man did not answer at once. Either this was a woman who was a consummate actress or she was indeed what she appeared, a lady of position. She might even be what she claimed, the wife of Mr Macleod. The question in the dingy man's mind was – which?

His dilemma was cut short by another voice.

'Marie, mon Dieu, is it really you?' Marie, startled to hear herself addressed in French and her name used, turned. The woman who had spoken came forward, took her arm, leaned forward and, before Marie could react, kissed her on the cheek. 'But come, my dear, we must sit and talk. It has been so long. Too long.' She turned to the man at the desk. 'You, is there a room where we can take coffee?'

The dingy man gestured to a door. 'There is a small sitting room, Madame. I will see that you are not disturbed.'

The woman turned to Marie. 'Your husband is with you, yes? You are not travelling alone?'

'No, I am not travelling alone.'

'Good. Now, come Marie. I have so much to tell you and I am sure you have just as much to tell me. Boston must have been such a change from New Orleans.' She turned to the dingy man. 'If there are any enquiries for Madame de Metz please say I am not to be disturbed.'

Marie, surprised by events and not willing to cause a scene,

112

allowed herself to be guided to the door by her sudden friend and the two women passed into the privacy of the hotel sitting room. Once inside Marie stopped. She had, at last, recovered herself.

'You!'

'Yes, my dear, me.' Madame de Metz, or Dolly Bawtry to ardent New York theatre-goers, was not in the least discomforted by the look that had accompanied Marie's single word. 'Come, sit down and let's talk. I thought it would be better to be private, first because I'm known by a few people in New York and *not* as Madame de Metz and secondly,' and here she gave Marie a nasty smile, 'because I'm sure you don't want me babbling about your husband's doings in public. He was always a naughty man and seems to have got naughtier as the last few years have passed. I regret that marriage has not improved him, not even marriage to you, my dear.'

Marie tried to look scornful. 'I have no idea what it is you are talking about and what is more I have no wish to know.'

'Of course you don't, dearie, that's why you're here sniffing about this hotel asking for him, isn't it? Of course it is, so why try to pretend otherwise? He's playing a deep and dangerous game and if I know what he's up to I'm sure others do as well. I don't think I need to name names ,do I? Not to you, dear, I'm sure.' She saw that Marie had become unsure of what to do, which was exactly where she wanted her. 'So, Marie, shall we sit and wait for our coffee or are you going to be silly and storm off? Not that running away will do you any good. If I can find you once I'll soon find you again.' She paused once more. She was a woman who knew her work. 'Or maybe I'll sell you on to the others.'

'Others?'

'Oh yes, dearie, there are others who are as keen as I am to meet up with Mr Macleod but I'm afraid they're a sight rougher in their methods than I am.'

It was enough. Marie sat down. But she was not defeated, she was still defiant. She did *not* remove her bonnet nor her gloves and she did *not* lay down her parasol by her chair.

113

'Well, Madame, you have, as you say, found me and have me at a disadvantage. What is it you want of me?'

'Why, to talk, to chat over the old times and gossip about the new. What else should friends do after a long separation?'

'We are not friends, we have never been friends, we never will be friends. I loathe and despise you. I think you are beneath contempt. I think you are the scum of the earth. I spit on your words.'

But, being truly a lady she did not, of course, carry out this rather vulgar act. Madame de Metz laid aside her parasol, removed her bonnet, shook out her abundant, dark ringlets and removed her gloves.

'Well, you can't say fairer than that, can you? Still, now you've got it off your tits you can loosen your stays and come down from your high horse because the great lady won't wash with me, will it? I know you of old, Marie. I know there's paper out on you in New Orleans for murder, two murders to be precise, and if I was to tell all I know I dare say it could be made three.'

'You lie.'

But Marie's voice lacked conviction and Dolly noticed it. 'No, no lies at all. It's old paper, true, and put out by Governor Salcedo, so Spanish and probably no good any more. But murder's murder, dear, and even if New Orleans is American now I still think there's those that'd like a word or two with you.'

Marie's eyes lowered. She didn't like being reminded of New Orleans nor of the death of her husband and his lover. But not liking it didn't make it less true.

'You are still cruel, I see.'

'Cruel but fair, Marie. And whatever I am, I'm not wanted for killing my husband and his boyfriend. Which brings us neatly back to where we started, the man you say is your husband, my old friend and adversary, Macleod.'

Marie raised her eyes.

'He *is* my husband. We were married in Rome.'

But her companion was unimpressed.

114

'If you say so, dear, and as for Rome, well, Rome, Boston or the moon, it's all one to me. I've claimed men as husbands myself and I know that all it takes is a yellow metal band on your finger and a few words. In my experience husbands come and go and I don't keep the ring on too long because copper soon turns green and leaves a stain.'

Marie pulled off her glove and held up her hand. 'It is not copper but gold. I am Mrs Jean Marie Macleod and all your sneering counts for nothing.'

But the anger of Marie's response was lost on her companion who gave her another nasty smile. All the more reason to get him back then isn't it?' Suddenly, as the door opened, she was Madame de Metz again. 'Ah, our coffee. Do take off your other glove and your bonnet, my dear, we must be cosy if we are to catch up on what the past few years have been doing to us both.' She smiled a winning smile at the waiter who put the tray on the table. 'Thank you. Leave it there, we'll see to it ourselves.'

'Certainly, Madame. Is there anything else I can get you?'

'No, that is all.' She looked across at Marie. 'Everything is as it should be I think, Marie. Do you not agree?'

Marie paused then nodded. 'Yes, as it should be.'

So the waiter gave a slight bow and left.

Once out of the room the waiter crossed to the desk. 'Here. You know who that is in there?'

The dingy man assumed an interested air. 'Madame de Metz she said.'

'De Metz, my Fanny Adams. That's Dolly Bawtry that is, from the Theatre House on Nassau Street. She's playing in The Ravished Maiden's Revenge just now. A very moving piece, very. She plays the maiden, Eugenie, who was ravished by the wicked Prince Rupert –'

'She's an actress?'

'Oh, yes, a very fine actress, very fine. With very fine …' and the waiter's hands fluttered to his chest ' …very fine indeed. I'm a regular there to see her, very regular.'

'Look after the desk.'

The waiter was somewhat taken aback at this request. 'Here, what do you mean, look after the desk? I'm not …'

'Do as you're told.'

The waiter spotted his mistake. It was not a request, it was an order. He began to untie the long white apron he was wearing and watched as the dingy man walked hurriedly to the main doors and left.

Chapter Twenty

In the small sitting room the coffee which Madame de Metz had poured for Marie was going cold.

'Suit yourself, dear, but if you want to find your husband you'll need help and it will have to be the kind of help that knows how to find people who don't want to be found.'

Marie remained stubbornly silent and the woman who was Madame de Metz to New Orleans society, Dolly Bawtry to New York's theatre-goers, and Molly O'Hara to London's underworld was, all three of her, getting both angry and frustrated. This meeting should have been worth its weight in gold but it was going nowhere.

She had come to the hotel because the previous evening Steuben Smith had been shooting his mouth off as usual. He had been angry and had too much liquor in him so it was easy for Dolly to coax out of him the cause of his spite, that Miranda had been summoned to Washington. Not his father, not Ogden, but Miranda.

'And what is he? No more than an untrustworthy Diego, full of false bravado and fancy words but like all of his race, underneath it all, he's a cheat and a coward.'

Dolly had let him rant for a while then turned the talk back to where she wanted it. 'I'm sure you're right. Here, have another drink. But why has he been summoned? Is it to do with your business?'

'Stands to reason, has to. And who do you think he's taking with him?'

'Who, my love?'

'Not my father, oh no. And not Ogden.'

'Then who, dearest?'

'That damn Macleod fellow, that's who.'

117

And that had been enough for Dolly to become active. Macleod was on the move with Miranda and to no less a place than Washington.

The next morning she had set herself to watch his hotel on the chance that she might pick him up and follow him. And if that could not be achieved then she would make enquiries about him. And her gamble paid off handsomely, though not in the coin she had anticipated for, lo and behold, who should walk up the street and go into the place but Madame Marie de Valois, her old friend and foe and accomplice of Macleod. But, having found her, Marie was proving obstinate.

'You know, I suppose, what Macleod is up to? He wouldn't keep it a secret from his wife, would he? Not if she really was his wife.'

Dolly watched Marie closely over the brim of her own coffee cup. The barb had struck home, she could see. Whatever the dog was up to the bitch wasn't in on it. She waited for the poison of her words to work. Marie tried to sound dismissive of her suggestion.

'Of course.'

Dolly gave a satisfied interior smile for she knew the answer was a black lie. Macleod hadn't shared his plans with her.

'Then that's all right, isn't it?' She put her cup down and picked up her bonnet. 'I see I was wrong. If you know where your husband is and what he's up to you don't need me after all.'

Dolly adjusted her bonnet and began to tie the ribbons under her chin. She tied slowly, she wanted to let Marie's mind turn. She picked up one glove and slowly slipped it on then smoothed each finger in turn. Marie watched her absently and Dolly watched Marie, her mind turning. Think on, dearie, think on. You need me, oh yes you do. You just need time to work it out for yourself.

She picked up her second glove and began again. But Marie didn't move or speak and Dolly felt a scream building up in her. If the cow didn't speak soon she would massacre her where she sat and damn the consequences. But she slowly stood up and

118

picked up her parasol. Under her gloves her knuckles showed white but her face was a mask of a gentle smile. She made as if to go.

'Wait.'

Dolly wanted to lift her parasol and wave it joyfully in the air, but instead she looked enquiringly down at Marie. 'Wait, my dear? What is there for me to wait for?'

'Perhaps, after all, I do need help.'

Dolly sat down. 'Of course you do. As far as the men-folk are concerned we women must always be ready to help each other or where would we all end up? In scrapes, my dear, that's where we'd be and, if I read your present situation right, that's exactly where your husband has left you at this very minute.'

This estimate of her present position was so very accurate in diagnosis that Marie's defences crumbled and her eyes filled with tears.

Dolly got up and went round the table and put an arm round Marie's shoulders. Marie's hands went to her face as the tears began to run down her cheeks.

She crooned softly into Marie's ear. 'There, there, my dear, we'll get your husband back for you.' But behind the soft words her thoughts were somewhat harder. *And when I get him I'll see the bastard pays heavy interest on some old debts, heavy interest indeed.* Dolly's hand patted Marie's shoulder gently as her thoughts ran on what she would do to Macleod when their paths re-crossed once more, now that the balance of advantage had swung her way. *I'll find you, Macleod, and I'll find out what you're up to and when I do not even God Almighty will be able to help you this time.* 'There, there, my dear, you've nothing to worry about now that I'm with you. Nothing at all. Let's go back to your hotel and we'll see what can be done, eh?'

Chapter Twenty-one

The Theatre House on Nassau Street was, in every sense of the word, true theatre. That is to say, everything about it was make-believe. Firstly, it was not a house. It boasted a street-front façade of two storeys which mixed Gothic with Classical and even had one or two flourishes of Tudor. It looked solid but was in fact mostly wooden board covered in painted rendering. The main doors in the façade opened on to a spacious if shabby lobby which had a sanded floor and a bar across the entire length of the left-hand wall. The roof was painted with substantial young women in coy positions wearing nothing more than smiles. These well-fed maidens were being eyed by chubby winged creatures who had the bodies of over-fed children but leered at the coy ladies with faces ancient in sin. The whole place was lit by a series of oil lamps around the walls and served as a saloon by night and a coffee house by day. Through a set of double doors opposite the main entrance all pretence at solidity was given up and tenting took over. The great canvas space, supported by none-too-substantial-looking poles, posts and ropes, was filled with bench seating divided by a main aisle which showed the floor to be hard-trodden earth. On either side of this seating rose two tiers of plain wooden booths each of which seated about eight people. At the far end of this space there was an ornate proscenium arch and a curtained stage.

In all, the great tent looked as if it could hold an absolute maximum of about two hundred and fifty people in safety, and when a performance sold out, which they regularly did, the management was always scrupulously careful to make sure that never much more than three hundred were allowed to attend.

The moving spirit which had caused this theatrical venture to come into existence, opening its doors only twelve months previously, was a British actor-manager, Sir Abercrombie Fitz-Peebles, who had chosen the establishment's title with some care, for the very name of the place, The Theatre House on Nassau Street, was make-believe. As a matter of cold fact the building was not on Nassau Street, which was a most respectable, even staid, address, but fronted onto an alley which ran behind a plain building of brick and stone which really was on Nassau Street and, though it matters not at all, was the offices of an import-export company specialising in Far Eastern trade.

Being that time of day when late afternoon is on the point of slipping into early evening, the coffee drinkers had departed and the saloon drinkers not yet arrived. Thus it was that the guiding genius of The Theatre House on Nassau Street was able to relax in peace and quiet and talk with his leading lady, Dolly Bawtry.

'It's hard, Dolly, damn me but it's hard. It seems those scoundrels Price and Simpson over at the Park Theatre are out to close us down. I wouldn't put it past them to report us to the authorities as a fire hazard.'

'Why not? We are a fire hazard.'

He ignored the riposte. 'Of course you know why they hound me so? They can't take the competition. Price is a mere mechanic, he has no vision, no grand design and as for Simpson, my dear, the man is no more than an accountant. They neither of them belong in the world of theatre, they are midgets in a world which requires giants.'

'And you're a giant, are you?'

Sir Abercrombie chose to ignore the irony and see the question as a compliment.

'Good of you to say so, Dolly, but I own it's no more than the truth.' He paused to wave a hand at the bar. A man in a soiled white apron stopped reading his newspaper and brought another bottle to the table. Sir Abercrombie refreshed his glass and offered the bottle to Dolly who shook her head. 'No? Well, perhaps you're wise. You're on in the first act.' He put down the bottle and took a drink. 'I, thank God, am not on until halfway through act two. And that, Dolly, encapsulates my greatness.'

'What? How much of that stuff you can put away and still get on stage and say your lines?'

The knight smirked.

'It's a gift, dear, one I've had from my earliest years. My late uncle, the Duke, lowered it by the pail-full and never, to my knowledge, collapsed under the strain until the apoplexy finally did for him. I, like him, hold up tolerably well. It's in the blood, and blood will tell.'

'Will they get anywhere?'

Sir Abercrombie looked puzzled. 'Will who get anywhere?'

'Price and Simpson from the Park.'

'Them? Oh, I think not. Palms have been greased and sweeteners spread like … like … well, let's just say money's been spent where it will do the most good. Added to that Simpson is well-known among the men at City Hall as a skinflint miser. No, Dolly, I don't think it will be Price and Simpson who will close us.'

A "but" hung unspoken at the end of his sentence.

'So who will?'

The knight pointed a finger upwards. 'A power higher than those scoundrels of the Park. A power higher even than myself.'

'What, God?'

'The very one, my dear. Closed we shall be and it will be an act of God that does the deed. No human hand could bring about our closure but the might of Divine Power cannot be resisted even by me.' He took another drink.

'Explain yourself.'

'The fever. This Yellow Fever is upsetting people. Too many of our local citizens fall prey to the pestilence and the cry goes up from the great unwashed, "City Hall is impotent". The murmur runs through the town, "City Hall cannot cope". It's all a matter of votes, my dear. Either the lordly ones do something or they face that most awful of political calamities, they have to take the blame.'

122

'So they'll close us?'

'Not just us. All places of entertainment. That's the word that was slipped to me and from a source I trust entirely. It is some small satisfaction that when New York is deprived of Sir Abercrombie Fitz-Peebles's Players those gutter-rats Price and Simpson will also perish.'

A figure suddenly appeared at their table, a woman. Dolly looked up and almost fell from her chair.

'By all that's holy, Kitty Mullen.' Dolly rose, knocking her chair carelessly back, stepped across to the newcomer and embraced her. 'My God, you're a sight for sore eyes. I was thinking about you this morning, God's truth I was, and now here you are, you're an answer to a prayer, my girl, that's what you are, an answer to a prayer. Where did you spring from?'

Kitty gave her long-time friend and sometime partner an old-fashioned look and when she spoke it wasn't to answer her question but to ask one of her own.

'Come on, gel, you know what they say, when ladies of quality meet, pleasantries are usually exchanged. Where's the refreshments?'

Dolly laughed.

'Of course. Sit down.' She looked across to the bar and called. 'Zeke, my bottle of the sweetened, quick, and clean glasses. And I mean clean ones, not one you've just wiped over with that rag of yours.'

Kitty had sat down and Dolly resumed her seat. Sir Abercrombie rose. 'May I have the pleasure of your friend's name?'

Dolly looked at Kitty. Her eyes said, "If he wants a name from you, then I leave you to choose it."

'Mrs Dashwood.'

Sir Abercrombie gave a small bow. 'Mrs Dashwood, an honour and a privilege.' He sat down as the bottle and clean glasses arrived and were placed on the table. 'Are you of the profession, dear lady?'

Kitty scowled at him. 'What d'you mean, of the profession? What do you take me for?'

The knight understood at once his error. 'No, really, dear lady, you mistake my meaning. What I meant was, do you perform?'

Worded as it was the question elicited another scowl.

Dolly came to his aid. 'He means no harm, Kitty, he just wants to know if you're an actress?'

Kitty shot the knight a withering look. 'No, I'm not an actress.'

Having settled the matter, Kitty waited while Dolly poured a glass of clear liquid and pushed the glass towards her.

She took a drink. 'My life, sweetened gin.' She raised her glass to Dolly. 'God bless you.' She took another long drink. 'I haven't had a pull at the sweetened since London.'

Dolly snatched the bottle away as Sir Abercrombie reached across the table for it.

'None for you. This is a ladies' reunion, no men needed, so push off. Mrs Dashwood and me has old times to catch up on and you'd only get bored.'

'Never, dear ladies, I could never get bored among such handsome company.'

Dolly gave him a meaningful look.

'Then bugger off and get bored among some ugly company. God knows there's enough of it about and if you can't find any to hand then sit and look at yourself in the mirror. That'll do the trick.'

Sir Abercrombie rose. 'I take the hint, Dolly, a nod's as good as a wink as they say.' He bowed to Kitty. 'Mrs Dashwood, your undying servant, Ma'am, yours, dear lady, until death.'

He turned and walked away to the bar with his bottle where he re-filled his glass and engaged the barman Zeke in conversation.

At the table the two friends had pulled their chairs closer together. There were no customers and though it had been some time since they had last seen each other they both naturally fell into the habit of making sure no one could overhear whatever it was they were discussing.

'How did you find me?'

'I was with Lady Muck when she went to the hotel but stayed at the corner of the street because I'd already been in there once asking about our old friend, Macleod, and I didn't want anyone inside to see me hanging round. I saw you go in straight after her.'

'What, you were with Marie? I didn't see you.'

'No one never sees me, do they? Not if I don't want to be seen. I waited till you both came out and followed you back to her hotel. I kept myself scarce after that and waited until you came out and then I followed you here.'

'Why wait? Why not come in to the hotel once you saw me and Marie were together?'

'I didn't know what your game was, did I? Nor what name you might be using? I didn't want to barge in on anything and maybe queer it. I waited downstairs and asked a few questions of a gadabout fellow who does the reception and found he'd recognised you as Dolly Bawtry, the actress, who worked in this place so I waited 'til you'd gone and then went up to her all innocent. She'd been weeping I could see but as the cow weeps easy and often I just went on as if nothing had happened.'

'Did she mention me?'

'No, didn't say anything. Seemed to be chewing on something tough that disagreed with her so I left it alone, waited a while and then told her I was going out to make more enquiries and here I am.'

'But why are you with her?'

'I'm her maid and housekeeper.'

Dolly was stunned.

'What! Servant to *her*?'

'Well, after we parted in Boston I did a bit of this and a bit of that but me heart wasn't in it. Boston's not London and somehow I couldn't bring myself to get properly into things. Then I found out that she was setting up with that old bastard Macleod. They wanted someone who spoke French and neither of them ever clapped a clear eye on me so I applied. I thought it might lead to something but until this lot blew up it didn't go

125

anywhere.'

'But Kitty, a servant? A talented girl like you. One of the best cut-purses ever to walk Covent Garden.'

'Well, it was like I told you. I was down, down with no prospects and never likely to see the price of a ticket home. I needed a billet and I speak French. I'd been mostly straight and clean so there was nothing known against me and it looked a comfortable crib. How about you?' She looked around the room. 'Don't tell me you're back on the game in a place like this? It's nothing more than a ...'

'Hold your gab and listen. It may not look like much to you but behind those doors is a theatre and I'm an actress. Not only an actress but New York's darling, that's what I am. I'm a regular queen among those as goes to the plays. Never mind gadabout reception clerks, ask any of the nibs who Dolly Bawtry is and see what they say.'

But Kitty was ready to get to business. Catching up is fine, but going forward is better.

'They'll say Dolly Bawtry met with her old friend Marie de Valois this morning and spent the rest of the morning in her hotel room.' Kitty leaned closer. 'You're on to our old friend Macleod, aren't you?'

Dolly smiled.

'I am.'

'I knew it as soon as I saw you. She's on the old dog's trail I said to myself. What is it? What's the villain up to this time?'

'If you're here I thought you'd know already.'

'No. Madame Merde thinks he's come down to New York chasing skirts but I know better. He's up to something and I smell money. What do you say? I cut her throat and we set off after him? Whatever he's into it could mean money for us and I'm damned if I'm going back to bloody Boston and service.'

'Croaking Marie would be one way, but the wrong way. We'll use her.'

Kitty shrugged.

'Just as you like, you were always the one with the brains. As far as I'm concerned you say what goes and I'll see that it gets done. It'll be like old times. So, what's the fox up to?'

'He's in with a funny crowd. There's an old Colonel called Smith and a merchant called Ogden who are putting a small army together under the Colonel's son and a man called Miranda. They're going to get themselves a kingdom down south somewhere, steal it off the Spanish.'

'S'truth, steal a kingdom? They don't think small over here, do they?'

'Miranda doesn't. He's a right Captain Huff and stands no nonsense. So long as he's in charge they may even get away with it. But he's got the Colonel's son alongside him, a cockscomb of a lad called Steuben and I reckon him for a jinxer.'

'So where does Macleod fit in?'

Dolly shook her head and took a thoughtful drink.

'I'm not sure. I never could make him out, devil or dolt, he was sometimes one and sometimes the other.'

'But he bested us.'

'Him or someone who was using him. But you've served in his house, Kitty. You must have been able to properly sconce him. What's your tally on him?'

'Difficult. In his own home he's much like any other husband. To see him from day to day you'd say he couldn't plan a pissing match in a pothouse, but that don't signify. We've seen him at work and he's like you say, sharp and stupid by turns. Is he with the Americans again on this one or is it others?'

'I think the Americans. You can't put together a small army, fit it out and put it to sea without the government knowing, so I think our friend Macleod might have been slipped on to the crew-sheet to keep an eye on things.' Dolly shook her head and gave a sardonic laugh. 'You could have knocked me over with a feather when Miranda introduced me to him. There he was, calm as you please.'

'You know this Miranda?'

'I let him inside my drawers now and again. He brasses up well and I thought it worth keeping an eye on him.'

'And it's paid off.'

'Not yet, but it will. Miranda's been invited to Washington and guess who's managed to tag along?'

'Macleod!'

'See, dull as a bucket one minute then sharp as a needle the next. But whether he's a fox or someone's making him look like one doesn't matter. There's business afoot, business a certain gent in London would pay well for.'

'Trent?'

'Mr Trent indeed. What we need to do is get to Washington double quick and find out how the land lies and get in touch with Trent through our Ambassador.'

Kitty jerked a thumb.

'And her at the hotel?'

'Marie? I told her I could find Macleod and I think she may be ready to take my help. God knows she'll get nowhere under her own sail. That's what she was thinking about when you went back to her. If we can get her to rely on us then we'll use her for the time being.'

'Use her how?'

'She's our ticket to follow Macleod without questions getting asked and while she's at it she can bankroll the trip.'

'And once we find him?'

'She's yours, Kitty, do with her as you wish.'

128

Chapter Twenty-two

Macleod and Miranda took ship on one of the many merchantmen which plied America's Eastern seaboard. Their ship was a small two-masted coaster carrying a mixed cargo of manufactured domestic goods, pots and pans, chairs and tables, knives, forks and spoons, curtains and sheets, anything and everything in fact that the factories of the north could produce cheaply and in quantity, and that the people of the south wanted and would buy.

At the front of the ship there had been added one cabin, an acknowledgement that in these restless times people, almost as much as merchandise, needed to be moved up and down the coast. The cabin was small with one window, designed more to withstand heavy seas than to give much light or air. The door was equally solid when shut tight against any waves breaking over the deck in rough weather. Inside, against either wall, were two sets of double bunks indicating that this small space, about four paces long by three paces wide, had been deemed fit for four adult passengers. Fortunately Macleod and Miranda were able to get it to themselves by the simple process of Miranda buying all four berths.

Macleod did not look forward to the journey. Georgetown, where they would disembark, was not a place of happy memories for him. He had made the journey once before when Bentley had ensnared him into the New Orleans business. It had been messy and dangerous, indeed almost fatal to both himself and Marie. Yet here he was and once again he was ensnared.

During their enforced idleness at sea Macleod had been happy to sit in the cabin if the weather was inclement or walk the deck if fine and listen to Miranda hold forth on his plans for the Venezuelan project as the ship slowly ploughed through the grey-green Atlantic waves and the wind sung through the rigging. Colonel Smith and Samuel Ogden were financing a small army and Miranda was confident that, once landed on South American soil, the local people would rise up in their support.

Macleod deferred to his friend's knowledge of South America and its peoples but he readily offered his views on one of Miranda's New York associates.

'I don't know your friends as you do, nor do I want to know them, but from what little I've seen I'd say that Steuben Smith will prove a sorry ally for you. He dislikes you and strikes me as a young man of ambition for himself rather than any cause.'

'You are right about Steuben. He thinks that once we have Venezuela he will eliminate me and take some grand title, King perhaps. Well, let him dream. I also have dreamt, and for too many years to be bothered by that young man. I needed his father and his political friends and I needed Ogden's money. The price was allowing Steuben to be involved, so I paid it. I will honour our contract until he breaks it, which he will, then I will kill him. You see, my dear old friend, my mission is not for Venezuela alone. It is for the whole of South America.'

As the ship was driven ever forward by the wind, so Miranda was driven back to his eternal hymn of freedom from Cape Horn to the Mississippi and Macleod would listen. So the days passed until the ship had docked at Georgetown and, after a night's rest, the last leg of their journey to the capital had begun. The last time Macleod had visited Washington it had been little more than a building site. Much had changed. It was now a true capital, a home of government. There were streets with rows of fine terraced houses each with a spacious, colonnaded front porch. There were parks, wide avenues and handsome buildings. And presiding over the new city, atop its own hill, the Capitol building. Macleod and Miranda rode through the city more or less in silence. Miranda, like Macleod, had been there before and both were occupied with past memories and thoughts of what was to come. Their first night in the capital found them in the dining room of the best hotel

Washington could offer, courtesy of the government. Newly-built and grand in scale and design it was located close to the heart of government and was used by important visitors both domestic and foreign. Miranda, from arrival, seemed at home in its atmosphere of deference and wealth. In fact he deported himself as if he were one of the foreign dignitaries whom the hotel was used to welcoming and carried it off so very well that he was treated as if he were the genuine article. Macleod, on the other hand, was accepted as some minor functionary who travelled with him. A secretary perhaps, or his valet.

The evening of their arrival, when dinner was over and they were relaxing, Macleod decided it was time to speak of a matter that had pressed hard on him for some time. 'Now we're here, Miranda, I need to tell you something.'

'Then tell me. But first more of this excellent wine.' Miranda waved his hand and a waiter was immediately at their table, he took the order and was gone. 'As guests of the Government we are treated with proper respect. Too often, alas, I have *not* been shown the respect I deserve.' Macleod sat back. He wasn't looking forward to what he wanted to say so, as long as his friend talked, he would let him. 'In Europe I sometimes styled myself Count Miranda.' He looked at Macleod. 'You think that arrogant, improper?' Macleod shrugged. 'You are right. It *was* arrogant and improper but it was meant as a joke, a suitable response to those who –' The waiter arrived with the bottle. Miranda poured himself a glass and offered the bottle to Macleod who shook his head. 'But insults and worse have never made me lose sight for one moment of my purpose. In England the Spanish tried to arrest me. They had pursued me across Europe from Sweden to Paris and on to London. But I defeated them. The Russian Ambassador told them I was in the service of Queen Catherine.'

'Were you?'

'Oh yes, it was no lie, I served her Majesty, among others.' Miranda made a dismissive gesture. 'I was a man of many parts, serving many governments, but only ever one cause.' He raised his glass. 'The cause of freedom, the cause of my country,

South America.' He drank. 'That is why the Spanish want me. They know that I will not rest until the whole of South America is free and that freedom stretches from Tierra del Fuego to the banks of the Mississippi.'

The mention of the Mississippi stirred Macleod into action.

'Look Miranda, I need to tell you something and I'm going to damn well tell you. I don't want to say it, but it must be said.'

Miranda put his glass down. 'Then speak, my friend.'

'Curse me for a weak coward, I'm not your friend. I'm an agent for a man named Bentley. He gave me that letter that invited you here and he told me to come with you to Washington. I wouldn't be at all surprised if he didn't write the damn thing himself. He's a powerful man, Miranda, more powerful than I can explain, and it seems he can do pretty much as he pleases, even issue invitations from the President. He got me into this and told me to stick by you and play the friend.' Macleod hung his head. 'And I did it.' He looked up again. 'I'm nothing more than a coward and a foul cheat and I have played my part in bringing you into what, for all I know, is a trap where you may well –'

'But my friend, my dear Jean Marie, I knew all of this.'

'What? You knew! How could you have known?'

Miranda gave a careless shrug. 'I knew of Bentley. I knew that you were working for him and as for coming to Washington being a trap, well, as a meeting with both the President and the Secretary of State is the bait, then I walk into it gladly.' Miranda reached across and put his hand onto Macleod's arm. 'Come, old friend, do not look so concerned, it is clear to me, as it has been for some time, you are not an agent of Bentley but merely someone he has found and used.' Miranda sat back and took another drink. 'No, no, you must not blame yourself for whatever happens, although nothing will happen, at least nothing as you imagine it.'

'You knew?'

'Of course.'

'But how did you know?'

'You told me.'

132

'Me!'

'Of course. I see you in the hotel in New York and I recognise you at once. It is my old friend from Boston, so I come to you and introduce myself. You are no actor, Jean Marie, your astonishment is genuine. And I have to know this. Too many times friends have appeared as if by accident, but are no accident. But you are indeed an accident. Then there is the incident with that imbecile Steuben and his friend. That was not managed by you. The next day you are taken away from your hotel to visit a most anonymous house. I know this. I have my own helpers who are my eyes and ears in New York. I make enquiries about your destination. I discover that the house is not at all what it seems. I make more enquiries and what do I find? Bentley. Now he *is* a man of consequence. He will never be an accident. I know of this Señor Bentley. He is a dangerous man, a man to be avoided. From then on I am very careful of you. I watch you, not in person of course, but you are watched. I am aware of every move you make. The rest you know. I introduce you to the lovely Dolly Bawtry and behold, you are already well known to each other. But not friends, I see that at once. She visits you and after that you visit Bentley. Then you bring me the letter which invites me to meet the President and the Secretary of State. You tell me that you must accompany me. You are cautious, you are secret. You say you can tell me nothing, only that the letter comes from the very highest level. Of course I accept. As I say, you have told me everything I need to know. You are in New York, why I do not know, but it is *not* as any sort of agent. We meet by chance and you are caught up in a net set by our mutual friend Bentley, a net from which you cannot escape. You do as you are told and here we are.' Miranda paused and looked at Macleod. 'I am right, am I not? I have missed nothing. It is all as I say it is?'

'It is.'

'Of course it is.' Miranda finished his wine and poured himself another glass. 'Such things have been my life for too long to be fooled so easily. No, Jean Marie, you are *not* an agent for Bentley and you *are* my friend. As for being a coward

133

and a cheat, some of the very best men I have known have been cowards and cheats. Now, please take a drink. To drink alone brings only melancholy and, now that we are here and I am to meet President Jefferson and Secretary Madison, it is not the time for sadness.'

Macleod was bewildered but he held his glass out and let his friend fill it.

'If you knew about Bentley, that he was using me, why did you go along with it all?'

'Why not? Look what it has brought me. Am I not the guest of your Government here in your very capital?'

'But why keep me by you? I work for Bentley, unwillingly, but I still am answerable to him. I must do as he bids me.'

'Of course you must. I would have it no other way.'

Macleod took a drink. It was indeed very good wine.

'I don't understand you, Miranda.'

'Of course you don't. But that is not important. What is important is that I understand you. If I had removed you –' Macleod looked at him '– not that it crossed my mind for a moment to do so. But if I had, then some other would undoubtedly have taken your place, perhaps a real agent, someone who could indeed do me and my cause harm.' Miranda offered the bottle to Macleod who held out his glass. 'As it is, I know where I stand. You will watch me for Bentley and report everything you see and hear to him. Good, let it be so. I will do what I must do and you will do what you must do and, God willing, all will be as it should be when the cards are finally played out. By the way, the lady I know as Dolly Bawtry and you know as Madame de Metz, she is someone I would like to hear about. Of Dolly the New York actress I know. Tell me all you know of Madame de Metz.'

Miranda emptied the bottle into their glasses and waved to the waiter who, anticipating their requirements, had another bottle ready and waiting.

'Madame de Metz, eh? Where shall I begin?'

'At the beginning, old friend, always begin at the beginning.'

134

'Well, I suppose you could say it all began in New Orleans, or maybe Georgetown, or maybe Boston.'

'Let's say New Orleans, that sounds by far the best place of those you have mentioned.'

'Yes, you're right. As far as that woman is concerned it *did* start in New Orleans, with some fancy handkerchiefs in a tailor's shop.'

Miranda refreshed their glasses from the new bottle once more and sat back.

'Indeed! Pray go on, old friend, I am already fascinated.'

Chapter Twenty three

That irrepressible impresario, Sir Abercrombie Fitz-Peebles, made an elaborate bow.

'Dear lady, it is a joy and a privilege to welcome you to our little company. I am the founder and fountainhead, the guiding spirit and presiding genius, in short, dear lady, I am Sir ...'

Marie looked on totally at a loss as to what she should do or say but Dolly, however, cut short his performance.

'Never mind the dramatics, Abe, Marie's not going to be impressed. Her late husband really was one of the nibs, youngest son of the Duke of Toulouse, so your little pantomime is pretty much wasted on her.'

Sir Abercrombie, Abe, rose from his bow. 'Really, Dolly, a little support, a little appreciation, it's not much to ask I think. As your leader and indeed your mentor I must insist –'

This time it was Kitty who interrupted. 'Does he go on like this all the time? Cos if he does we'll get to Washington in time to die of old age.'

Sir Abercrombie gave Kitty a poisonous look. They had not been in each other's company more than a few times but he did not like her and made no attempt to hide how he felt. From Kitty's tone it was clear that her feelings were returned in kind.

Dolly intervened. This was no time for fallings out.

'Now look, both of you. Marie's paying for this outing so, Abe, no more ogling from you. She's off limits. And Kitty, we've all got to rub along so no more getting your knife into Abe. He ain't much I'll admit but he knows the stage and he'll get us through. We're all agreed we need to go to Washington?'

Kitty nodded reluctantly and Marie added a heartfelt endorsement. 'We must, if we are to find my husband, we must.'

Sir Abercrombie gestured to Marie. '*You* must, dear lady, if you wish to find your husband. You, Dolly, and your friend must because you say you must. But I? Why should I go to Washington? Really, Dolly, if I am to lead you ladies as an ensemble I must have my position acknowledged by all.' He shot another nasty glance at Kitty. 'From the lowest,' he turned and bestowed a smile on Marie, 'to the highest.' Then he turned back to Dolly. 'Really, Dolly, if I am to go, and I remind you of your own words, I and I alone know the stage sufficiently well to carry off the venture. I must insist, nay demand, that my position be acknowledged by all.'

Dolly stood looking at him for a moment. 'Now listen, Abe, because I'm not going to repeat this. You agreed to go and you agreed the price. As for not going, you're finished here in New York. Your theatre's being closed on you by Price and Simpson because they've rubbed City Hall's noses in the fact that you run a public knocking-shop in those cosy side boxes. And if that hadn't got you closed then the fever would have done it or the fact this tinderbox of a theatre would have gone up in a merry blaze sooner or later. As for Kitty,' Dolly gave her friend a meaningful look, 'she knows which side her bread's buttered. She don't like you and you don't like her. Very well, stay out of each other's hair and both do your jobs. And if all that wasn't enough, then let's say you'll go for good-fellowship, for my sake who's been alongside you for over a year, and whatever our Park Theatre friends know about you and your Theatre House is nothing compared to what I know.'

Sir Abercrombie capitulated. 'Dolly, you are, as always, in the right of it. I agreed to go and, as a gentleman of the blood, I can do no less than honour my word. *Noblesse oblige*, dear ladies, *noblesse oblige*. I shall lead you to Washington and there we shall bring high culture to an otherwise barbarian corner of this great land. Dear ladies all, ever your humble servant.' And the actor-manager gave his followers a deep bow. As he rose he somehow changed and the grand manner dropped away like some sort of costume. 'Well, if we're going, we ought to scoot. Travel light and travel fast have always been my watchwords and Price and Simpson will have me in the Bridewell if I stay but, by God, it's been tried before. They'll have to catch me first which is easier said than done. I'm packed, one valise and a bag, how about the rest of you?'

'Me and Kitty are done.' Dolly turned to Kitty, 'How about Marie?'

'She's done, I saw to it myself.'

Sir Abercrombie had a final question. 'One last thing. I can act and you, Dolly, can act. What about these two?'

Kitty shook her head. 'No fear, I'm not going out on any stage.'

They all looked at Marie.

'I can sing a little.'

Sir Abercrombie looked at her thoughtfully. 'Well, a pretty song-bird might be useful. We'll see. In the right dress the men will be looking rather than listening so we might find a use for you. We'll be a small troupe and it's a pity we've got to run out on our colleagues but as you say, Dolly, it was all up here anyway. Well, that's that then, so let it be ho for Washington and new audiences, and may God rot the precious Park Theatre and all who perform in her.' He waved a hand. 'Farewell, New York, you ain't been a bad old town to me and I wish you good fortune. Come, ladies, the world awaits.'

And what was left of Sir Abercrombie Fitz-Peebles's strolling band left the Theatre House on Nassau Street by the back exit and, each carrying their own bags, silently slipped away in the dark, heading for the docks.

Chapter Twenty Four

James Madison, the Secretary of State for the Union of America, had dark, penetrating eyes, a high forehead and a strong chin. It would have been a handsome face had it not been suffused in an angry scowl. He sat in his office with his hands clasped in front of him on his desk glaring at Miranda who sat calmly opposite him. Miranda had received angry looks from powerful men in many countries, a number of whom had tried to do considerably worse than scowl at him. He smiled ingratiatingly because he knew it would annoy Secretary Madison even further.

'As I say, I found President Jefferson to be, as he always was, a most charming man, a man of culture and refinement. A man of superb good manners which is so much more important, do you not think, Mr Secretary, than mere brains?' Madison's scowl deepened and he seemed about to reply so Miranda hurried on. 'In the sometimes difficult world of international politics it is too easy, I have found, to become, how shall I put it, to become coarse, to forget those little touches of courtesy that separate the gentleman from the barbarian.'

Madison stood up. Miranda slowly followed his example.

'You, sir, are a scoundrel. I know it, you know it and Jefferson knows it.' Miranda smiled and bowed as if Madison had just paid him the most generous of compliments. 'You have lived by your wits across Europe and now you're up to your tricks here in America.'

'I assure you, Mr Secretary ...'

Madison snapped his fingers.

'And I don't give that for your assurances. You think yourself high-born? Well I have better-bred horses pulling my carriage. You think yourself a hero? Well I have braver hounds in my kennels. You think you serve a cause? Well, sir, I say that the only cause you serve or have ever served is Sebastián Francisco de Miranda. As for any little touches of courtesy, you can have them when I finish wiping my arse with them. If you're an example of a gentleman, sir, then thank God I'm a barbarian.'

Miranda smiled and bowed again as if Madison had heaped an embarrassment of praise on him.

'What can I say, Mr Secretary? If one of your exalted position has taken the time and trouble to acquaint himself so closely with my humble life I can only say that I am as honoured by your efforts and interest as much as I regret your choice of sources of information.'

And once again Miranda bowed and smiled.

Madison stood for a second then burst out laughing and slapped a hand hard on the desk. 'By God, Miranda, they weren't wrong about you, were they?'

This laughter and the big grin on Madison's face that followed it achieved what the previous tirade had so failed to accomplish and a disconcerted look spread across Miranda's face.

Madison sat down waving a hand at Miranda for him to do the same.

'To business. I was told you could handle yourself. I now see that you can. I was also told that you were sharp and capable. You'll need to be. Yesterday you met Jefferson and he told you that we'd continue to ignore your little adventure with Smith and Ogden. He went further and gave you his blessing up to a point.'

'His private and utterly deniable blessing.'

'Well what do you expect? We can't be seen to be sponsoring an invasion of a Spanish colony can we? Apart from anything else there's the 1793 Proclamation of Neutrality.' A smile returned to Madison's face as he sat back. 'We're not at war with Spain, not yet. We're not at war with anyone. We've made our position clear and we stick to it. America stands neutral.'

'And if others, who choose not to be so neutral, take actions which will be in America's interest?'

'We don't interfere in anything we don't know about and officially we don't know about your little project.'

Miranda spread his hands. 'Ah, politics and diplomacy. What a wonderful game of lies, hypocrisy and deceit. Truly a profession for gentlemen.'

The smile disappeared and the frown returned. 'Don't play your hand too strong, Miranda. You need us more than we need you. We could squash your enterprise in a second if we chose to.'

'But then Colonel Smith would not be able get you your own little foothold in South America.'

'As to that,' Madison shrugged, 'things will turn out as they turn out. Yesterday Jefferson told you that we'd let your project go ahead. He even hinted that we'd smooth your way a little. Today I tell you the price.'

'Of course. America always has its price.'

'We need a man of experience in certain matters. A man who has judgement and resource. To be short, we need you. President Jefferson's late Vice President, Aaron Burr, is proving a difficulty for the present administration. Not putting too fine a point on it, he is plotting treason.' Miranda's eyebrows rose, not because the news surprised him, treachery among politicians never surprised him, but being told about it in such clear terms by Secretary of State Madison certainly did.

'You have proof?'

'Some, a little, not enough. That's where you come in. Your coming here was arranged in such a way that, so far as anyone knows, it is concerned with your Venezuelan project. It was arranged by a man named Bentley. He arranges things for us, things like dealing with Burr, things that can't go through the books, as it were. We need to know what Burr's up to, how far it's got, and who else of importance is involved. He's been given forty thousand acres by the Spanish on the Ouachita River and he's taken what he calls farmers there and armed them, so now he has land and the beginnings of an army set up

141

on it. We also know that he's been in negotiations with the Spanish to turn his bit of land into an independent state to stand in the way of any possible American incursion into New Spain now that we have the Louisiana Territories.'

'And where is this Ouachita River?'

'Out west.'

'Texas or California?'

'Texas way.'

'Then I wish Mr Burr joy of his land. Texas has nothing of value on it nor under it. His army will have to be very good farmers indeed if they are to feed themselves.'

'Burr's not interested in farming. Jefferson ditched him from the Vice Presidency and he lost out in New York when he ran for Governor. He's lost out all down the line. He's finished in American politics and that means his money's dried up. He's had to make a new start for himself. The Spanish can't get settlers from their South American territories to move up into New Spain and they need people to live there if they're to protect it. They want Burr to sit on their American border for them, but Burr isn't a man for small thinking. He'll want more than just a land-grant and what he can pick up from the Spanish. What we need to know is where he'll go next, who he'll recruit and where his money will come from.'

'It seems to me that if you know so much already you are somewhat tardy in asking these questions.'

'We tried using one of our own agents, a capable and experienced man.'

'And?'

'He's dead. Burr's no fool, in fact he's as shrewd as they come, so he knows we're trying to stop him and he'll be expecting us to try again. That means we need to use somebody whose motives would be beyond question.'

'And you think that I am your man?'

'You are widely known as a man who is politically unattached except to your own notions of freedom for South America. If Burr is meddling in New Spain it would be natural for you to ask what he's up to and see if his plans and yours

142

might coincide.'

'I see. I am to wander off into New Spain in search of evidence of treasonable activities carried out by your ex-Vice President Burr? Of course, why not? How hard can it be to find him? It's only a thousand miles and more from your Louisiana Territories to the Pacific.'

'Oh, we know where to start you off and it's not New Spain. We got that much from our agent before he took a ball in the back of his head. We know Burr's on the look-out for further financing and he doesn't want it to come from the Spanish.'

'Why not? If they are already ...'

'Because Burr is planning to double-cross them. Burr has no intention of becoming a poor relation existing on Spanish handouts. What he wants is his own country and it won't be some piece of Texas wilderness. We want you to go and see a man called Harman Blennerhasset. He's an English aristocrat who got kicked out of Ireland for bedding his own niece, came over here and settled on an island in the Ohio River about two miles below a settlement called Newport. He's set it up as his own little kingdom and he has enough money to help make Burr another of the same only in a bigger way of business. You have a man named Macleod with you?'

'An old friend, he has no connection with the Venezuelan project.'

'Whether he does or no, would you rate him as a capable man? It would be a better proposition for you if you had someone you could trust alongside you.'

Miranda gave it a little thought. Madison obviously wanted Macleod to go with him. Well, why not?

'In my opinion a most capable man.'

'Then take him with you. He can act as your go-between to an agent Bentley will have trailing you both.' Madison sat back as if the meeting were now concluded. 'Start with Blennerhasset and see where you go from there.'

'And if I refuse?'

'Refuse!'

'I have not yet agreed to go.'

143

'Well, let me see. If I were in a forgiving mood I would have you thrown into prison and leave you there to rot. But that would only be if I were in a forgiving mood. As for any part you might play in the Venezuelan project ...'

Miranda held up his hand. 'Enough. I agree, I am persuaded. But there is one thing. I will do this work of yours, but I must be back in New York in no less than three months. We are working to a schedule and so are the British. You know of the Maitland Plan?' Madison nodded. 'Then you will know that the British intend to commence with that plan by spring of next year. If we have not taken Venezuela before the British arrive we will have failed completely.'

'That should be no problem. If you get what you need from Blennerhasset and follow it up, you should bring us enough to settle this Burr business and then you can get on your way back to New York.' Madison stood up and put out his hand. 'Good luck, but I hope you don't need it.'

They shook hands.

'One always needs luck, Mr Secretary, luck and reliable friends wouldn't you say?'

Madison didn't reply, so Miranda picked up his hat from the desk and left.

Madison sat down and rang a small bell on his desk. A moment later the door opened and a man appeared. It was Cedric Bentley.

'Did it go well?'

Madison thought for a second.

'Maybe. If Miranda's as sharp as they say he is then it will need to have gone well. He said something before he left, about needing luck and reliable friends.'

'It means nothing.'

'Maybe, maybe not. Timing is our great problem. London will have the Maitland Plan ready by late spring of next year. We need the Venezuelan venture to have succeeded before that happens. I'm not sure this business with Miranda isn't a trick too hard to win with the cards we hold.'

'And if we don't use Miranda then how do you suggest we

deal with Burr?'

Madison waved an angry hand at Bentley.

'I know, I know. We've been through it God knows how many times. Well, we are committed now, so I hope you can see to it that everything goes to plan and God help you if it doesn't because no one else will. Are you sure this man Macleod can be trusted to play his part in this?'

'He doesn't need to be trusted. I'm using him like I did in New Orleans and Paris in the Territories affair. It all went well enough then and it will again.'

'I'm not so sure. Miranda has only one loyalty and that is to South America. If, when he gets close enough to find out what's going on, he decides that Burr is a better ally than Smith and Ogden he might change allegiance. You'll need to be very careful that any information he passes on to us can be checked. This affair is bad enough already. The President would be decidedly angry if it were to get any worse.'

'One spy to spy on the other?'

'Exactly, and remember, this is your affair, exclusively the work of the Contingent Fund. Neither the President nor I know anything of it officially, except that you asked for the necessary finance.' The look on Bentley's face assured Secretary Madison that Bentley fully understood the consequences of any failure. 'Politics and diplomacy. What a wonderful game of lies, hypocrisy, and deceit. Miranda's words not mine, but he wasn't far wrong, was he?'

'But justified if used in the cause of America.'

'Yes, it's the way it has to be I suppose, and the way it will always be.'

'Until we're strong enough.'

The Secretary of State gave a grunting laugh.

'No, Bentley, no country ever gets that strong, not America not anyone. Lies, hypocrisy, and deceit it will always be, but as you say, in a good cause, the cause of America.'

Chapter Twenty-five

'No, positively no.' Sir Abercrombie waved a hand as if to dismiss any further argument.

Marie's angry response hit the knight at his most vulnerable point. 'Then there will be no more money.'

'But my dear lady, reflect. Have I not explained? We cannot go to Washington. We must stay here in Georgetown. Be reasonable. Washington's no more than a carriage ride away. Be reasonable, dear lady.'

But Marie was in no mood to be reasonable. 'Then if it is so close why is it not that we go there?'

Dolly intervened.

'Because, Marie, we'd have nowhere to perform in Washington and, even if we had, there's not enough of the right sort to provide an audience.' She gave a sidelong look at Sir Abercrombie. 'Abe's methods aren't exactly designed to appeal to those nibs who are used to high culture. His talents are more for what you might call, those who like it broad.'

Marie stamped her foot. 'No. I allowed myself to be persuaded. I did not trust you, I would never trust you. But Kitty is good, she has helped me. She said if I pay enough then you will do what you say and help me find my husband. I listened to her. Very well, I pay so you will do as I say. My husband has gone to Washington with this Miranda so we must go.'

Kitty stepped closer to her friend and made a whispered observation. 'I know a way to sort it. Sort it for good.'

Dolly turned and gave a brief shake of her head. 'Look, Marie, it's like you say, you're paying, so you're in charge. Kitty was right, if you pay then we'll find your husband for you. And we will go to Washington, it's what we all came for.

146

But Abe's right as well. If we're passing ourselves off as a theatre troupe we need to put on shows and get an audience. If we roll into Washington saying we're actors and don't put on a show we'll stick out like nuns in a knocking shop and any chance of finding either your husband or Miranda will be gone.'

Marie wanted to dismiss Dolly's words, to demand they all do as she commanded but the truth was she was out of her depth and had been ever since she had allowed Kitty to overcome her mistrust of the woman she had known as Madame de Metz and knew now as Dolly Bawtry.

'How else can we get anywhere, Ma'am? This sort of thing needs the likes of Madame de Metz if she's all you say she is. I've done what I can, you know that, but by ourselves we'd get no further and New York isn't a healthy place to spend any more time. Pay her, Ma'am, that's my advice. Pay her well and she'll do as you wish. You can't trust her I know, but you can buy her. People like her are only true to one thing, money.'

So, reluctantly, Marie had sent Kitty to make the necessary arrangements and agree a price and as a result had become part of Sir Abercrombie's ensemble. True, she was closer now to finding her husband, but she still felt that things were beyond her control or understanding.

'Why must we pretend? Why will he run away from me? I am his wife. No, I have had enough. I want no more of this play-acting. I want to find my husband and return to Boston.' It was pure petulance. Marie knew it and she saw from the wry smile on Dolly's face that she knew it also. 'I say I will go to Washington with you or without you.'

'But, but, but –' The knight looked helplessly at Dolly who went to the table and sat down.

'Get out the bottle, Kitty, all this yap has given me a thirst.'

Kitty went to a drawer and obliged by bringing a bottle and mug to the table. As she put them down her head went down close to Dolly's and words were spoken at which Dolly quickly shook her head again.

Dolly poured herself a drink and took a good pull then looked up at Marie as if surprised. 'What, still here? I thought you said you were through with us and off to Washington taking your money with you? Well, go on, get going. I've had enough of carting you about, nurse-maiding you and listening to your whining. I'm finished with you, wash my hands of you and kiss you a fond farewell.' Here she put her hand to her lips and blew Marie a kiss, then took another drink. 'And you, Kitty, are you staying or going with her?'

Kitty took her cue and looked scornfully at Marie. 'No. I've had enough of her. I've had enough of her moods and her tantrums. I'll stay on here with you. No amount of wages is worth going back to Boston and that big empty house and listen to her weeping and watch her fading away. I've had all I can stand of that.'

Her words were carefully chosen and did their work.

'Very well. Then sling her stuff in a bag and then heave it out of the door. She's had enough of Georgetown and our company and she's going to make her own way in the world. Do her one last act of kindness and see that she takes everything that belongs to her. We don't want her claiming we robbed her.'

Kitty gave a satisfied laugh.

'She ain't got much, but what she's got I'll gladly put in a bag for her.' She turned to Marie. 'It'll be on the street outside in ten minutes and if you aren't out straight after it I'll put my boot up your arse and kick you out alongside it.'

Smiling broadly to Dolly she left the room. Sir Abercrombie, with an actor's sense of scene, followed Dolly's lead. 'Well, well. The parting of the ways. How sad, but in life we know that every new beginning must have its ending. For each curtain up there is a curtain down.' The knight turned from Marie and gave a conspiratorial smirk at Dolly. He was, if nothing else, an actor and could take a prompt on the fly as well as the next man. 'It's hard, Dolly, damned hard. We had a fine business in New York, damned fine, and we give it up to come here to do this lady a good turn. To see if, through our poor efforts, we can re-unite two sundered hearts.' He turned back to Marie, struck a pose and slowly raised his arm and pointed a finger at Marie. 'How sharper than a serpent's tooth is …'

148

Dolly saw that the knight was getting carried away. 'As you say, Abe. She can't see where her own good lies so there's no helping her.'

Abe looked round annoyed, realised Dolly was right, let his arm drop, relaxed his pose and smiled at Marie. 'Well, dear lady, on your own you may achieve what it is you set out to do. You may, but I doubt it. Still, that is your decision and I honour it. You may go.'

He turned away from her to face a blank wall his hand to his face with his head slightly bowed. With his free hand he pointed to the door. He had used the pose before in "The Woman Who Had Sinned" and it always went down well. Of course the line leading into the pose should have been ... "Go, you leave knowing that you have broken a father's heart ..." still, you had to make the best of whatever prompts came to hand.

Marie looked at him bewildered and anxious. Her petulance had gone and she was beginning to realise once more that she had agreed to join this group because she had no other way of finding her husband. It had been Kitty who had brought her to New York, she would not have gone on her own. It had been Kitty who had found Macleod's hotel. It had been Kitty who had arranged for her to join with Dolly and Sir Abercrombie. She, herself, had done nothing. And it was Dolly who had been able to find out that her husband had left New York with this man Miranda and headed for Washington. Without Kitty and Dolly she was lost. 'But if we go to Washington why will he run away from me?' she said

Marie did not notice but the door through which Kitty had left opened slightly. Dolly, however, did notice.

'Because he's at his old games. He's up to something for the government. What it is I don't know and don't want to know but he's hooked into a desperate character in this Miranda. To my way of thinking Miranda has drawn him into something and, if I know Miranda, it'll be something dangerous. If Miranda gets a sniff of anyone following him he'll cut his losses.'

Marie thought she understood, but didn't want to believe what it was she thought. 'In what way cut his losses?'

Dolly drew her finger across her throat. 'He'll croak your precious husband, that's what he'll do. Miranda's a villain, but he's a crafty villain. Your husband must be of some use to him but if things get tight it'll be Miranda first, last and always. Mark me well, Marie, Macleod could be in this for the government. I don't say I know for sure, all I say is it's likely. Why else would he run off from Boston and send you that letter? Why else would he flit to Washington? But whatever his reasons he's in bad company, the worst sort. It could turn out very nasty for him if it isn't handled just right.'

Marie didn't say anything. She wasn't quite convinced, but Dolly could see she was getting there. Dolly gave a small, almost imperceptible nod and the door burst open.

'What, still here?' The bag Kitty was carrying went flying across the room. 'Think I didn't mean it about my boot up your backside?' Kitty hitched up her skirts and made as if to come at Marie who gave a small frightened scream.

Abe turned, stepped between them, faced Kitty and threw out his arms.

'Never.' He gave Kitty a big wink which Marie could not see. 'Never, I say, not while I have life and breath. I have promised, nay vowed, to protect this lady.' He turned and clasped an arm round Marie's shoulders. He lifted his free arm slowly and finally uncurled a finger and pointed it at Kitty. 'Begone, foul fiend, for knowest thou that –' and he suddenly realised he was playing Sir Jack Goodheart from "Only a Lowly Maiden" and it was all wrong for this scene. He removed his arm from Marie's shoulders and dropped the other. 'That is to say, well, humph, no violence, eh? All friends together, eh? What do you say, Dolly?'

'I say it's up to you, Marie, go if you want or stay if you want. But if you stay we do this my way or not at all. That's how it is and that's how it must be, take it or leave it.'

Dolly poured herself another drink and took a long pull. Marie gazed at the floor. It was all too much for her, it was like

150

some awful dream, some nightmare. But what else was there after coming so far and being so close?

Kitty resolved things by walking to the bag she had thrown, picking it up and turning to Dolly. 'What about this? In the street or what?'

Dolly looked at Marie. 'Well?'

Marie looked at Kitty.

'Well?'

She had been abandoned. She was alone. She let her eyes fall to the floor and capitulated.

Dolly smiled to Kitty. 'Back in the room with it. Marie's seen sense. She'll be no more trouble.' Dolly decided the mood needed changing. Marie was beaten and now it was important to move on. 'Now then, Abe, we came here as actors so what are we going to give them and where?'

Sir Abercrombie revived at once. His had been a life filled with alarums and excursions great and small. This latest little scene had discommoded him not at all. 'It is all in hand, Dolly. I can't see any place yet for this good lady's French songs,' he turned to Marie and smiled, 'lovely though I'm sure they are, so there's only you and me. That being so we must give them selections of great love scenes from the Bard. High words, higher hemlines and the lowest of necklines, that should do I think. As for a venue, why not here? It's not a positively bad house, not got such a very bad name, and there's a room I've seen upstairs as would take almost a hundred if we had standees at the back and round the sides. Not what I'm used to but it would suffice. It's not in a good part of the town, I'll admit, but that's not necessarily against us. Gentry like a roll in the mud from time to time but they need to have the right occasion to be induced to do it, so we'll provide. We'll start the prograMadame with the balcony scene from Romeo and Juliet, something to catch the eye in the posters. Yes, I can see the posters, red I think, bold red. I can probably get them on account and once we're off and running my account can keep running as well. Of course we'll need to make sure that among all that culture and high art they get plenty of what they're

151

expecting. If they part with ready money they must get value so, Dolly, when you're Juliet and you lean down to me from the balcony *do* try to reveal as much of your great talent as you can.'

Kitty picked up Marie's bag and carried it back into the bedroom and Marie quietly went to a corner and sat down while Sir Abercrombie held forth and began to hit his stride.

'Life can be hard for the tragedian, so full of the divine fire and yet so often misunderstood, so often harassed by narrow minds. The great thing is to keep one's spirits up. Talent will always find a way if it is deployed in the service of art and beauty. Great art must always prevail even in the rudest of …'

Dolly took another drink as the knight continued and Marie sat thinking. Would she prevail? Perhaps he was right, the only thing to do, the only thing left for her to do, was to try and keep her spirits up. So she sat and tried while Sir Abercrombie Fitz-Peebles continued outlining his plans for their coming success with scenes from the Bard which would showcase Dolly's undeniable talent.

Chapter Twenty-six

His Excellency Anthony Merry, Envoy from the Court of St James to the American Republic, was standing by the windows looking out. The room in which he stood was large, ornate and comfortably furnished with both style and elegance yet it somehow maintained that air of order and purpose so necessary to the upper echelons of the British Diplomatic Service. Anthony Merry fitted the room perfectly having, like the room, both style and elegance although lacking, at the moment, any air of order and purpose.

There was a gentle knock at the door which opened to admit a man of middle age, soberly dressed in black. Anthony Merry turned as the man entered and waited for him to speak. The man paused, then spoke with obvious reluctance. 'There is a woman below who wishes to see you.'

'A woman, Mellors?'

'Yes, sir, a woman.'

'Not a lady?'

'No, sir, in my opinion *not* a lady.'

The Envoy left the window and sat at his desk. 'And does this woman have a name?'

Mellors responded with a distinct reserve as if distancing himself from the answer. 'She *gave* a name, sir, Madame de Metz.'

'Gave a name did she, eh? French would you say?'

'She did not say and I did not enquire.'

'What sort of woman is she?'

Mellors considered the question. 'Apart from a certain superficial attractiveness I would say that she is –'

'Superficial attractiveness, eh? Well, what business did our superficially attractive woman say she had with me?'

153

'She did not say, sir.'

'Didn't state her business? Then I suppose you must throw her out. Superficially attractive or not we can't have mysterious women wandering in and out of the offices of His Britannic Majesty's Minister in Washington, can we?'

'She did ask me to mention a name to you, sir.'

'A name? What name?'

'Mr Jasper Trent of London.'

Anthony Merry's light manner changed abruptly. 'Did she by God! Hmm, Jasper Trent, that might make a difference.' He thought for a moment. 'Show her up, but be near at hand and have one of our bigger footmen by you while she's in here with me.'

'Very good, sir.'

Mellors left and Anthony Merry once again stood up and went to the window but stood facing the door this time, awaiting his visitor. A few minutes later the door opened and Mellors entered once more.

'Person calling herself Madame de Metz, your Excellency.'

Madame de Metz entered, waited until Mellors had left, then crossed to the desk. 'Thank you for agreeing to see me, your Excellency.'

Anthony Merry looked at the new arrival. Yes, he thought, she certainly had superficial attractions, but he made no attempt to move away from the window and examine them more closely.

She was on the other side of his very substantial desk and the desk was a goodish distance from the window and until he knew what this woman wanted he felt it wise for things to stay that way. The name Jasper Trent of London had got her in but it also had set him on his guard. Trent dealt in important matters, matters sometimes of the highest diplomacy, but his methods were often not at all diplomatic, indeed, Merry knew they could be at times downright brutal.

'Well, Madame, you used a name to get in and see me but you will need more than that to stay. What is your business?'

'Won't you ask me to sit?'

154

'No, and I won't ask you to leave. I'll just call to my men outside and have them throw you into the street out of this very window if you don't give me good reason to let you stay. Come, Madame, you've used up Jasper Trent, what more?'

'Well, sir, another name then, Lord Melford, younger son of the Earl of Glentrool and trusted agent of Jasper Trent. How's that for a good reason.'

'Not much. Lord Melford's name is well known. I don't think that it alone will save you from the street.'

His threat seemed not to unsettle his visitor in the least. In fact on hearing it she gave him a beaming smile. 'Oh dear, and I had hoped to be well received on the strength of those two names, as I'm afraid I can offer you very little more in the way of people of consequence. But perhaps you're right to be cautious. You don't know me and I might be here to do, oh, all manner of wicked things.' She paused as if in thought. 'Yes, on reflection I'm sure you're right, caution first and questions, if there be any, after. Safety must always be first. That being so, you'd better carry out your threat and call in your bully-boys to throw me out of the window, hadn't you?' She allowed herself a fraction of a moment's pause. 'But, if you know Mr Trent at all, you'll know he isn't a forgiving man. He can be hard on those he thinks have let him down by any misjudgement. For instance, if he finds out I came to you and you wouldn't listen but threw me down into the street, he might blame you for it. I've worked for him, you see, and I know his ways. That's why I came here. I came to you because it's my opinion that, if you'd have listened to what I have to say, I'd soon be working for Mr Trent again. But as you're adamant, and I can see you are, I'll leave before you have me thrown out. It's a long way down to the street below and, soft as I am, I don't believe I'd bounce.'

She turned as if to leave.

'Wait.' Madame de Metz, who had turned and started for the door, turned back. Anthony Merry waved a hand at her signalling her to stay. 'I'll hear you out, but I warn you, if I don't like what I hear …'

155

The guise of Madame de Metz fell away and Dolly Bawtry took her place, her speech clear, hard, and without refinement, her manner boldly familiar and direct.

'You'll have me thrown out into the street. I know, you've already told me so there's no point in you repeating it.' She walked to a nearby chair, picked it up, set it down facing the desk and sat down. 'Now tell your men outside to sling their hooks. I don't want anything I say overheard and carried as tittle-tattle elsewhere.'

Merry looked at her for a second, then called out, 'Mellors', and at once the door burst open and a large, liveried footman entered followed by the soberly dressed Mellors.

They both stopped short when they saw Merry by the window and his visitor sitting by his desk.

'Get out and clear off and make sure we're not disturbed.' He turned his eyes on Mellors. 'Not disturbed or overheard, is that clear?'

'Yes, sir.'

The two men withdrew and the door closed. Merry advanced to the desk and sat down. 'Well then, Madame, state your business.'

'My business is a man named Miranda who has come to Washington from New York to see President Jefferson and Secretary of State Madison. In New York he was part of a group fitting out a venture to go south and take a small kingdom away from the Spanish. As to what the President and the Secretary of State want with him I couldn't say for sure at this moment. But if I was given the right kind of support and finance I think I could find out what it is that's made Miranda wander off from gathering together his little home-made army. Whatever it is, it almost certainly don't bode well for King George. There, it may be something or it may be nothing but I've put in time and money aplenty already finding out what I've just told you. Now I need someone who can put the thing on a proper footing and that man is Mr Trent or someone who can act in his name.'

Anthony Merry put the tips of his fingers together and

waited a short while. It didn't do to seem too enthusiastic.

'Well, Madame, we may after all do some business together. As it happens I am already well aware of Señor Miranda's presence here and, unlike you, I can say for sure the reason for his meeting with Jefferson and Madison. I also know he is accompanied by a fellow called Macleod and that they're close as brothers. From what I've learned, Macleod is a Boston lawyer, nothing more. Now, if we're to work together, if I'm to offer you support and finance, tell me something I don't already know. Tell me, for instance, why Mr Macleod is here and what he is to Miranda?'

Dolly gave a laugh, almost clapped with delight, and the actress in her wanted to get up and take a bow. He couldn't have asked her a better question.

'He's a Boston lawyer all right. He's also an American agent for a man named Bentley. He acted for Bentley before in a matter in New Orleans and killed at least two people, or had them killed. I and Lord Melford were sent after him by Trent but he bested us and got away. He's as crafty as a fox and twice as sly. He comes on as if he's the biggest innocent since the baby Jesus but, when you think you've nailed him, he slips you. If he's alongside Miranda then it's because Bentley's involved and whatever it is it's important.'

'Hmm. I know of Bentley, a most able man. This Macleod killed for him, you say?'

'Two that I know of for sure and one more fished out of the river almost certainly down to him.'

'A man of many parts, one minute the simple lawyer, the next an associate of a known adventurer, and now an American agent and occasional murderer.'

Merry stood up and began to slowly walk around the office. 'Miranda has been recruited by the Secretary of State to discover a plot that is being hatched by a man named Aaron Burr, until recently Jefferson's Vice President. The plan is beautifully simple. He intends to steal the Louisiana Territories and New Orleans from the Americans and set up an independent state of his own. Naturally Burr has the sympathy of His Majesty's government though not, of course, its active support. Madison wants conclusive proof of Burr's treachery and the names of those who have agreed to join him. We, the British, on the other hand would prefer if that information did not fall into the Secretary of State's hands. As to Señor Miranda's ambitions in South America, they are of no interest to me nor His Majesty's government. What I *would* recommend to Mr Trent, and what I'm sure he would agree to, is that Miranda and his friend Mr Macleod of Boston are frustrated in their search for evidence of Aaron Burr's treachery. To anyone who could do *that* I would be prepared to offer support and finance. What do you say? Is it something you might undertake?'

'You want me to kill Miranda and Macleod?'

'I want them stopped. How you might do it would be none of my concern.'

'You won't stop Miranda without killing him and, if Miranda goes so must Macleod.'

Merry waved a hand. 'The details would be your business. I don't wish to hear them. If Miranda and Macleod are stopped then you will have done a service to His Majesty and will be rewarded. If not, or if you are taken by the Americans, I never met you.'

'Fair enough. But I'll need working money, there's travel and there's recruiting –'

Another wave.

'My Private Secretary, Mellors, will provide a certain sum, modest but sufficient. If you need more I must have results to justify it. Come, Madame, enough discussion. Are you in the service of the King or are you not?'

It was what she had come to hear so she didn't pause in replying.

'I am.'

'Good.' Merry pulled a pen out of an inkwell and pulled a sheet of paper to him. 'Where and under what name can Mellors contact you?'

'I'm at the Eagle Tavern in Georgetown, name of Dolly

Bawtry.'

Merry looked up from his writing.

'Dolly Bawtry! Ecod, I was planning to come and see you myself. I've heard good reports of your performances. Very, erm, very –'

'Artistic?'

'Quite so. Very artistic. Mellors will be a fortunate man that both duty and entertainment should so comfortably coincide, though knowing Mellors I doubt if the artistic is something that would appeal to him. Once the payment is made I might visit your performance myself with one or two friends who understand and appreciate –'

'Art?'

'Precisely.'

Madame de Metz, now fully revealed as Dolly Bawtry, stood up. 'Where are Miranda and Macleod now?'

'Mellors will provide all the information you need.'

'And the money?'

'Mellors will also provide the money.'

'Well then, our business concluded I'll bid you good day, your Excellency.'

Merry rose. 'Good day to you, Miss Bawtry, and I look forward with eager anticipation to seeing your ...'

'I'm sure you do and I'm equally sure you won't be disappointed. What I promise I generally deliver.' Dolly turned and left the room.

Anthony Merry sat down and, after a moment of quiet reflection, rang a small bell on his desk. A moment later the door opened and Mellors entered.

'You made sure you heard it all?'

'Of course.'

'And?'

'Don't you think you may have been somewhat precipitate?'

'In what?'

'In telling her about Miranda's mission for Madison.'

'No, Mellors, not in the least. Aaron Burr, though he doesn't realise it, is going to hand us the greater part of the Territories and New Orleans. Burr can't hold New Orleans without sea power and he has none. He's relying on us to keep the mouth of the Mississippi closed. Well, we shall do that and when Burr has his new kingdom we'll open it again but only to His Majesty's Navy and his troops. America will undoubtedly be attacking him from the East and with our forces ready to come up from New Orleans and down from Canada how long do you think Mr Burr's grand scheme will flourish? If he's any sense he'll cede any claim he has to us.' Mellors gave an indifferent shrug. If Merry wanted to declaim to the air what a fine piece of diplomacy he had arranged with Mr Burr then, as Private Secretary, he was obliged to be an audience, but he didn't have to enjoy it.

'Will he have any legitimate claim?'

'Actually, no. But then, who has?'

'The Americans paid for it so I suppose they might think they have.'

'So they did. But what right had France to sell or, if it comes to that, Spain to give it to France? If anyone could be said to be the legal owners I suppose the tribes of savages who live there have the best one and nobody seems to have consulted them. As far as London is concerned the whole of the Louisiana Territories belongs to whoever sits on them. At the moment it's the Americans. Soon it will be Aaron Burr. Then it will be us.'

'And the Americans?'

'Oh they'll fight. But that fight, for one reason or another, will happen anyway. These American colonies are still unfinished business between us. London knows it and Washington knows it. All that remains is, when and what will cause the resumption of hostilities? Trent, and I agree with him, wants the time and place to be of our choosing and Vice President Aaron Burr has given us what we want.'

'Indeed? You think so?'

Mellors' obvious indifference to Jasper Trent's plan somewhat damped Merry's enthusiasm and his tone became brusque and businesslike as if it had been Mellors who had been wandering from the point.

'That being the case, London wants Burr to succeed. Trent's last communiqué gave strict instructions to scupper any attempts by the Americans to frustrate his plans. He has a man on the way. But a man at sea is no good to me because at this precise moment Miranda and that shadow of his, Macleod, are on the move, heading for Blennerhasset. Fate has dropped this Madame de Metz or Dolly Bawtry into my lap so, by God, I'll use her. If she trailed Miranda here from New York why not let her trail him further until Trent's man arrives from London?'

Asked a relevant question, Mellors responded, 'It would suffice, I suppose.'

'Oh you suppose, do you? Well Miranda has gone and if someone doesn't follow him how the hell am I to know what he's up to? Would you prefer that I sent you?' Mellors gave him a startled look. 'No, I thought not.'

'And what if this de Metz woman kills Miranda?'

'Well, it's unlikely but just about possible I suppose. She seems a determined and resourceful individual.'

'London wouldn't be happy with such an outcome.'

'Well, nothing in life is certain, and if Miranda dies then he's dead and the Burr business is safe for the time being. London will have to settle for that.'

'Mr Trent won't like it. If he wanted Miranda dead he'd have made it clear. It's my belief that Mr Trent considers Miranda to be of some importance, perhaps of even more importance than Mr ex-Vice President Aaron Burr.'

Anthony Merry lost patience.

'Dammit, Mellors, Mr Trent is in London and I'm here dealing with things as best I can, so we'll do as I say and I want to hear no more about it. Get three hundred dollars in gold and take it to Georgetown and hand it over to the Bawtry woman.'

'Three hundred!'

'For God's sake, man, we need her to think we've pinned our hopes on her. Anyway, when Trent's man arrives and takes over I dare say we'll get most of it back.'

'Indeed I hope so.'

'Then go to it, and while you're at it you can let me know

what the show is like. If it's all I've heard, I really might go across and take a look for myself.'

Chapter Twenty-seven

The upper room of the Eagle Tavern was dark and empty. The show was over and the audience departed. Only a single lamp gave light as Sir Abercrombie Fitz-Peebles and his leading lady, Dolly Bawtry, rested after their latest triumph.

'Can you put her off, Dolly?'

'Why should I, Abe? We promised to find her husband and now I know where he is.'

'Come, Dolly, it's me you're talking to. We've had her money and now we're set up to do well. What's a promise against cold cash coming in with plenty more on the way? Dolly, my dear, be reasonable. Jolly her along a bit more.'

'No, Abe, things have moved on. There's others to consider now.'

'That fellow, Mellors, who came at the end of last week?' Dolly nodded. 'Not a man I could take to, lacking as he was in manners, respect, or any proper appreciation of the theatre.'

'He was here on business not to ogle me, so what you think of him and what he thinks of you is of no interest.'

Sir Abercrombie quickly changed his manner. Dolly had to be made to see sense. They had been performing to full houses and were an undoubted success. Now was definitely not the time to think of moving on, no matter what might have been promised or who else Dolly had become involved with.

Dolly's assessment concerning Sir Abercrombie's talent for his kind of theatre had proved absolutely correct. With nothing in the way of competition, the shows had proved little less than a sensation among a certain section of Georgetown's citizens. Not least because whatever scenes from the pen of the Bard Sir Abercrombie selected, re-wrote and staged, he was always careful to make sure that Dolly was well showcased.

The ladies of Georgetown might purse their lips and raise their eyebrows at such goings-on but their menfolk pointed out that it was high art, Shakespeare no less, and flocked to the upper room of the Eagle Tavern where they happily parted with their money to listen to those immortal words and look at those undoubted talents.

'Dolly, try and see sense, look at the crowd we had in tonight.' He gestured to the rows of chairs packed closely together in the darkened room. 'With more space for standees we could have pulled in twice as many and more. Why, I could double the price of admission and still be a sell-out. I don't say we actually give up on finding this Macleod fellow. As you know I would no more go back on my sacred word than I would —'

'Fiddle the receipts when it came to divvying up.'

'Dolly, you wound me. Have I ever tried to pull anything on you?'

'No, Abe, you haven't, but only because I keep a close eye on things.' She paused and Sir Abercrombie stayed silent. If she was thinking things over that was all to the good. Dolly finally spoke. 'Double the admission?'

'Treble it, why not? Who else can give 'em what they get from my pen and your acting? Why, with any luck they might try and close us down.' Suddenly he stood up. He had been sitting on a chair in the front row facing Dolly who was sitting on the edge of the raised platform which fulfilled the role of stage. He stepped forward across the narrow, heavily sanded gap between the row of chairs and the stage and threw out his arms. 'Good, God, I'm a genius. A positive genius.' He let his outstretched arms sweep dramatically around the darkness of the room not lit now by the solitary lamp beside Dolly. 'We won't stay here, we'll go to a bigger place.'

'That would mean more rent.'

Sir Abercrombie dismissed it with a gesture. 'Rent, pah! With my credit I could get anywhere I wanted on tick but, by God, to get the right place I'd even pay ready money.' He returned from the gloom into the lamplight and sat down again.

'Two more months, Dolly, that's all that I ask.' He leaned forward, all eagerness. 'Two months at most. We'll cream them, my dear, we'll squeeze them 'til the pips squeak. Why we'll make so much money that we'll –'

'You haven't told me why you're a genius yet.'

'Oh that.' He sat back with a grin on his face. 'I'll arrange for a Morality League to get set up.'

'A what?'

'A Morality League. I did it once before. We give 'em stronger and stronger stuff and suddenly somebody says what Georgetown needs is a Morality League to protect the innocence of the youth and the purity of the womenfolk.'

'And everybody agrees and they close us down. Brilliant, Abe, true genius.'

'No, the leader of the Morality League will be a newcomer shocked by what she has found. She gets the League going, gets a few of the mothers of consequence on board. That's when I reveal that the League's leading light was herself a lady of the night in New York or somewhere,' and he threw up his arms, 'shock, horror.' He let his arms drop, 'And bang goes your Morality League and we're fireproof for a while so we juice up the shows, put our prices up and play to bigger and better houses. There, ain't that genius?'

'Hmm, it's a clever move, Abe, damn clever I'll give you that. And the funny thing is that giving them something a bit stronger chimes in with an idea Kitty dreamed up.' Sir Abercrombie scowled. 'She thinks we ought to do the dagger scene from Macbeth.'

'I'm surprised she's even heard of it.'

Dolly got up. 'Stay here, I'll call her and let her tell you herself. After all, it was her idea.'

'If you must.'

Dolly went to a stairway and shouted down. Kitty's voice answered and there was the noise of feet on the stairs as Kitty came up and joined them.

'Go on, Kitty, tell him your idea.'

Kitty looked at Sir Abe and then at Dolly. 'No, you tell him, you'll do it better.'

'If that's how you want it. Look around, Abe, and imagine the scene. It's night, dark like it is now. Lady Macbeth comes onto the stage and a light goes up. She's holding a dagger –'

'I know the scene, get on with the idea.'

Dolly stood up and took the lamp to the back of the platform. 'Did you bring a knife?' Kitty pulled one out from the recesses of her costume and handed it over. Dolly struck a pose in front of the lamp and looked at the knife. 'Is this a dagger I see before me ...'

There was petulance in Sir Abercrombie's voice.

'I know the lines but I still can't see any idea.'

'That's because you'll have to use your imagination. Just now I'm wearing a dress, but what would you see if I was on the stage wearing a nightdress of some nice, flimsy material. Use your imagination, Abe. With the house-lights out and the only light in the place behind me, not too much light but enough, what would you see then?'

Abe stood up.

'By God I see what you mean. Why they'd tear up the seats, they'd pull the place down around their own ears and then bay for more. This is first-rate, stupendous. I can see it all now.'

Dolly picked up the lamp.

'And they'll see it all as well.' She came off the stage and handed the knife back to Kitty. 'Well, Abe, what do you think of Kitty's idea now?'

'Dolly, as you know, I'm a man of few words, but I've said it before and I'll say it again ...'

But the words were indeed few, in fact they remained unspoken, their place taken by a choking gurgle as Kitty who had slipped behind him reached round and cut his throat with a strong single slash. Dolly jumped back and Kitty stood away as the blood spurted out of the gash. The choking gurgle spluttered into silence and the body of the late Sir Abercrombie Fitz-Peebles fell with a crash among the front row of chairs.

'Quick, get something on the wound or we'll be walking ankle deep in the bugger's blood.'

Kitty dropped the knife and pulled a towel from under her skirts, pushed away the chairs, stooped down beside the corpse and smothered the blood with the towel.

The towel quickly darkened but the flow of blood was restricted and the sanded floor round the dead man's head absorbed what had already run on to it. Kitty stood up.

'Where's the crate?'

'Over there by the wall.' Dolly held up the lamp and Kitty crossed to a big wicker basket by the side of the stage and dragged it to the body where she opened the lid and began pulling out an assortment of costumes. Dolly watched until the crate was about half empty. 'That'll do, we need enough under him to soak up the blood.' She put the lamp down and took hold of Sir Abercrombie's legs. Kitty put her hands under his arms and both women heaved. 'In he goes.'

With the body in the basket Kitty then picked up one of the costumes and started to rub the blood off her hands while Dolly took up the lamp and went round the crate looking carefully. After two of three circuits she stopped. Kitty threw the stained costume into the basket.

'No leaks?'

Dolly shook her head.

'No, I can't see anything. It should hold him well enough. Wipe over the handle and then go down and wash your hands and sort out Marie. I'll finish here.'

Kitty picked up another of the costumes, wiped the basket handle and lid, threw the garment into the basket then picked up the knife and disappeared down the stairs. Dolly put the lamp back onto the stage then pushed the rest of the costumes in onto the body. The last few she used to gather up most of the bloodied sand and when they'd gone in she shut the lid then kicked her foot through the remaining dark patches so they scattered. She then picked up the chairs and set them back into order. Finally she slowly pulled the now heavy basket back to its original position and then went back to the lamp kicking the sand as she went to remove any signs that the crate had been moved. Holding up the lamp she surveyed the scene of Sir

Abercrombie Fitz-Peebles's final performance.

'It was a good death scene, Abe, nice and gory. Pity only me and Kitty got to see it. Still you can't have everything can you? We need to be on our way and we couldn't very well take you along, could we? And if we left you here you'd have sold us out as sure as sin. Sorry, Abe, but business, as you always said, is business.'

And Dolly went down the stairs leaving the upper room, which had so recently echoed loudly with cheers and applause, to darkness, death and silence.

Chapter Twenty-eight

Downstairs Marie was sitting sewing. The success of Sir Abercrombie's efforts brought with it work for her. Each show required that Dolly had the right kind of costume and that meant rapid adaptation from their limited stock. This was where Marie found that she could be of some real use. She had been brought up to know the lady-like pastime of delicate sewing so, while Kitty did the rough work, Marie made sure it could not be seen by adding pretty flourishes over hastily tacked seams. Strangely, Marie found some comfort in this labour. Her hands and mind were occupied, she was mostly left alone, and the work brought back a sense of innocent childhood. Dolly was careful to make sure that Marie's temporary comfort was, as far as could be managed, protected by a small but sufficient stream of information concerning the whereabouts of her husband so Marie could tell herself all was going ahead for the best. And that was indeed what Marie told herself, because what else could she say? She was too committed now to turn back and she knew she could not strike out on her own.

Kitty came in. 'Here, make yourself useful. Clean this knife and put it away in a drawer.'

'But it has blood on it.'

'So it has, and plenty of it.'

'But blood! What has happened?'

'For God's sake, it's pig's blood. Abe wants Dolly to do the dagger scene from Macbeth because he can put her in a flimsy nightdress that hides nothing but her thoughts. And for the dagger scene you need a bloody knife, although who'll be looking at the knife I couldn't say. Still, Abe's a stickler for detail so a bloody knife we had to have. Now here, clean it and put it in a drawer like I said and be careful, it's sharp. We don't want no one hurt, do we?'

Marie gingerly took the knife trying to get as little blood on her hand as possible. Kitty took up Marie's skirt and rubbed her hands on it and let it drop back.

'Don't worry, if you'd bothered to look you'd see there's already drops of blood on your skirts so it'll need washing anyway. When the knife's put away give me the dress and I'll get it clean for you.'

Marie looked thoughtfully at the knife. 'But why is Sir Abercrombie rehearsing something new? Dolly told me she knows where my husband is and that we were to set off at once. Why do we need a new scene?'

'Because we don't need Abe no more, he'd be in the way and slow us down, so we've got to make sure he thinks we're staying on here awhile. Now do you see?'

Marie was still doubtful, but her spirit was now so thoroughly subdued to the will of Dolly and Kitty that she asked no more questions.

'Yes, I see.'

'Give the knife a quick wipe over on your skirts, they're soiled already, and then rinse it off. Dry it proper before you put it in the drawer. It's a good blade and I don't want it rusting.' Marie hesitated, a vestige of her old life remained and the thought of picking up her skirts and wiping blood, even pig's blood, on to them filled her with distaste. But she could see it was as Kitty said, the dress was already stained so she picked up her skirt and wiped the knife. Kitty gave her a satisfied smile. 'Right, when you've finished get the dress off and I'll wash it.'

Just after Marie left the room Dolly came in. 'It's all done up there. What about Madame?'

'All done. She's got the blood on her dress.'

'Good girl. Now, when she comes back get us packed and ready to travel. You have the horses?'

'Ready at the back in the stables. How long before Abe begins to smell and draws somebody's attention to his new lodgings?'

'How should I know? He's mixed in with plenty of clothes so he's comfortable, I should think. Apart from having his throat cut from ear to ear, I'd say he's very snug.'

Kitty grinned.

'You're sure they'll think we all did a flit long enough for us to get clear?'

'Oh yes, I've been salting the trail for a week, dropping hints about how Abe should be watched as one who's known for his sudden urges. How he sets off unexpected-like. And that he has a shocking memory so he often forgets to settle up on debts before he packs his bags and leaves. That upper room wasn't used for much before we took it so until Abe forces himself on their attention they'll assume he's done a runner.'

'But they'll come after him, won't they?'

'No. Abe didn't know but I saw to it that the Eagle got more or less paid up to date. There's debts for materials and a few bits and pieces but not enough to get anyone up in the air and go to the trouble and expense of running after us. We'll be clear, don't you worry, and when we are we'll have our pretty Madame Macleod exactly where we want her. As far as she'll know there'll be a blood-stained dress left behind in a drawer with the knife that did the deed and a body in the big basket. As far as Marie will be concerned it will be – do as you're told or we hand you over to the law and you swing by your pretty neck.'

Kitty thought about it. 'But if we leave the dress and the knife they might get found and set people to thinking.'

'Kitty, my sweet girl, you're an artist with a knife but don't try to think. Leave the thinking to me. There'll be no dress, nor no knife left but what we put into Marie's mind. We'll know there's nothing left to get anybody wondering but she won't. The way we'll tell it, we left the dress and the knife in the drawer. She saw the knife, she saw the blood and she knows there's blood on her dress. After that we let her imagination do the rest, the way we've got her now she'd believe in fairies if we told her to. Abe was a good teacher and I was a good pupil. I really can act, Kitty, it doesn't all have to be tits and leg. I can

171

tell this tale so Madame will swallow it, don't you worry. Now off you go and get her ready to move quick. I want us to be well away as soon as it's light enough. You slipped the stable lad enough to see we can do it all right, quick and quiet?'

'Oh yes, he's squared.'

'Then let's finish off here, we've a long road ahead and a hard one.'

Kitty smiled. 'But profitable I hope.'

'Oh yes. If all goes well, very profitable.'

Chapter Twenty-nine

Lord Melford passed through Georgetown on his way to Washington three days after Marie, Kitty and Dolly had slipped quietly away and the sudden and unexpected departure of Sir Abercrombie Fitz-Peebles's Players had already become stale news. Their passing had caused a momentary pang of regret among those gentlemen of the town who had developed a high regard for art but an air of quiet satisfaction among their wives. There were a few grumbles of discontent from several suppliers who had not been paid in full but, all in all, the loss of Sir Abercrombie and his Players passed off much as Dolly had predicted and no one, even for a moment, suspected anything other than that they had all flitted. Certainly no one suggested that they be followed. The Eagle Tavern returned to being a beer house of low repute and Abe rested in peace in his basket in a dark corner of the now empty and unused upper room.

On the night of Lord Melford's arrival in Washington, Anthony Merry gave him dinner. No one else was present as Merry wanted to waste no time in passing over the matter of Sebastián Miranda to hands other than his own. Over dinner, however, the conversation had been somewhat neutral, each man sizing up the other and, as both men were well versed in the art of using a great many words to say almost nothing at all, no real business was done until the table had been cleared and the decanter of port placed before them.

'It's a pity there was no way of knowing when you'd arrive. Trent said he was sending someone, but circumstances rather forced my hand.'

Lord Melford took a sip of his wine. 'Trent dropped the thing in my lap rather suddenly.'

'Often sudden is he, Trent? I would have thought him a man

of method.'

But Lord Melford was not interested in going down yet one more conversational side-alley by discussing the author of his present excursion. He was tired and wanted their business concluded. That being the case he became direct. 'So, the woman who described herself as Madame de Metz gave you our names, Trent's and mine?'

'She did.'

'And on the strength of that you gave her money and sent her off after Miranda.'

'Not on the strength of that alone.'

'Then what else?'

'As I said, circumstances. Miranda had suddenly arrived in Washington and Secretary of State Madison had equally suddenly shot him off to collect information on Burr's project from a man named Harman Blennerhasset. That much I was able to find out, but I had no way of safely making direct contact with Miranda. This is, after all, their capital and I am the British Minister here which limits my scope for such action.'

'Were there no other resources you could draw on?'

'None safe enough. I had no way of knowing what specific arrangements Miranda had come to in his meeting with Madison nor if those arrangements represented a threat to Burr's project. If they did then I judged it would be a serious one. So when Madame de Metz popped up like some children's toy out of a trap I decided to make use of her.'

'On no more than the basis of my name and Trent's?'

'No, she gave me two more names which, shall we say, tipped the balance in favour of using her.'

'And these were?'

'Bentley, a name which I'm sure is well known to you, and Macleod, a Boston lawyer.'

Melford reached forward and poured himself another glass of wine. 'Damn good port, Merry.'

'It is good, isn't it? I have to have it specially shipped in. America is a barbarous place and Washington, despite all its

174

fine new building, is pretty much filled with barbarians, and as for Jefferson ...'

But Melford had only mentioned the wine to give himself a brief thinking space. The name Bentley had come as no surprise. He had known Bentley's hand would show sooner or later. But Macleod! That it had to be the same Macleod was beyond doubt. A Boston lawyer. It had to be the same man. Good God, first Madame de Metz, now Lawyer Macleod. The whole thing was becoming like some sort of damn reunion.

'This Macleod? What do you know of him?'

'Nothing except that he arrived with Miranda and stuck to him closer than a brother. The de Metz woman told me he was an agent for Bentley and had more than a few bodies to his credit. A dangerous man if what she says is right. Is she right?'

'Hmm. I know the man but I can't say whether he's a good agent or a natural fool. He has to be one or the other as I doubt he can be both, but as to which it is I can't decide.'

And they both took a thoughtful drink.

'Yes, that's pretty much what the de Metz woman said. Anyway, with Madison's people keeping a close eye and this Macleod always at his side there was no way of talking to Miranda privately. Then both he and Macleod were gone. I needed someone to follow and the de Metz woman turned up so I used her. Even if I'd known you'd be here so soon I could have done nothing to delay Miranda. As it is we can assume that they are on their way to see this Blennerhasset with my new recruit following.' Merry smiled pointedly at Lord Melford. 'And now you're here to pick up the reins on the whole thing so, with great pleasure, I hand it all over to you.' He raised his glass. 'Good health and good fortune. I don't envy you your task.'

'What instructions did you give to Madame de Metz?'

'To stop Miranda.'

'Kill him?'

'I doubt she could, but I ruled nothing out.'

'Trent wouldn't want him dead and nor would he want him thinking the British would send assassins after him. Trent wants

175

him well-disposed to us whatever his more immediate designs might be either here or in New York.'

'Trent playing a long game as usual?'

Melford ignored the question. 'De Metz may prove to be a problem.'

'Then it will be your problem, Melford. My instructions, unless you have brought new ones, in writing and duly endorsed, are to see that Burr's plan prospers and, from what I hear from London, time is not on our side. Pitt's government won't last and if Addington gets back in then whoever he wishes on us as Foreign Secretary may not look so kindly on our support for Burr as Mulgrave does now and as Harrowby did before him.'

Melford nodded in agreement. 'The talk is that Fox wants it.'

'Is it, by God? Then that settles it. Fox would soon scuttle anything that might harm America. The man's a damned republican through and through.'

'They must give him something.'

'I suppose they must. They couldn't give him the Home Office, I suppose?'

Melford shook his head. 'No. If they did then Catholic Emancipation is inevitable.'

'Hell's teeth, what a choice? Either we get a Foreign Secretary who's more of a republican than Danton or a Home Secretary who's more of a Papist than the Pope.'

Melford finished his wine and stood up. 'Well, that's for London and the future to decide. For the present I'll busy myself here trying to see that Madame de Metz doesn't kill Miranda and that Miranda doesn't get Aaron Burr hanged for treason. It's enough to be going on with I think.'

Anthony Merry rose. 'Aye, Melford, enough and more than enough.'

'Where is this Harman Blennerhasset?'

'On an island in the Ohio River not so very far from a place called Marietta in Virginia. He's a British exile apparently, but more than that I don't know. By the way, how's your brother? I heard he'd been wounded.'

'Lost a leg.'

'Leg eh? Mean an end to his soldiering, I suppose?'

'It will.'

'Shame, damned shame.'

'Yes, my father and I both thought it so.'

And business being over and conversation having come to a civilised end on family matters the two men shook hands and parted.

Chapter Thirty

Harman Blennerhasset was a man of many parts. A wealthy British aristocrat, a man of education and culture and a qualified lawyer. He was also a social leper. He had been driven from his estates in Ireland by his fellow wealthy aristocrats who were also men of education and culture, though not all of them were lawyers. His fault? The trivial misdemeanour of marrying his niece, Margaret Agnew.

Harman's response to their condemnation of his conduct was to turn his back on society. He and his niece-wife, Margaret, left the ostracism of their neighbours and of their immediate families and set out to find a congenial location in which to pass their exile. Europe being in something of a turmoil they settled on America but, American polite society being, if anything, even more rigid on moral questions than their British cousins, the Blennerhassets eschewed the more comfortable and sophisticated towns and cities of the Eastern seaboard and, in 1798, Harman bought a large island on the Ohio river which he and Margaret proceeded to turn into their own small kingdom.

Miranda and Macleod travelled the three hundred miles to the Ohio River on horseback, taking with them only a single packhorse. The journey from Washington to Frederick was rapid and uneventful, the late April weather was clement and, the country being well-settled and thriving, the trails were all well used and clear. It was much the same as they passed through the Great Appalachian Valley between the Allegheny and Blue Ridge Mountains. Nature, in the spirit of a glorious spring, seemed to smile on them. The trail was firm and, as the rain held off, they were able to make excellent time. From Morgantown, where they rested themselves and their horses, the country became less populated and more frontier-like but there were still plenty of villages and settlements and the trail was still sufficiently clear to present no problems. After ten days pretty well constantly in the saddle it was with some relief and satisfaction that they arrived in the mid-afternoon at Newport on the eastern bank of the Ohio River. Not so big or advanced as Marietta, fourteen miles further upriver, Newport was nonetheless a substantial settlement and the nearest to Blennerhasset's island kingdom. They found a room in a clean and well-furnished lodging house and eased the pain of too many days spent in the saddle in a warm tub after first arranging for a message to be sent to Harman Blennerhasset informing him of their arrival and requesting permission to visit him the following day. Before dinner a message arrived for them that they were welcome and should come to the island at ten the next day. They were to bring their luggage as they would be most welcome to stay for a few days if their time permitted of it.

The following morning, after breakfast, they hired one of the local boatmen to take them downriver to the island. They tied up at a small landing stage, paid off the boatman, left their bags on the landing and set off along a gravelled pathway which led to a large white house set back behind trees and flowering shrubs. As they walked they saw several black slaves cutting back some of the shrubs and raking in the cuttings, and began to realise that what they were walking through was no natural woodland but planned and well-kept grounds.

As the path ended it opened on to a large expanse of lawns beyond which was a large white porticoed mansion in the classical style, the whole front of which was given over to a porch at ground level. In the middle of this porch, between two classical pillars, was a wide set of steps leading up from the gravelled path to the front doors. Newport had not been a backwater, indeed it had several substantial buildings to its credit, but nothing there had prepared Miranda or Macleod for this magnificence.

Standing on the porch at the top of the stairs stood a man, slim, elegantly dressed, aged about thirty. Miranda led the way up the steps and held out his hand.

'Mr Harman Blennerhasset, I presume.'

'You presume correctly, sir.' The two men shook hands. 'And you are Señor Sebastián Francisco de Miranda Rodríguez, are you not?'

'I am.'

'Then let me say at once, sir, that it is an honour and a privilege to meet you and welcome you to my house.'

'Allow me to introduce my friend,' Miranda turned to Macleod, 'Mr Jean Marie Macleod of Boston.'

Blennerhasset looked at Macleod for a second then held out his hand and spoke with a singular lack of sincerity or conviction. 'Any friend of Señor Miranda is, of course, most welcome.' He then proceeded to dismiss Macleod from his mind and turned once again to Miranda. 'Come, sit down, sir, take some refreshment, some tea.'

Miranda followed Blennerhasset to a table and four chairs beside which stood a black servant in footman's uniform. Macleod stood still.

'What about our bags? They're still at the landing.'

Blennerhasset turned and looked at him. 'Then I will have them brought up and put in your room.' He sat down and was joined by Miranda. 'See to it, Claudius.'

The black footman left the porch and set off down the gravel path. Macleod waited for a moment unsure what to do.

'Come, Jean, do not dally, sit down.'

Macleod, with some reluctance, joined the other two men and sat down. Blennerhasset, ignoring him, at once began to talk to Miranda as if they were old acquaintances and Macleod's arrival had interrupted a conversation already well underway.

'We are quite independent here, Señor Miranda. We answer to no overlord, something that will, I know, appeal to you.' Miranda made a slight bow in acknowledgement of the compliment. 'You, like myself, sir, have suffered at the hands of those with a narrow-minded fixation on outdated social shibboleths. In your case the tyrannies of Old World empires, in

180

mine the tyranny of Christian morality. I look forward to discussing with you many of the subjects in which I am sure we share a common interest.'

'As do I, sir.'

'And may I ask, pray, what brought you to my island?'

'My friend and I are travelling to Cincinnati from New York. Naturally, as we came so close to your island, we wished to make your acquaintance.'

'Indeed, sir? Your name is well known to all who are interested in the times we live in and the changes being wrought. But myself? I am not such a person of note, I think.'

'You do not do yourself justice, sir. You are known widely as a free-thinker and a man of science. Merely by leaving the more settled parts of civilisation and coming here to establish a … a what shall I call it? A new state? A new republic? A domain of your own?'

'Call it what you will, sir, I still cannot bring myself to believe that my situation here is something the wider world cares to talk about overmuch.'

Macleod felt distinctly uncomfortable. Miranda, as always, carried himself with supreme confidence, but even Macleod could see that Blennerhasset was not in the least convinced with his explanation of their arrival. He struggled to find something to say which would help his friend, but nothing presented itself to him other than what Miranda had already offered. But why Cincinnati he wondered?

Fortunately at this moment the black footman returned accompanying the two gardeners they had passed on the gravelled path who now carried their bags. Macleod at once took advantage of this relief column.

'Ah, Miranda, see our luggage has come.' Macleod made as if to stand up but Miranda waved him back to his seat.

'Sit down, Jean, the bags will go to our room. For myself, I am happy to sit with our host and talk. As he has so kindly said, we have much to talk about.'

'Indeed we have, Señor, more than I at first suspected. But I think your friend is correct. Perhaps you should go and unpack your things. We can talk later.' Blennerhasset stood up and Miranda and Macleod followed suit. 'Claudius, take these gentlemen to their room. Now excuse me, gentlemen, I have some business to attend to. We will meet again at luncheon at mid-day.'

It seemed more of a dismissal than a farewell but, whatever it was, Miranda and Macleod obeyed and followed the gardeners and the footman into the house, up a wide staircase and into a large, comfortable room where the gardeners set down the bags. After they had left, the footman, Claudius, bowed and made his way silently out of the room, closing the door behind him.

'Well, Jean, we are arrived, are we not?'

'But not welcomed.'

'No? I thought our host most gracious on our meeting.'

'At first, to you perhaps, but that story you told him, and why, for God's sake, Cincinnati?'

'Why not? It was a little story, something, nothing, a temporary fiction, no more, not meant to be believed.'

'No?'

'Of course not, merely something to whet his appetite. Would you rather I had said straight out that we were hunting Aaron Burr on behalf of the United States Government?'

'No, of course not. But it seemed a bit weak even to me.'

'Yes, and it was intended to be so. Jean, trust me, this is my trade not yours. Leave it to me.'

'Glad to. From what I've seen of the man, Blennerhasset has no interest in me whatsoever. I might as well be one of the paintings on a wall rather than his guest.'

'Or his prisoner.'

'What?'

'Well, are we not? This is his island. How are we to leave if he chooses to keep us here?'

'Damn, you're right. I hadn't thought of that.'

'Then sit and think about it now, Jean, think about it until mid-day when we shall rejoin our host for luncheon.'

'Not a meal I'm looking forward to, especially if we are

182

prisoners.'

'Oh I think it will prove a most interesting meal, most interesting indeed.'

Chapter Thirty-one

Miranda was proved wrong about luncheon, it was not in the least an interesting meal. The food was excellent but the conversation was somewhat limited with none of the three men at table apparently too keen to rejoin the subject of the purpose of the visit and, as no other topic arose, was eaten in what amounted to an almost funereal silence. After luncheon Blennerhasset rose and suggested that they go and sit on the porch. Once outside, Miranda and Blennerhasset sat at the table while Macleod, not caring to sit down, stood by the balustrade.

Miranda at once returned to the conversation Blennerhasset and he had begun on arrival. 'I congratulate you, sir, on the magnificence of your house. It would grace any European city.' Blennerhasset nodded in acknowledgement of the compliment but did not speak. 'And your grounds, as nature intended but guided by a wise hand. Tell me, sir, apart from a fine house, what is it you intend here? A retreat? A shelter from a world you reject? Or shall it become something more?'

'More?'

'You are a man of vision, sir, and I suspect of ambition. I cannot believe that you have come here to sit and grow old.'

'Perhaps not.'

'Your mind, sir, ranging as it does over science, morality, politics, is not one to vegetate. I suspect that what you intend here is ...' Here Miranda paused and, correctly, guessed his pause would bring Blennerhasset on into conversation.

'Is what, Señor?'

'Something more grand.'

'And if it is, what might it be?'

'A new state? A new domain? Perhaps even ...' and Miranda paused once more as if looking for the right word,

184

'… a new kingdom,' he smiled, 'shall I say kingdom?'

Blennerhasset returned the smile.

'Do, sir, say kingdom if you will, for understand I rule here absolutely with my wife as queen.'

The point was not lost on Macleod although Miranda seemed to not notice the emphasis Blennerhasset had laid on the remark.

'Very well, then let it be kingdom and I look forward with anticipation to meeting its queen. Does this island kingdom yet have a name?'

'As to names, my wife and I have not settled the matter to our satisfaction. Blennerhassetland, I fear, is too much to slip gracefully off the tongue. In fact Blennerhasset-anything is too much, so for the present it is The Kingdom, no more no less.'

Miranda raised his hand as if he had been holding a glass.

'To The Kingdom then, and its monarchs. And do you get many visitors here to your court, sir?'

'Few, which is just as we would have it. I, like you, have seen the world and I, again like you, have rejected what I have seen. Unlike you, I do not seek to change what I have seen. I merely reject it and here, on this island, have created a place in which a man of independent spirit and freedom of thought may live and breathe.'

'And yet, my friend,' Miranda paused, 'you do not object to "friend" on so small an acquaintance?'

Blennerhasset waved a dismissive hand. 'No, sir, let it indeed be friend if it pleases you.'

'Then that being so, I will speak out as one friend to another. I am here for a reason.'

'I never doubted it, Señor. We are somewhat out of the way here and no one calls in mere passing even if they are on their way to Cincinnati. Those who come generally have a reason and usually a pressing one, the journey to this remote place being what it is.'

'Very well, sir, I see you are as astute as you are hospitable so I will do you the courtesy of frankness. I am looking for Aaron Burr.'

If the news in any way startled their host it did not show. 'Aaron Burr? Vice President Aaron Burr?'

'No other.'

'Indeed? Then why here? Why not in Washington?'

'Because he is not in Washington.'

'Indeed?'

'I have been to Washington.'

'Have you, sir?'

'It was in Washington that I was given your name and your name brought me here.'

For the first time in this conversation Blennerhasset's eyes turned to Macleod.

'Not alone, sir, you didn't come alone.'

'No gentleman travels these parts alone.'

'No, some have guides, some have body-guards, some have slaves and some have servants. You have,' Blennerhasset turned his gaze on Macleod, 'Mr Macleod?'

'I do indeed. My good friend travels with me for companionship alone for he has no part in the great cause of South American freedom and wants none. We met in New York after many years apart and he agreed to accompany me on this present little adventure but, as I say, he does it for companionship.'

'He is fortunate to have so few calls on his time that he can wander with you in search of Aaron Burr. I find it hard to believe his interest can be so altruistic as mere friendship.'

'I assure you that is the case. He is my companion, no more, except a true American and one I would trust with my life.'

'Indeed?'

'I swear it.'

'In that case let him *be* your companion and take a full share in the consequences of your visit here.'

'The consequences?'

'Señor Miranda, it was by your own choice that you came to this island. But it will be by my choosing whether you leave it or remain to take up permanent residence. Any business I might have with Mr Burr can be no concern of yours. There is a place

186

on this island where a few unwanted visitors have found complete rest from the troubles of this world. It is an orchard, a quiet, charming spot not far from the house. They tell me the trees were originally planted by Johnny Appleseed. Well, they may have been. But it is a place I can see clearly from my study window and I keep an eye on my orchard to make sure the guests who reside there stay quite settled. And settled they must be because, sir, none has yet got up and left.'

Miranda's response to this threat was brutally direct. He swept aside Blennerhasset's threat and Macleod could do no more than watch as his tone and manner changed dramatically.

'As for orchards, I leave them to those who care for apples. I am here to ask for the whereabouts of Aaron Burr. You, sir, will provide an answer,' and before Blennerhasset could reply, which it was obvious he fully intended, Miranda went on. 'You think that I, Sebastián Francisco de Miranda Rodríguez could be in ignorance of Burr's plans? You think that his ambitions are not already well documented by those of us who seek something more than petty, personal kingdoms. Pah! Burr's horizon is no better than your own, sir. A sorry plot of soil, some piece of Texas wilderness which he can, like you, sit on like a cockerel to call himself a King. And bought with mere money, sir, not fought for, not paid for in blood. If you are any gauge of Vice President Burr's allies in his scheme I pity you both. As for your threats, I blow them away' and he lifted his hand palm upwards and blew, 'there, they are gone. Kill me, sir? Would you kill me? Then by all means do so and bury me in your orchard. But if you do, please be sure and let Aaron Burr know that he will have made mortal enemies of men whose names you no doubt know as well as my own, O'Higgins, Bolívar, San Martín All men who will return the favour of giving him a piece of soil somewhere for his eternal rest. As for you and this island, it will not last until the apples in your orchard fall. It will be like your threats, sir, blown away.' He repeated the gesture and fell silent.

Macleod was impressed. Miranda's act had been delivered with total conviction and authority. Then Macleod realised wherein lay that conviction and authority. He had meant every word. He was indeed inviting Blennerhasset to kill him. And Macleod was suddenly aware that he also, for companionship's sake, was very much included in the invitation.

Harman Blennerhasset was, as has already been said, many things, but a fool was not one of them. Had Miranda's sudden tirade been the only factor he had to weigh in deciding what to do with them, then Miranda and Macleod would have quickly made their way to the orchard.

When Aaron Burr had visited him and laid out his plans, Blennerhasset had questioned him closely concerning not only the likely American response, but also what help if any would be forthcoming from the British. Burr had assured him of British support. They wanted and would have a new ally standing in the way of any western expansion, and America would lose access to the Ohio and Mississippi Rivers with the attendant damage to their cotton and tobacco exports. America, with its way west blocked and its revenues diminished, would be weakened economically and, more importantly, politically. As for Spain they would also welcome a block on American expansion. As Vice President he knew there already existed detailed plans for American inspired annexations, provocations and incursions which would escalate, if necessary, into full-scale invasions. He did not doubt that Spain was equally aware of American intentions if not the details of how they would be brought about. But although Burr believed Spain would support him in his project he also believed that the eventual liberation of Spanish and Portuguese possessions was not only a possibility but an inevitability and named Miranda along with Bernardo O'Higgins, Simón Bolívar, and José de San Martín as the men who would bring about such an outcome for South America.

Blennerhasset remembered how Burr had spoken with passion and conviction. New American countries, north and south, would emerge. Free and independent countries. And Burr was determined, as determined as O'Higgins and the rest, that one of them would be his own.

Harman Blennerhasset was not a man easily swayed by fine

words. He was a trained lawyer who had qualified for the bar in Dublin. But Aaron Burr was also a trained lawyer and, more than that, he was without doubt a man on a mission, a crusade, and he already had behind him resources which could make his crusade a reality. Harman Blennerhasset had enthusiastically agreed to support him with money and the provision of a safe and secure base on his island for equipment and, when they were ready, men.

But Burr had not only convinced Harman of the prospects of his own plan. He had also convinced him of the abilities of those men who would lead the great South American liberation. Now one of them was sitting on his porch, entirely at his mercy, threatened with death, surrounded by servants and slaves who would obey their master without question and, when threatened, had not only defied him but had heaped scorn on him.

Magnificent! Wonderful! A man who, every inch, lived up to Burr's description, a Liberator indeed, if ever there was one.

Blennerhasset looked at Miranda for a short while, then clapped.

'Bravo, sir, bravo. I salute you. You are all I had been led to expect.' He turned to the black footman who, throughout, had been standing silently by the main door. 'Claudius, champagne.'

The man bowed slightly and went inside.

Miranda sat unmoved as Macleod looked on, uncomprehending but relieved. Unfortunately his relief was short-lived as Miranda spoke.

'I dismiss your salutations, sir. I do not care what is your opinion of me. I withdraw not one word of what I have said.'

'I would not have it any other way, sir, no other way 'pon my life. Your description of me was decidedly accurate, a man sitting on a piece of soil in the wilderness playing at being a king. From you, sir, it is no more than the truth. Had it come from any other then the orchard would indeed have had another settler, one delivered there by my own hand. Now, come, sir, I have made my little test and you have passed through it with flying colours. You will allow, I think, as a reasonable man, that

189

given the business in which we both have an interest, a little reassurance on my part was in order. Come, sir, as one reasonable man to another?'

Miranda gave a great laugh and, as he did so, Claudius came out with a silver tray on which were a champagne bottle and three crystal flutes. He put them on the table and silently withdrew.

'Why not? Why not indeed?' But then his manner changed once more to that with which he had delivered his harangue. 'So long as I get an answer to my question. Where is Aaron Burr?'

But Harman Blennerhasset was still no fool and his lawyer's training stood him in good stead. He leaned forward and, with a loud report, sent the cork of the bottle flying onto the grass. He then poured three glasses, replaced the bottle on the table and sat back.

'Well, as to questions, let me ask you one first, sir. Why does the whereabouts of Aaron Burr interest you?'

'Because I may find myself in conflict with him. He plans to set up some sort of kingdom, some sort of country with him at its head. Very well, if he succeeds with Spanish aid he would become a vassal of Spain and he would become my enemy. I would oppose him and oppose all who stood with him in his project. In fact, sir, I would be forced to bring his project down about his ears. That is why I am interested in his whereabouts. I need to meet with Aaron Burr and discover whether we shall be enemies or allies. In pursuit of my cause, sir, I cannot admit of neutrals. If Burr has involved himself in any way in the matter of Colombia then he is for us or against us. There can be no middle way.'

'Colombia?'

'A country, sir, free and independent from Cape Horn to the Mississippi.'

'A big place then? Not at all a small piece of soil lost in some wilderness?'

Miranda sat for a moment and Macleod feared the worst. Was Miranda about to resume his verbal attack on their host?

190

Then Miranda gave another great laugh. 'Sir, we have champagne I see, a wine the best hotel in New York could not provide, so I know I am in the company of a truly civilised man. With your permission I give you a toast.' Blennerhasset nodded and Miranda took up a glass. 'To Colombia, and to all who help in her creation.'

Blennerhasset took up another of the glasses.

'And I give you one, sir. To freedom and independence for all new countries and kingdoms, from the greatest to the smallest.'

'Yes, sir, it is enough. I will drink to that.'

Macleod, ignored by the two men at the table, stood watching them. Miranda drank with gusto but Blennerhasset, it seemed, thoughtfully. As he stood, Macleod pondered. After all the mutual congratulations and the toast drinking the orchard still lay not so very far away and he wondered whether it might not yet acquire two more settlers. Were they now welcome guests or still prisoners? It was an interesting question.

Chapter Thirty-two

That evening before dinner Harman went to his wife's boudoir. 'What do you think, my dear, shall we trust this Miranda?'

Margaret Blennerhasset sat at her dressing mirror putting the final touches to her hair. She was a beautiful young woman with pale skin, hazel eyes and thick locks of vivid-red hair.

'My dear, I have not yet seen either of them and therefore can have no means of coming to a judgement about this Miranda. You asked me to leave the matter to you and I have done so.'

The manner of her answer was so mild, so very wifely but Harman Blennerhasset knew that the fiery colour of her hair could be, and often was, a true signal of what her temperament could be when roused, so he proceeded cautiously.

'Remember, my love, this is business, very important business, not some social visit …'

His wife turned sharply. 'And I am no domestic ornament to be brought out and displayed like some table decoration or put away in a room and hidden from view.'

'No, my dear, of course not. All I meant was, well I would value your opinion in this as in all things.'

Her point made, his wife turned back to the mirror. 'As to my opinion, according to you we have a most distinguished visitor, a man well-versed in revolution and bold escapades. That being so, tell him everything.'

'Everything?'

'Why not? I would have thought that much was obvious from his arrival.'

'But everything?'

His wife turned again. 'And again, why not? If he is as powerful as you say, or will be, let him know who he is dealing with and what it is we seek to achieve. If he opposes us, well, Burr will deal with him. If he joins us then we have a new ally.'

'And if he chooses to share what I tell him?'

'With whom?'

'Why, Washington of course.'

'Harman, you are the lawyer not I. If our friend Miranda goes to Washington and reveals Burr's full intention, then what?'

'Why treason, my dear, treason at the very least and our involvement in it.'

'How so? On what grounds?'

'Why, on his.'

'Exactly. On Señor Miranda's word supported by his companion. They will say one thing and we will say another. Would you go into a court of law on such tittle-tattle?' Harman thought about it and decided that his wife, though no trained lawyer like himself, had a point and a very good one. 'And who would they be taking into court? Only the Vice President of their Union.'

'Ex-Vice President, my dear.'

But his wife dismissed the detail. 'A man who has been at the heart of government. A man who knows all its secrets, such as America's intentions against Spanish territory. A man who can say in court, as he said here, that the American government fully intends to take all Spanish possessions from Florida to the Pacific coast for its own. That every settlement of American citizens in what is now New Spain is regarded by Washington as the advanced guard of an invading army.'

It was enough. Harman agreed. 'Quite so, my dear, it is as you say. Even if Jefferson were convinced of Burr's treason he could not easily move against him. Not in any court of law, that is.'

Margaret gave her hair one last look and stood up, satisfied. 'Then tell your new friend Miranda everything and send him and his companion on their way. Give them all the help you can to meet with Aaron Burr. Be their friend in everything and withhold nothing.'

'I do believe you're right, my love. After all, it is as you say. Other than their word against ours who can say what passed here during their visit? And if Miranda is genuine about supporting our cause he will undoubtedly repay whatever help we give him.'

'I'm glad that you have finally made up your mind, my dear, but now let us go down to dinner and, please God, farewells.'

'But they are only just arrived.'

'And have business elsewhere, have they not?'

'They have, but I will need to show them what we have achieved here, to show them our part in Burr's plan. Then their transport arrangements will have to be made.'

'Well, if not for the morrow then as soon as it can be managed and in the meantime make my excuses. I will dine with them tonight but then I wish to be left alone and will leave everything to you,' she smiled, 'as you said you I should.'

'Quite so, my dear, quite so.'

Chapter Thirty-three

Dinner, unlike lunch, had been a resounding success. Mrs Blennerhasset was vivacious and charming, Miranda was gallant and charming, and Blennerhasset himself managed to be quietly charming. Macleod alone felt thoroughly out of place and uncomfortable and failed to provide any discernible charm whatsoever, though none of the other three seemed to either notice or care. The dinner party eventually broke up with Blennerhasset promising to show his visitors some parts of his island kingdom the following day.

Next morning after breakfast three horses were brought to the front of the house. Harman asked Miranda and Macleod to accompany him across the island to the shore farthest from the house where he said he had something of particular interest to show them. Once the three men were mounted they walked their mounts along the gravel path that was neatly raked in front of the house. Then they turned on to a grassy track which ran past what was obviously a considerable and well-stocked kitchen garden being tended by two black women, one with a sleeping baby strapped to her back.

'We are completely self-sufficient for food and I take an interest in breeding strains of native vegetables so that they fit more closely to European tastes. As yet my researches have not been blessed with any marked success but as a man of science I press on.'

Once past this garden they came to a white picket fence within which stood the orchard and by which they all rode in silence. Away from the house and gardens they moved into cultivated fields where rows of black women and children were bent over crops, clearing weeds and keeping irrigation ditches clear. Beyond these fields they could see stands of well-tended maize.

'I grow nothing commercially, you understand. These fields of produce are for the house and then to feed the cattle. What is left feeds the slaves. But apart from their obvious practical use, my main interest is to scientifically test for pest-resistance and yield.'

Miranda rode alongside Blennerhasset with Macleod silent at the rear.

'You are a trained scientist?'

'Self-taught but, yes, I would say I am a trained scientist. The key to science is method. Observation, measurement, recording. That is science. Facts are won by method and facts are the only truth. I have established at my home a laboratory and it is there, if anywhere, you could say I worship. My laboratory is my church. Even here in this semi-wilderness we must not let ourselves forget this is an Age of Reason. God is dead and religion has died with him, thank God.'

And Miranda joined Blennerhasset in laughing at his joke.

They rode on past a landscape that was one of orderly agriculture and Macleod noted that there was no sign of any men among the slaves working the land. That seemed odd to him but, as neither Blennerhasset nor Miranda had once turned to speak to him, he kept his observation to himself.

They left the fields and rode into the dappled shade of a well-wooded area through which there was a wide, clear trail, obviously well used.

'You have a plentiful supply of timber I see.'

'Not as much as I need. I have to have a steady supply sent over.' Macleod, hearing this, looked around at the mature trees wearing the bright green of new leaves which stretched away on either side of them. What project, he wondered, would require more timber than presently surrounded them in what to him seemed an abundance?

They rode on and Macleod began to hear noises coming from ahead, voices and banging. Miranda also heard them. 'There is work going on, by the sound of it, quite a lot of work,' he said.

'That there is, as you will see for yourself soon enough.'

After a short while the trees ended and the trail opened up on to a large cleared area full of tree stumps beyond which was the river. The whole place was a hive of activity. A slave ran forward ready to hold their horses. All three dismounted and the man took the reins. Blennerhasset stood and looked around him.

'This, Señor, it what I wanted you to see. The beginnings of my barracks.'

Miranda and Macleod looked around them.

The trees had been cleared for about a hundred yards back from the river bank and sawn tree-trunks lay about between the stumps of felled trees. Nearer the river banks were stacks of rough-cut timbers and at one side of the clearing several black slaves were busy working a long saw vertically over a pit, turning the trunks into timbers. A horse grazed at a hay byre, its harness and tackle hanging loose. Well back from the river's edge men were working on two half-built sheds big enough to house several coaches. On the river bank itself there was already a substantial landing stage which men were busy extending along the bank. There were black men everywhere, directed by several white overseers, digging, laying planks, hammering, wading with heavy timbers at the river's edge, or fetching and carrying. It was a place full of activity and purpose.

Harman Blennerhasset looked on proudly. 'At present as far as anyone passing can tell, I am building a landing-stage and setting up warehousing.'

'Does much river traffic pass this side of the island?'

'Not so much. That is why I chose the spot. The current's faster on this side because the channel is narrower, so craft stay over yonder in the other channel where it's easier to navigate, but what few craft come this side see only a landing stage and warehouses going up. There are settlements all along the river now and new ones starting all the time. This whole valley will bustle soon, mark my words. There'll be towns here one day, aye and maybe even cities. Indeed, once Burr's plan has been put into effect my island could become a major trading point on this part of the Ohio River and after that, who knows what I may do?'

'Who indeed?'

'Once the landing area is complete and the warehouses finished the weapons can come in to be stored. Back there where there are still trees, and well away from the warehouses, we will throw up the earth-works to surround the powder-house, but that will all be done when our plans are more advanced. Then, last of all, the barracks will go up. Once the men arrive all need for secrecy will be gone for we shall house a small army here. The plans for the whole place were drawn up by Burr himself when he was here.' Blennerhasset turned to Miranda. 'What do you think?'

'I think the army will be very small indeed to fit on to this piece of your island.'

Blennerhasset seemed not to mind the criticism. 'So it will, quite small. No more than eighty to a hundred men. But it will be a well-armed, well-trained, mobile force to be deployed where it will be most needed. Aaron Burr has more in mind than simply becoming master of a small part of Texas, he has gained considerable support here in the Ohio Valley, enough support to raise a substantial militia. With this militia we can control the Ohio river and from that base we can take the whole of the Mississippi valley.'

The words were out of Macleod's mouth before he knew it and he at once regretted them. 'The Mississippi valley!'

Blennerhasset turned to Macleod.

'You doubt me, sir?'

Miranda shot Macleod a warning look who quickly tried to recover his lost ground. 'Well, Mr Blennerhasset, the whole of the Mississippi valley. It's no backwater.'

'No more is the Ohio.'

'No, true, but –'

Miranda saw that Macleod was struggling. 'What my friend is trying to say is that controlling the Mississippi and Ohio valleys is a great undertaking. The American government would certainly have something to say about it, would they not?'

'True, but so would the British. Burr has seen Anthony Merry, the British Minister in Washington, and through him has been promised the support of London.' Blennerhasset turned once again to Macleod. 'If Anthony Merry and the British Government believe that Aaron Burr can deliver the Ohio and Mississippi valleys would you still doubt it, sir? If so, then of course I defer to your better judgement in such matters. Aaron Burr has been a soldier and has held the post of Vice President, he has sat at the very heart of government. You, no doubt, have some superior experience on which to base your assessment.'

But Miranda was impatient and uninterested in Blennerhasset's humiliation of Macleod.

'A grand design, sir, I agree, but as yet all we have seen is,' and he waved an arm at work around them, 'a lot of blacks who, it is true, are working very hard, but all you have to show for their labours is a landing stage and the beginnings of some warehousing.'

'True, but there will be other small and mobile armies such as the one we will be garrisoning. Together they will make a western force capable of creating –'

'Nothing more than a slightly bigger kingdom than you already possess. In fact no more than hills, forests and rivers in which there are a few frontier settlements, the whole stretching God knows how far and which, even if taken, could never be consolidated, never mind held. Come, sir, there is more. Aaron Burr is not a man to set himself up as ruler of a rag-bag collection of backwoods forests and Texas scrub wilderness.'

Blennerhasset gave a self-satisfied smile.

'Yes, Señor, *you* of course are too discerning, too experienced in such matters to think otherwise, and you are in the right of it. There is indeed more. More than most men could imagine. But you, sir, will understand the breadth of Burr's vision. He intends to take all of New Spain from Florida to Mexico.'

And Blennerhasset stood, as if he was a magician on a stage and had performed some impossible trick and now awaited deserved applause.

'But that's unbelievable.'

Blennerhasset, pleased with Macleod's response went so far as to bestow a patronising smile on him. 'But nonetheless true, Mr Macleod, quite true.'

Miranda, however, took it all in his stride as if it was the merest commonplace.

'Why not? Spain cannot hold it. Someone will take it. The Americans certainly intend to do so. Why not Burr?'

To Macleod's surprise this response seemed to please Blennerhasset.

'Why not indeed, sir?'

'Because, sir, Burr has no organised army. He may well have here on this island, at some future time, a hundred men. There may be other small armies. He may have some settlers from these parts and elsewhere who will fire a musket for him so long as not too many people fire back. But to take New Spain will require a real army, not a raggle-taggle of free-booters and farmers. And without an army, a trained, equipped and professionally-officered army, even the Spanish, who know only too well the weakness of their grip on New Spain, would laugh at his plans.'

'Do you laugh at them, sir?'

'No. I do not laugh. I weep. I had been told Aaron Burr was a man of consequence, a soldier, a visionary, a man of audacity. I had hoped that he and I might form an alliance. But now it seems he is no more than a dreamer.'

'And if, sir, I told you that Burr does indeed have an army, equipped and trained, not only professionally-officered but generalled? What then, sir?'

'Then I would not need to weep and I would not laugh.'

'Then let me tell you it is so. As we speak Aaron Burr is meeting with General James Wilkinson, Commander-in-Chief of the Army at New Orleans and American Governor of the Louisiana Territory. Now, sir, what of that? With General Wilkinson at our side and at the head of the New Orleans Army, with militias ready to rise here on the Ohio and along the Mississippi and with an army already assembled in Texas what do you say of Aaron Burr's vision. Is it that of a dreamer, sir, no more than a fancy? Or is it the boldest, bravest and best-laid plan you have ever heard of, sir?'

And Harman Blennerhasset stood looking at them for all the world as if he himself were at the head of that army in their moment of victory which, in his imagination, he probably was.

Miranda paused for a moment, then threw up an arm. 'Bravo, sir, bravo indeed. It is a most accomplished plan. A masterpiece.'

Macleod thought it all a shade too theatrical, but Harman Blennerhasset seemed delighted. 'Yes, sir, you have used the exact word. A masterpiece indeed.'

'But tell me, is this General Wilkinson committed, truly committed?'

'He is, sir, he will be with us to the hilt.'

Macleod tried to take in what he had just heard. Aaron Burr, who had served as Vice President to Thomas Jefferson, an American and a veteran of the Revolutionary War, was about to betray his country, to commit treason and become a renegade! And almost as bad, he would be aided in this dastardly enterprise by a serving American officer, a General no less, and one who had been charged with the safety of the new Louisiana Territory. Macleod was appalled, so appalled he was speechless. Which was probably all to the good for, if had been able to utter any one of the many thoughts surging in his brain then, surrounded as they were by Blennerhasset's men and slaves, it would have been the orchard for him and in double-quick time.

As it was, Miranda, well aware of what Macleod might be thinking and of what he might be rash enough to say, took control of the situation.

'Come, my friend, we must make all speed to New Orleans to meet with Aaron Burr and this General Wilkinson. I, Sebastián Francisco de Miranda Rodríguez will offer my full support and that of my friends in South America to this most admirable project.'

'Admirable!' Macleod managed to get the word out but,

before he could get any more, Miranda stepped to his side and caught hold of his arm and looked him straight in the eyes.

'Of course, Jean Marie, as you say, admirable. Remember why we came. Try to remember. Spain is the enemy of liberty and freedom. If Spain is to be driven out of her lands then the hand that performs the task must also be given the hand of friendship by those who wish the same for all South America.'

'But, but –'

'But what, you ask, of America? It is like you, old friend, ever loyal, ever honourable.'

'I, I –'

'I see your question. America loses New Orleans and some of the Louisiana Territories. Well, is that so bad considering what they gain?'

'Gain?'

At this point, Blennerhasset, who had been watching Macleod carefully, intervened. 'Yes, sir, a good question from your so very loyal American companion. What gain?'

'Why, America gains a secure southern border. Not Spanish, not French and never British. America will be free to take everything to the north of it. Burr is a soldier. He knows he cannot hold all he takes, the Louisiana Territory is too vast. Once he has the Ohio and Mississippi valleys he will consolidate his possession of the south and leave America to take the north. If Burr's new Kingdom blocks Spain, then America could march to the Pacific coast without firing a shot.'

'You think so, sir? You think that what you have said is Burr's plan?'

'I have not met him. I cannot know. But now, when I meet him, I will urge my idea on him. Why make an enemy of America if you can have her as a friend? I have been to Washington, I have spoken to President Jefferson and Secretary Madison. They want living space for their new country. They want settlers to move west. As Aaron Burr has told you already they want New Spain, but they don't want to fight for it and they cannot afford to buy it as they did the Louisiana Territories. If Aaron Burr by his actions gives them everything

202

north of what he takes for himself, they will thank him for it, thank him most heartily. Do you not think it is so, sir?'

Blennerhasset thought about it. It might be so. Miranda was a man well-schooled in such things.

'It might be as you say.'

'And you, Jean Marie, do you not think it might be so?'

Finally, with Miranda's eyes firmly holding his own and his hand equally firmly holding his arm, Macleod realised the part he was being called on to play. 'Yes, I'm sure it will be just as you say. Just as you say.'

It was no great speech, it lacked enthusiasm and authority, but Miranda had those in full measure and turned now to use them on Blennerhasset. 'I bless you, sir, I bless you in the name of freedom and liberty. This day you have done me a great service. If ever I can repay it, you have only to ask. You have my word, sir, my sworn word that what you have given me I will use for the great cause which I serve.'

And Miranda held out his hand to Blennerhasset, who, after the briefest of pauses, took it.

Harman Blennerhasset was silent and thoughtful as they rode back to the house. He was pleased that Miranda felt so sure the venture would prosper, but was disturbed that his interpretation of Burr's great plan differed so materially from the one Burr himself had given him.

'Well, Señor Miranda, you go now to New Orleans?'

'With all speed, sir, this very day if I could find a boat.'

'That is easily done, though not in one day. I will furnish you with a boat and pole-men. They will get you down to the confluence of the Ohio and the Mississippi and from there you will be easily able to find onward transport to take you to New Orleans. You could be there in no more than a matter of a few weeks.'

'You are a true friend, sir, a true and gracious friend. When will the boat be ready?'

'In two days.'

'A boat in two days?'

Blennerhasset laughed. 'Two days is adequate for this kind

of boat, I assure you. I will get my men started on it at once.'

Blennerhasset and Miranda rode side by side and talked of various erudite topics which, had he listened carefully would, no doubt, have considerably improved Macleod's mind. But Macleod wasn't interested in listening to anything they might say, however improving. He had heard enough already and all of it treason and betrayal. Miranda might be accomplished at wearing the mask, if that was indeed what he was doing, but he was not, so he remained silent and let his thoughts keep him company, reflecting on what, if anything, he and Miranda had actually achieved.

They now knew for certain what Burr was planning, or did they? They also knew that General James Wilkinson was party to the plot, or was he? It all depended on how reliable Blennerhasset was as a source of information. But even if what they knew was true, only they knew it. Bentley didn't and nor did Madison. So, had they achieved anything? And as Macleod asked himself that question they passed the white picket fence beyond which stood the grove of apple trees, the orchard.

Well, they had avoided taking up residence in the orchard. There was always that.

The day and a half's waiting proved tedious for Macleod. Miranda spent his time either in conversation with Blennerhasset about Burr's plans or talking science with him in his laboratory. No one was interested in Macleod nor took any pains to occupy or divert him, and so he passed his time as best he could in Blennerhasset's library or walking in the gardens trying to think of ways that the information they had collected might be passed back to Washington. In this pursuit he failed so miserably it led him to feel somewhat aggrieved that no arrangements had been put in place for this necessary task by those who had sent them. After lunch on the second day, finding Miranda alone in the library, he confided his concerns to him.

'It's too bad, here we are with vital information and no way to send it. I cannot think how such a simple requirement was overlooked.'

And here he paused, a little embarrassed that he was required to criticise his friend, so Miranda finished the sentence for him. 'By me and by Secretary Madison.'

'Yes, by both of you.'

'But it was not overlooked, as you say. We are followed and at some point contact will be effected. Our courier could hardly come to this island and ask if we had discovered anything, could he?'

Macleod considered the question. 'No, I suppose not.'

'Our invisible friend must stay invisible until there are circumstances under which we can safely meet. No, we must be patient.' He made an expansive gesture with his arm. 'Out there somewhere our friend is waiting and watching. We can do no more than wait as well.'

And Macleod, seeing the sense of this, agreed that waiting patiently was all that could be done.

Chapter Thirty-four

Before dinner on the second day of waiting their host announced that the promised boat would be ready the following morning and his guests could depart at first light. On hearing this, Macleod felt his spirits lift. He also noticed that Mrs Blennerhasset, who had joined them at the meal, seemed as cheered as he was at the news and even managed a few pleasant words to him while Miranda was his usual self and talked, laughed and drank. The only somewhat sombre note was struck by the lack of conversation of their host, for Harman Blennerhasset was thinking. He had done his best. Now it would be for Aaron Burr to decide whether Francisco Miranda would make a safe and useful ally or turn out to be a dangerous enemy.

The following morning, having been awakened and risen before dawn, Blennerhasset, Miranda, and Macleod breakfasted together although, for the amount of conversation that took place, each might have eaten alone. The house slaves had made everything ready and, after their meal, in the pale light of dawn, they mounted the horses that were held waiting for them by the front steps. No breeze stirred the trees and shrubs and a stillness surrounded the house. They rode slowly out of the grounds and once more passed the white picket fence of the orchard. It had about it an eerie, almost ghost-like aspect in the early half-light which left Macleod somewhat unnerved. That he was out of his depth he knew, but there was something else. Miranda seemed so confident, Blennerhasset so accommodating, in fact all seemed to be going well, too well. Should it all have been so easy? His thoughts were interrupted as he heard a strange ethereal sound. Someone was singing. It was a slow, almost mournful, rhythm, not unlike a dirge, sorrowful yet hauntingly beautiful. The three riders were approaching the fields and in the dawn light he saw that it was the slave women who were singing as they arrived with their children to begin their day's work. As Macleod rode past he felt a twinge of envy. For them, as for him, another day was beginning, but they knew for a certainty what lay ahead. He did not. Yet as he rode on he found that their singing comforted him and he left the fields with an uplifted heart. If they sang, surely they must be happy, or, if not happy at least content. It was a good omen on which to begin the next stage of their journey.

The clearing was already busy when they arrived and dismounted. One part of the landing stage was free of workmen where, tied up beside their luggage, was their transport, the boat that would take them down the Ohio to the Mississippi. Miranda and Macleod walked across, stood beside their baggage and looked at their craft. Both felt the same sense of impending disaster. Miranda turned to Blennerhasset.

'What is this?'

'Your craft.'

'But it is nothing more than a great box, a box with a shed at the end. No, not even a shed, a stable and one hardly fit for a horse if it were on dry land. It is only the ropes holding it to the landing stage that keep it afloat, is it not?'

Blennerhasset laughed.

'Oh she'll float all right and hold together all the way to the Mississippi unless you pole her onto snags or rocks, which won't happen with the men I've given you. They're two good men, reliable and experienced.'

'But where is the sail, where are the oars, where's the rudder and –'

'My dear Señor, this is the Ohio River, not the open sea nor some great lake.' He gestured at the craft which was indeed a shed of planks nailed roughly together which sat at the back end of a similarly constructed, shallow box hull with a blunt, sloping prow. But obviously, as it floated well enough, it was watertight. 'The Ohio's a shallow river and mostly a kindly one.

The current will float you all the way and you'll make good time, much better than you would if you made your journey on horse-back.'

Miranda looked again and considered the boat. If all it had to do was float, it might manage its task.

'And if we get to the Mississippi how will you get your craft back?'

'My God, sir, you don't think any of these flat-boats are built to do more than one journey? They take the load down to wherever it's going and then get sold as fuel or timber, which is all they're fit for once they've arrived. The pole men will make their way back on the trails by mule or on foot. You and your friend here will quickly find a more substantial craft that will take you on to New Orleans. Now, sir, if you're ready, I'll have your things put on board and send you on your way. Quick partings are the best, so farewell and may good fortune attend you. My regards to Burr when you see him.'

Miranda shook hands with Blennerhasset and then went to superintend the stowing of their baggage in the flat-roofed shed-like cabin which occupied the rear part of the craft. Macleod stood forward and held out his hand. Blennerhasset took it. Neither felt the need for words. Macleod joined Miranda in the boat and they looked on while Blennerhasset mounted his horse, turned it and rode away.

'Well, Jean Marie, we trusted ourselves to Señor Blennerhasset and survived, so now we must trust ourselves to this wooden bucket and pray that it will take us as far as the Mississippi.'

'Oh she'll get your down river, sir, never fear.'

The man who had spoken had appeared out of the cabin structure and stood smiling at them. He was a white man with a weathered face, stocky and strong-looking. He wore a canvas shirt and calf-length trousers held up by a wide, black leather belt. Macleod felt he had something of a sea-faring look about him. They were then joined by another man holding two long poles who clambered on to the cabin roof and passed one of them down.

'Here you are, Clem. All stowed and ready?'

'All done, Joe. I was just telling these gentlemen that she'll do us well all the way down to the Mississippi. They seemed a bit on the doubtful side.'

'Well, gents, I grant you she ain't like a regular keelboat. She ain't handsome but she's solid enough and she'll serve if'n we don't bump her round too much.'

Joe laughed. 'Sounds like you're a-talking about some woman, Clem.'

'Boat's *is* like women, Joe. Fair and fancy will let you down when the rough times come, tough and plain will see you through.'

'If you say so, mate, for myself I'll stick to being single.'

Miranda interrupted their erudite discussion of female virtues. 'You, I take it, are our pole men?'

'We are, sir.'

'Just two?'

'Well, sir, she's a small craft built quick for you, gentlemen, so two should be able to handle her, but on the easier stretches Joe and I thought you might spell us a while. No offence intended, but this craft is as full as she's safe to be with four on board so two poles is all it can be. I guess you're in a hurry, havin' her built special like, so I'll say what I must straight off. It's either you gentlemen take your turn with the pole or we have to lay up periodic for Joe and me to get our rest and victuals. As I say, sir,' and the man knuckled his forehead in the universal gesture of men of the sea, 'no offence intended but if you want to get down quickest, then all hands to the work is best and no idle passengers.'

Miranda laughed. 'Of course, my friend and I will stand our turns, is that not so, Jean Marie?'

Macleod was less enthusiastic about the prospect but nodded in agreement.

'Well then, gentlemen, you're stowed and ready so we'll be off as soon as you give the word, Captain.'

Miranda, obviously delighted to be addressed by the title, beamed a smile at the man. 'As soon as you like my friend, as soon as you like.'

As Miranda and Macleod got into the boat, Clem turned to his colleague on the roof. 'Ropes away, Joe. We're shovin' off at once.'

Clem put down his pole and Joe jumped down from the roof of the craft on to the landing stage. They untied the lines at the bow and stern and threw the ropes on board. Clem stepped back into the square open area of the boat in front of the cabin while Joe returned to the roof. Both then took up their poles and planted them on the edge of the landing and pushed. The craft slowly eased away from the landing stage and almost at once began to drift forward in the current.

Chapter Thirty-five

Blennerhasset had said that most craft favoured the other, wider channel of the island where the current ran more slowly, and it soon proved necessary for Clem and Joe to pole hard to keep control of the craft once it had been picked up by the full speed of the current. Miranda and Macleod stood silent as the pole men worked, and they watched as Blennerhasset's island slipped past them.

Finally the craft reached the confluence of the two channels at the end of the island and the river became wider and more slow-moving. Clem and Joe eased the boat closer to the nearer shore and settled to a slower, steadier rhythm. Safely in the gentler waters, they let the stream do the work using their poles only to keep the boat far enough away from the shore to avoid any possible snags or rocks. The boat was now comfortably in motion and, as the two pole-men had settled to an easier rhythm, Miranda was inclined to talk.

'Now we are begun, perhaps you could tell me exactly where it is you are taking us?'

Clem answered. 'As to your destination, sirs, we'll take you down to what we call Little Egypt.'

'Little Egypt?'

'Yes, sir, that part of the river where the Ohio and the Mississippi join hands as it were. There's a fair few settlements there and bigger craft a'plenty running on down to New Orleans which is where I'm told you're both heading.'

'And why do you call it Little Egypt?'

'Because the folk down there is very Egyptian-minded. Lot of book-learned people in those parts as knows all about ancient kings and such. I reckon they have a fancy to begin a new kingdom in those parts like as it might be a new Egypt, so they go in for names as fit their fancy.'

'Such as?'

'Ah, there you have me, sir. I have no learning, not of any sort except what a common sailor can pick up, and ropes and rigging is too vulgar for any of your Egyptian-minded kind. The likes of me don't bother with different names. We lump all the settlements along that part of the river together, call 'em Little Egypt, and leave it at that.'

Macleod was not interested in the conversation that sprang up between Miranda and the pole men so he stood at the side of the craft and looked at the countryside through which they were passing. It was low-lying and heavily wooded right down to the riverside.

Above the treetops was a blue sky which managed to dwarf and dominate the landscape and, beginning to appear above the tree tops, the sun was climbing and the day was already pleasantly warm. The craft seemed to travel at no real pace at all as it moved with the river. But careful study of the passing bank showed Macleod that they were, in fact, making very good progress.

The morning passed, and every so often they would see a clearing cut back into the trees. Sometimes there was no further sign of life and Clem, when asked, said that these were well-used landing places which led into nearby trails that ran through the forests, often connecting the main river with other, smaller rivers, individual homesteads or small settlements. Sometimes the clearing had a log cabin and other signs of habitation such as out-houses, fencing and even small fields. One or two of these were obviously not only homesteads but served some commercial purpose, trading or supply points, as they had provided themselves with landing stages and small warehouse outbuildings.

As the day wore on it became apparent that while the Ohio valley might seem to any city-dweller's superficial glance a backwoods wilderness, it was in fact liberally dotted on both banks with the beginnings of a thriving community. Out of sight of the river, hundreds of souls, possibly even thousands, lived,

212

worked, and had their being.

As the morning turned to noon Clem ventured a question. 'Now, gentlemen, this part of the river is shallow and clear of danger and the current's nice and steady. Who'll be first to get to know how to do a bit of poling?'

Miranda stood up. 'Give me your pole. I have been watching you. I will take a turn.'

Clem pulled the pole up clear of the water and held it out. 'Here you are, sir, but beware, it might look as a child could do it but there's a knack, as there is to most things that look simple.'

Miranda took the pole and walked to the front of the boat where he dropped it into the water took a strong grip and calmly walked back to the cabin where he retrieved the pole, walked back to the front and repeated the operation. 'Like so, my friend?'

From on top of the cabin Joe had been watching and now laughed. 'Ah, he's cotched you out fairly, Clem. He's been and done it before, ain't you, sir?'

Miranda continued to work the pole as he talked. 'True. I have worked a boat with a pole before. Never such a boat as this, I admit, but the principal is the same whatever the looks of the craft.'

'And where would that have been, sir, here in the Americas or elsewhere?'

'Russia.'

'Ah, Russia. Very mysterious place so I've heard. Very cold, they tell me.'

'Yes, my friend, mysterious, cold, and often dangerous.'

Clem came forward and took the pole once more. 'Well, sir, you'll be able to do your turn all right.' He turned to Macleod. 'What about you, sir? Ever poled a craft like your friend here?'

'No, I have not.'

'Would you like to try your hand at it a bit, sir?'

And Clem held out the pole, the end of which was still trailing in the water.

Macleod left the doorway and took hold of it. To his

surprise, it was a considerable weight.

He took a firm grip on it and went to the front of the boat as Miranda had done and jammed the pole down into the water until he felt it firmly strike bottom. Then he walked along the boat to the cabin where he pulled the pole up. Or rather, where he would have pulled the pole up, except that it seemed reluctant to leave the water and he was left with the choice of either holding on to the pole and parting company with the deck or parting company with the pole.

Macleod let go.

There was a clatter as Joe dropped his pole, quickly moved to the rear of the cabin, dropped on his front, leaned down and caught the pole that stood upright in the water as the boat slipped past. With a sharp twist Joe released it and pulled it up out of the water.

He stood up, walked back to where Macleod was looking up at him and handed the pole down to him.

'There you are, sir, no harm done. If you'll be guided by me, sir, not quite so much violence when you plant your pole. You're not runnin' through some foe with a sword. Just find bottom and gentle her along.'

Macleod took the pole and turned.

Miranda looked at him. 'Do not look so grim, old friend, it is a trick that is always played on a novice. The first time I poled a raft I had it played on me with almost the same result except that I refused to let the pole go and finished in the water. Yours was the wiser choice.'

'You knew what would happen?'

'But of course.'

'Then, dammit, you might have told me.'

'Oh no, to have told you would have spoilt the whole effect. We will be on this craft for long enough to make every little chance of diversion valuable indeed. Come now, Jean, a little laughter among comrades is not such a terrible thing is it?'

'I suppose not.'

The words provided the required sentiment, but the look directed at Clem gave the intended meaning. But Clem's hide was too thick to be penetrated by mere looks so, with a smile, he took back the pole and resumed his work.

Chapter Thirty-six

The wide, gently-flowing Ohio's surface was darkening as the day ended and the sun settled behind the tops of the trees and the pole-men brought the craft to a sandy shore where it could be safely tied up. A small fire was soon built on the bank and from the cabin of the craft Clem brought out the box of provisions while Joe gathered more wood to feed the fire. Both were men of experience and, as the sun's last light finally disappeared from the sky and the shadow of night covered them, there was a cheerful blaze around which the four men sat while Joe passed out the meat and poured their drink into four tin cups.

Macleod looked at the meat. Even allowing for the firelight which gave everything a yellowish tinge it did not look wholesome.

'What is this meat?'

Clem, chewing, looked at his own portion. 'Well, sir, as to what it might have been in life I couldn't say, but my guess is deer.'

'It doesn't look like deer.'

'No more it does, sir, and it might not be.'

'Mr Blennerhasset has cattle on his island. Could it be beef?'

'It might be, but I doubt it.'

'Why?'

'Beef comes high, sir, mighty high. There's few enough cattle brought out here, and those that are ain't meant for trail food or river men.'

Miranda was lounging back, leaning up on one elbow, looking perfectly content and at home. 'Jean, we are not in Boston or New York now, we are in the wilderness, we eat

216

what we are given and give thanks for it. Why do you care what sort of animal your food began life as. It is now as you see it. It is food. Eat.'

Macleod took a suspicious bite. It didn't taste like anything he'd ever eaten, except for the salt. It was impossible not to notice the salt.

He took a drink of his rum and water to wash away the taste then threw the piece of meat onto the sand by the fire.

'I'm damned if I'm going to be poisoned by such as that. If it's meat of any sort, which I doubt, it's not fit to pass the lips of any Christian.'

Joe, being nearest, reached forward and took up the discarded meat, wiped it roughly on his trousers and threw it back into the provisions box and looked with a mild censure at Macleod. 'I'll admit it ain't something that church-going folk might set on a Sunday table, sir, but it lasts. It'll travel along of us and be there when it's needed.'

'Come, Jean, it is all we have, try another piece.'

'No, you might as well ask me to take plain salt.'

Clem gave a small laugh. 'It *is* salty, sir, as you say. But any meat that has to stay fit to eat over days and weeks must be that way, it has to last and it has to be able to take the heat without turning, and any victuals that can do that need proper doctorin'.'

'Doctoring?'

'Just an expression, sir. I don't know exactly what they do to corn this meat, apart from as you say, plenty of salt, but it's kept many a man alive when there was nothing else to be had.'

But Macleod would not be persuaded, so the meal carried on until each had eaten as much of the corned meat as he wanted and all four then relaxed to drink a few more cups of rum and water.

Miranda, seeing that Macleod was going to sulk, engaged the two pole men in conversation to while away the evening until sleep beckoned. 'How did you come to be in these parts? You,' he looked at Clem, 'from your accent are English.' He looked at Joe. 'And you, Spanish? French?'

'Portuguese originally but that was a lifetime ago, sir. I was born in a fishing village in the south but it was raided by a Barbary ship and I was taken while still a child. I was a slave in a household for a few years then sold back to the pirates. I crewed a Corsair for three years but they were cruel men, sir, devilish cruel and I managed to slip them on a raid in Italy. Knowing only the sea as a trade I signed up on a British slaver. Crews weren't easy to come by so no questions were asked if a man knew his job. The money was good and I couldn't afford to be any too nice about choosing my work. Besides, having been a slave myself, I can't say the cargo we carried troubled me overmuch. We ran slaves from the African ports up to Liverpool where they were sold on and loaded into ships as would be taking them to the Americas. It was in Liverpool that I fell in with Clem. He got me alongside him on one of the American-bound boats. Ah, sir, they was comfortable ships –'

'For the crew no doubt, I hardly think your cargo would have described their accommodation as comfortable.'

Clem joined in. 'No, sir, them blackbirders, even the best of them, were hell ships. The things I've seen happen on them ships would make your blood run cold. Evil things, sir, things as a good Christian would never believe could happen.'

But the Liverpool slave trade and its concomitant horrors were of little or no interest to Miranda. 'And here you are, a long way from Liverpool but still working with slaves. You are overseers for Mr Blennerhasset, are you not?'

Clem nodded. 'Aye, sir, we are, but working with slaves ain't the same as bringing them in. Here a slave may work and sleep and eat. Why, they're even allowed to choose partners and have families. It's my opinion, sir, that one day the slave-ships will be put out of business because all the slaves needed will be born and bred to it as it should be in a Christian country.' He put a knuckled finger to his forehead. 'Beg your pardon, sir, if such a sentiment seems a bit forward from a man such as myself to a gentleman like you.'

'Not at all, friend, your sentiment does you honour but it will never happen.'

218

'No sir?'

'No. Mr Blennerhasset is a man of liberal mind, a humanitarian. He treats his slaves as he treats his cattle, with care and respect, because he recognises their intrinsic worth to him. As you pointed out earlier, cattle brought with such great difficulty and expense to these parts are not lightly slaughtered to provide food for the trail. They are cherished, they breed, they are valued. But there are places where this is not so, I assure you. There are cities where cattle are slaughtered in their hundreds, nay thousands, so that beef can be set on the humblest table.'

'I know, sir. Why, we all ate beef in Liverpool. Even the poorest got the taste of meat in their broth from the skimmings.'

'And there are places where slaves are worked in their hundreds and thousands until they drop and are replaced with others who in their turn will drop. No, not all slaves are owned by civilised men like Mr Blennerhasset. Your blackbirders, as you call them, will keep ferrying their cargo. Slaves are as old as time and the trade may change but it will never stop.'

Joe spat into the fire and pulled his blanket out. 'Well, sir, whether you or Clem are in the right of it is all one to me. I've found a comfortable berth with Mr Blennerhasset and I'll settle for it until my time is up and I'm the one to drop. So now, goodnight to all.' And with that he pulled the blanket across himself and seemed to fall at once to sleep.

Miranda looked at the inert figure only dimly discernible now in the light of the camp fire. 'Is he asleep already?'

'Bless you, sir, Joe can fall asleep in an instant. It's a gift he's always had and a great blessing it is.'

'And can he wake so readily?'

'Oh yes, trust Joe to rouse himself as soon as the sun is pulling itself over the horizon. When you awake, sir, there'll be a fire and warm rum and water ready to get you started, count on it, sir, count on it.'

'I will, and after having relieved myself I will also try to imitate our friend here and fall at once asleep.'

Miranda stood up and walked to the edge of the river and

219

opened his breeches. As he stood relieving himself he was joined by Macleod who also opened his breeches and added to the gentle splashing while speaking in a low tone.

'Are we safe in this place? Do you not have a pistol by you?'

Miranda secured his breeches. 'No, there are a brace in our baggage but I have no pistol by me, but even unarmed I think we are quite safe.'

Macleod, having finished, also adjusted his costume. 'Well, if you say so.'

'I do, my friend, I do. This river has had settlers on it for many years and is no longer any more dangerous than some French forest. Now try to sleep and dream of beef and gravy and any other Christian food you may care to think of, for tomorrow morning it will be more salt-meat to break our fast.'

They walked back to the dying fire where Clem was now also under his blanket and also apparently fast asleep.

Miranda looked at them then at Macleod. 'No, Jean Marie, I do not think there will be any need for pistols tonight.' He lay down and pulled his own blanket over him. Macleod did the same and lay still until he heard Miranda's voice once more. 'Unless the Indians come, but then a pistol would be of no use. I have heard that they come so quietly that you do not even know you have had your throat cut and been scalped until you wake the next morning and find your hair gone. Goodnight my friend. Sleep well.'

Chapter Thirty-seven

Macleod's dream was disturbed by someone pushing the toe of a boot in his back but he did not mind so very much. He had been dining at a fine house where the waiter had just poured the entire contents of the salt-cellar onto his plate of beef and gravy. He was about to explain to his host, who was a black man, that he needed his meal replaced but Indians with huge knives had begun creeping from the wallpaper towards the back of his host's chair. He could not shout any warning because the waiter, Miranda, kept on trying to force more salt on him.

Then the toe of the boot had arrived. Once awake Macleod's first thought was that he was incredibly hungry. He was also the last of the four to awake. The sun was still behind the tree tops but would soon be above them and its warmth was making itself felt. Already Clem and Joe were packing away their provisions box.

'Wait. What about me?'

Clem looked at him. 'You, sir?'

'My breakfast.'

'Of course, sir, I ain't forgotten. There's your mug and I'll warm you some rum and water in the ashes of the fire as soon as you like. Joe'll roll up your blanket while you slip down to the river to do what's needful.'

Joe was taking three rolled-up blankets to the boat and nodded to Macleod as he passed. 'Slept sound I trust, sir?' And he passed on without waiting for any answer.

Macleod's stomach put in its order of an immediate need for something solid and sustaining.

Macleod looked at the provisions box. 'What about that salt stuff?'

'The corned meat, sir?'

'If that's what the wretched stuff is called.'

'What about it, sir? I thought as you'd set your face against it?'

'Well, as it's all there is, I might as well try to force a little down.'

Clem opened up the box. 'Just as you like, sir. You go down to the river and see to yourself and I'll have some warm rum and water and some meat ready for you when you come back.'

Miranda emerged from the trees. 'Ah, my friend, up at last. I was afraid we'd have to carry you on board fast asleep as neither Clem nor Joe were willing to kiss you to bring you back from your dreams.'

Clem gave a short laugh looking at Miranda and then at Macleod. 'He's a rare one, your friend, sir, tells us that you're a true prince and that once you're asleep then only a kiss will wake you, and he can't do it 'cos he's a fallen angel trying to work his way back up to heaven. Reckons he must get you back your true kingdom as is called Colombia what was stolen from you as a baby by your wicked Spanish uncle. Fair had Joe and me doubled up with his tales while we breakfasted.'

But Macleod was unimpressed with the tale of Miranda's entertainment. 'Where have you been, Miranda? Why did you leave me sleep so long?'

'As to where, I have been at nature's business among the trees. As to why I let you sleep? Why not? What was there to wake you for? But as you are now awake I suggest you get yourself ready to continue our journey. The craft is almost ready, I am ready, we all wait for you.'

Macleod saw that Miranda was indeed right and that they were indeed waiting for him. The sun had not yet cleared the trees but there was plenty of light and they should have been on their way. He went down to the river, washed his face, then returned to the smoking ashes of the fire where Clem had warm rum and water ready with a piece of corned meat.

'Take them with you, sir, into the woods and finish off while you relieve yourself then when you return we can be on our way.'

222

Macleod did as he was bid and disappeared into the woods carrying his mug and meat. On his return his companions were waiting by the boat.

'If you gents will get aboard, me and Joe'll shove us off, and if you're minded to take up a pole each and lend a hand we'd be grateful.' Macleod and Miranda did as they were bid and the craft was soon once more gently gliding along with the current. After a couple of hours, at a shallow bend in the river, an island came into view.

'We'll go port of the island, sirs, the channel's narrower and the current faster so we'll make better time and make up for our late start. Settle yourselves where you will as there may be a bump or two as we run through.'

Macleod and Miranda both went and sat on either side of the cabin door out of the way of Joe who was taking turn as the lower pole-man. Both pole-men worked together skilfully to guide the boat into the faster water of the left channel and, once into it, worked to keep it on the island side away from the main shore which was heavily wooded right down to the water's edge, which was strewn with roots and rocks.

Miranda looked at the shore then at Macleod. 'A dangerous place for such a craft. I hope our crew know their work or we will end up swimming to New Orleans.'

Macleod nodded, he too felt the time saved might not have been worth the obvious risk.

Suddenly both Macleod and Miranda were thrown sideways onto the deck. Macleod banged his head hard on the cabin wall before hitting the side of his face on the deck floor. The two heavy blows almost made him lose consciousness but he was vaguely aware of shouting on board and cries from further off. He struggled to rise but the boat was moving wildly, rocking and lurching.

Dimly Macleod knew that the craft was in trouble and any moment expected to find himself in the water. He began to fumble with the buttons of his coat which, once waterlogged, would be enough to pull him under, but his fingers failed to function properly. Then there was a sharp shudder which threw him forward and he collided with another body. At first he thought he was being attacked and attempted to struggle free but then Miranda's voice penetrated.

'Hold, Jean, we have been –'

But then the grip on his arm was gone and Macleod saw that Miranda had fallen on his back. Standing over them both and looking down was a man holding a cudgel.

The man turned to unseen others.

'Here they are, lads, all ready to take and truss.' Macleod attempted to rise but the man with the cudgel pushed him back roughly by putting the sole of his boot on his chest.

'Stay down, mister, it'll be better for you. Try any heroics and you'll get a taste of this.' He held out his cudgel.

Macleod realised that he was not in any condition to resist so he lay still until two men came, pulled him upright and began to manhandle him off the boat. Their craft lay at an angle, the bow raised up where it had run hard on to the bank. There was no sign of Clem or Joe. Once he'd waded on to the shore, each arm firmly held by the men who had pulled him to his feet, he looked back at the boat, but all he saw was the man with the cudgel still standing looking down. Miranda, it was obvious, had not recovered consciousness. Then, from the far side of the river he saw an Indian canoe put out with two men in it paddling towards them, towing something in the water behind them. But his guards pushed him onward in to trees where, after a short while they came to a clearing. One of the guards produced some stout cord and pulled Macleod's hands behind his back, bound up his wrists and then pushed him back against the trunk of a tree.

'Sit there and behave yourself.' Macleod let his legs lower him down until he was sitting at the foot of the tree. The guards turned and left, only to return some few minutes later carrying the inert form of Miranda who, Macleod noticed, had a thin trickle of blood running down the side of his face. The party walked past Macleod followed by the man with the cudgel who smiled at him.

'Don't you worry, friend, your mate's not dead. I know my

work. He'll have a sore head for a time but he'll wake soon enough.'

The party passed on out of the clearing with their burden and some moments later two more men arrived carrying between them an enormous coil of thick, wet rope. Neither looked at Macleod but passed on by, following the group who had carried Miranda.

Macleod sat thinking. What had happened? Who were these brigands? Where were Clem and Joe and were they accomplices in what had occurred? None of which he knew. Did his head hurt? He knew that all right. His head hurt like hell.

But Macleod was not left alone with his thoughts for very long. Arriving from where the brigands had carried the inert form of Miranda came a man in a tall hat and long cloak and, under the cloak, Macleod could see that the man used a stick to aid his walking.

Jeremiah Jones limped up, stopped and looked down at Macleod. 'Knocked about a bit, eh? It looks like your eye will come up nicely.' He examined him further. 'That scrape on your cheek could get nasty if it becomes infected which, out here in this God-forsaken country, must be reckoned a possibility. Still, that's all in the future, now to business. I've got you here because I need a report, Bentley wants to know exactly what Burr and Blennerhasset have arranged.'

'You mean that business on the river was your doing?'

Jones gave a rather self-satisfied smirk. 'Oh yes. A good plan and carried out to the letter. I admit you may think my methods a little extreme but I assure you they were completely necessary,' he said

'You damned lunatic. You might well have killed us.'

'Not so. These men know their work believe me. Come, come, Macleod, no sulking. You and Miranda were bound downriver which meant your investigations on Blennerhasset's island were finished and done and you had some reason to head for New Orleans. That much I could find out for myself, but I needed to find a way of having a private word, a meeting which could remain unknown to our friend Miranda.' Jones paused to raise his stick in a wide gesture. 'And here it is. Private as one could wish.'

'Those damned brigands are your men?'

'Temporarily, yes. I saw the whole thing from the shore, stout rope diagonally across the narrow channel. Ran you ashore sweet as a songbird. Nice work, very professional, especially for men who only took up the trade of river-piracy so recently.'

'Blast you, Jones, you could have turned us over and drowned us.'

'Oh no, I don't think so. Those flat-bottomed boats are pretty stable craft even though they're roughly built. The plan had my full approval.'

'Damn you and damn your approvals.' But slowly, through the pain in his head, Macleod began to think through what Jones had been saying. 'But why should Miranda not know of our meeting? He was told to expect a contact.'

'True, but the fact of the matter is that we don't altogether trust Señor Miranda. He has distinctly divided loyalties and Bentley felt it would be better if the report on Blennerhasset came first from you and that Miranda was unaware of it. You were a party to all that was said, I hope?'

Macleod squirmed as the ropes bit into his wrists but, despite the pain, conceded that if Jones needed to arrange a meeting without Miranda's knowledge his plan seemed to have accomplished that difficult task admirably, if not comfortably. He conceded it, but nothing would make him like it, and his attitude showed clearly in his voice. 'What's done is done I suppose, now let me loose of these ropes and I'll make your damned report.'

'Come now, Macleod, your attitude is unfriendly, as if you alone have been the one to suffer. I've been on this pestilential island three nights waiting for you, and I assure you that the company was as primitive as the accommodation. It wasn't pleasant for me here while you relaxed in luxury with Blennerhasset.'

'To hell with your idle talking. Untie me.'

226

'Ah, now there I fear I must refuse. I went to no little trouble to arrange this charade. You and I needed to talk without Miranda knowing and then I needed you both on your way. River-pirates seemed a damned good ruse and it will work, too, but only if we make it look like the real thing. You'll stay tied here and Miranda will wake up tied elsewhere. Tomorrow morning one of the men will come and loosen your ropes enough for you to wriggle free. He'll show you where Miranda is and you can free him, then both of you can jump into the canoe that's been conveniently left by your flatboat and paddle off down to the nearest settlement which is Hocking's Landing – not so very far downriver. Miranda's a sharp fellow and if he's been tied up all night he'll know what it feels like so he must see that you look and feel as he does. If he's all aches and pains, so must you be, so sit as you are, tell me what you found out, and make it quick. I must be on my way.'

Macleod reluctantly saw the sense of it. A night sitting without cover and your hands tied behind your back would be no easy thing to counterfeit especially to a man just freed from that exacting position himself. He didn't like it but he decided that he must accept it.

'Blennerhasset is building a landing-stage and warehousing for weapons. Next he'll build powder stores and then barracks. The landing-stage and the warehousing will be up and ready inside a month, by my guess. As to when the rest will get built or the men arrive I have no idea.'

'Good, go on.'

'He says Burr has recruited a sufficient following in the Ohio and Mississippi valleys to raise a considerable militia which, together with well-armed, well-trained, small mobile forces like the one to be assembled on his island, Burr will be able to take and hold the whole area.'

'He does, does he? Well, let them dream. Anything else?'

Jones seemed singularly unimpressed with the information he had so far been given, but as Macleod went on and eventually finished, Jones's manner changed dramatically.

'Are you sure? He's got Wilkinson and the New Orleans

Army in on his plan?'

'It's what he claimed. It may be true or it may be all a fantasy that he chooses to believe, how would I know?'

'What does Miranda think?'

'He seemed to believe it.'

'Did he indeed?'

'He must have. It was why he was dead set on going to New Orleans.'

'Then to New Orleans you must both go, and I to Bentley. This is a turn we hadn't expected and a nasty one.' With difficulty Jones squatted down beside Macleod. 'Now listen well. You will be freed tomorrow, early. Get Miranda and be on your way in that canoe. About three hours paddling downriver is Hocking's Landing, quite a big place as settlements hereabouts go. I have a man waiting there to contact you, just as Miranda is expecting. Be sure and let Miranda make the report. Best if you're not even present when he does it so he feels he can say exactly what he wants us to know.'

'Blast your eyes, Jones, why go to all this trouble if there's a man waiting –'

'Because, my dull friend, Miranda expects a contact and he must have one. Also, when he makes his report it can be compared to yours. If it varies we'll know he's playing a double game. If not, well, it may only mean he's still not made up his mind which way to jump as yet. Once he's spoken to our man, get on your way to New Orleans.'

'To do what?'

'That, as yet, I don't know so cannot say. I'll need to get to Bentley and give him this latest information. Once he has it he'll decide what to do. Whatever he decides, we'll need you and Miranda where we can lay our hands on you, and that means New Orleans.' Jones struggled up and stood, leaning on his stick, looking at Macleod. 'You've done well, Macleod. Bentley will be pleased. Now I must go. I have a canoe of my own on the other side of the island and I need to get on my way.'

A question surfaced in Macleod's mind. 'Can you trust these

228

villains you've hired? They won't cut our throats after you've gone?'

'No. Once you and Miranda are safe at Hocking's Landing they'll all be paid off handsomely, but only if you get to the settlement safely. So be careful in the canoe, don't drown yourself or Miranda or you'll do my villains out of their honest wages. Good luck.'

And Jones turned and limped away.

Macleod sat thinking. His head hurt. His wrists hurt. His legs were getting cramp and he was to spend the whole night in such a condition until he was released in the morning. If he was released.

All this he knew. What he didn't know was what it was he was really doing. Helping Miranda gain information for Secretary Madison? Perhaps, if that was what Miranda was really doing. Helping Jones gain information for Bentley? Certainly. But did that mean he was betraying Miranda? What was Bentley really up to? What was Miranda really up to? And most of all, what was Aaron Burr really up to?

He felt alone and confused. He thought about how he had stumbled into this awful thing. He wondered if he would come out of it alive, if he would ever see his home again and, thinking of Boston and home, his thoughts turned to Marie. There she sat, alone except for a maid and manservant in that big house in Boston with no news of him since the letter Bentley had dictated for him. God's blood, she must be worried. Any woman would be. Yet what could he do?

Macleod determined that once they had arrived at the settlement he would contrive somehow to get a letter on its way to Boston, to his beloved wife. She must not be left to sit and worry on her own with no news. He would write something to comfort her. But what? No matter. He would think of something, some story that would set her mind at ease. He was a heartless wretch not to have thought of it before.

She was a poor, weak woman and it was for him, her husband, to make sure that she did not suffer any more unnecessary fears. Women, he knew, should not be too exposed

229

to the roughness of the world. He would write a letter and say –
Well, he would think of what to say.

Chapter Thirty-eight

The day passed slowly. Twice Macleod was visited by his captors and inspected to check the cords binding him. Neither time was he offered food nor water and Macleod began to discover just how much discomfort his body could generate. His wrists hurt, his head throbbed with pain, his cheek stung, he ached everywhere and, despite his pain, he felt both hungry and thirsty. But as there was nothing he could do about any of it his weariness eventually overwhelmed all his other discomforts and he fell into something between a swoon and a sleep and his mind began to fill with weird fancies. It was a world full of distortions and alarms, of drowning in salty water and being chased by wild Indians through the rooms of Blennerhasset's house where, in each room, Mrs Blennerhasset looked at him with loathing in her eyes. Then, suddenly, it all changed. He was home in Boston, sitting at the dining table. Opposite him sat Marie who was speaking to him, but he could not make out what it was she was saying. From her face it was obviously urgent, yet as her lips moved no voice came. Then she was at his side, whispering gently. 'Dearest Jean.' She was breathing words of endearment. 'Jean, my love.' Her arms enfolded him and her lips ... then he fell sideways and hit his head on the hard ground. The pain rushed back as he suddenly returned to consciousness and he realised that he was not dreaming. Marie *was* whispering to him, she was leaning down close to him with her lips almost touching his cheek and shaking him.

'Jean, Jean, for God's sake wake.'

Seeing his eyes open and looking at her she pulled him up into a sitting position. Behind her, the first light of a new morning was visible through the leaves above her head.

Looking up at her, Macleod was as stunned as if the blows to his head on the boat had been repeated, but finally found speech. 'Good God. How did it happen?'

Marie was fumbling with his wrists. 'Please, Jean, try to help. There is not much time.'

'I'm not dreaming? You are here?'

'Of course. Please lean further forward or I will not be able to loosen your cords.'

Macleod leant forward as best he could.

He'd heard of things, strange stories from the East, of people who could dissolve their bodies and move them from one place to another, but had always discounted such tales as fantastic. He had wanted to contact her, to reassure her, to comfort her, and here she was. Had he done it by will-power? Was it some kind of miraculous …

Marie stood up. 'There, you are free. Now we must hurry. I have a canoe.'

Macleod sat and stared.

'You're not in Boston?'

'Oh, Jean, come, please come quickly. There is a canoe and we have no time.'

She stooped down and began, with difficulty, to help him to his feet. Once upright Marie pulled at his arm but he was fuddled, dazed and his legs were so stiff that he nearly fell as he took his first step. This managed to rally his faculties somewhat and he bent down and rubbed them vigorously. Marie stood nervously waiting, speaking to him in a low voice. 'Kitty has not been well, Dolly stayed up with her last night and this morning while they both slept I crossed the river by canoe. But they will follow and when they do …'

Macleod, a little feeling restored, straightened up. 'Kitty? Dolly?'

Neither name meant anything to him in his confused state.

'They have made plans. They are in league with these cut-throats. She found out what was planned and bribed them to work for her. I felt sure they meant to kill you after they killed your friend Miranda, so I stole the canoe and came. Now we must go.'

Slowly, but only very slowly, in Macleod's head reason was returning. 'Kill Miranda? Why would they kill Miranda?'

'Oh, Jean, why do you stand asking questions when time is running away for us? What if the cut-throats come? We will be discovered and we will die. For the love of God, let us go.'

Marie pulled him forward and Macleod allowed himself to be led. They moved reasonably quietly along the path which the pirates had carried Miranda. After a short while Marie stopped, crouched then turned to him, put a finger to her lips, then pointed away to her left and lifted five fingers. Then she beckoned Macleod to follow.

Macleod watched the dumb-show bewildered. He wondered if he was hallucinating. He had heard that people saw strange things, unreal things after a blow to the head. Marie looked back anxiously, then gave a silent groan of despair and came back to him, took his hand and led him on.

After a few minutes they reached the shore where, pulled up on the sand, there was an Indian canoe.

'Here is my canoe. Get in, we must depart.'

'In that?'

'But of course, what else is there?'

But it was already too late. From the far bank another canoe emerged from the shadow of the trees into the dawn light on the river. Marie looked at it carefully but not for long.

'Mon Dieu, it is Dolly and Kitty. They are coming. We are lost. What shall we do?' She grabbed hold of Macleod's arm and clung to him. 'They will kill us, Jean. What shall we do?'

Had she been a doctor specialising in mental disorders she could not have chosen a better cure for Macleod. He didn't understand her sudden appearance from nowhere. He didn't understand her dumb-show games. He didn't understand why Dolly and Kitty, whoever they were, were coming to kill them. But he understood the terror in his wife's voice and her cry for help.

He took her arm.

'Come. I know where there is another canoe on the other side of the island. I saw two of the villains crossing the river in it. They'd stretched a damn rope –'

Marie was about to cut short his explanation but, before she could speak, a voice carried across the river from the approaching canoe.

'Rouse yourselves there. Hi, you bastards on the island. Rouse yourselves, damn you.'

The morning was still, without any breeze, so the voice carried well across the water.

'Ah, Dolly is calling them. We will be taken.'

'No, dearest, we will not. Follow me.' Macleod led the way but soon stopped, unsure of which way to go. Marie pulled his arm and pointed to the trail. 'Good. Follow me.' Macleod led the way once again until they came to the place where Marie had gone into her dumb-show. Macleod suddenly realised what it was she had been trying to signal to him. Over there, now to his right, was the pirate camp and there were five of them. What of that? The way he felt, let there be twenty-five.

'Wait here.'

'But Jean –'

'I must find Miranda.'

Before Marie could protest further Macleod had clattered off through the trees.

Marie waited and then, once more almost in despair, followed.

Macleod emerged into the camp-site. It was empty except for Miranda who sat bound as Macleod had been under a tree. Macleod looked around furiously.

'Where are they?'

'Gone for the moment. They heard calls from the river and left. By all that is holy I'm glad you were watching for your chance. Come, free me,' Miranda answered and squirmed round so his wrists were in the open.

Macleod was still standing looking furious with his fists clenched.

Marie arrived and made a decision. She didn't want Miranda with them but she needed to get Macleod moving and, as he seemed determined to stay and get them all killed, she needed whatever ally she could find and the only one present was Miranda. She went to him and began to untie his wrists, then helped him to his feet. Macleod was still looking angrily around.

'I'll kill the bastards, every last man jack of them.'

Miranda caught Macleod's arm. 'Of course you will, Jean, but some other time. Now we must go. Madame, who you are and why you are here I do not know, but the thanks I owe you must wait. We must find some way of …'

'Jean says he has a canoe.'

'A canoe? You have a canoe?' Miranda asked, switching naturally to French.

'Yes. It's by the flat-boat. I saw two of the villains …'

'Then let us go.'

Miranda set off and Marie grabbed Macleod's arm and pulled. 'Jean, come. We *must* go.'

Reluctantly Macleod allowed himself to be led away muttering, 'cowardly swine', and followed Marie and Miranda to the shore and the canoe.

Not more than a few minutes after Marie, Miranda and Macleod had left the camp, the man who had wielded the cudgel on the boat ran out of the trees and looked around, a pistol in his hand. Four more men joined him followed by Dolly who was supporting Kitty, helping her to walk and remain upright. They all stood and looked as the man with the pistol went to where Miranda had been left bound. He kicked the cords which lay on the ground.

Dolly looked scornfully at the five men. 'Fools, blunderers. Couldn't you even nursemaid two unarmed men?'

The man holding the pistol, obviously the leader, looked at her sullenly. 'We heard the calling and we went to see what it was. They was both well trussed.'

'They're still gone though, aren't they, or are we all suddenly made blind?'

Kitty spoke quietly to Dolly. 'Marie. This is her doing. When I get my hands on that –'

But then she fell to coughing. Dolly looked at her,

concerned. 'You're ill, girl.' She put a hand to Kitty's forehead. 'You're burning.' She turned angrily to the men standing looking at her, waiting. 'Don't stand there like a bunch of idiot children. Get after them. This is an island, isn't it? Unless they swim for it they have to still be here. You,' she looked at one of the men, 'go and stand guard on the canoe in case they try for it.' The man hesitated. 'Well, dolt?'

'Which one?'

The meaning of the question dawned. 'Dear Lord, there's another one?'

'There's yourn as you came on and there's the one we used to set the rope.'

'Go and look after ours, the rest of you after the other one. Look lively, you simpleton bastards, or they'll be away.'

The four men ran off in the direction Macleod, Marie and Miranda had taken and the remaining man went back the way he had come, leaving Dolly and Kitty alone.

Kitty looked at the fire which was burning well in the middle of the camp. 'I'm cold, Dolly, fearful cold. Can I sit by the fire for a moment to warm myself?'

''Course, my dear. Come and sit.'

Dolly helped Kitty to the fire and both women sat down. Kitty turned and looked at her. 'Have we missed them, Dolly?'

'Forget them, dear, sit and rest. You're not well.' Dolly reached forward and put another couple of sticks on the fire and with another stirred it up so that it burnt even brighter. 'Still feel cold?'

Kitty shook as she answered. 'To the bone.' She looked at Dolly with real fear in her eyes. 'My God, I ain't goin' to die, am I? Dolly, I'm afeared. I ain't ready to die.'

Dolly pulled off her own shawl and added it to the one Kitty wore. The sun was up now and it was going to be a fine day. The fire was more for cooking once the morning chill had gone and already the day's warmth could be felt, but Kitty got off the log and went nearer to it, kneeling with her hands out trying to absorb some of its heat. Dolly joined her and put her arms round her. Kitty looked at her again. The fear was still there. 'I

236

ain't ready to go, Dolly. I've been a bad girl, I know I have. I've done things. Oh, Dolly, I ain't ready.' Tears began to run down her cheeks.

Dolly put her arms about her and hugged her close. 'You'll not die, Kitty. I won't let you.'

From the direction the four men had gone a shot was fired and both waited but there was nothing more, only silence. Then Kitty collapsed into an untidy heap, weeping again and Dolly could hear the fear back in her voice. 'They're gone, ain't they?' Dolly nodded. 'He's the Devil, that Macleod, the Devil himself, that's who he is. How else could he do it?'

'Marie, that's how. She gave us the slip and came over. I underestimated that madam and now we've damn well paid for it.'

Kitty looked up at her. 'But he always does it, Marie or no Marie. He always slips away just when we have him in our grip.' Kitty shuddered and looked around. 'He's the Devil, that's who he is and he'll come back for me. I know he will. He'll take me, Dolly, he'll take me down below with him. Oh, God, I ain't been good and the Devil will have me and when he does I shall burn. The nuns in Dublin said it was so when I was a child, that the wicked blossomed for a time but then burned for ever. I ain't been good, Dolly, and I'll burn just like the nuns said.'

And Kitty put her face in her hands and started sobbing. Dolly gently took her once again in her arms and began to rock her gently like a little child. 'No you won't, girl, and I'll tell you for why?' Kitty looked up with hopeful eyes. 'Because you ain't blossomed yet, have you? How can you be classed among the proper wicked if you ain't blossomed yet?'

Kitty managed a weak smile. 'You're right, I ain't, have I, not like the real wicked? I've been a bad girl I know, but not more than most and not so bad as many. And I don't remember ever blossoming so I can't really and truly be so wicked can I?'

'You ain't no more wicked than what I am.'

'Ah, but you've blossomed in your time, Dolly, you've blossomed.'

'Maybe I have but I ain't the one with fever, feared of dying and Macleod coming to carry off my immortal soul, am I? So I ain't worrying and neither should you be. And it all makes no difference because I won't let you die, so leave it alone and try to stay warm.'

Through the trees the four men came back into the camp and stood round the fire.

'What's up with her?'

'She taken with the fever.'

The leader, still holding his pistol, seemed uninterested. 'Well, they're away. They got free somehow and while we was at the shore waiting for you they got the canoe and they're away. I got one shot at them but it did no good.'

Dolly looked at them one by one. 'God save me from big, strong bully boys who keep their brains in their breeches. Why in God's name I thought you wouldn't botch the thing, I don't know. Well, what's done is done. Where are Blennerhasset's men?'

'A good few leagues downriver by now both with their throats cut. They'll keep their own council, never fear.'

'Will they then? And if either of them gets found won't people start asking questions? And when they don't return might Blennerhasset make enquiries, do you think? And that flat-boat of theirs, what if it's seen abandoned? Or are you thinking of taking it downriver yourselves?' Her points obviously struck home for the men looked anxiously at each other. 'Fools. Why didn't you bury them here? But no, you're too idle. Sling 'em in the river, take the easy way. Well, one of you can take us back to shore. I need to get care for my friend.'

'What about our money?'

'What about it?'

'We ain't been paid.'

'No, and you won't be, not by me. Why? Because you've snarled up everything so well that there's nothing now that I can do to unsnarl it, is there? For all the good you've done me you might as well have stayed loyal to your limp-along friend as hired you in the first place. What I said I'd pay for is for you to

238

cross him and do my bidding, but as things stand it looks like he's the one you've served well enough after all. The men I wanted dead are alive and back on their way downriver where they were headed in the first place. Added to that there's two bodies floating in the river with their throats cut. Give it one or two days or, if you're lucky, a few more and the whole valley hereabouts could be up and shouting 'river-pirates' and then they'll come looking and, if you ain't very lively in skidaddling, they'll take you and you'll all find out how pleasant it is to swing in the breeze at the end of a rope.'

The leader fingered his pistol and began to regret the shot he had made.

'We may have lost your men but we still have you.'

'Well, well, well. A threat. What a brave man you are and no mistake especially with a weapon in your hand.' The man glanced down at his empty weapon and when he looked back at Dolly there was a small pistol in her hand. She stood up and, cocking the flint, took a step towards the leader. 'Pity it's discharged or you might have been the one who did for me.' And she shot him square in the chest. With a look of surprise the man dropped his empty pistol and fell back stone dead. Dolly put the small pistol back in her pocket and calmly looked at the other three. 'Any more brave bullies want to make threats against two poor defenceless women?' But it was clear there weren't. They looked at Dolly, then at their dead leader then at each other. These men had had enough, they wanted to be gone. The fifth man ran into the camp.

'I heard a shot.'

'So you did,' and she nodded at the dead man, 'and now you see where the shot went.' Dolly went back to Kitty. 'Come on, girl, we need to get going and get you some doctoring.' She looked up at the three men still standing by their dead leader. 'She's weak and getting weaker. Can you get her into the canoe?' They were men who had always taken orders, always followed. The leader in their latest venture was lying stretched dead on the dirt so, after the briefest pause, they accepted that Dolly had taken charge.

'No, it won't work. With her as she is she might do anything and it takes nothing to upset a canoe.'

'Then it will have to be the boat. Any of you handled a pole?' Three of the men answered that they had. 'Good. Then get the boat ready and get me whatever will pass for bedding and I'll want blankets, all you've got, and water. Clean water, mind, no river stuff.' The men stood listening. She was in charge now, she was their leader.

'And me?'

It was the man without any pole experience.

'You clear up here and I mean clear up. I want old bully boy there buried and deep enough so he won't be easily found. Then knock this camp down so as it won't easily show whether it's fresh or months old. Can you do that?'

'Aye, sir.' The man looked at Dolly sheepishly. 'Sorry, I mean ...' but he didn't know what he meant. He'd never followed a woman before.

'Use any damn name you choose so long as you do as you're told and, if you don't, then God have mercy on your soul because I bloody well won't. Now hop to it all of you, and you,' the man charged with clearing the camp stopped, 'after we're clear, bully's planted and the camp's sorted, take our canoe and go downstream as far as the second or third settlement and wait for your mates there. Make up your own story as you go along but have the brains to keep it simple. Understand?'

'Aye, sir.'

All the men left to go about their business. Dolly stooped down by Kitty who was staring at the fire shivering and muttering. Dolly put a hand to her forehead then to her cheeks.

'By God it's come on you quick, you're burning up.'

But Kitty wasn't listening. The fever had driven her into a land that existed only inside her own delirious brain. 'He'll come for me, I know he will. He'll take me. He can do it. He can do anything, he's the Devil himself. No one can take him but he can take who he likes.' She suddenly turned to Dolly and grabbed her arm. 'Don't let him come for me, Sister, I meant no harm. I'll say my prayers and tell my beads. I'll not be sinful,

I'll be a good girl. Don't let him come for me.'

Dolly pulled the sobbing shivering Kitty into her arms and held her close, rocking her gently once more. After a short while Kitty's sobbing ceased and she fell silent.

'You bastard, Macleod, you've beaten us and we're done for this time. Well, good riddance to you and may you rot in hell and, as for that bitch of a wife, I hope she joins you in the flames and I wish you good company of each other.'

One of the men sent to get the boat ready returned. 'She'll float and she's watertight as she stands but I wouldn't answer for her making it far. We'll need to put in at the first settlement we come to.'

'We'll have to anyway. This one here is burning up and needs a bed and proper tending.'

The man shuffled his feet uneasily. 'Aye, but what if it's as you say and one of those bodies has run ashore or been fished out.'

'Leave the thinking to me. If anyone can get you pack of witless fools through this, I will. Just get us to the settlement without drowning us and I'll not only see you get free and clear but I'll give you enough of a stake to be on your way.'

'That's fair I reckon.'

Suddenly all the passion, anger and hate stoked up in Dolly flared out at the unfortunate who stood before her. 'Fair! Fair? By God it's generous, it's lavish. Fair, you backward arsehole, you turd in trousers, God rot your eyes and –'

But a whimper from Kitty at once had all of Dolly's attention. 'Where am I? I'm so hot, I'm burning. Am I dead? Oh, Mother of Mercy, Holy Mary Mother of God,' she made a grab for Dolly's arm, 'say that I'm not dead.'

Dolly's voice was all gentleness and kindness as she rested her hand on Kitty's forehead. 'No, no, dearest, you're not dead. You're sick of the fever but I'll care for you and see you get proper tending. Rest my love, here put your head against my breast and close your eyes.' The man took advantage of the change in Dolly's attention and hurried off to gather what there was for bedding and Dolly began to quietly croon a lullaby.

After a few minutes she carefully looked down at Kitty. 'That's right, my love, my dearest, you sleep. We're done chasing and running now. There'll be no more roving for you and me. This is where we fetch up and make the best of it. Sleep my angel, sleep and rest and get well.'

And Dolly began to slowly rock to and fro while on her breast Kitty lay still, now sleeping that everlasting sleep from which no one awakes and in which all questions are finally answered or lost in an eternal silence.

Chapter Thirty-nine

'It's no good you holding her like a baby. She's dead.'

Dolly looked up angrily. 'I know she's dead and she won't be the only one if you don't hold your gab.'

The man who had spoken looked at the others then at the ground. He didn't know what to do any more than they did, so they waited.

Dolly sat holding Kitty's body. She needed to think. Kitty's dying didn't change anything. She'd sickened over the past two days and the signs had got worse but Dolly hadn't expected the end to be so soon nor so sudden. Now she was gone. Well, everyone went some time.

'Should we dig a hole for her?' Another of the waiting men spoke.

This time Dolly looked up but there was no anger. 'No. We'll take her with us.'

The men looked at each other. 'Why? She's dead.'

Dolly carefully laid Kitty on the ground and stood up.

'Because I said so. And why do I say so? Because we need her.' She looked at the men who clearly had no idea what she was talking about. 'Let's say one of those bodies has been found. Or the men I came for, the ones you fools let slip through your fingers, let's say they've raised the alarm. Then the good folks will be looking for a bunch of rough, tough, river-pirate, cut-throats, won't they?' The men nodded gloomily. 'And what will we be? We'll be a lady, a grieving lady who's just lost her dear sister while travelling, that's who me and her'll be. And you three? You'll be kind-hearted God-fearing men who agreed to ferry me and my dear departed down river to a settlement to see that she got a Christian burial. That'll be our story and I don't want any of you opening his

243

trap wide enough to put all our heads in a noose, so I'll do all the talking that's needed, understand?' The men nodded. 'And you'll all try to look like honest Johns. Say no more than you have to, if that. Now, if the boat's as ready as she'll ever be we'd best be on our way.' She nodded down to Kitty. 'Load her on to the boat and make ready.'

The men did as they were bid and took away the body between them. Dolly went across to the man who was busy digging the grave for the fallen captain of the band. He stood in the hole and looked up at her.

'You're about ready to be on your way, I guess?' Dolly nodded. 'I'm heartily sorry, Ma'am, that your friend died but once the fever takes a good hold there's not many as pull through.'

Dolly put her hand into a recess in her dress. The man gave her a worried look but when her hand came back into view she held a small purse. She opened it, took out a coin and flipped it into the hole beside the man's feet.

'That'll get you on your way when all's done here.'

The man bent down, picked up the coin, wiped it and looked at it. It was a silver dollar. He looked up gratefully. 'God bless you, Ma'am.'

But almost before the words were out of his mouth Dolly had stepped forward, leaned towards him and driven a knife deep into his throat. The man gave a strangled gargle and blood foamed at his lips. Dolly pulled away the knife and the man fell sideways. Dolly stepped down into the shallow grave, retrieved the dollar from his closed hand and wiped her blade clean on the dead man's jacket. Then she put both knife and coin away, stepped out of the grave and walked away towards the boat.

The men had the craft in the water ready to go, holding it steady with the poles. One stood at the side waiting.

'All finished back there?'

Dolly took the hand that was outstretched to help her on board. 'He'll stay until it's done then he'll take the canoe I came across in and make himself scarce.'

'Do you trust him to keep his mouth shut? If you gave him

244

money he'll spend it on drink, and who knows what he might say?'

'I know what he'll say, and I know he'll say nothing that will harm any of us, and that's all any of you needs to know. Now get this tub out into the river and let's get where we're going before it all falls to bits and we float all the way to New Orleans face down.' The two men holding the poles began their work and soon the boat was out in the water and moving well. Dolly looked back. 'Does that place have a name?'

The man who had handed her aboard looked at the island as it slid past.

'Mustapha Island. No idea why, but that's its name.'

'Well then, farewell Mustapha Island, the last resting place of Dolly Bawtry.'

'How do you mean? You're alive, and you're Dolly Bawtry. At least that's the name you gave us when we signed up with you. How can it be your last resting place if you're here?'

'Because Dolly Bawtry is dead and buried and this lady you see before you is now Miss Fanny Dashwood, late of Boston and before that of London.' She nodded to Kitty's body. 'I was travelling with my sister looking for a place to settle, a place where we might find honest Christians and help them build up God's kingdom here in God's country. There, now you all know. The Misses Fanny and Kitty Dashwood, ladies from Boston and, before that, London. We contracted with two guides at Marietta to take us onwards downriver but my sister Kitty fell ill and we were left in the lurch by the villains who had undertaken to guide us to a settlement. They took our belongings and left us to die. You kind men found us after, let's see, three days, that'll do. You found us on the riverside as you poled down river looking to pick up passengers or cargo, I leave those details to you. You undertook to get us to a settlement but my sister, having been without food or clean water or proper shelter for so long, became much worse and on the boat she sadly passed away.' A sudden thought struck her. 'How did your limping friend intend to pay you off? He wouldn't have been so stupid as to put all the money up front, of that much I'm

245

sure.'

'If both men got safe off the island and down to Hocking's Landing, he said a man there would have our money.'

Dolly laughed. 'And you dull bastards believed him. This Hocking's Landing, is it the first settlement, the one we're making for?' The man nodded. 'Well, don't go looking for any man nor any money, not if either exist, which I doubt. We have our story and our necks may depend on it. We're ladies and you're God-fearing Christians. That has to be our tale so get it stuck into those blocks of wood you call your heads. Misses Fanny and Kitty Dashwood, got it?'

The men all nodded and the man standing by her leaned towards her and dropped his voice. 'I dare say Tom, what we left digging a grave back there on Mustapha Island, is as dead and buried as Dolly Bawtry. Not that I care, in fact it settles my mind to know that Tom is taken care of. He was always one for the drink and in drink he was given to talking. No, Miss Dashwood, it was the clever thing to do.'

Fanny Dashwood smiled at him and spoke in an equally low voice. 'Would you like me to show you how it was done?'

The man stood back sharply.

'No, captain, your word is good enough for me.' He turned to the pole-men who were finding the going easier as the island slipped away behind them, the channel spread out and the current slackened. 'Now, lads, Miss Dashwood here, what's just lost her dear sister, says she thanks God that she has found three true Christian souls to see her through her ordeal.'

The pole men looked at each other then laughed. 'Arr, Billy, true Christians, that's us all right.'

Fanny Dashwood looked at the three of them. 'Then everything will be fine and when I get to wherever we're going you'll find me grateful. Now, if this tub holds together will we make our destination before sunset?'

'We will, Miss.'

'And what sort of place is this Hocking's Landing?'

'Busy place, where the Hocking River joins the Ohio. Getting to be big. The folks there reckon to make it into

246

something more than a settlement before long.'

'Busy you say?'

'Aye, very busy.'

'That's good for us. If those who slipped away from us have fetched up there, we need not run into one another, not if we're discreet.'

'How do you mean?'

'My guess is that they won't want any fuss or delay. If I tell our story before they know we've arrived there's a good chance that even if they get to hear of us they'll leave it lie. Blowin' the gaff will only delay them and they don't want no delay.'

'Sounds risky.' It was the man who had congratulated her on her handling of the late Tom who had spoken and he immediately regretted it. 'But what you say goes. We'll do it your way, captain. Miss Dashwood can stand on us, eh, boys?'

And the others readily agreed and Fanny continued, 'Then it must be careful and quiet. You land me and my sister there, I'll tell my tale, pay you off and you get on your way.'

'Aye, Miss, if it goes as you say.'

'It will, or close enough to it. Just get me there and leave the rest to me.'

The two pole men kept the boat in the shallow water not far out from the shore. Fanny Dashwood, as she now had to think of herself, sat down beside Kitty's body. She was feeling weak in the legs, she was also hot. Then she shuddered slightly. Soon she would begin to feel cold and hot by turns. The coughing would follow as it had done with Kitty. She hadn't been sure before but now she was, the fever was upon her too.

247

Chapter Forty

On reaching the canoe to make their escape from Mustapha Island, Macleod and Miranda, as the men of the party, naturally took the paddles and Marie had sat in the middle between them. Neither man had used a canoe before and they managed it as well as could be expected, that is to say, badly. Marie accepted her passive role and was grateful that at least they did not capsize the small craft.

For the first, furious minutes Macleod and Miranda did a lot of splashing with the paddles, all producing very little result, but the canoe was light and the current sufficiently swift so that by the time their pursuers burst on to the shore they were far enough away for the one shot that was fired to be no more than a gesture. Once clear of the island and in slower, less dangerous water, Marie had insisted that both use their paddles only to keep the craft steady and far enough from the bank to avoid any hidden rocks or snags. They had no idea how far away the nearest settlement would be and Miranda, seated in the front of the canoe, kept alert for any sign of dwelling along the riverside.

One came into view after about half an hour. Miranda shouted back to Macleod and pointed and both men began again to splash water about. They managed nothing in the way of navigation and the river gently took them past the cabin that stood back from the water's edge in a clearing. Macleod, seeing a woman standing at the front of the cabin waved his hand and then his paddle. The woman responded by waving back. Marie then insisted that he stop his waving as he was almost sure to upset the canoe. And so they drifted on.

At last, after about two or three hours, they sighted the substantial settlement of Hocking's Landing. Marie was determined that they would make landfall and not drift past, and under her guidance the two men managed to get safely to the shore about two hundred yards below the main wharfage of the settlement. This was just as well as some short distance beyond the wharfage another substantial river emptied itself into the Ohio and, had they gone much further, its current would have carried them away from the shore and on down river.

On reaching shallow water near the bank Miranda scrambled as best he could out of the canoe and pulled it up on to the muddy shore. Marie went forward and got out followed by Macleod. The black mud of the bank went back for about twenty yards or so, rising steeply. At the top, above their heads, were wooden buildings of two storeys with shingled roofs built on thick wooden piles driven into the ground. These buildings lined the upper bank all the way back to the wharfage where a considerable number of large flat-bottomed boats were moored. Scattered across the wooden decking were crates and bales containing all the many domestic necessities which were needed for people living in the fast-growing settlement and the farms and homesteads beyond it. Men and carts were busy collecting these unloaded cargoes to be carried into the settlement, and other men and carts were equally busy bringing new cargoes of timber and farm produce to be stored on the wharf until they could be loaded for carriage downriver.

The men working on the wharf and those on the boats had taken little or no interest in the canoe as it had made its erratic landfall, nor did they seem in the least bit interested in its three occupants as they walked through the shoreline mud, climbed up on to the wooden wharf and stood looking around them.

Miranda, as always, seemed well contented and satisfied with their situation. Marie looked concerned and uncertain, and Macleod looked angry, which indeed he was, although he was finding it hard to find a satisfactory target for his anger.

'Well, my friends, here we are safe at last.'

Macleod begged to disagree with his friend. 'Indeed! Our possessions gone, no money, probably pursued by those black-hearted villains and you call that safe?'

Marie tried to calm her husband. 'But at least we are on land and among civilised people. Surely we are safe here?'

'Madame, I assure you that we are indeed safe.' Miranda turned to Macleod. 'As for our possessions, we have lost nothing that cannot be easily replaced.'

'With what, kind words and charm of manner?'

'Leave that to me and as for those black-hearted villains, they will not follow us.'

'Will they not?'

'Look around you, Jean Marie, take a good look. This is a settlement filled with honest, God-fearing people. If those river pirates came anywhere near here they would be putting their own heads into the noose. No, my friend, and you Madame, I assure you we are safe here. Now, let us go and examine more closely what it is we have come to.'

They left the wharf, still ignored by the men working there, for many people came and went at Hocking's Landing, all sorts of people. Indians still came by canoe to trade, settlers came to buy, traders came to sell. Families came with a mountain of baggage and people came singly or in small groups with no baggage at all. Hocking's Landing welcomed them all. It was a bustling place, a growing place, already a place of consequence and known as such up and down the river. There were even those who speculated that one day, and one day soon at that, the name Hocking's Landing would mean something, not just on this part of the Ohio River, but all over the territory.

The three stood together where the wharf met the town. In front of them stood a wide dirt road, dry and rutted in the sun. The carts travelling to and from the wharf on this road threw up a haze of dust which settled on the wooden buildings and boardwalks either side of it, giving them a not altogether unattractive patina of light ochre. Miranda, Marie, and Macleod set off into the nearest part of the town which consisted of warehousing, shops, and taverns interspersed with the offices of suppliers who catered to the river trade. Further on were stores, dwelling houses, more offices and all the usual trappings of trade and domestication, in a word, civilisation.

250

At each side of the main dirt road, in front of the buildings, were raised board-walks, obviously necessary when the road itself became a sea of mud in any heavy rain. Some women on these boardwalks wore dresses and bonnets which would not have disgraced New York or even Boston, while others wore homespun, plain dresses and Puritan bonnets not seen for many, many years in the more sophisticated East. The men were the same, some in well-cut suits and fashionable hats, some in Puritan plain broadcloth and some even in buckskin and wide-brimmed hats. The whole place seemed to be in some sort of half-way state between a frontier settlement and an established town, for elements of both jostled each other almost everywhere.

Macleod looked at the place to which the river and fate had combined to deposit them. It didn't look so very bad and he found his anger had faded as they walked.

'Do you suppose there's any law here? It looks like it might have law.'

Miranda turned to him. 'Law? And why do you ask that? What business have we with the law?'

'Dammit, we need to get some sort of constables on to those swine who captured us. They're damn pirates. We need –'

'Stop.' Macleod stopped. 'Jean Marie, we need to get to New Orleans and that is all we need. If there are river pirates hereabouts, we leave them to these good folk to deal with.'

'What do you mean, if? We were taken by them, weren't we?'

'Were we? Well, if you say so. But now we are free of them and we must make haste to resume our journey.'

Marie looked back up the river. 'Will they follow us, do you think, if we take to the river again?'

'No, Madame, as I have said, they will not follow.' Miranda gave her a reassuring smile.

But Macleod was not satisfied. 'Now look here, Miranda, if we don't make their presence known, then some other poor souls may fall into their hands.'

'And if they do, my friend, it will be someone else's duty to rescue such poor souls. Our duty lies elsewhere, in New Orleans. We must leave your other poor souls to someone as equally brave and resourceful as this most daring and capable young lady to whom I have not yet been formally introduced.' Miranda bowed. 'Our first meeting was somewhat constrained by circumstances as you no doubt remember, but, now that we are safe, may I offer you my sincere and heartfelt thanks. It is you who have rescued us, Madame, and brought us to safety. Having done so you have earned the undying gratitude of Sebastián Francisco –'

Macleod interrupted. 'Miranda, this is my wife, Marie.'

'Your wife?' Miranda looked at Macleod.

'My wife.'

'But I do not understand.'

'No more do I.'

They both turned and looked at Marie.

'Gentlemen, could we leave standing here and go where we might refresh ourselves and take rest? Once we have found somewhere to eat and perhaps repair our appearances I will be happy to answer any and all questions you may wish to ask.'

Chapter Forty-one

On making enquiries concerning their need for respectable lodgings they were directed to a two-storey building about two hundred yards up the main street which, when they arrived at it, had a large sign above the doorway on which was painted in red and green the legend "Dillon's Boarding House and Livery Stables".

They entered and were met by a matronly lady of about five foot with a round figure, a kind face, grey hair done up behind in a tight bun, and wearing a spotless gingham apron. This, it transpired, was Mrs Gerda Dillon who owned and presided over the establishment. She welcomed them in good English but with a strong German accent; upon which Miranda began to talk to her in that language. Her delight at someone speaking her own native tongue was apparent and seemed to uncork a veritable onslaught of words as if they had been banked up and waiting in her for years to finally burst forth. Eventually Miranda forced her back into English and made her aware they were tired, muddy, needed restoration, rest and refreshment. With much waving of hands and with still more German in amongst her English, she apologised for the delay then hurried off to arrange two rooms, one for Mr and Mrs Macleod and one for Herr Miranda.

'I didn't know you spoke German, Miranda.'

'My dear friend, there is a great deal you do not know about me.'

'Mrs Dillon seems to have taken to you, sir.' Marie said.

Miranda gave a slight bow to Marie. 'I try to spread a little joy as I pass on my way. Why not? There is, I fear, too much sorrow in this world to let any opportunity go by.'

'She seemed to talk for a long time just to say welcome and

ask what it was we wanted.'

'True. In our very brief acquaintance Mrs Dillon has already informed me that her husband was an Irish sailor whom she met in Hamburg and married. They came out here to seek a new life. Alas they were successful.'

'Alas?'

'Yes, Madame. Her husband used his success to develop his thirst rather than promote further their business. One night he fell off the wharf into the river and was never seen again. Now she is alone but still successful.'

'She told you all that?'

Miranda shrugged. 'I speak German, Madame, so I listened. It was a small thing to do.'

Mrs Dillon returned with a beaming smile for them all. 'The rooms are ready. There's only the one bath house out back but I'll get Betsy to put the water on the stove. I guess you'll go first, Ma'am, and the men can follow just as they like. The water will be hot for you and warm enough for the men, I suppose, if you don't dally.'

'But surely there will be fresh hot water for each person?' Macleod seemed a little shocked.

Mrs Dillon laughed. 'God bless you, sir, if I was to do that then how would anything else get done? Betsy is all the help I've got. Once she's made up water for one tub there's the cooking to see to and plenty more to do as well. Fresh hot water for each tub, indeed! Why, sir, anyone would think you was at some Marietta hotel. You're city folks, I can see, but you can't expect things here to be the match of wherever it is you hail from.'

'As it happens, Madame, I am from Boston.'

'Well, I won't hold it against you, sir, but nor will it get you enough hot water for three fresh tubs. Take it or leave it,' she looked at Marie, 'or maybe your good lady would let you take the first tub seeing as how you're so particular.'

Macleod almost reeled under this assault on his manners. 'Good God, no. If there is to be only one –'

Miranda intervened. 'Frau Dillon, you are kindness itself.

254

We will take with gratitude what you have offered and my friend's wife will most assuredly have the first tub. Please inform us once it is ready.'

Mrs Dillon almost made a curtsey to him, but not quite. 'Very well, sir, and as to meals they'll be ready as soon as you're all three cleaned up.'

'Perfect. Now, in the matter of clothes. We will need to refurbish ourselves almost completely. Could you arrange for someone to visit us, a lady who could provide for Madame Macleod and a gentlemen who could provide for my friend and myself?'

'I can send a boy to Mrs Chaney, her husband runs the general store near here.' She turned to Marie. 'There won't be anything very fine. That sort of thing has to be sent off for, but what there is'll be hard-wearing and comfortable. As for you gentlemen, if you give a list of your needs to Mrs Chaney when she comes, her husband will do his best to fill it. Now, if you will be so good as to follow me.' Mrs Dillon led them upstairs, showed Miranda into his room then led Marie and Macleod further down the corridor to theirs. It was a large room with a chest of drawers, wardrobe, a stand with an urn and ewer on it and a big, brass double bed. Mrs Dillon pointed to the bed with an air of pride. 'It has been with me always. It came from my parents' home in Lübeck. They gave it to me on my marriage.'

Marie felt some sort of response was required. 'I understand from Señor Miranda your husband, sadly, is no longer alive.'

'He was given to drink and he fell into the river.' Mrs Dillon dismissed her late husband with a gesture, and added something in German. The door was still open and Miranda entered and looked around.

'Palatial.'

Mrs Dillon smirked at him. 'A fine room, yes, but too big for one woman alone. Now I must go. There are other guests to see to and food to get ready. I will send Betsy to you as soon as the tub is ready.'

Mrs Dillon left, closing the door behind her, and Miranda crossed to the bed, bent down and pushed his hand into the mattress which hardly yielded.

'Well, as Frau Dillon has said, one cannot expect Paris comfort on the frontier. My own is no more comfortable, but it will suffice.'

Macleod, however, seemed uninterested in mattresses. 'Well now we're here what do we do?'

Marie obviously felt the same. 'Yes, Señor Miranda, what do we do? I have no money. How can we pay for these lodgings? How can we pay for clothes? How do we pay for a passage if we are, as you said, to go to New Orleans?'

Miranda looked at Marie. 'With your permission, Madame,' then pulled his shirt front out from his breeches and revealed underneath a wide leather belt which Macleod at once recognised as a money-belt.

'My God, have you had that on all the time?' Miranda smiled and nodded. 'And how much have you got in there?'

'Enough and all in gold.'

'But if you'd gone in the water with that round you you'd have sunk like a stone.'

Miranda shrugged and tucked his shirt back in. 'Undoubtedly, but it was a necessary risk. And now, Madame Macleod, if you will allow me a rather forward observation. As I remember it, you said that if we found you a place to rest and refresh yourself, then it would be you who would answer our questions, not I who would answer yours.'

'Yes, that is true. Very well, Señor Miranda, ask me your questions.'

But Miranda did not have a chance. It was Macleod who exploded into words as if touched off like some firecracker by being reminded of Marie's sudden and completely inexplicable appearance. 'Yes, dammit, Marie, what's this all about? What in God's name are you doing here? Where on earth did you spring from? Why aren't you still in Boston? What the hell has been happening?'

Miranda took Macleod's arm gently.

'Please, my friend, we must have a system or we will get nowhere. I suggest we let your wife tell us her story in her own

256

words and in her own way. Once she has done that, we may begin to understand. Do you not agree?'

And Macleod found that he did, so the two men sat down and Marie began.

Chapter Forty-two

'I got your letter from New York, Jean. It was in your hand but they were not your words. I thought you had left me, that you had found another woman. I thought …'

Macleod leaned forward and took her hands in his. 'But Marie, darling, dearest. Another woman? How could you think such a thing?'

Miranda gently intruded. 'Please, please, both of you, I know what reunions between husband and wife should be, especially after a long parting, but the bath house will soon be ready. We must make progress. Let your wife continue.' He turned to Marie. 'Please, Madame.'

'Kitty, our servant, persuaded me that …'

And the men listened as Marie quietly told them of her adventures. Finally she fell silent. For a minute no one spoke then Miranda burst into applause.

'Bravo, Madame, bravissimo. If I had a dozen like you, Colombia would already be a free country.'

Macleod looked on. Was this his wife, his Marie? The woman he had thought alone and worried? Was this the helpless woman who should not be exposed to …

There was a knock at the door and a girl's voice called. 'Tub's hot and ready, Ma'am.'

Miranda went to the door and opened it.

A girl of about sixteen stood there in a mob cap and a plain linen apron over her rough dress.

'Ah, the delightful Betsy no doubt?'

'Yes, sir. Missus says I'm to take the lady down and do all as is needful for her.'

'Of course. Madame is ready. Come, Mrs Macleod, your servant and your hot tub await.' Marie went to the door and

Miranda smiled at the servant, Betsy. 'And when Madame is complete come and let me know, Betsy,' and he leaned forward, his smile becoming confidential, 'and you can take me down and do for me also all that is needful.'

Betsy returned Miranda's grin.

'Go on, sir, don't you be a wicked gentleman.'

'Ah, but I am, Betsy, a very wicked gentleman.'

Betsy moved to one side as Marie left the room and pulled the door shut. Miranda returned to the bed where he sat down.

'Well, Jean Marie, what do you make of it all?'

'Madness, it's all madness. It can't be true, it can't really be happening.'

'Alas it is only too true and, if it is madness, it is the madness of politics and diplomacy prettily spiced by treason.'

'I don't mean our business. I mean my wife, Marie. I hardly know what to think. It's all too incredible.'

'No, not incredible. Amazing yes, wonderful, yes, but incredible no. It is happening and it continues to happen as we speak. Aaron Burr does not stop so we cannot stop which means we must go with all haste to New Orleans. If it is as your wife says and the British Ambassador sent Dolly and her friend to stop us, he will not have relied on them alone. He will have sent others. Tomorrow we must make our arrangements for departure.'

'Good God, man, you don't think we can just go on, do you?'

'But we must, now more than ever.'

'But Marie. We can't put Marie in any more danger.'

'My friend, she has most assuredly placed herself there already. But fear not, from what she has told us she is more than capable.'

There was a knock at the door.

Miranda went and opened it. Betsy stood there. Miranda grinned at her. 'Ah, Betsy, surely you and the tub are not ready for me so soon?'

But Betsy was not in the mood for any humour. 'I'm sorry, sir, but Missis says you'll have to give up your room.'

'But why?'

'We need to lay out a body in it, sir.'

Macleod heard her. 'A body? What body?'

'One that's just in on a boat from up river, sir. A lady what died of fever on her travels accompanied by her sister who, from what I heard, has the fever herself now. We'll need a room for the body to be attended to and laid out proper. Dillon's does it for most folks as can't have the body laid out in their own home and does it for all the respectable ones who have no kin hereabouts, so the men have been told to bring it here. If you please, sir, as you're last in we'll have to take your room. There's a small outhouse as I can make up for you, sir, until the body's taken and buried. It ain't what you'd call a proper room, but it can be made comfortable if you'll agree to use it. That's what Missis says.'

'But of course, Betsy. Move my belongings to the outhouse as soon as you like.'

Betsy gave a small curtsey. 'Thanking you kindly for as co-operating, sir.'

'This lady, the sick lady whose sister died, do you know her name?'

'No, no name as I heard, sir. Now I must be going. They'll be bringing the body up before long and I've got things to do to make ready.'

Betsy disappeared and Miranda closed the door.

'What do you think?'

'About what?'

'Oh come, Jean, use your brains for God's sake. Marie tells us of her friends Dolly and Kitty. She tells us that Kitty falls ill and thus she is able to slip away while they both sleep. Now a lady turns up with a dead sister. Do you not think that that these ladies are all one and the same?'

'Great heavens, you don't think it's them, do you?'

'I think we must know for sure one way or the other.'

'Damn right we must. If it is them we must make sure that the law takes her, fever or no fever.'

Miranda gave a sigh. 'No, Jean, we must find out what she

260

knows.'

Macleod was about to argue but, on reflection saw the sense of Miranda's words. 'How will we do that?'

'Yes, that is an interesting question. I will consider it.'

Miranda went to the window and stood looking out in silence. After some minutes the door opened and Marie came in.

'The water is still warm.'

Miranda turned and quickly went to the door. 'Good, it will help me think.' He was gone.

Suddenly it dawned on Macleod that he would be the last to use the tub.

Marie stood and looked at him. 'Jean, are you not glad to see me?'

'Of course I am.'

'But you do not show it.'

'No, well, I, er …'

Marie came forward and took his face in her hands and kissed him. 'Would you not care to show it?'

Macleod thought about it. The water would be twice used and almost certainly cold.

Marie kissed him gently again and suddenly Macleod found he didn't give a hang about the bath-house. There were other things in life than tubs and water, hot *or* cold.

Chapter Forty-three

There was no doctor in Hocking's Landing nor anyone with any formal medical training. But there were older members of the community who, in the earlier days of the settlement, had lost family or friends to the fever and by force of necessity had learnt how to treat it. These days it was uncommon, almost unknown, for any settlement-dweller to fall victim, but travellers did and so did poorer folk who lived in the more remote and unhealthy homesteads on low-lying, boggy land.

Miss Fanny Dashwood, when she arrived, was taken straight away to the home of a widow lady, one of those older folk who understood the fever only too well. Two years married, three months pregnant with her second child and settled in Hocking's Landing only two months, she had nursed her husband but failed to save his life. From then on she made it her business to study the fever. She had lost a husband and didn't intend to lose a child nor, if she could help it, watch as some other wife suffered as she had. Over the years her knowledge grew, not only of the fever, but of many other ailments and afflictions, especially female, and she was now acknowledged as the closest thing Hocking's Landing had to a medical practitioner.

This kind and competent soul took in the unfortunate Fanny Dashwood, put her to bed and immediately began to prepare her treatments. The three men from the boat told the story they had been given and told it well enough, not only to be believed, but congratulated on their Christian charity and rewarded with money to go on their way. They left Hocking's Landing well satisfied, with only the slightest regret that they had, in such a short time, lost two such able and resourceful captains.

Miss Fanny Dashwood lay sick with the fever for several days, but she did not die. She became very ill indeed but, as she had skilled tending, a warm bed and constant attention, she survived and, a few days after her sister was interred with all due Christian ceremony, Fanny passed her crisis and began to recover.

The old lady who had nursed her through her illness had hardly slept during her care and it was decided that, as all Fanny needed, now the fever was beaten, was rest and quiet, Dillon's was the most suitable place for her to recuperate back to full health. Mrs Dillon was considerably influenced in allowing a fever victim, even a recovering fever victim, into her establishment by Miranda who told her that he would fully meet all expenses.

When Fanny awoke, well again, she could just about remember landing and being helped out of the boat, but after that she could remember nothing. She lay in bed too weak to move and looked around her. She saw a bright room with the afternoon sun streaming in through the window and, sitting by the bed, a young woman of about sixteen in a mob cap and an apron. Betsy looked at her patient and seeing her eyes open stood up and left the room to inform Mrs Dillon. Her disappearance gave Fanny, as she remembered she now was, time to collect her thoughts and, when Mrs Dillon came bustling into the room, she was ready. Her mind was back to normal even if her weak and helpless body would take some considerable time longer to achieve the same status. Mrs Dillon stood by the bed.

'How do you feel, Ma'am?'

'Weak.'

'You will be, weak as a new-born kitten for a while, but we'll build you up and before too long you'll be as bright as a pearly button.'

Fanny felt relieved. The way this woman was speaking, nothing was known here against her, in fact the woman spoke to her as if she was a servant talking to a lady.

'And my sister?'

Mrs Dillon gave her a gentle reminder. 'Your late sister?'

'Yes, my late sister.'

'She was given a Christian burial two days after they brought you up here from the river.'

Fanny's arms lay on the bedspread. She tried to lift one so as to cross herself but found she couldn't. Was I very ill?'

'Ill enough, but it was caught in time to tend you properly. With God's help you'll make a full recovery.'

'The men who brought me, where are they?'

'Gone, Ma'am, gone on downriver about their business. But they told us the story.'

'The story?'

'As to how you and your sister were travelling west and how she fell ill and you were robbed and abandoned until they found you.'

'I trust they were rewarded for their kindness.'

'They was handsomely paid, more than handsome, generous.'

'And to whom do I owe gratitude for such handsome generosity?'

'The kindness of strangers, Ma'am. I swear it was Gospel-like.'

Fanny felt confused. 'Was it someone from this place?'

'No, it was as I said, strangers. Two men and a woman, husband and wife and a Spanish gentleman. They came the same day you did, no more than a couple of hours before you. When they heard of your sister dying and you being in such a way as was, they sort of took over. They got the full story from the men and settled with them. They paid for your sister's burying and left enough money to see that you would be well tended until you were all to rights once more. Like I say, Ma'am, it was Gospel-like, the Good Samaritan on this very river. Folks here was mighty impressed.'

'And where are these good people now?'

'Gone, headed on down to the Mississippi. Their business here, whatever it was, was quickly done.'

'And what, pray, was their business?'

'I don't rightly know. Not much, I guess. A man came to visit them, that was all I saw. Been waiting for them, it seemed

264

to me.'

'They were expected?'

'Must have been, leastways by their visitor. The Spanish gentleman and this man talked for a good while and then the man left. Once he was gone, they seemed in a hurry to be off again, bought supplies, got a boat and took off for Cairo to pick up a Mississippi boat. But the Spanish gentleman left money to make sure you'd lack for nothing whilst you stayed here. He seemed to be in charge of their party, a Señor Miranda by name. He went himself to look at you and, when he came back, said you were obviously a lady of quality and was firm that you be treated proper, kept here and tended 'til you was fully well. The Spanish gentleman went so far as to leave a message for you as I was to tell you when you revived enough to understand it.'

'What was his message?'

'He said you was to stay here, stay here and rest, stay here for as long as you liked, as further travel might be …' and here she paused getting her words ready, '… most injurious to your state of health. Most insistent he was that I use his very words.'

'And those were his very words?'

'Indeed Ma'am, most injurious to your state of health. You was to stay here for your health's sake. And twenty dollars in silver to see you had all the care and comfort as was fitting to a lady. As it says in the Good Book, in meeting strangers we may meet angels. Halleluiah.'

Fanny needed to think over what she had been told. 'Thank you for all you have done, but now I feel tired. I will rest.'

She closed her eyes. Mrs Dillon was dismissed. But she didn't mind. This woman was quality, a lady, and besides, she had already been well-paid, more than well, handsome, generous. And she was a good Christian. She would earn those silver dollars, every cent. She would keep the lady in Dillon's long enough to earn it all out if she had to knock her down and tie her to the bed.

Fanny lay with her eyes closed, but not closed in sleep. She was thinking. Well, girl, here you are on your own again. But here you're thought of as a lady. Well, why not? You've been quality in Paris and London and no one here knows you did it all by working on your back. Here there's no reason why you couldn't be the real thing. How would these backwoods peasants know any difference?

Fanny considered her position and, considering it, found it quite acceptable. She didn't need to be warned off by Miranda. She had her own head on her shoulders and it told her she was out of the game. They'd had their meeting with the man who was waiting for them, were gone and were days ahead of her even if she'd wanted to follow. But she didn't want to. She wanted rest and peace. She'd had enough. She'd seen it all, the palaces and the whore-houses, the false finery, the wickedness and the lies, the cheating, the cruelty, the getting and spending, the killing and the dying. She'd seen it all and she wanted no more of it. She wanted a place to settle. A place like this. A growing place that might even be somewhere one day and in which she might become someone. But what?

So it was that Miss Fanny Dashwood, a lady of quality fallen on misfortune, lay with her eyes closed dreaming of what she might one day become in Hocking's Landing on the Ohio river.

Chapter Forty-four

Jeremiah Jones had left Mustapha Island pleased with the way his plan had been carried out and set about getting Macleod's news about General Wilkinson to Cedric Bentley with all possible speed. He returned by canoe to the place on the bank where he had left his horse hobbled, and set off on the trail which led back upriver to Newport, where he had based himself and would be able to acquire fresh mounts for the journey which lay before him. The news of Wilkinson's possible involvement gave him plenty to dwell on. He had not anticipated such a move by Aaron Burr and he was sure it would come as an equally nasty surprise to Bentley. That it was a serious possibility he did not doubt. Burr had served with Wilkinson during the Revolutionary War and a friendship, an enduring friendship, may have ensued. If it turned out that it had been at Burr's prompting that President Jefferson had appointed Wilkinson Governor of the Louisiana Territories and, unusually, also given him command of the army at New Orleans, then this new link between Burr and Wilkinson became all the more sinister.

Jones reached Newport with sufficient of the day before him to arrange for two fresh horses to be made ready while he ate a hasty meal. He then set off on the next stage of his journey, to Clarksburg, some seventy miles east through heavily wooded but fairly level country. It was a bold decision by Jones and he knew it was a gamble. He had made his way to Newport along that same trail so he knew it to be well-used and clear of any serious difficulties, but he would have to ride hard, changing horses when necessary. His mounts both seemed sound of wind and limb but were livery saddle-horses and were used to a more sedentary pace of travel. Either or both might become winded or suffer a strain when pushed into a continuous gallop and, even on such a good trail, a fall was always a possibility. But the news he carried drove him on. Bentley needed to be told as soon as possible. At Clarksburg, if he could make it before nightfall, he would be able to use the official papers he carried to send a galloper on to Washington. That would be a journey of some two hundred and fifty miles and cross the Appalachian Mountains, but it was along well-marked and well-maintained trails and where relays of horses would be available. A good man should be in Washington in no more than three days.

Jones's first mount soon gave him concern by showing signs that it would prove inadequate to its task, so Jones decided to drive it hard until its wind gave out when he would abandon it and change mounts. The spring rains had not been so heavy as to make the trail at all treacherous, and Jones was more fortunate in the second horse which he found both strong and willing. As the light faded, tired and saddle-sore, he finally eased up on his horse and rode into the busy town of Clarksburg.

He dismounted outside the substantial courthouse across the road from an equally substantial Town Jail. At the courthouse Jones made enquiries and, having secured the address and directions, walked as swiftly as his game leg and weary condition would permit to the home of the local magistrate. Here the door was answered by the magistrate himself, angry at being disturbed in his own home at his evening meal. The magistrate, seeing only a travel-stained stranger was at first inclined to make his feelings abundantly clear to this importunate young man but, on being presented with and reading Jones's papers of identification and authority, and recognising the name on the bottom, at once changed his attitude. He invited Jones into his home and was all willingness and courtesy. Once Jones had made his requirements clear, a galloper was sent for, while Jones wrote a message in cipher for Bentley. He required an urgent meeting. There was news, important news. For a meeting place, he chose Morgantown which lay forty miles to the north of Clarksburg and on the main trail between Washington and Pittsburgh. The galloper was given the sealed message in a leather satchel and told to be ready to depart at first light. Speed, it was made abundantly clear to him, was of the essence. The man departed to the stables where he would sleep that night and where a lightly built but strong and fast saddle-pony would be made ready before dawn to make the earliest possible start.

Jones thanked the magistrate but refused his offer of hospitality for as long as he needed it. He wanted no conversation and certainly no questions over the next few days. As for the present, his leg hurt damnably, his buttocks felt on fire and his back hurt. In short he was one great ache and all he wanted was his own company in a hot tub, a hearty dinner and then a soft bed. He was taken by the magistrate himself to a hotel where, all his needs having been met, Jones lay down to a deserved night's rest. He was pleased with himself. If all went well he and Bentley should meet up in no more than a matter of a week. Tomorrow and the next day he could rest and recover. His leg was still painful as were his buttocks but, all in all, he was well satisfied. Macleod, he reflected as he waited for his brain to wind down and sleep to come, had done well. Confoundedly well, and he admitted to himself that he was surprised. Macleod was an enigma. Was it simply luck as Bentley had suggested or was there something more to Lawyer Macleod? Well, no matter, as soon as he and Miranda were freed by his pirates they would go on down to, where was it? Hocking's Landing, that was it. They would go down to Hocking's Landing where his man waited to receive Miranda's version of their meeting with Blennerhasset. That report, when he eventually saw it, might make very interesting reading, very interesting indeed.

Chapter Forty-five

Jones's message to Cedric Bentley was delivered at once, as were all messages addressed to the small office allocated to the Office of the Comptroller of the Contingent Fund. It was late, already dark, but Bentley kept long hours and was still at his desk when it arrived. Once deciphered it posed for him something of a problem. Jones had some important news concerning Aaron Burr and desired an immediate meeting with him in Morgantown. That meant that the news, whatever it was, was too important even to be committed to department cipher. However, Bentley was loath to leave Washington. Now was not a good time to be away, too much was happening. But his small department, known by the cumbersome but suitably opaque title of The Administrative Agency of the Contingent Fund of Foreign Intercourse, was not a large one. In fact its permanent and full-time Washington staff consisted only of himself and Jones. There were many other people used by the Department scattered around the country but they were employed only on a temporary or casual basis depending on what, if anything, the President decided to use the Contingent Fund for. For the most part these people provided background reports on developing situations that interested Bentley or, more routinely, on the private, personal or commercial activities of people with sufficient power and influence to cast them as allies or enemies of whatever administration was currently in office.

With Jones away on this Burr business, Bentley alone kept his superiors informed of the information that sometimes flowed but often trickled into his office, and took any instructions on any desired response. But the message from Jones had been phrased in the strongest terms. Something must have been found out by Miranda and Macleod which had caused Jones to summon him away at once.

Bentley was not long in deciding. The most vital thing on his desk by far was the Aaron Burr business so, if Jones wanted him, then he must go and go quickly. The fastest method of travelling over the Appalachian Mountains, the first part of his journey, would be by light carriage and team of four. He ordered one to be made ready for the following morning and also ordered that an armed escort travel with him. He then sent a request to the Secretary of State's office for an urgent appointment.

The following morning, arriving at his desk he found he had an appointment with Secretary of State at nine-thirty. There he informed Secretary Madison that there were developments, as yet not known to him, which required his personal attention and that he would be forced to be away perhaps for over a week and, depending on the report he would receive from his deputy, even longer. That meeting concluded, he and a sergeant-at-arms, though not in uniform, got into their carriage and set off.

Bentley and his escort changed their carriage for saddle horses once they were over the mountains. Travelling through the Great Appalachian Valley would be faster on horseback. This was all well-settled land with clear, well-maintained trails and, with fast, strong saddle-ponies at the relay stations, they made excellent time.

When Jones arrived in Morgantown he made himself known to the authorities and arranged for two sets of rooms to be made available at the best hotel the town had to offer. Once established there he arranged with the Town Constable that a look-out be kept for Bentley, of whom he gave a full description, and that the moment he was sighted he should be brought to Jones's hotel.

Bentley arrived in the afternoon two days after Jones and was, as arranged, brought at once to the hotel where he left his escort to see to the horses and what little baggage each had carried and was taken up to the privacy of Jones's room. There, stiff and saddle-sore, he met his deputy.

Jeremiah Jones saw all too clearly that his superior was

271

suffering very much as he had done and felt that, however urgent the business of their meeting, some easing of Bentley's immediate discomfort might reasonably take priority. 'A hot tub, sir, and then something to eat or drink before we begin?'

Bentley testily waved away his well-meant suggestions. He had ridden almost one hundred and fifty miles in two and a half days and his mood was not the sunniest. He was travel-soiled and, as it had been many a long year since he had spent quite so long in the saddle, suffering a sore backside. He took off his hat and cloak and threw them on a chair.

'Jones, I'm tired, dirty, sore and hungry but what I need most at this moment is to know what's so damned important that I have to leave Washington and ride what feels like half-way across the confounded continent. A hot tub, a good dinner and a soft bed will have to wait and I warn you, if this news of yours is not all you have led me to believe, it might be the last report you will ever deliver, so get on with it.'

'Very well, sir. Macleod claims that Burr now has as his ally in his plot General James Wilkinson, Governor of the Louisiana –'

'Dammit, I know who Wilkinson is.' Bentley walked across the room slowly. His legs were stiff and sore and movement hurt them but this news made him restless. While in motion he gave thought to what Jones had just said. Jones waited. 'That's as bad as it is unexpected.'

'My feelings entirely, sir. Quite unexpected.'

'Alright, go on, let's have all of it.'

'I arrived in Newport, just upriver from Blennerhasset's island, not long after Miranda and Macleod had crossed over. I set about making myself generous company in the local drinking shops, put it about that I was looking for some rising place to open a General Store, that I owned three back East and wanted to expand into somewhere that had prospects.'

'And they swallowed it?'

'They seemed to.'

'Do you know anything about store-keeping?'

'No, but when asked, which I was, I said I didn't need to

272

know anything about running an actual store as I had inherited the business from my father and all the stores were well managed for me. The impression I gave was that of the spoiled son who wanted to do something to show everyone what a devil of a businessman he was.'

'Good, people generally trust a fool not to be a knave.'

'I asked about Blennerhasset, who was he, what was he up to? Would he represent any kind of opposition or competition to my enterprise? I especially asked if he had visitors and if he did of what sort? The locals weren't too shy of talking about him and his doings, which they seemed to know well enough.'

'How so?'

'His overseers regularly came over and mixed freely. Seems Blennerhasset kept a quiet house himself and expected all in his employ to do likewise so, if any of them wanted to be sociable, they had to come across and do it in Newport and, while being sociable, they talked.'

'And Miranda and Macleod?'

'No one knew who they were or why they were there.'

'Anyone suspicious or curious of what they might be up to?'

Jones was pleased to see that at this point Bentley lowered himself gingerly into an easy chair. His mood was obviously mellowing.

'No, no one knew anything and they didn't care. Blennerhasset was a mystery to them. A British gentleman who had arrived from nowhere with his wife. He was rich and educated but had chosen to build his fine house well away from his own kind and to live in seclusion on his island. Those few visitors who came to see him were equally alien to the locals, so two more were nothing special.'

'I see. You mentioned a drink when I arrived, Jones. Do you have something here in your room?'

Jones went to a cupboard and took out a bottle of brandy and two glasses, poured two drinks, handed one to Bentley and sat down himself. Two of Blennerhasset's overseers came across to the settlement for a drink one night and I fell into company with them. They told me that he was arranging to send Miranda and

Macleod downriver in a boat he was having specially built for them. They were experienced river men and had been told to act as the pole-men down to the Mississippi, a task they both clearly resented. I suggested that I would like a private word with one of the gentlemen they would be carrying, that I was fairly sure that the Spanish one was a rival who wanted to expand all down the Ohio. His friend, however, might be open to persuasion and supply me with the names of the locations the Spaniard thought most promising. Why do all the looking myself, I said, if I could have someone else do it for me and at the same time let me know all that he was doing and planning.'

'Sounds thin.'

'It *was* thin and damnably so. But they were simple, uneducated men and easy to persuade that such methods were standard business practice and, when I mentioned what the thing might be worth to me, they were happy to put any doubts well out of mind.'

'And how did you explain Miranda's visit to Blennerhasset?'

'I said Blennerhasset was interested in putting money into his venture.'

'And that satisfied them?'

'They needed little satisfying once money had been mentioned. It was they who suggested the best method of bringing about a private talk with Macleod and a damn good method it proved. They knew the river and said the best way would be to take the boat in the narrow back channel by an island, Mustapha Island, so that it might be snared by a stout cable laid across the channel.'

'And who would do this?'

'River pirates.'

Bentley held out his empty glass and laughed. 'Pirates. That's deuced good. Where did you find them?'

Jones took their glasses, went back to the bottle and re-filled both. 'Newport is a flourishing enough place but still has its fair share of frontier riff-raff who aren't too particular about how they earn a dollar, so I selected a group of local toughs, told

274

them much the same story and arranged with them that they should act as the pirates. They were to lay the rope, get the boat to the island and knock Miranda on the head so I was free to talk to Macleod.'

Bentley took his glass. 'And they swallowed it just like Blennerhasset's men?'

'They did, but only because they'd already swallowed a good deal of my hospitality and, as men of no moral worth, didn't care too much one way or the other about the truth or otherwise of my tale so long as the pay was good. And it all went as sweetly as a Sunday afternoon tea party. I was able to talk to Macleod while Miranda was knocked cold, trussed up and laid elsewhere.'

The brandy was doing its work and Bentley felt that his journey, after all, may have been worth it. 'Good work. And what was to become of Macleod and Miranda?'

'I'd arranged that they should be freed by the pole-men next morning who'd say the pirates were sleeping off the previous night's drinking and they had worked themselves loose. They'd all get back in their boat and set off. The pirates were to fire off a couple of pistol shots to make it look as if they'd been roused and had given chase. I went down to the island with the toughs and we crossed in a couple of canoes and waited until the heavy work was over, then I spoke to Macleod. I must admit his information staggered me more than a little, but if it was true, which I think he believed it to be, I knew it was vital, so I left and got word to you as soon as I could.'

'And now you say they should both be well on their way and no harm done.'

'Exactly.'

Bentley drained the last of his brandy. 'You did well, Jeremiah, and you were right to summon me as you did. Now, anything else before I send for that hot tub?'

'Not much, nothing we didn't already know. He confirmed that Blennerhasset was building a supply depot and barracks and that Burr had been at work in the Ohio and Mississippi valleys setting up militias. There was some confused rubbish about Burr creating a kingdom from Spanish Florida to the Pacific. Truly it was poor stuff, more fantasy than anything else and all laughable.'

'So, nothing else that was new except the business about Wilkinson?'

'No, nothing else.'

'Well, Jeremiah, what are your thoughts on this matter? You had some time to reflect on it? Can we put any credence in the story?'

'Macleod may be many things but a man of imagination he is not, nor any kind of deceiver. What he told me was what he had heard. He was convinced that Blennerhasset was fully committed and believed Burr had indeed drawn General Wilkinson into his plot. But Wilkinson was appointed by Jefferson himself and even if his name was put forward by Burr I can't believe that a general, a serving senior officer, would countenance getting involved in treason on such a scale.'

'Can't you?' Bentley held out his glass, Jones took it and re-filled it. 'What if I told you Wilkinson has already not only countenanced it but made a try for it once before.'

'Surely not!'

'Oh yes. General James Wilkinson is a choice piece of work, an inveterate schemer, but I'm damned if I've ever been able to nail anything to him which might free America of a man I wouldn't trust to sweep a shit-house floor. He'd damn well steal the broom.'

Jones was surprised at the bitterness of Bentley's denunciation and felt, not unreasonably, that the tiredness had combined with the brandy to loosen Bentley's tongue a little more than was usual. That being so, he felt his way forward with a certain amount of care. 'But Jefferson must trust him, surely?'

Bentley snorted. 'Ha! Jefferson trusts him all right. Jefferson trusts anyone who'll agree with him and tell him what a wise fellow he is. Wilkinson has always been a great one for agreeing with anyone powerful enough to do James Wilkinson some good.'

It was clear to Jones that it was more than professional judgement that fed Bentley's bitterness. 'You have personal experience of Wilkinson?'

'I do. I served with him under Horatio Gates. He came to us with Benedict Arnold after the siege of Quebec. Burgoyne had arrived at the head of the British reinforcements and Arnold's force had to make a run for it.'

'He was with Benedict Arnold?'

'He was, and it has crossed my mind more than once that it was Wilkinson as much as anyone else who began to turn Arnold's mind against us.'

'How so?'

'Wilkinson was sent to Congress with news of Gates's victory at Saratoga and the way he told the story it was really all his doing. Arnold had fought well in that engagement and was badly wounded. By rights he should have been honoured for the part he played. But when Wilkinson came back he was the one promoted, gazetted brigadier-general, no less. And Arnold wasn't the only officer senior to him who had their nose put out of joint.'

'I see.'

'No you damn well don't. Wilkinson was a good soldier, no one ever doubted him on the field of battle. But as a man, away from the battle, he worshipped only one God, himself, and if he wanted something, and could see a way to get it, then as far as he was concerned, it was his to take. Gates got sick of his scheming and kicked him out, so he wormed his way to the post of Clothier General for the Army, but had to give that up when people started checking his accounts too closely.'

'And yet he was chosen by Jefferson for Governor of Louisiana and General of the New Orleans Army?'

'I told you, Jefferson likes people who like him. He likes to hear people tell him what a great man he is. Jefferson wants America to see him as a father-figure, he wants to be admired and loved. He'll probably have Father of the Nation engraved on his damn tombstone. Wilkinson was always no less than charming and always damnably plausible. The way he told

277

things they usually got believed. He knew that if he told Jefferson what a loyal fellow he was and how he'd be a reliable support against any opposition if given the Louisiana Governorship and the Generalship of the Army Jefferson would swallow it whole, which he did. My understanding is that it was done before anyone could oppose it and we all had to live with the decision because our President wasn't about to listen to anybody telling him what a serious mistake he'd made.'

'And this other business you mentioned?'

'That came up during some government work I was doing in '88. I was asked to look into Kentucky's opposition to the new Constitution. At first it seemed no more than a natural grievance at having their separation from Virginia delayed yet again. But then I found that Wilkinson was behind a scheme to get Kentucky to cede from the Union and become a Spanish vassal state, with him as its overlord of course.'

'But that's treason surely?'

'Of course it was.'

'But I never heard of it nor anyone even hint at it.'

'No, and no one will, trust Wilkinson for that. It was George Washington himself who got him the job of Assemblyman. That appointment gave him his chance to make his try for Kentucky. Washington wasn't about to have Wilkinson arraigned for treason and be made to look a fool in a public trial. And no more will Jefferson if it turns out that Wilkinson has hitched himself a ride with Burr. Whatever happens now, and a great deal may happen, Jefferson will do what he's best at.'

'Which is?'

'He'll shuffle.'

'Shuffle?'

'Aye, he'll look at the cards and, when he sees he may hold a losing hand that may damage him personally, he'll shuffle those cards and re-shuffle them until they deal out in a way that leaves him looking the wise and honourable President and somebody else can takes any blame.'

'And in the meantime?'

'In the meantime we must see that Burr is stopped and this time stopped dead. No more waiting and watching, Burr's made a clever move, but it's finally shown his hand in a way that cannot be revoked.'

'In what way not revoked?'

'Jones, why have we not moved against Burr? He's accepted land from the Spanish and put armed men on it. He's been busy raising militias in the Ohio and Mississippi valleys. He's been getting money and support from the likes of Blennerhasset and he's cosied up to the British through their Envoy, Anthony Merry. All of which we can prove if we have to. Why haven't we put him in the dock, do you think?'

'Because none of it made any sense. He almost certainly couldn't take the amount of land involved and, even if by some miracle he did, he definitely couldn't hold it. We'd take it back from him with no effort at all.'

'Exactly. I knew that Burr was up to something and I needed to know what it was. Now, with this information about Wilkinson, I think I know.'

'And what is it?'

'He doesn't want some straggling, impossible kingdom. He wants what he's always wanted, America. By all that's holy and glorious I take my hat off to the man. Jefferson dropped him as Vice President because Burr opposed him whenever he thought him wrong, which was too often. But Burr was the better mind and the stronger character. By thunder, Burr is twice the man Jefferson was or ever will be,' but Bentley, realising that he had, perhaps, let his tiredness and the brandy run away with his mouth somewhat, paused in his eulogy, 'however, my opinions of the men involved count for nothing. Jefferson is our President and it's Jefferson we serve so, Jones, we'll bring Burr down and with luck we'll bring down Wilkinson as well.'

'How?'

'Good question, Jones, and it will need a damn good answer,' Bentley stood and picked up his hat and cloak from the chair on which they lay, 'and I must go and find that answer. Which I will do as soon as I've enjoyed my tub and then a good meal. My room?'

'Next door, sir.'

'Good. Order me a tub and make arrangements for us to leave tomorrow morning.'

'Leave for where?'

'New Orleans, of course, where else? Wilkinson is there, Burr may still be there and Miranda and Macleod are headed there. There's only one place left to be in this game, Jones, and that's New Orleans, so be ready to move at dawn. By then, please God, I'll know how I'm to bring down our birds and finish this business once and for all.'

Chapter Forty-six

The next morning the sun was not quite up and the lamps were lit when Bentley arrived in the hotel dining room. Jones was already there eating his breakfast.

Bentley sat down and poured himself some coffee. 'Well, Jones, I have my plan and the horses will be ready for us to leave as soon as it's light.'

'New Orleans still?'

'Yes. There are good trails from here to Washington with plenty of places to change mounts so we can make good time. Miranda and Macleod will have to stick to the river, it's the only way for them now they're that far down the Ohio. From Washington I'll arrange a fast boat to New Orleans. Once there I want you to go immediately to General Wilkinson and give him a verbal instruction from President Jefferson to arrest Miranda and Macleod.'

'On what charge?'

'On any charge Wilkinson wishes. Let him choose.'

'Why arrest them? How will that help?'

'Because I know him, I've studied the man. Wilkinson is greedy but not stupid. He's always been careful to stay well on the right side of Jefferson and his efforts in that quarter have paid off handsomely. Jefferson couldn't have done more for Wilkinson if he'd been a blood relative. He's closed his eyes and his ears to anything anybody has said that places Wilkinson in a bad light. More than a few have tried, believe me. Your job will be to convince Wilkinson that the instruction for Miranda's arrest is genuinely from the President. Wilkinson loves to scheme, so I'll give him a bit of scheming to chew on. Tell him that the President has been made aware that there is a powerful cabal of senior men, Federalists, who intend to use Miranda and

281

Colonel Smith's venture in Venezuela against Secretary Madison.'

'Madison, not Jefferson himself?'

'No. If Wilkinson was made to think for one second that Jefferson's patronage was in any way compromised, he'd do what he always does, sit tight, do nothing and wait and see who comes out on top. This way we're asking him to do Jefferson a favour and he'll be the more inclined to agree because he'll expect a handsome favour in return.'

'And what charge am I to level at Madison on behalf of our imaginary cabal?'

'Say they're going to claim he's using Government funds and other resources to promote a private adventure led by a foreign national and that he's doing it for personal gain.'

'That should work well. It's actually not so very far from the truth.'

'Yes. The only actual lie is that Smith's venture has Madison's backing and it's being mounted for his personal gain. Tell Wilkinson that Jefferson needs time to break up the cabal and in the meantime he needs to ensure that the Venezuelan venture goes ahead, but under the sole authority of Colonel Smith, and is led by his son Steuben and no one else. Tell him Miranda must be held secure for at least three months.'

Jones turned the story over in his mind.

'It might work, but that's only might, not will.'

'It'll work all right if you play your part well enough. Wilkinson will be quite happy to detain Miranda if he thinks Jefferson wants it, more than happy. If Wilkinson can be made to think that he's doing Jefferson's bidding he'll take Miranda and sit on him until he's told what Jefferson wants done with him. And when he's made the arrest I'll pop up telling him that Miranda is in New Orleans on a secret mission, sanctioned by the President himself, looking into a possible case of treason by a very senior figure who, until recently, was in the Government but cannot, as yet, be named. I'll have papers to prove that Miranda's mission had Jefferson's full approval.'

Bentley's breakfast arrived as Jones pushed away his empty

plate and poured himself another coffee.

'I like it. Wilkinson's detention of Miranda puts him in a difficult position and at the same time you let him know that Burr's treason is suspected in Washington and being investigated. Damned good, it should make the fellow sweat more than a little.'

'Indeed it will. And I'll make sure I carry the authority to institute, if I choose, an investigation into Wilkinson's arrest of Miranda.'

'Wonderful. At this particular moment he would hardly welcome anyone representing Washington nosing about too much into his affairs. The chances of his connection to Burr coming to light would be too great to risk.'

'If I know our General he'll be quick to look out for his own hide.'

'Will he take your word for all you say, even if you have papers to give you the authority?'

'No, he's not so easily taken in. He'll want thorough enquiries made in Washington and he has the friends who can do it. As I say, Madison's support for Miranda's Venezuelan adventure could easily be verified by anyone with government contacts in Washington. Secretary Madison will confirm ordering Miranda's mission and Jefferson will say it has his full support. But the real convincer, the one thing that will make Wilkinson absolutely certain will be Macleod.'

'How so?'

'Wilkinson is sure to question Miranda, who's an old hand at intrigue, so he'll have some sort of story and he'll stick to it. But I doubt Macleod will give such a good account of himself. If he's questioned, I have every confidence that our Lawyer Macleod will confirm to the hilt his, Wilkinson's, involvement with Burr. That it was given to Miranda by Blennerhasset and that it has been passed on, through you, to Washington.'

'Macleod! Of course. He'll blunder out the truth like a trumpeter and all the time think he's being as close as an oyster. And when Wilkinson realises his part in the plot is known, what then?'

Bentley gave a derisory laugh. 'Oh I think we can trust Wilkinson to run true to form. He'll resign and try to worm his way out of the whole thing by getting his high and mighty friends to speak up for him.'

'No more than that? It's not much considering what he's done.'

'It's enough for me. I'll settle for him being ready and willing to do a deal to save his own hide. It's Burr we're after, not General James Wilkinson.'

'Will he resign, though?'

'He always has before.'

'I hope you're sure of that. There's a lot at stake here for any misjudgements.'

'He'll resign. He won't need his nose rubbed too hard into the seriousness of his situation. Joining Burr in his scheme has carried him too far even for Jefferson to turn a blind eye. If I can threaten him with any sort of official investigation, what else can he do? He'll know it wouldn't take too much sifting to turn up his involvement, put him in a court-martial and then in front of a firing squad. He'll resign all right, but only if you do your part, Jeremiah. Remember, he's greedy but clever and he's schemed his way to the top so he'll be sniffing very closely for any whiff of conspiracy against him. He'll try every way he can to wrong-foot you and this is too important to make any mistakes.'

'I'll do my best.'

'I know you will, Jeremiah, and I hope your best will be good enough.'

'As do I. But tell me, if we take General Wilkinson out of the equation, where does that leave us with Burr?'

'Exactly where we want him to be. Burr will have lost his key asset so the plot fails, but he'll not have been officially implicated in anything, so there need be no trial and I will be able to assure our noble President that nothing will come out that he would prefer to stay hidden.'

'But Burr will be free to continue his plans at least as far as Texas and maybe the Mississippi and Ohio valleys.'

284

'No. Burr will be finished. He only ever had one plan, a beautifully crafted and very clever plan.'

'Well I can't see it and I've been at your side all the way on this.'

'That's because you have never really understood what sort of man is Aaron Burr, a true American and a patriot. He despises all those politicians who twist and turn at every opportunity to serve their own ends. He despises weak men who pretend strength, stupid men who wear a mask of wisdom, and men who believe that an image of respectability excuses the reality of betrayal.'

'All fine sentiments, but don't they clash somewhat with what you told me, that Burr wants America for himself?'

'No. I said Burr wants America, and if we hadn't stumbled on Wilkinson he would have got America. But not for himself. He wants to be President. He knew he was a better man than Jefferson and should have won the candidacy for President when they ran together for it. He damn nearly did, they had to ballot thirty-six times before Jefferson shaved it and was chosen. Burr accepted the lesser role of Vice President and served under Jefferson and he did it loyally, although in private he let Jefferson know too many times exactly what he thought of his judgement. Jefferson likes admirers round him, not critics, so he made sure that Burr's name was dropped from the ticket for the second term. That was the thanks Burr got and he took it badly, any man would. So he set out to find his own way into office. He created a wonderful fantasy. His own kingdom. He got the support of the British through Envoy Merry. That support persuaded Wilkinson. He dangled Wilkinson and his army in front of Blennerhasset and that got him the finance he needed. Blennerhasset's money was what took him to New Orleans to finally put Wilkinson securely in his pocket. With Wilkinson firmly convinced that he was going to become the joint ruler of a new kingdom stretching from the Atlantic to the Pacific, he had an army sitting on the mouth of the Mississippi and British naval support promised. All of that would give him Jefferson and his cronies by the balls and Burr could squeeze.'

The breadth of the plan and the simplicity of its final act almost took Jones's breath away.

'By God, yes. If he had control of New Orleans, a real army at his back and ships in support, he could slam the door on all trade coming down or going up the river. He could cripple the Union financially in a matter of months.'

'That's what all this has been about. Once he was sure of Wilkinson, all he had to do was sit tight and Jefferson and the others would have to meet his terms.'

'Which would be?'

'His name at the top of the next Presidential ticket with his own choice of Vice President alongside him.'

'But surely Jefferson and the others would renege?'

'No. He's not only been a soldier, he's been a lawyer and a politician. He'd make sure enough of the right signatures, led by Jefferson and Madison, were on documents which would bring them all down if they tried to revoke on him. In three years, at the end of this current term, he'd be where he thinks he always rightfully belonged, President of the Union.'

'Well, thank God I know now what I'm about.'

'And better equipped for your task?'

'Aye, a damn sight better. Where will you be?'

'There's a plantation about six miles upriver from the city owned by a man named Burrell. I've used the house before and it's safe and handy for our purposes. Report to me there as soon as Miranda's taken.' Bentley looked at the window. The dawn light was showing. Bentley stood up. 'On our way then, Jones, back to Washington to get you the papers you'll need, then on to New Orleans to get that scheming bastard Wilkinson into our hands.'

Chapter Forty-Seven

The great city of New Orleans was the natural market for Ohio Valley farmers, and the Mississippi and Ohio Rivers gave them a year-round highway to transport their goods there. Corn, flour, potatoes, tobacco, beans and even whiskey were carried on flatboats downriver. And these boats were not the small, makeshift craft that Blennerhasset had had made in two days. These New Orleans boats, sometimes called Mississippi Broadhorns, were big, up to and even over fifty feet in length and some sixteen feet wide. Many were roofed over and carried passengers as well as cargo. They were crewed by oarsmen and carried a steersman and a pilot. The distance as the crow flies from Cairo to New Orleans is about six hundred miles and was a journey of four to six weeks. The river was busy, nearly two thousand flatboats a year went down to New Orleans; the number was rising and the boats getting bigger all the time.

Demand for passage on the Mississippi boats outstripped supply and it took three days before Miranda, Macleod and Marie could buy exclusive passage on a craft. Their boat was forty feet long, the rear half roofed over for passengers and a cooking space, the front half open for cargo. Having left Cairo, the journey proved slow and uneventful, which was exactly as Macleod and Marie would have it be, while Miranda suffered the passing of these lazy days with a good grace, that is to say, he left Macleod and Marie largely to each other's company.

As to them, Marie told her husband more of her adventures and Macleod told his wife of his and both determined that they had been utterly foolish to ever doubt they loved one another, would always love one another and, well, that is enough. They were husband and wife, re-united.

However, even the slowest barge on the laziest river will in time finally wind its way to a destination which, to Marie's surprise, proved not to be New Orleans but Baton Rouge.

The crew tied up the boat on the busy, bustling wharf and, having suggested a hotel where the gentry were wont to stay, set off with their passengers' luggage which now consisted of a small chest and three bags.

Marie stood on the wharf beside Macleod and Miranda. She was gazing at the town beyond the busy harbour. 'This was my childhood home.'

Macleod felt awkward. There was a certain sadness in the way Marie spoke and he wasn't quite sure what he should say by way of reply, or if indeed a reply was needed. 'Yes, I know.'

'But now Boston is my home and you are my family and I want no other. You know that, do you not, Jean?' Marie turned and looked at him with a gentle smile.

'Yes. I know that now. I was a fool to think otherwise.'

'We were both foolish, but that is past. We will never be so foolish again. But I must ask, why have we stopped here?'

'Well, the fact is, and I agree with him,' Macleod paused. This was going to be damned difficult. 'You see, Marie, Miranda and I, well we have spoken about it all and he suggested, but I must say I have to agree with him –'

'Come now, my friends.' Miranda had been patient throughout their journey down the Mississippi, of necessity perhaps, but patient nonetheless. Now, however, they were almost at journey's end and his patience had evaporated.

Macleod looked at him. 'What do you mean, come now? Come where?'

'I mean, Jean Marie, that there are arrangements to make. Tomorrow you and I will set off for New Orleans. Is it your wish that your wife should accompany us? For myself of course I feel that the safest thing to do would be to find Marie a good hotel here in Baton Rouge where she can await in comfort for our return,' and here he paused to make sure Macleod would understand his meaning, 'when our business, our very important business in New Orleans, is complete.'

During the journey and in a vague way Macleod had known

that there would be a problem with Marie when they reached New Orleans. But he had preferred the problem to remain vague and the answer to be postponed. It was not until the previous day that Miranda had forced a decision on him. Their work was not without the possibility of some little danger. Did he want his wife exposed to whatever hazards awaited them? Of course not. Then should she not be made comfortable and left at Baton Rouge? Macleod supposed, reluctantly, that she should, but he hadn't looked forward to explaining to her that, so recently reunited, he chose that they once again be parted, and now it was proving as difficult as he had anticipated. It was with considerable gratitude that he found his friend had put the matter into a nutshell for him.

'Absolutely. She must be found safe and comfortable lodgings and rest here until our business is completed.' He turned to Marie. 'Dearest, you must remain here for a time. Miranda and I must ... we must ... we have business ...' Macleod had not spoken very fully of what he and Miranda would actually do in New Orleans during their journey down the Mississippi. This was not because he wished to keep it secret from Marie but rather because he had never asked himself what it was that he and Miranda would decide to do when they arrived. But now he asked himself that very question and found, as usual, he had no idea what the answer might be. He turned to Miranda. 'Do you know what our business will be?'

Miranda, unusually for him, nearly lost patience with his friend but, with an effort, controlled himself and spoke slowly and calmly. 'I do, and when we have settled your wife comfortably I will tell you.'

Macleod turned back to Marie. 'Dearest, do not think that I lack trust in you, you know I would trust you with my life.'

'I know, Jean.'

'Nor that my leaving you here is in any way other than a necessity. Were it not so, then nothing in the world would part us.'

'I know, Jean.'

'It's just that the nature of our business is somewhat difficult to explain.'

But as usual, Marie already had control of the situation. The thing, she could see, had been decided and she must make the best of it. She must also make her husband comfortable with his decision by hiding her own true feelings at yet another, and to her mind, quite unnecessary parting.

'Dearest Jean, I knew from the beginning of our journey that I would not be able to accompany you to New Orleans.'

'You did? How?'

It took only a moment's hesitation for Marie to think up a suitable response, which came to her courtesy of the meeting in New York with Dolly Bawtry in her Madame de Metz role.

'Might I still be known in New Orleans? Once I was very well known. Now I may still be remembered as the lady who fled and whose husband and lover were found in bed shot to death. There may still be those in New Orleans who would like to talk to me about that circumstance and, if I was questioned, I would find it most difficult to provide suitable answers, would I not? There may even be a warrant for me, an old Spanish warrant, no doubt, but enough to cause considerable inconvenience to any business you might have.'

It was enough for Macleod and satisfied him completely that he had indeed made the right and proper decision. 'Yes, of course, your husband and St. Clair. I should have thought of it myself.'

'So I must stay in Baton Rouge and you and Señor Miranda must go to New Orleans without me and attend to the business on which you have travelled so far and already risked so much. I know that you and Señor Miranda do work for the government. I already know it is hazardous. So be it. You must do your duty and go, I must do my duty and await your safe return, and whilst I wait, what prayer and hope can do shall be done. Now, the day is well advanced and you two must make your plans. Tomorrow we will be parted, my love, but we still have tonight to say our farewells.'

Miranda, looking on, was reminded very much of Dolly

Bawtry for Marie had spoken her piece with great charm and accomplishment and captivated her audience though she played only to an audience of one. His only regret was that it would be inappropriate to applaud, but surely some sort of compliment was in order?

'Madame Macleod, you combine beauty with good sense in a degree almost unique in my experience. Let us go and find this hotel recommended to us and assure ourselves that you are provided with the best lodgings available in this town.'

'Thank you, Señor. Come, Jean, it is time to go.'

And together, they left the busy wharf to its bustling business, passing through the bales and crates and, as obvious gentry, were made way for by both black and white.

This city had been Marie's childhood home but, coming from the family she had, she had known nothing of these swarming docks. Once into the city proper, with its terraces of two-storey houses with balconies surrounded by delicate and elaborate iron trimmings, it became more familiar to her. She remembered well the carriages with uniformed black coachmen pulled by handsome matched pairs, ladies in fashionable dress walking with opened parasols against the afternoon May sun followed dutifully by black maidservants carrying their pretty purchases. And all round them, in the architecture, in the language, in the style and the manners, French mixed with English, a happy marriage between the Old World and the New.

The hotel more than fulfilled the crewmen's recommendation. Three storeys, in the very best colonial style, the walls washed with a light pink to which the sun gave an almost magical glow. Long ago it had been the home of an aristocrat of the French nobility but time and the French Revolution had taken their toll and for many years now it had been one of the premier hotels of Baton Rouge.

Their boatmen were waiting patiently outside the main entrance and took off their hats to welcome their ex-passengers as they arrived. Baton Rouge was an old-fashioned city where proper manners were not only expected but required. On the boat their manner had been easy and relaxed. But they were no longer on the boat and, more importantly, their payment was due. After Miranda had made a cursory inspection of the hotel, he settled their account and they went their way rejoicing. Once inside the hotel, Miranda had taken the management by storm. He had thrown down a gold piece and demanded that his friends be immediately shown the best room and by none less than the manager himself. Even in a city of nobility and wealth, a gold piece cast so carelessly causes a response especially when the promise of more to follow is made. The manager arrived. He had seen all sorts arrive at his hotel, from the genuine article to the cheap fake, and his judgement in these matters was honed to an almost supernatural degree. Himself a man of fashion, he looked at the arrivals. The clothes were wrong, the baggage was wrong, the second man, the American was most decidedly wrong. But the Spanish gentleman and the lady were most decidedly right. Clothes can be bought, baggage can be acquired, but the grand manner and the ability to carry it off successfully could not be bought nor even taught. Señor Miranda was the genuine article. What puzzled the manager was that the lady appeared not to be his wife nor companion, but the wife of the American. Still, times were changing. Many northerners came to Baton Rouge with their coarse ways and their uncouth talk but with real money to invest. It was sad, felt the manager, but it was progress.

'If you will permit me, Señor, Madame,' he allowed his eyes to include Macleod since his words had not, 'I will take you all to your rooms. I am sure you will find them satisfactory.

He clicked his fingers and a liveried black boy hurried up. The manager indicated the baggage but in such a manner as to make clear to the menial that he dissociated himself from it entirely. The black boy summoned a twin and between them they picked up the trunk and bags and followed the party. Led by the manager up the impressive staircase they were watched in some wonderment by the ladies and gentlemen in the lobby who had all noticed, like the manager, the clothes of the new guests.

'But my dear,' quietly whispered one well-attired lady to her equally well-upholstered husband, 'they are dressed like frontier people, positively backwoods folk. Who on earth can they be for Pierre to treat them in such a manner?'

But the husband had nothing to suggest, not that his wife minded. Having seen what she had seen, she now had the most intriguing topic for her dinner table that evening. A group of three mysterious people, people moreover in disguise with virtually no luggage whatsoever, had arrived, thrown handfuls of gold coins about and been welcomed lavishly by Pierre himself. What could it mean? Who could they be? And the lady left the hotel more than satisfied.

Miranda inspected the rooms for himself and his companions.

'They will do, they will suffice. Tomorrow my friend, M'sieur Macleod, and I leave for New Orleans. Madame Macleod will remain for an indefinite period. She is to be cared for, no expense must be spared. Understand?'

Gold changed hands. Pierre understood. Oh yes, with the gold in his hand, Pierre understood completely.

That night they dined together but, excusing themselves, Macleod and Marie retired early. Miranda had expected no less and wished them a good night's repose and, once they were gone, summoned the manager to his table.

'Now, M'sieur, to go over what is required of you. Madame, the wife of my friend, is to be cared for. She is not to be disturbed or in any way discomposed. Is that understood?'

'Oh yes, sir, understood completely.'

'Good, then when my friend and I return I will further reward you according to how well you show that you have understood completely.' Miranda smiled at the manager. 'Be aware, sir, that I carry a brace of pistols in my baggage as well as gold on my person.' Pierre nodded his understanding. He had expected no less. This man would reward extravagantly, but he would also punish in the same manner without a second thought. 'Have hot water, towels, soap and a razor sent up to my friend's room soon after dawn, but not too soon. You understand?'

Pierre smiled knowingly.

'Completely, Señor.'

'Good. Now, bring me my coffee.'

Chapter Forty-Eight

The sun blazed from an endless blue sky and the muddy green river, almost a mile wide, seemed to stretch out to meet it creating a landscape almost devoid of land. On either side were dark, irregular ribbons of shore which seemed far too trivial to contain the mighty river.

Macleod and Miranda were sitting on the cotton bales as their boat made its gentle way. The heat of the day was beginning to make itself felt and the four oarsmen had stripped to the waist. Both Macleod and Miranda had taken off their jackets.

'Jean Marie, there is something troubling you. Is it leaving your wife alone back there? I assure you she will be well cared for, I have made all the necessary arrangements.'

'I know you have and I thank you heartily for it. No. I am of course concerned for Marie, what husband wouldn't be? But that is not what troubles me.'

'Then tell me what does trouble you.'

Macleod picked at the edge of a cotton bale. 'It's difficult to know how to put it.'

'Then put it plainly.'

'Look here, Miranda, do you trust me?'

'With my life, Jean, you know that. You are honest, loyal and true. How could I not trust you?'

'Dammit, because I am not worthy of your trust. I have betrayed you. There, that's plain enough I think. I am a traitor to our friendship.' Whatever Macleod had expected, it wasn't the laugh which Miranda gave. 'Damn you, Miranda, this is no laughing matter. I say I've betrayed you. I betrayed you to a man named Jones, Bentley's agent, way back there on the island when the pirates took us.'

'Of course you did.'

'You knew?'

'Not the detail, but I knew it was not what it appeared. Why take us at all in the first place, if not to rob us then cut our throats and send our bodies on their way down the river? Why take us if not for gain? Why be captured together yet so carefully kept apart? Why else but that the so-called pirates were working for someone who wanted the whole charade cleverly staged.'

'Yes, I suppose it would have looked that way to someone like you.'

'And if it was arranged so that you might have your meeting, as you say it was, then I am not surprised. I do not think I am wholly trusted by Secretary Madison. And he is right to think so. I do his bidding, certainly, but I am true to my cause. It does not surprise me that he has us watched and asks you, oh so secretly, to inform on me. I would do no less in his position.'

Macleod was a bit aggrieved that his reluctant confession had fallen so flat. 'Well, I'm glad I told you anyway.'

'And I also am glad. Jean, one day it will dawn on you that all this secrecy and play-acting is my world. Intrigue and deception are things I have lived with for many years. I have been the hunted and the hunter, I have been an agent and a counter-agent, I have played the false friend and been betrayed by true friends. You are no traitor to our friendship, you are an innocent who has been caught up in a web of deceit. Of course I trust you because, in all of this, you alone are true. You alone would never betray me.'

'But on the island I told Bentley's agent all I knew, all about Blennerhasset and his army, about the militias and about Burr getting Wilkinson to join him in the treachery. Once Bentley knows all that he will …'

Miranda waited, but Macleod, found he had no idea how to finish his sentence.

'Well, Jean, and what will your Mr Bentley do when he learns that Burr has managed to get the Union Army of New

Orleans in his pocket?'

Macleod thought about it. There seemed only one answer. 'He'll arrest Wilkinson on a charge of treason of course. What else would you expect?'

'I thought you might say that, but alas, I must disagree with you.'

Macleod, however, felt that what he had said made solid, sound sense and he was rather pleased with himself. 'Of course he'll have him arrested. Bentley may be many things but he's no traitor. He'll arrest Wilkinson and Burr and they will both stand trial in a court of law.'

'No, they will not, and for two reasons. First your courts are not like so many I have known. They provide justice, and it is a justice based on evidence. What evidence do you think your Mr Bentley will be able to provide to this court in which Wilkinson and Burr will appear?'

'Blennerhasset. He can tell what he knows.'

'And put a noose round his own neck? I think not.'

'Then there's the buildings he's making to house his army.'

'All of which he will say are requirements for supplies and stores, a wharf and warehousing.'

'The militias, somebody must be in a position to testify that Burr has made preparations to raise militias.'

'True. But ask yourself, if it is so easy to know why has it not already been discovered and used against him?'

'I don't know, but it could be used now.'

'Which brings me to my second reason. Aaron Burr will not be charged by your Government because they dare not put him in open court. He knows too much for one thing and he can call people to give evidence who would not wish to speak the truth in open court.'

'No one is above the law. Any true American called to give evidence would be in duty bound to do so.'

'As you say, no one is above your law, but there are those who may choose to stand outside it, to circumvent it.'

'Who?'

'President Jefferson, Secretary Madison, Mr Bentley

himself. None of them would cut too fine a figure if all that is involved in this business were to become public property. Think of what we know, what we have found out and, thinking of that, try to imagine how much more there could be. How many others might be involved and the positions those others might hold? Need I go on?'

No, thought Macleod, he needn't go on. There were indeed men, great men, for whom it would do untold harm to appear in a witness box and face an antagonistic lawyer. A man of the law himself, he didn't need Miranda to tell him what a clever lawyer's questioning could do to even the most honest and blameless of men. But Macleod was unwilling to leave it as it stood. 'So, if not arrest and trial, what do you think Bentley will do? You said back in New York that you knew him to be a man of consequence in your world of intrigue and I know him to be both able and ruthless. What can he do?'

'If Burr has indeed turned Wilkinson then Bentley will try to turn him back. He will find some way to apply pressure and, if he is the man I think he is, he will succeed. Wilkinson will hand Burr to Bentley with enough evidence against him to ensure that Vice President Aaron Burr will choose to retire into private life with his honour still intact and leave politics alone.'

'I see.' The two men sat in silence as the boat drifted lazily on the current, comfortably managed by the crew. Suddenly something occurred to Macleod. 'But if it's like you say …'

'It is, I assure you.'

'Well then, what are we going to New Orleans for?'

'Because we must go and confirm Blennerhasset's story. We must be certain that Burr has Wilkinson as part of his plot.'

'But now you say you're sure it won't come to anything. That Bentley will find some way of putting an end to Burr's activities. Dammit, I'm confused as hell. If Bentley now knows what I told Jones, and if he can do as you say with Wilkinson, then aren't we redundant?'

'To Bentley, yes, we probably are.'

'And Bentley must have made known to Secretary Madison what's afoot, so we don't have to report any of what we've found to him because he'll already have been told.' Miranda nodded in agreement. 'So if we're no use to Bentley and no more use to Madison, what the hell are we going on with this thing for?'

'To finish our business. What I may think, Jean, is not the same as what I must know for certain. Suspicions and speculations are not facts. Secretary Madison sent me to find out what I could about Aaron Burr's scheme, so I do it for him. But I also do it for myself and for my cause. I need to find out what, if anything, Burr has arranged with the Spanish. To find out who, if anyone, he has taken into his plot from among those who work for my country's freedom. If Vice President Burr is clever enough to ensnare this General Wilkinson, who can say who else he has not ensnared? I need to find out how all of this tangled web may help or hinder the great cause I serve.'

'But that's you, not me. I don't serve any such crack-pot cause. I don't care a hoot whether Spain or Portugal or the Devil in a tall hat rules your precious Colombia. All I care about is America.'

Miranda smiled indulgently at this outburst. 'Surely not America alone? Your wife too, I hope.'

'Laugh at me if you like but I'm telling you the truth. I only came along with you from New York because Bentley gave me no choice. I stayed with you after Washington because I thought we were doing work for America. But if all we're doing now is running off after some half-baked hope that whatever we find may help your damned dreams of freedom, then I want no part of it.'

'But, Jean, you are already part of it. As you say, you have been at my side since New York. We have faced dangers together. You cannot leave me now.'

'Can't I? Just watch me go.'

'Very well. I see that your mind is made up. Adieu, old friend.' Miranda sat and looked at him.

As Miranda sat, waiting, it dawned on Macleod that no matter how fine and firm his words, they could not, in any practical way, be put into effect. Both men were sitting on a cotton barge that only went one way and only made one more stop. Like it or not Macleod was going to New Orleans and like it or not he would arrive there at Miranda's side. He looked out at the wide, calm, slow river. It wasn't a wild, raging thing, yet it had something about it of overwhelming force. It was calm but it was also unstoppable. There was no point whatsoever in opposing the mighty Mississippi. Either you went with it or you stood aside and went nowhere.

'Come, Jean, we have been together all this way. Bear me company to the end, for the end is very close, I assure you.'

Macleod made a last stand. 'Why? Why should I?'

'For friendship's sake.'

Macleod looked again at the mighty river. It was an unanswerable response and Macleod knew it. Friendship. How could you oppose such a force?

Chapter Forty-nine

General Wilkinson stared angrily at the man facing him, much as he might at a junior officer to whom he was about to give a severe reprimand. But the man standing before him seemed unconcerned by the General's fierce look.

The General was a chubby man of middle height with fair, curly hair who looked as if he would smile easily and who, if he hadn't been wearing a uniform, no one would have taken for a soldier. However, as he was wearing a uniform, wasn't smiling and was sitting behind an imposing desk, he looked very much the soldier and Jeremiah Jones was under no illusions that this man, if he chose, had the power of life and death over him.

'General Wilkinson, you have seen my papers. Do you accept them?'

'Such things can be forged.'

'They can indeed. Are those forged would you say?'

General James Wilkinson thought for a moment whether to respond to the man's insolence, but instead he picked up the two sheets, read them slowly once again, carefully examined the signatures at the foot of each sheet, then held them out to Jeremiah Jones. 'They seem genuine.'

Jones folded them and slipped them inside his coat.

'Thank you, General. Then perhaps you will permit me to sit. My leg is troubling me.'

'An old wound?'

Jeremiah Jones, though not actually invited, sat down.

'No, I never soldiered. An illness in early childhood that left me lame.'

'You never soldiered?'

'No.'

'Yet there is a General's signature on one of those

documents.'

'So there is, and the name of a man equally influential in politics on the other.'

Jeremiah Jones waited. He had Wilkinson at a disadvantage and wanted to keep him there, but he didn't want to antagonise him. It would be a very fine line to walk. General Wilkinson sat back in his chair and studied his visitor for a moment.

'Well, Mr Jones, perhaps you will be so good as to tell me what it is you wanted to see me about.'

'I wish to ask you a favour.'

That got a smile although not a nice one.

'A favour! And why should I do you any favours?'

'Because it saves me the embarrassment and discomfort of having to make it a command.' Jones returned the smile but tried to make it as genuine as he could.

General Wilkinson, as Bentley had said, was no fool and had served a long and hard apprenticeship in double-dealing. He lied well himself and had been lied to often by experts. He knew what to look for in any man he suspected. He was cautious as only the guilty are cautious. Above all he knew to the minutest detail both the extent of his power and its limits. He could, here and now, order this man taken out and shot, and it would be done. But he also knew that if the papers the man carried were indeed genuine he would have to answer for it to people who would in turn have the power of life and death over him.

The General decided that if this man was a counterfeit then he was a damn good one and, in matters of such judgements, General Wilkinson rightly prized his own opinion above all others.

'Well then, what's your favour, Mr Jones.'

'Two men will arrive in New Orleans or may already be here. I am instructed to see that they are detained.'

'Arrested?'

'Not necessarily, that would be for you to decide. They are to be detained though not harmed in any way. Once taken they are to be kept incommunicado but may be allowed all the

302

necessities of comfort appropriate to gentlemen except, of course, freedom of movement and communication with each other and anyone else at all.'

'And does either of these men have a name?'

'One is of no consequence, a Boston lawyer called Macleod. The other is of considerable consequence, Sebastiàn Francisco de Miranda Rodríguez.'

Jones saw a look of surprise in Wilkinson's eyes. It was gone in an instant, but it had been there and Wilkinson continued as if the name meant nothing to him. 'Spanish grandee is he?'

'Born in South America. Have you never heard of him? He is, in his own way, quite well known.'

Wilkinson evaded the question. 'And what would be his own way?'

'A leader of those who are dedicated to bringing about the independence of all the Spanish and Portuguese possessions in the Americas.'

'And is that why you want me to detain him? Are we suddenly such allies of the Spanish or Portuguese?'

'No. My reason is more domestic and has, in part, something to do with a project which at this moment is being brought to fruition by a Colonel Smith in New York.'

'What project?'

'The invasion of the Spanish Province of Venezuela by a group of filibusters. In the normal run of things such a matter would be of no particular concern, in fact under more normal circumstances the whole scheme would probably have been ignored or quashed. But a situation has developed whereby it is regarded as in our interest that such a project be allowed, quite unofficially, to proceed and, if possible, succeed.'

'You speak of "our interest" as if you yourself were part of the government, Mr Jones.'

'No, not part of the government, not officially. I represent a small administrative agency in Washington which deals with those little nuisances that arise from time to time and which the government needs to have resolved without any direct involvement of themselves or their more official representatives.'

Wilkinson gave a short, derisory laugh. 'An agent, eh? One of those grubby little men who do the politicians' dirty work?'

Jones slightly bent his head in acknowledgement. 'An agent if you will.'

'Well then, Agent Jones. What grubby little thing do your political masters wish me to do for them?'

'A nuisance has arisen in connection with Colonel Smith's Venezuelan project and I have been sent to you to resolve it.'

Jones paused. So far he had done reasonably well and felt he had carried his listener with him. But Wilkinson was a cautious man and now he needed to be taken from the edge of doubt into belief. This was the critical moment and judgement was everything. Jones waited until Wilkinson's impatience caused him to speak.

'Well? Go on.'

'Before I go on, General, I have to lay on you a condition. It is not my condition you understand, but one imposed on me personally by the gentleman who sent me.'

'Some Washington politico?'

'In a way.'

'The one whose name is on your papers?'

'No, neither he nor the general whose name is on the other paper know me at all. I have never seen or spoken to either of them. They signed those papers because a certain person asked them to.'

'What certain person?'

'A tobacco planter from Virginia who temporarily resides elsewhere until his present occupation comes to the end of its term. When that happens he may consider a trip to Italy, they say Monticello is a place he's fond of. I don't know it myself, do you, General?'

Wilkinson's face betrayed no change, but Jones sensed most clearly that the identity of President Jefferson, whose home was named Monticello, was now fully established as the "person" for whom Jones acted.

'And the name of this planter from Virginia?'

'I cannot say it out loud, sir, but I think you have good reason to know it well enough.' Wilkinson said nothing so Jones continued. 'And my condition, the condition laid on me by our Virginian tobacco planter, is that no names are to be used and no written records whatsoever to be made. None, absolutely none. If anyone asks, I came here to provide you with intelligence of the movements of a man named Miranda. He is a known agitator and wanted, I believe, by the Spanish Government. It was decided that his presence here, his secret presence here, should be made known to you and you were to use your judgement as to what, if any action, you might take.' In his little speech Jones's manner had been all caution and tact with not a little deference thrown in. Now it changed. It was time to show the whip. 'There, General, you have all you need to comply with the request of our planter friend. Will you accommodate him or not? I need an answer and I cannot delay too long. Come, sir, make your choice.'

Jones sat back. The tale had been told as he had rehearsed it and now all he could do was see what result he had achieved. General Wilkinson looked at him thoughtfully for a moment then rang a small bell which stood by his hand on his desk. The door opened and an officer entered.

'This gentleman is Mr Jones. In a moment we will have finished our business and, when we have, see to it that Mr Jones is found somewhere comfortable and private to stay, here inside the barracks. Somewhere he won't be disturbed.'

The officer looked at Jones.

'I understand, sir.'

'Good. I'll ring when I want you and, when I do, have a couple of men to accompany you and then let them keep watch at Mr Jones's door, in relays if necessary, to see that he is left in peace until I need to see him again.'

The officer and General Wilkinson returned his gaze to Jeremiah who held it without concern. He had done his job well, Wilkinson was won over. If he had not been then Jones knew he would already be under guard and on his way to some cell. As it was, Wilkinson wanted to know more.

'Well, General, am I to be thrown into captivity?'

'You will be made comfortable as my guest, Mr Jones.' Wilkinson held out a hand. 'And now I will take those papers.'

'If you take them, General, it will have to be by force for I will not give them up. If they have served their purpose I will happily destroy them in your presence, but I will not give them up willingly.' The General slowly withdrew his hand. Jones was satisfied and, being satisfied, was prepared to be conciliatory. He knew he had to be careful not to push this man too far or too fast.

'General, it seems that you must trust me and I must trust you. One of us must first show that trust so let it be me. I can go so far as to tell you the nature of the problem, the nuisance I have been asked to help resolve. I can name no specific names, partly because I am constrained, but mostly because the names are not all known to me. I know my own part in this but only my own part. Only one person sees the whole picture, knows all the parts. You understand?' Wilkinson nodded. 'The project undertaken by Colonel Smith is, of itself, a comparatively small matter but important in its own way and, if successful, may lead to greater things. But it is not of any serious political importance currently. Being of some potential value it goes ahead with the unofficial support of the government. However, such an undertaking, the raising and equipping of a small army cannot be kept a secret. There are those within the government and close to it who would use this project to do harm to a certain senior figure within the present administration, a figure very close to our mutual friend from Virginia. They would wish to distort the facts and present the project as being designed for personal gain rather than for the national interest. Señor Miranda has been an essential part of Colonel Smith's project. He knows Venezuela intimately, has the contacts needed there and has made all necessary local arrangements. However, because of the centrality of his role in the planning and setting up of the project, the whole thing can be represented as mounted and led by him and, if shown in such a light, would

306

create the false idea that this is a private project under the leadership of a foreign national organised solely for profit. Were that supposition to gain credence among unsympathetic minds it is entirely possible that a resignation might be called for, perhaps worse. Whatever the outcome, serious political harm would inevitably be done. On balance it has been decided that the main part of Señor Miranda's role is now substantially over and his services, though still of undoubted value, are best dispensed with. If he were to become unavailable to continue for any reason, then the project could go forward under the exclusive sponsorship of Colonel Smith, a man above suspicion and unconnected with politics. Also it would fall under the sole leadership of his son, Steuben Smith. Such being the case, the calumny being organised is temporarily thwarted. Time is gained to put in place more complete and effective counter-measures which can eliminate the possibility of a certain person suffering political harm. There, General, now you have it all, at least all that I know of the matter. You can have me taken from this office and have me questioned in whatever manner you choose, there's no more or, if there is, none that I know.'

There. It was done.

Wilkinson took several minutes to think through what Jones had told him and then finally rang his bell. The officer entered and Jones noticed two armed soldiers waiting outside.

'Take Mr Jones to his room. See that he has everything he needs or wants and see that he has complete privacy.'

'Yes, sir.'

Jones stood.

'Thank you for your time, General. I hope the information I have delivered to you is of help.'

The officer moved to one side and Jones left the office. The two soldiers immediately took up station beside him and all three followed the officer down the corridor. Jones was satisfied. He had succeeded. And yet, had he? Wilkinson was a shrewd man, a man used to lying and being lied to, a man who knew scheming better than most. A sneaking doubt crept into Jeremiah's mind, a small but troubling doubt. Had it not, perhaps, been all been a bit easy? Had it not, in fact, been all a bit too easy?

Chapter Fifty

The flatboats were moored three deep and more beside the New Orleans dock and Macleod and Miranda had to cross two other boats loaded with cotton bales before they could step on to the wooden dock. What confronted them was a wharf crammed with slaves, horses, carts and wagons all filling the air with their clamour. They looked about them, it was as if some New Orleans buildings had spilled from the city on to the wharfage and would at any minute tumble into the Mississippi which, behind them, stretched the better part of a mile to the far bank. But these "buildings" were not made of stone or wood. Their walls rose up solidly enough from the wooden decking to the equivalent of two storeys but were in fact cotton and tobacco bales stacked into great blocks. The "streets" running between these blocks were filled with an army of black bodies who toiled at bringing more bales from the flatboats to build yet more enormous stacks while others dismantled those already built to cart them away to warehouses or to the other great dock where ocean-going ships, also moored several deep, awaited their cargoes. The air had a sickly tinge to it which came from islands of molasses barrels which stood among the blocks of bales.

All was activity, with black men doing the hauling and carrying, the pulling of handcarts, the rolling of barrels from flatboats to build new pungent-smelling islands, while white overseers in linen coats and wide-brimmed straw hats directed and shouted and generally attempted the seemingly impossible task of creating some system among the chaos.

Downriver at the furthest end of this city of cargoes there was also the graveyard of the flat-bottomed boats. Having delivered their cargoes they could never, without overwhelming effort, be got back to wherever they had come from. The hulks of this graveyard reached well out into the river, tied together with chains against the pull of the current. Visible on the wharf where they were chained, even above the blocks of bales, were mighty stacks of timber into which previous boats had already been rendered and, beyond these, equally high stacks of what seemed mere debris, the detritus of destruction. Yet even this was useable, for the debris would become the fuel of uncountable domestic hearths which lay beyond the great, grey, stone warehouses which lined the rear of the docks. The good timber would be hauled away and used in building new parts to this restless, ever-growing city. By the miracle of man's ingenuity many homes and even a whole church had risen, built entirely from timber which had, not so very long before, brought passengers and cargoes down the Mississippi river.

Macleod and Miranda set off and picked their way forward between the slaves and the bales that were rising round them, aiming for the warehouses beyond which the city began. They had not gone more than a few yards when a man suddenly stepped out from behind an immense pile of cotton bales and, blocking their progress, confronted them.

'Pardon me, gentlemen. Am I addressing a Señor Miranda?' This importunate stranger wasn't such a big man but he somehow gave the impression of considerable strength. He wore a dark, loose-fitting suit and a shabby tall hat and one of his eyes wandered randomly giving his face a slight air of madness. The other eye, under control and totally sane, was fixed on Miranda. The man took off his hat and held it at his side. 'I think I am, sir, from the description given me. And this gentleman with you –' the roving eye flashed across the horizon but the good eye fixed itself on Macleod, '– would be Mr Macleod, lawyer of Boston. You're a long way from home, sir, a very long way.'

Macleod gripped Miranda's arm and spoke in a low voice.

'Beware. This has happened to me before.' He turned to the man. 'On your way, you blackguard, we want nothing to do with you.' But the man stood his ground with a half-smile and continued to block their passage. 'Be off with you, I say, before I take my boots to you or worse.'

The man continued his smile. 'Dear me, sir, don't be hasty. I own I'm not much to look at but looks may mislead, sir, indeed they may.'

Macleod was about to speak again when Miranda interposed. 'What is it you want?'

'I want you to come along with me, gents, and I want you to be sharp about it. I was sent to collect you by –'

Macleod laughed.

'Go with you, ha! And what? Be attacked by your fellows in some back alley, robbed, murdered or worse.'

'Well, sir, in my experience there's not much worse than being murdered but let it be as you say.' The man turned to Miranda. 'Time's not on our side, sir, and, if you stay here, you'll not only be attacked but you'll be taken. Now, Señor Miranda, the gentleman who sent me said to tell you …'

Before Miranda could speak, Macleod had stepped forward and caught the man a blow with his fist on the side of the head which sent him sprawling into a wall of cotton bales beside which they were standing.

Miranda caught Macleod's arm as he was about to step forward and inflict further mayhem on the man calmly now dusting off his coat.

'Jean, wait –'

'Never fear, I know his sort.' Macleod turned again to the man. 'Sent by a gentleman, were you? Sent to lead us somewhere? By God I know what your game is.'

The man picked up his tall hat which he had dropped and dusted it off on his sleeve and resumed as if nothing at all had happened. 'Sent I was, gents, sent to bring you. And I tell you squarely that you'd better come before –' But either his one good eye caught some movement in the throng or he heard something. Whatever it was his manner abruptly changed. He jammed his tall hat back on his head. 'Come along, gents, the time for gabbing is done.' Macleod and Miranda turned and saw a group of soldiers coming towards them, forcing their way

311

through the cargoes, slaves and carts. 'Be quick now or the bullies will have us all.' He turned and moved off, shouting over his shoulder. 'Follow me and keep close.'

Macleod didn't move. Miranda grabbed his arm and dragged him a couple of paces.

'For God's sake, Jean, be quick or we'll be taken.'

But Macleod was not quick. His was a slow mind and he shook off Miranda's arm. Why should he run from his own country's soldiers? 'Good grief, Miranda, surely you don't believe that ...'

But Miranda, with a despairing look left him and followed where the tall-hatted man was waiting to lead. Macleod stood where he was, with no idea what to do but wait.

The first of what he could now see was a group of six soldiers came up to him and Macleod noted the three chevrons on his sleeve.

'Sergeant, I'm glad you and your men ...'

But the Sergeant didn't wait to find out what it was that Macleod was glad about. He struck him hard across the temple with the butt of his musket.

Macleod collapsed to the ground, unconscious and bleeding. The Sergeant shouted to the other men who had gathered round.

'Right, you and you, see this one is taken back as soon as he wakes. The rest of you, with me after the other one.'

The sergeant and soldiers ran forward pushing through the busy workers whom they jostled aside but, because of their long muskets, making much slower progress than any unencumbered individual.

One of the two men left to guard Macleod looked down at the prone form at their feet and spat sideways.

'They'll not catch them now. They're away.'

'I reckon so. What do we do with this one?'

The first soldier leaned his musket against the bales and got out a short, stubby pipe from his pocket which he began to fill from a small packet pulled from the ammunition pouch on his belt. The other soldier added his weapon to that of his companion, looked down at the prone form on the ground, then

312

turned back to his comrade. 'You get fourteen days hard if the Sergeant finds you've baccy in there instead of ball.'

'Then I won't let him find out, will I? How was we to shoot anyone through this crowd. I knowed when we did our first stretch of watchin' there'd be no firing of weapons, at least none to speak of.'

And he lit his pipe and fell to smoking.

The two men stood still and waited, glancing from time to time at their charge who lay still, blood congealing and matting his hair from the wound on the side of his head. The world of commerce and trade rolled on busily around them uncaring, uninterested and unimpressed, black bodies sweating in the hot sun and straw-hatted overseers shouting. This was New Orleans docks and the business of business had no time for anything *but* business, so Macleod lay, and the soldiers waited, all equally ignored among the noise and bustle as life went on.

Chapter Fifty-one

The tall-hatted man was surprisingly agile and seemed sufficiently familiar with the dock area that, by weaving through cargoes, they soon made the warehouse yards. Here were many places two men might conceal themselves and the soldiers would be faced with the dilemma of stop and search or press on.

Miranda, not used to such sudden exertion, was slowing badly. The tall-hatted man paused so as not to outdistance him. Miranda came up and stopped.

'Can we not hide in one of these yards, my friend?'

But the crack of a musket and a ball smacking into the wall only a few feet from the tall-hatted man answered Miranda's question and once again they ran, the shot having marvellously renewed Miranda's energy

Once past the warehouses they were into the city proper in a maze of by-ways. With so many possible turns the soldiers would soon be lost. Miranda managed to keep up, but only by the greatest exertion, as the other took him first one way then another. Then suddenly he found himself alone. The man had disappeared.

He was standing in a dark, cobbled passage between two great, windowless, stone walls where, high above him, the sky was no more than a thin, blue ribbon of light. He put out a hand and rested it against one of the walls which he found cold, damp and somewhat slimy. He tried to regain his breath and weighed the possibility that Macleod, after all, might have been right and, having been brought thus far into this place, he was to be robbed or worse. After a moment he spoke loudly into the shadows in front of him.

'My friend, if you are there you must come and get me. I am

too old for such games.'

Round a corner not far from where Miranda leaned against his wall the tall-hatted man slowly emerged and came towards him, then stood and looked back along the passageway and listened.

'Well, sir, no harm in getting your wind back now, I suppose. The bullies are well behind us and won't give us any more bother.'

Miranda took his hand from the wall and wiped it on his coat.

'You seem to know your way about these docks, but you do not sound like a native of this city nor of this country.'

'No more I am, sir. I'm from London, but docks is docks and the people who work them is much the same the world over, I reckon. I fitted in comfortable enough when my gentleman settled us here.'

'Your gentleman?'

'Him as I work for, sir, him as brought me across, and him as I'm taking you to.'

'And has this gentleman a name?'

'Everyone has a name, sir, and, in my experience, there's many as has quite a few names. But you'll excuse me if I don't supply my gentleman's to you just yet. If he wants you to have a name then he'll give you one of his own choosing. Now, if you're rested?'

'Yes, quite rested.'

'Good.' The two men resumed their journey, but now at a more leisurely pace. 'Our soldier friends what was so keen to make your acquaintance won't follow, but there'll soon be others out looking, so it's best to get you off these streets as quick as possible.'

'You say your gentleman brought you here from London?'

'I did, sir, and, in saying so, may have said too much, so we'll leave it alone if you please.' And with that they walked on and soon came out of the alley into a street of shabby, ill-repaired dwelling houses and run-down shops, punctuated by two disreputable-looking taverns. The tall-hatted man stopped by a door. 'Here we are, sir.'

He knocked and, after a wait, the door was partially opened. The woman, from what Miranda could see of her, was of grubby aspect and suspicious countenance. She looked at the tall-hatted man and then spoke in rapid French. 'It is you, is it, you pig, you villain, you piece of filthy excrement?'

The tall-hatted man smiled and replied calmly in English. 'Open up, mother, can't you see we've a guest?'

The woman began in French again, so Miranda intervened. 'You do not speak French, my friend?'

'Don't need to, do I, sir? When the likes of her speaks at you like that it don't matter whether she talks, French, Chinese or Hindoo. You can't mistake the meaning, can you?' The woman stood aside muttering as the tall-hatted man pushed the door open and led them across a tiny hallway to a flight of stairs. As soon as they were inside the door slammed shut and the hallway was plunged into darkness. 'Steady as you go, sir, there are stairs here, just feel your way after me.'

Miranda did as he was bid and they left the mutterings of the grubby woman in the darkness. At the top of the stairs a door led them into a large, well-lit, uncarpeted room. In the centre there was a bare pine table at which stood two plain wooden chairs. By the window, which was large and looked out over the street, there was an unmade truckle bed at the foot of which was a substantial traveller's chest. In another corner was another sleeping place consisting just of blankets. There was nothing else except a large, empty fireplace which had obviously not seen a fire in a long time.

A man stood by the window, youngish, well-dressed and handsome. He smiled at Miranda and came forward.

'Welcome, Señor Miranda, I was watching for you and saw you arrive. Allow me to introduce myself, Lord Melford, currently in the service of his Majesty King George. May I say it is a pleasure and an honour to meet you, sir. Your reputation is well known to me as it is, indeed, to many.'

'I thank you, Lord Melford, and I also thank you for arranging my rescue at the wharf.'

Melford waved a hand. 'A mere nothing. But I see that your friend Mr Macleod is not with you.' Lord Melford turned to the tall-hatted man who stood still, his arms straight down at his sides with his tall hat clutched in one hand. His good eye gazed steadily into the middle distance looking at nothing in particular while his other eye roved at will as if looking at everything in great detail. 'What happened?'

'It all went smooth until Mr Macleod knocked me down.'

'Knocked you down?'

'I had to let him, m'lord. You told me no verlance on my part, so I had to take the blow. I tried to explain but he wouldn't let me speak. Short of taking him by the throat to shut him up, there was nothing I could do and, as you'd said no verlance, I was handicapped.'

And he gave the smallest of shrugs as if distancing himself from the wisdom of not allowing this.

'Never mind what I said. What happened?'

'The other gentleman, Mr Macleod, wouldn't come, sir.' The man turned to Miranda. 'Ask this gentleman if it weren't as I say.'

Miranda was happy to back up the account of his tall-hatted saviour.

'It was as he says. My friend Macleod was too sudden with his reactions and, when we saw the soldiers, he refused to come with us so we were forced to leave him.'

'Oh well, I'm sorry about Macleod but I see he has not changed. I remember him as an awkward and a stubborn man who did not always know where his best interests lay.'

'You know him?'

'Slightly. Our paths crossed in Boston some few years ago. I never thought to see him again but it seems Mr Macleod has a way of popping out at you when you least expect it. Oh well, if the soldiers have him, they have him. Please, Señor Miranda, take a seat. We are humbly situated here, as you see, but secure.'

'Tell me, who ordered the soldiers to the wharf?'

'General James Wilkinson. He commands the army here.'

317

'I know of this General Wilkinson. But why would General Wilkinson want me or Jean Macleod?'

'Oh I don't think he wants Macleod. He wanted you.'

'Explain.'

'Of course, but first let me order you some refreshment. Gregory, get us a bottle and two clean glasses and then get that harridan downstairs to make something to eat for Señor Miranda.'

Gregory went and carefully placed his tall hat on the floor beside the truckle bed, opened the chest and pulled out a bottle. He then took two glasses which stood on the window ledge, brought them all to the table then left the room.

Lord Melford pulled the cork from the bottle and poured two glasses.

'Wine, sir, not too good a vintage, I'm afraid, but it's better than spirits and safer than the water.' He raised his glass. 'To you, sir, and your safe arrival.'

Miranda picked up his glass and drank.

'So, Lord Melford, you tell me General Wilkinson wants me, but instead, it seems you have me. That being the case, what is it you intend to do with me?'

'Whatever you want me to. Get you on a boat to wherever you want to go, get you a horse, give you money. I am, sir, entirely at your service as is Gregory who, though unprepossessing to look at, is an invaluable aid.'

'And if I choose to walk out of this place?'

'Anything. Leave if you wish, but I warn you, Wilkinson will have orders out for you. If you appear on the streets you will be taken inside twenty-four hours. He had shifts of four men watching the incoming boats at the docks all round the clock, they were there even at night. That, I think, will give you some idea of how badly he would like to get his hands on you.'

'And you had Gregory watching?'

'Yes, but I had the sense to send two men upriver on horseback to Baton Rouge to look out for you. Once you and Mr and Mrs Macleod arrived there I was informed and made sure I was ready for your arrival. I'm glad Mrs Macleod did not accompany you. That would have complicated things. As it was, one of Wilkinson's men saw your boat coming in and sent off for the soldiers. My man Gregory picked you up before they could arrive, but unfortunately it seems Mr Macleod took things into his own hands and here we are.'

'And where would my friend be?'

'Almost certainly they will take him to the barracks and hold him there. But he can do you no harm. He does not know of my presence here nor has he any information which might lead General Wilkinson to this place. I think we can forget about Mr Macleod.'

'No.'

'No?'

'He has stood by me, so now I must stand by him.'

Lord Melford rubbed his chin thoughtfully. 'Your sentiment does you honour, Señor. But to secure the release of your friend would be well nigh impossible.'

'You would help me in any attempt?'

'I am instructed to be entirely at your service. I do not recommend it, in fact I recommend strongly against it. But, if it is your intention to try and free your friend, then Gregory and I and all the other resources I have gathered round me since my arrival here are at your disposal.'

Miranda thought it over. Brave words were cheap, lies were cheaper still. Before he trusted this man he needed to hear him speak something he could be sure was the truth.

'Why are you here, Lord Melford?'

'I was sent from London by a Mr Jasper Trent who serves in a somewhat –'

'I know Mr Trent. We met more than once when I was in London. Please go on.'

'Mr Trent was concerned that a project in New Spain and the Louisiana Territories, sponsored by Mr Aaron Burr, until lately the Vice President of America, might be in danger of encountering considerable opposition. It is a project that the British Government would like to see succeed, indeed it is dear to their hearts. I was sent by Mr Trent to gather information and render what assistance I could. Our Envoy in Washington told me of your presence there with Mr Macleod and that you had been in discussions, secret discussions, with Secretary of State Madison.' The door opened and Gregory came in with a tray which he brought to the table, set down then stood back and fell into a statue-like trance. 'The woman is unspeakable in many ways but she *can* cook. I hope you enjoy your meal and, if you'll allow me, we'll talk as you eat.' Melford picked up the bottle, refreshed Miranda's glass and continued while Miranda began to eat. 'Merry was aware that you had set off to see a man called Blennerhasset and from that presumed you were involved in Mr Burr's project from the American side. He had been approached by an ex-agent of Mr Trent calling herself Dolly Bawtry who offered her services. Merry gave her money to follow you and prevent you causing any nuisance to Mr Burr. Although this Dolly Bawtry seemed an able and determined woman, I considered that she represented no material threat to a man of your wide experience, so I left the matter as it stood. I knew that, once your business with Mr Blennerhasset was concluded, New Orleans had to be your destination, so I came and established myself and began to collect what information I could. One interesting fact that came my way was that General Wilkinson, for some reason I could not understand nor find out, had set a watch for you at the docks. I made my counter-plans and here you are safe and well.'

Miranda paused in his eating.

'You came to New Orleans because you anticipated that I would come here?'

'I did.'

'You anticipated that I would be in danger?'

Melford saw that Miranda was less than convinced by his story as told so far. 'No. I will be frank with you, Señor. You, though undoubtedly important, were very largely a secondary consideration to my coming here. I came here because Mr Trent wanted confirmation that Mr Aaron Burr's arrangements were all that he claimed them to be, in short that he had a sufficient force to carry out his plan.'

'And have you met with Mr Burr?'

'I have.'

'And no doubt he told you that General Wilkinson was now fully and irrevocably committed to join with him.'

Melford did not try to hide his surprise.

'Ecod, Señor, you're damned well informed. How did you come by that particular piece of information?'

Miranda waved a dismissive fork. 'No matter. I know, it is enough. Where is Mr Burr now?'

'Gone about his business, so I waited here for you.'

'To assist me?'

'In a way, yes. As I said, your coming here was something of a side-issue for me but if you were indeed working in the American interest I wanted to be ready and able to see that you caused no, how shall I put it …?'

'Friction? That I generated no friction in the smooth running of Mr Burr's project which is so dear to the heart of your Government in London?'

'Exactly so. Even though a man of undoubted talent and resource I calculated there was little of real damage you could do, but, as your reputation is well known, I thought it best to be here and ready just in case.'

'And what actually happened was that General Wilkinson made careful plans to take me and my friend as soon as we arrived?'

'Yes, and that disturbed me. Burr's plans do not, as I understand them, conflict with your own ambitions. The British Government, as you well know, looks with favour on the aspiration for freedom for South America which you, and others like you, share. In addition Mr Trent impressed on me that, should our paths cross, you were to be given all possible protection and assistance except, of course, in any attempt to frustrate the Burr project. As I say, I was relieved that Merry had not chosen some more professional assassin to follow you.'

'You seem to have been given conflicting instructions by Mr Trent.'

'Not really. As I said, Mr Burr's preparations are well

321

advanced, indeed almost accomplished. However, as you were working for the American interest and against Mr Burr, General Wilkinson's wanting to take you seemed to bode ill for your safety so I decided to intervene. There, I have laid all my cards on the table before you and I hope you will now regard me as an ally.'

Miranda pushed away his empty plate and finished the wine in his glass. Everything he had heard chimed in with what he himself knew to be true. But he still needed to be cautious. 'If General Wilkinson is holding my friend, could a rescue be at all possible?'

'No, not if he's held in the barracks.'

'I see. You say Burr confirmed to you that General Wilkinson was committed?'

'Totally and irrevocably.'

'And you believed him?'

'I did.'

Miranda made up his mind. He needed to finish what he had come to New Orleans to achieve and be on his way back to New York. The best way to do that, the only way to do that, was to accept this man's help.

'Lord Melford, let me tell you something interesting about this wonderful project so carefully constructed by ex-Vice President Aaron Burr. He has no intention of creating some new country.'

'No? He has convinced me.'

'And it seems he has convinced General Wilkinson. But it is my opinion, and one which I would wish you to convey urgently to Mr Jasper Trent, that Aaron Burr is not interested in acquiring any new country for himself.'

Melford almost allowed himself a small derisive laugh. 'Then what, pray, would you say all the scheming and planning has been for?'

'To make himself President of America.'

Lord Melford now began to laugh, but the laugh didn't fully materialise when he looked at Miranda. 'By God, you're serious.'

'I am.'

And Miranda explained, in almost exactly the same terms as Bentley had used to Jeremiah Jones, what it was that Vice President Aaron Burr was really planning. When he had finished, Lord Melford sat for a moment, then banged the flat of his hand on the table. 'By all that's holy, Señor, if you're correct in this then the man's a damned genius.'

'I am sure I am right. It is the only outcome that makes any sense.'

'And, if he pulls it off, he'll have taken in everybody. He'll use an American army and the Royal Navy to bottle up the Mississippi, and Jefferson and all the rest in Washington will have to drop into his lap within a couple of months. The alternative would be certain financial chaos and a possible war. It's the most wonderful plan I've ever heard. I almost wish he could get away with it, he damn well deserves it.'

'But he cannot be allowed to get away with it, can he, Lord Melford?'

'Oh no, I don't think we could allow that. There'd be too many red faces in London if that happened. There's some very powerful people who've put the full weight of their support behind Burr. If he gets to be President of America and then thumbs his nose at King George, heads will roll.' Lord Melford stood up and went to the window where he stood for a moment looking out. Then he turned. 'You have placed me in something of a dilemma, Señor. If you're right then I must do my best to frustrate Mr Burr. And if you're wrong I must do my best to see that he prospers.'

'Yes, Lord Melford, a pretty dilemma indeed, and no time to consult with either Mr Trent or Ambassador Merry. I do not envy you your task.'

Chapter Fifty-two

James Wilkinson was not a happy man. Neither was Jeremiah Jones. The General turned from the window from where he had been looking down across the barracks parade square.

'Who the hell knew he was coming here?'

Jones avoided a direct answer. 'That will entirely depend on who Miranda himself told.'

'Then who would want to take him when he got here?'

'Shouldn't you know more about that than I, General? I arrived only recently and know the city and its doings hardly at all, whereas you are Governor here.'

But General Wilkinson wasn't going to be criticised by some limp-along messenger boy and turned back towards the window. 'Well whoever's got him is damn well stuck with him. If Miranda tries to slip away he'll be taken. I'll have this whole city stoppered-up tight and have my men beat through the place until they flush him out. Unless he can grow wings and fly away I'll take the bastard yet.'

'Don't you think all that effort may cause some small annoyance to the people of New Orleans?'

Wilkinson turned sharply. 'I'm the law here, Jones, high, middle and low. If I want to bottle up this city then it gets corked. And as for annoyance, I'll order my men to shoot, aye shoot to kill, if anyone tries to interfere with what I've ordered. I'll take our precious Señor Miranda, never fear.'

'I feel sure you will, General, and I will convey to our planter friend that you are making every effort and more to fulfil his request. However, I presume the corking of the city will not be so tightly done as to stop ordinary citizens from going about their legitimate business? I doubt even you can make New Orleans come to a standstill without causing a considerable upheaval, an upheaval which would reach as far as Washington.'

'Make your point.'

'Our friend doesn't want attention drawn to what we are doing. If your efforts in New Orleans are too sudden, too strenuous, too precipitate, questions will undoubtedly be asked and people will be alerted. As a military man, General, with a military man's mind, I assume you fully appreciate the value of surprise when confronting a well-organised enemy. Discretion, as they say, can sometimes be the better part, can it not?'

Jones could see that Wilkinson had taken his point.

'I'll have Miranda's description at every checkpoint and with every patrol. There'll be no need for any upheaval. These things can be managed well enough with the men I have available to me,' and, after a short pause, Wilkinson added grudgingly, 'anyone with good reason to leave will be able to do so.'

'And your beating through the city?'

But Wilkinson had given enough ground. 'What my men do in this city when under my orders is no damn business of anyone but myself. If I have to break down the door of every house then I will.'

Jones saw that his limit for negotiation had been reached.

'Quite. As you say, General, you are the law here and you must do as you see fit. But now, with your permission, I fear I must withdraw and leave your kind but somewhat close hospitality for a time.'

'Must you? Then you'll need a good reason for me to let you go off a-roaming. We may be working in the same cause but keeping you close by me until this thing is done is still my preferred option.'

'For you it may be but alas not for me. Miranda's arrival was known. Well, that by itself could have happened in any one of many ways. But your intention to take him was not only known but known sufficiently well to thwart it. Now I must report that failure and, of course, your future efforts to redress it. To do that safely I need to be where there can be no chance of my words being intercepted. To be frank, I would not feel confident of sending any report from these barracks nor even from New Orleans. My surest course would be to leave the city and send the report by my own choice of safe hand. Would you not agree that would be the sensible course, General?'

Wilkinson considered for a moment. He didn't trust this man, but then again, he would never fully trust any man in a situation such as this. When intrigue was involved a healthy all-embracing mistrust was no more than a necessary first precaution.

'A report must be made I suppose.'

'Indeed it must. Our friend will be anxious for news and, although I must advise him that we have suffered a set-back, I will also assure him it will be rectified very soon.'

'Where will you go?'

'I have not yet decided.'

'I'll see you have an escort.'

'Thank you, General, but wouldn't that rather defeat the object of the exercise? It would enable you to keep an eye on me, to be sure, but it would also draw attention to me. No, no escort. I fear that you must trust me on my own in this matter.'

That General Wilkinson did not trust him and was never likely to trust him was obvious to Jeremiah. But it was also obvious that Wilkinson was faced with the choice of keeping him secure, in which case no report would be sent, or allowing him freedom. He waited.

'Very well. It seems I must trust you, Mr Jones.' The General came to his desk and rang his bell. The door opened and his aide entered. 'Mr Jones will be leaving us. See that a horse is made ready for him.'

'Yes, sir.'

The door closed behind the aide and Wilkinson sat down at his desk.

'Thank you, General, be assured you have made the right decision.'

'Do you think so, Mr Jones? I am not at all so sure. I will

give you twenty-four hours. If you are not back one day after you leave here, I'll send men out to look for you and, believe me they will find you. As for a ship,' Wilkinson gave Jeremiah a nasty smile, 'avoid any of the docks, Mr Jones, it will prove unhealthy for you, perhaps even fatal if you are seen anywhere near them. Now go and make your report and remember, twenty-four hours, not a minute more.'

Chapter Fifty-three

Jeremiah Jones rode out of New Orleans no more than an hour after leaving General Wilkinson and headed up the river trail which ran along the bank of the Mississippi all the way to Baton Rouge. This carriage and cart trail was well-used and kept in good order as it served the plantations along it. At the entrance to each plantation, facing the river but behind well-maintained grounds, stood a substantial house. All were in the same classical style as that favoured by Harman Blennerhasset. These homes spoke eloquently of leisured wealth and Southern gentility and the house at Burrell's plantation was no different, varying, as they all did, only in the smallest details.

Jones rode up the wide drive to find Bentley sitting by himself on the veranda with a tall glass on a table at his side. Bentley stood up and walked to the balustrade as a black-liveried servant hurried out and held Jones's horse as he climbed out of the saddle on to the mounting block by the veranda steps.

'Well, Jeremiah, good news I hope?'

Jones limped onto the veranda and rubbed his weak leg as he replied, 'Odd news, damned suspicious news.'

'Miranda and Macleod not taken?'

'Macleod's been taken all right and is being held in the barracks.'

'And Miranda?'

'Taken, but not by our General.'

'What?'

'Snatched from the dock under the noses of Wilkinson's men.'

'Damn and blast. Who took him?'

'May I sit? I haven't my stick with me and my leg is

328

troublesome.'

Bentley led them to the table where they both sat down. The servant, having tied Jones horse to the hitching rail, came to them.

'A drink for your visitor, sir?'

Bentley, without consulting Jones, waved the man away. 'No, nothing.' The servant left them. 'So who's got Miranda if Wilkinson missed him?'

'Ah, that's what we'd all like to know, not least Wilkinson. But that's not all. When I arrived, Wilkinson was suspicious, as you'd expect. I told him my tale and, though I say so myself, told it well, and he seemed to accept it, and when I explained what Jefferson wanted of him he not only agreed to take Miranda into custody but agreed all too easily.'

'But, if he got Macleod, how the devil did he miss Miranda? Had they parted?'

'Apparently not. Wilkinson told me that Macleod was taken almost as soon as they got off the boat, but Miranda was led away by someone who had been waiting for them.'

'Miranda left Macleod behind? I don't believe it.'

'Nonetheless it's true, unless Wilkinson lied to me, which I doubt.'

Bentley took a drink while Jones looked on enviously. The day was warm and it had been a hot, hurried ride.

'Has Macleod been questioned?'

'Briefly. Wilkinson's letting him stew in a cell for a while to get him in a more co-operative frame of mind.'

'So, what does Wilkinson propose to do?'

'He's getting ready to move heaven and earth. He'll put check points on the roads and send out patrols, then he says he'll send his men to beat through the city and flush Miranda out.' Jones paused, obviously undecided about whether to speak his mind, but Bentley was impatient of his hesitance.

'And? Come on, Jones, spit it out, whatever it is.'

'Well, what I ask myself is, why? Why is General James Wilkinson who, if we are right about him, is about to betray our President in favour of Aaron Burr, making such an almighty effort to do Jefferson this favour? If all goes as Burr has planned Jefferson won't be in a position to do anyone any favours. It makes no sense.'

Bentley stood, and for a couple of minutes he walked up and down the veranda, then came back to Jones and sat down. 'The only answer I can see is that he isn't doing it for Jefferson.'

'But if not Jefferson then who the hell for? Burr certainly doesn't want him.'

'No. But Miranda is wanted nonetheless, and has been wanted rather badly for some time, has he not?'

'By God, of course he has. You think Wilkinson wants to take him and hand him over to the Spanish?'

'It has to be. Who else would want him and, more importantly, pay well for him? The Spanish have been after Miranda for years. They almost took him in London but he slipped through their fingers. They'd pay a handsome price for him, a very handsome price.'

'But, if Wilkinson thinks he's going to get his own kingdom, what in the Devil's name is he doing side-tracking himself in such a way?'

'Money, what else? Understand your man, Jones, always be able to know how he'll jump. Wilkinson would walk ten miles in tight boots to pick up two cents. That's the sort of man he is. He may think that he and Burr are about to gain a country stretching from the Atlantic to the Pacific but, if there's a chance of pocketing Spanish gold, then Wilkinson will grab at it from sheer habit. He wouldn't be able to help himself.'

'But if he succeeds and hands Miranda over to the Spanish, what then?'

'Then we lose the one man who might pull off Smith's Venezuelan project. And worse than that, all Miranda's friends in South America, O'Higgins, Bolívar and the rest of them, will blame us for it and we'll need all the friends we can get in that part of the world with the British about to send a force there.'

Jones added his own thoughts, 'And if Wilkinson intends to give Miranda to the Spanish, rather than hold him as I said Jefferson wanted, it means he is prepared to show his hand against Jefferson to the point where he cannot withdraw.'

'Exactly, so my plan of arriving and using Miranda's arrest to threaten an investigation would be pointless. The only option left to us would be arrest him for treason on the evidence we already hold. That would mean the whole mess spilling out in the courts. If that happens, no one will be able to avoid getting caught up in the consequences.' Bentley looked at Jones in such a way as to make his meaning abundantly clear. 'No one, understand? No matter what their rank or position.' He could see that Jones fully understood. 'And those who allowed the whole stinking business to finish up as public property would be made to pay dearly, very dearly indeed.'

'I see. So now we cannot allow Miranda to be taken by Wilkinson?'

'No, Jones, unfortunately we cannot. But we can still salvage something from this wreck if we're quick, careful and clever. You say Wilkinson's bottling up the city and will send his troops rummaging through the whole place?'

'That's what he said. Kick in doors if necessary. Might that work for us?'

'In the absence of anything else it will have to. If Wilkinson is to set up check points and use his troops in the city as he says, that will allow me to send to Washington and inform them of his extraordinary behaviour in disrupting trade and commerce which can do no other than spread alarm among the populace. Once that message is sent, I can use my own authority to go to New Orleans and confront him.'

'It's slim, is it not?'

'Perhaps, but what else do we have?'

The question required little or no thought. 'Nothing, but that doesn't make me any the more confident.'

'It has some merit. New Orleans is too newly come to us to have some heavy-handed clod of a general boiling up discontent among our new citizens by disrupting the smooth running of their city for some petty end of his own. I'll get a message off to Washington and wait a few days for Wilkinson to get on with his searching. Then I'll arrive.'

'And do what?'

'Whatever I can to discommode our general's search for Miranda.'

Jones could see Bentley was putting a brave face on what might well be a losing hand. But he had no alternative to suggest. 'It will need fine judgement on your part. He already acts like a king in his own domain, maybe because he thinks that soon enough he'll actually be one. What's to stop him simply throwing you in a cell or having you shot?'

'Because, please God, he's not ready yet to take such action against an accredited envoy of the President. I carry a warrant of authority signed by Jefferson himself and Wilkinson's been a senior officer long enough to know what the Contingent Fund is and what it is used for, and he is well aware that I administer those projects which call on the Fund's resources. To do violence to me would be to act directly against the President, for only he can authorise the deployment of the Fund.'

'And if you're wrong? He can't have gone this far without having gained the support of at least some of his senior staff, so perhaps he's gone too far this time to do other than go on.'

'True. But if he's got some of his senior men to join him, he might be persuaded to think of them as so many witnesses against him if he were somehow brought to trial. Maybe I can still make the bastard believe that resigning is a better choice than a rope's end or a firing squad.'

'You're risking a considerable amount on your ability to guess. No less than your life and mine.'

'Perhaps so, but we must play this as the cards have fallen. Our duty is to tidy up all this deceit, treason and villainy even if it is only so that men like Jefferson can write themselves into history. But it damn well sticks in my gullet. Hell's teeth, we're a Union not blessed with so many of the men we need that we can afford to bring down the likes of Burr and let that traitor Wilkinson resign and walk away.'

'But that, God willing, is what we shall do.'

'Yes, that is what we shall do. I'll make sure that Secretary Madison is fully informed so that, whatever happens to us,

332

Burr's plan to take New Orleans and use it should go nowhere. Now, off you go back to Wilkinson and do your damnedest to see Miranda is not taken.'

They stood up.

'And Macleod?'

'God's blood, Jones, I can't give any thought to Macleod. Wilkinson's got him, so Wilkinson can decide what to do with him. Your orders are to stop Wilkinson getting Miranda, that and nothing else. Now go.'

And, once more mounting his horse, Jones was gone.

Chapter Fifty-four

General James Wilkinson proved as good as his word. All roads from the city were guarded and patrols regularly covered the outskirts. No city such as New Orleans can be truly "bottled up", but Wilkinson was an able and experienced soldier and had a substantial army at his disposal which he had deployed to the very best advantage. In this he was assisted by the topography of the city itself which lay between the Mississippi and Lake Pontchartrain. To leave by either would require a boat and experienced boatmen and presented little or no opportunities for any secret escape. Between these waters there were natural levees which were easily guarded and patrolled. For the rest, much of the land was cypress groves barely above the level of the lake and known locally as the "back swamp", a treacherous place even to those familiar with it. A desperate fugitive, hoping for luck to be on his side, might have risked the guards or patrols on safe ground, but it would be a considerable risk and offered only the slimmest of chances of getting through safely. Night would, of course, be the safest time to cross the unguardable swamp, but even with a light the swamp at night could be a death trap. When Jones returned in the fading light of evening he found that, as far as was humanly possible, the city was indeed bottled up as he passed by a guard of four soldiers already checking anyone leaving the city.

Over the next few days groups of armed soldiers moved through those seedier parts of New Orleans where it was most likely that a fugitive might be in hiding. And they found and broke up a great many cheap lodging houses, taverns of low repute, illegal gambling houses, opium dens, bordellos and many establishments near the docks whose trade consisted mainly in finding ingenious or violent ways of parting sailors and rivermen from their hard-earned wages. Not all of these businesses paid good money to be left undisturbed in their various trades, but many did and the owners of these violated establishments complained loudly to the officials whom they had paid. These officials in turn complained to their seniors who had been happy to supplement their salaries with the levy they charged from their juniors. These senior men, through intermediaries, complained loudly to General Wilkinson that the activities of his soldiery were causing great and unnecessary financial hardship and distress. Wilkinson dismissed all such complaints out of hand. If he wanted to ransack New Orleans, then it would be well and truly ransacked.

But, if bordellos and other illegal establishments could be broken up with impunity, the solid citizenry of New Orleans were another matter.

The seamy underbelly of New Orleans, its back alleys and run-down areas, was one natural target of Wilkinson's men. Another was the docks. All ships leaving were thoroughly searched. Cargoes were checked and re-checked and passengers carefully scrutinised. All of which slowed things down to such an extent that the docks, already chaotic, stood in danger of coming to a standstill. Cargoes slowed down in clearance from the wharves blocked cargoes awaiting unloading. Incoming ships were made to wait, forced to ride at anchor awaiting a berth, and laden flatboats tied together awaiting unloading became so congested that those further out in the river were in real danger of breaking loose and being taken downriver to the sea. Those whose businesses were affected, and there were many, became vocal to an extent which could not easily be long ignored, even by Wilkinson.

After four days of furious effort there was no sign of Miranda, and the mounting discontent threw up more than one strange alliance. Brothel owners combined with tobacco exporters at public meetings got up to demand an explanation from the general as to why New Orleans was being subjected to such an onslaught. Owners of opium dens stood shoulder to shoulder with slave importers to demand a cessation to the activities of the soldiery. Sugar cane planters found themselves in alliance with saloon keepers in their protest. Yet still General Wilkinson pressed on with his search and New Orleans remained "bottled up tight".

Throughout all the disturbances of General Wilkinson's search, Lord Melford remained in the room with Miranda, partly in order to keep him company in his enforced idleness, and partly to see that he didn't submit to any urge to go out. Each day Gregory passed through the streets observing the soldiery at their work and mixing with anyone who might have news. He returned on the fifth morning to make his regular report.

'Well, Gregory, what news?'

'They'll flush this street and those around us tomorrow. The docks is still tight as a drum, all highways out of the city well guarded and travellers thoroughly checked.'

Melford turned to Miranda. 'So, no change, and the hounds getting closer, one might say almost upon us.'

'So it seems.'

'It would be better to move you, but I fear I have no safer place to suggest. I must admit I hadn't anticipated such an overwhelming response. It seems, Señor, that General Wilkinson will not rest until he has you. And have you he will unless we can move you to some safer spot.'

'And do you know, sir, why he makes such an extraordinary effort?'

'No, that's the odd thing in all of this. Wilkinson seems set on tearing the place apart and yet no one knows why. There's clamour on all sides for some sort of explanation and I dare say questions may even get asked in Washington. But that will take time, and time is the one thing denied us. We must move you, Señor. The question is how and to where?'

And all three men bent their minds to those vital questions.

In General Wilkinson's office another man was asking another but related question. 'General, you do not know me personally but you know the office I hold and to whom I answer, answer directly and solely.'

'Well then, I know it. But you and your office are nothing to me nor is your visit at this time a welcome one.'

'Perhaps so but it seems a necessary one.'

'How so?'

'I was in Baton Rouge on business and word came to me of your actions here in New Orleans. I must admit that at first I thought the report somewhat wild and overstated. But a further enquiry confirmed that you were carrying out some sort of military action against the populace here. New Orleans and the Louisiana Territories are only recently come into our Union and Secretary of State Madison is most concerned that no disaffection be allowed to rise up among those who live in these new territories, that they see their status as Americans as a blessing. That, in part, was why I was in Baton Rouge. And what do I find? That you are treating the people of New Orleans as if you were some occupying power and they a subject people. I must insist on knowing, General, why you seem hell-bent on bringing New Orleans to a stand-still.'

General Wilkinson looked at Bentley. His office and the papers he had presented gave him full authority to demand the explanation he required.

'And were you sent all the way down here to ask that question, Mr Bentley? It seems a long way to come for so little.'

'No, General, I was sent by Secretary Madison to assess the present condition of the Territories, to report on any possible points of friction. I would have come to New Orleans anyway to examine the warehousing facilities. The Treasury Department wants to further develop sugar cane plantations and molasses production in this region. To do that there has to be adequate transport, processing and warehousing here in New Orleans.'

'Really? You surprise me, Mr Bentley. I wasn't aware that the Administrative Office of the Contingent Fund now also worked for the Secretary of State and the Treasury Department.'

'No more it does. But, if we are to develop the Territories, New Orleans is the key. The availability of facilities here must

337

not cause any friction of interests as it has done in the past, as I'm sure you're well aware.'

'Then I suggest you stick to that business, sir, and let me get on with mine.'

'I fear your business, as you call it, *is* my business. How can I recommend the development of New Orleans facilities if I find them snarled up on no more than some whim and the people treated as if they were an occupied enemy.'

Wilkinson slapped his hand onto the desk. 'Confound you, sir, remember who it is you address. I'm Governor here, military and civil, and I do as I see fit.'

But Bentley remained calm, he even chanced a slight smile. 'Even if it means bringing the city to a halt?'

Wilkinson regretted his outburst. Bully tactics, he had already decided, would not work with this man so his voice became calm and reasonable.

'Mr Bentley, for decades the scum of the earth have been made welcome here, first by the French and then by the Spanish. They've trooped in from all over Europe, settled down and grown fat on every kind of loathsome crime you can imagine. Well, this place, as you have pointed out, is part of America now and I'm charged with seeing that it learns to live by American standards, so by God it'll be cleaned up and made wholesome if I have to break down the door of every vice, rum, and gambling shop and drive the vermin who run those establishments into the Mississippi.' Now he allowed himself a smile. 'Yes, sir, and I'll do it with fixed bayonets and musket fire if need be. There, I hope that's plain enough for you.'

'Plain and laudable, General. But while I can understand your men in every back street and side alley doing as you say, I ask myself why they also work so very hard at the docks.'

Wilkinson had expected the question, but that made it no easier to answer. 'You've heard of contraband I dare say?'

'Aye, General. But I note that your men don't look at what's coming in, only what's going out and, more importantly, who's going out. What exactly is the contraband that you think is being smuggled out of New Orleans, General?'

338

Wilkinson stood up. This man Bentley was too sure of himself and possessed too much authority to be allowed to continue his cross-examination.

'Mr Bentley, as you say, I know of you and your office and out of courtesy I have listened to you and answered your questions. But I am responsible directly to President Jefferson, not to Secretary Madison and certainly not to the Treasury Department, so if you have any concerns about the way I discharge my duties here or anywhere in the Louisiana Territories take it up with the President. Now, sir, my time is precious and I have work to do.' He rang the bell on his desk. 'You will be shown off the barracks and thereafter you may do as you see fit.'

The door opened and an officer stood waiting. Although Bentley was well satisfied with his progress, he decided some sort response to his dismissal would do no harm.

'General Wilkinson. I fear I must protest –'

'Protest all you like, Mr Bentley, but do it in Washington or any other place you choose. If you do not leave now I'll have you thrown into a cell and you can do all the protesting you like there.' General Wilkinson looked at the waiting officer. 'See this man off the barracks.'

Bentley went to the door and quietly allowed himself to be led away. He had done all he could and had not finished up in a cell. It was progress, but only of a sort.

Chapter Fifty-five

Jeremiah Jones was taking lunch in his hotel. There was nothing for him to do until Bentley had confronted Wilkinson. Until that was done all he could do was await developments. And they were not slow in coming. His meal, and that of his fellow diners, was interrupted by the noisy arrival of a sergeant and four armed soldiers who marched through the dining room to Jones's table. It was the sergeant who spoke and his manner was abrupt. 'On your feet, you, and come with us.'

Jones rose slowly. 'Come where?'

'Never mind where.'

'On whose authority?'

The sergeant gripped his arm and pulled him roughly from the table and pushed him at the soldiers who immediately fell into a guard, one at either side and two behind. Jones felt a musket butt pushed into his back and he lurched forward.

'On that authority, so look lively.'

'If I'm to do as you say, at least do me the kindness of handing me my stick.' Jones nodded to his cane which lay resting against the table. 'I'm lame and without it I fear our progress will be slow. These men of yours may even have to assist me.'

The sergeant looked at Jones, then at the stick and finally grabbed up the cane and handed it to him.

'Right, lads, let's have him on his way.'

Jones, now holding his cane, felt the urging of the musket butt again and, to the interest and amazement of his fellow diners, left the room.

General Wilkinson was behind his desk as Jones was brought in. He waved away the sergeant and looked at Jones

340

until the door closed. 'Do you know a man called Bentley?'

'Not personally, but I know there is a Cedric Bentley who runs the Administrative Office of the Contingent Fund.'

'And you know what that Office is?'

'The nearest thing we've got to a secret service?'

'Yes. Well it might interest you to know, Jones, that Cedric Bentley came to see me this morning.'

'Indeed? May I sit, General?'

'No. It's interesting, is it not, that he arrives so soon after you have been away to make your report, your so very private report that could not be safely made here in New Orleans?'

Jones felt distinctly uneasy at the question, and his remark to Bentley about their lives being put at risk came back to him forcefully.

'It's damned suspicious. What reason did he give for coming here?'

'Oh he had some story but, seeing as how the man's a spy, he would have, wouldn't he? Although I must say I found the one he used a little weak. He says he's here for Secretary Madison and the Treasury Department.'

Jones forced conviction into his voice. Bentley's arrival had to be as much an unpleasant surprise to him as it had been to Wilkinson.

'But how could anyone have known so soon what was going on here? My report to Washington went several days ago, as you know, but no one could have been despatched here because of that. There's not been enough time.'

'Well, Bentley's here and making a nuisance of himself and it seems to me that two sudden arrivals, yours and his, can't easily be written off as coincidence.'

'General, I assure you –'

'And I damn your assurances. I don't care who Bentley is. I intend to have Miranda and no one, no one at all will stand in my way.'

Jones felt singularly exposed. He did not have the protection of high office as did Bentley.

'And have him you will, General. It is a thing I wish for as much as you do. But your methods, though thoroughly sound in their own way, do tend to provoke opposition, and my task, if you remember, is to avoid publicity, not create it. We don't want to provide reasons for any more Washington folk to stick their noses into New Orleans business at this particular moment, do we? Bentley is already one too many.'

Wilkinson sat back and folded his hands together and regarded Jones for a moment with what Jones clearly discerned were hostile eyes.

'Well, Mr Jones, you want Miranda taken you say, yet you seem to oppose me in the only way I have of taking him. Why is that, I ask myself? You leave New Orleans and in a matter of days Bentley appears and opposes me alongside you. Again I ask myself why? Do you know, Mr Jones, the only answer seems to be that you and Bentley are in league against me, that this whole business of Miranda is some sort of elaborate ploy. I cannot act directly against Mr Bentley as I might wish, holding the position that he does. But you, Mr Jones are an altogether different matter. You I can deal with as I like.'

Jones felt his poise slipping even further and struggled for words. He had always known that working for the Contingent Fund sometimes entailed the regrettable but necessary premature termination of lives. Indeed, he had participated in more than one such unfortunate event himself. But it was not until now that he had given his fullest consideration to the fact that one day the life terminated might be his own. He gave it consideration now as he was profoundly disturbed, not only by Wilkinson's stare, but by what he had said, which was, after all, no more than the truth.

'Good heavens, General, me in league with Bentley? Why, the idea is – it is –'

'Yes, Mr Jones? You have something to say?'

Jones forced out the first words that came to him. 'Only that while I would not wish in any way to impugn your deductive abilities, all I wished to say is, as we are working together in our search for Miranda,' and, suddenly remembering that Miranda had been accompanied by Macleod, he saw a way

342

forward and forced confidence to return to his speech, 'I think I have a better way to take Miranda.'

'Indeed! A better way?'

'I think so. And even if it is not better it would certainly be more discreet.'

'Go on then.'

'We have the man Macleod.'

'What of him?'

'He and Miranda travelled together. Whatever were Miranda's intentions here in New Orleans, Macleod was obviously part of them. I suggest we use our Mr Macleod as bait.'

'Bait?'

'Put him out somewhere on display. Stop ransacking the city and bring your men back to barracks as if you've given up on whatever it was you were after. Use your troops to make your watch on the docks certain but less obvious. Try to create the impression that all has returned to normal. If Miranda needs Macleod for whatever his purpose is here, once he is out in the open Miranda may well try to contact him and, when he does, you take him'

The hostility had not left Wilkinson's eyes as Jones spoke, but it had diminished. He even managed a small smile of satisfaction. 'It's a thought, Jones.'

'More than just a thought, General. I feel it may work.'

Wilkinson stood up and went to the window and looked down on the barrack square. The parade ground was empty and the stars and stripes hung from the flagpole. The squat, two-storey, stone buildings which housed the troops and their materials were of a military grimness with small windows, those on the ground floor barred. Wilkinson liked this view. His office was in the three-storey administrative block, his window looking down from the top floor. From it he had a good view of everything below. Looking from this window he always felt in control.

He wanted Miranda. But this was not the time to get Washington worked up about anything and sticking their noses in. Burr had told him to be ready soon, no more than two months, three at the most. Was Bentley's arrival at this moment in time a serious complication? Were he and Jones in league? Whatever the answer, Jones was right. Now was not the time to get anyone from Washington looking into the state of things in New Orleans. Jones he could eliminate. Indeed he had already half made up his mind to do so. That had been why he had sent men for him. But now he wasn't so sure if that would be his best course of action. But no matter. He would keep Jones exactly where he could see him and that would suffice for the time being. And he would follow his advice and use this Macleod to try and tempt out Miranda. That would allow him to take his troops off the streets and Bentley would have no reason to prolong his stay. Once Bentley was gone he would be free to resume whatever methods he chose. It was not as he might wish and it left too many questions unanswered, but it would serve for the moment. Of one thing he was certain, he wanted Miranda, and one way or another he would have him.

He turned from the window. 'How could it be done?'

Jones silently uttered a small prayer of thanks.

'Come, General, sit down and I will explain.'

Chapter Fifty-six

Macleod sat on the wooden slats of the cell bed. There was no mattress. His clothes stank, he wasn't at all sure that the wound to his head had healed and was not infected, he was hungry, thirsty and utterly confused. He had awoken on the docks only to be hustled by two soldiers to some sort of barracks where he had been promptly thrown into this cell. That had been some days ago and no one had given him the slightest idea of why he was there or what would happen to him. Food and water had been given him by a soldier, backed up by another one who was armed, both of whom refused him even a single word of communication. The small, barred window was too high to look out from, the stone walls of the cell were damp and the bucket provided for his necessary relief sat almost full by the wall of the cell, forcing itself more each day upon his attention. His situation was, by any standards, dire, yet he could see no way of making any improvement in it.

The key turned in the lock and the door creaked open. Jeremiah Jones entered, the door closed behind him and the key turned once more.

'By God, Macleod, you look a mess.'

'You!'

'Yes, as you say, me.'

Of all the many emotions circulating in Macleod's mind, anger managed to gain the upper hand.

'Damn you, I might have guessed you'd be behind this, you and Bentley, no doubt.'

'Macleod, please keep your voice down. If I am to get you out of this place and restored to some sort of normality it won't do to have anything we say heard outside this cell.'

'The last time we met I had been knocked unconscious by

brigands, was bound and held prisoner. This time I was knocked unconscious by American soldiers and am held in this filthy cell. Tell me, Jones, considering the circumstances of our meetings, why in the name of Hades should I listen to one word you say?'

'Because I didn't have any part in putting you here, but I *can* secure your release if you help me, so for God's sake stop thinking like a block of wood for a moment and try to behave like a rational being. General Wilkinson had men waiting for Miranda, unfortunately all he got was you. How did Miranda give the soldiers the slip?'

Macleod sat trying to think. Jones always sounded plausible. And Bentley, he supposed, still worked for the American Government. As for General Wilkinson, he knew he was a traitor in league with Aaron Burr. So, if Wilkinson knew Miranda had been sent by Secretary Madison he would naturally –

But Macleod's thought processes were too slow for Jones.

'Damn it, man, speak up, or have you gone to sleep?'

'A man met us at the docks as soon as we left our boat. He told us to go with him.'

'And Miranda did?'

'Yes.'

'But you didn't?'

'No.'

'Why not?'

'I suspected him of having friends waiting who would do us harm.'

'So you stood and, by the look of your head, let the soldiers do you harm instead?'

Macleod sullenly touched his head where the blood had congealed. 'I had been approached like that before, in Charleston. There was this man –'

'Stop, Macleod, no more, my brain isn't up to your methods of reasoning. Now listen. You know what General Wilkinson is up to and I am here with Bentley to see that his and Burr's plans come to nothing. We had intended to use Miranda, but missing

346

him at the docks put an end to that.'

'You organised that?'

'In a way. I persuaded General Wilkinson that he should detain Miranda.'

'But –'

Jones held up a hand. 'No, Macleod, no explanations, we haven't the time and you wouldn't understand. Since you were taken things have changed. Now we want to make sure Miranda is *not* taken by the General.'

'Not taken?'

'No. And to do that I will need your help, your willing help.'

Macleod was anything but reassured, but one swift glance at the bucket made his mind up. His first priority was to get out of this cell, get a bath and get a good meal inside him. To achieve those three things he was ready to agree to almost anything Jones might ask of him. 'Very well, Jones. What is it you want me to do?'

Two hours later the two men sat in Jones's rooms in the barracks. Macleod had bathed, shaved and been provided with clean clothes. A doctor had seen to his wounds and he now sat at a table, an empty plate in front of him and a tankard of ale in his hand. For the first time in days he felt human. Jones had sat in silence while Macleod had demolished the hearty meal that had been set before him. Now it was time to explain to Macleod what was required of him.

'Well, Macleod, now that you're back among the living we must get down to business. The General wants Miranda. Bentley wants to prevent that. Bentley has put pressure on Wilkinson to stop him using his soldiers to scour the city but he'll start again soon if he doesn't have any other way. So I've suggested another way.'

'What other way?'

'You.'

'How do you mean, me?'

'We set a trap and use you as the bait.'

'What?'

347

'Think about it, man. You have been at Miranda's side all along. If he hasn't dropped you yet I'm hoping he won't drop you now. I want you to be where Miranda can see you. I want him to see that you are free and in no danger. When he sees that, I think he will make contact with you.'

'And General Wilkinson will take him. Good God, Jones, I may not be the intriguer you and Bentley are but even I can see that me walking around on display would be no more than a trap. And Miranda's an old hand at this sort of thing. He'd never be taken in by it.'

'No, of course not. All we want is for him to make contact. As you say, Miranda's an old hand at this sort of thing so if he makes contact it will be in a way that is secure for him. But once he does make contact, I need you to tell him that I can get him out of this city and away to safety.'

'How?'

'General Wilkinson has the city pretty much sewn up. He'll stop his men breaking down doors but he'll still keep a close watch on the docks and on all other ways of leaving the city. Miranda can try and leave but it would be a risk, a severe risk and he knows it. Bentley, however, is probably the one person who can get round Wilkinson's orders.'

'And he's here in New Orleans?'

'Yes, and he can leave New Orleans on his own authority.'

'Are you sure?'

Jones was anything but sure but he decided not to bother Macleod with any doubts.

'At this point in time Wilkinson will not dare challenge that authority. Bentley can get Miranda out with him if anyone can and, as things stand, Wilkinson will be only too glad to send him on his way. Bentley will find some way to put Miranda alongside him on a boat bound out of here.'

'What way?'

Jones felt his anger rising at Macleod's dogged, lawyer-like question. As a simple matter of cold fact he had no idea what way Bentley might use but as his own life hung on the necessity of Macleod's co-operation he forced himself to remain calm

348

and patient and lied.

'Bentley has a pass signed by President Jefferson and countersigned by Madison. It cannot be challenged. If Miranda meets with him Bentley will take him out of the city and get him safely back to New York.'

After all, it wasn't a complete lie. Bentley *did* have papers of authority and it was quite possible that if Miranda were to place himself in Bentley's hands an escape might be effected. All things were possible and the alternative would be to let Wilkinson carry on, in which case Miranda would almost certainly be taken.

Macleod put down his empty tankard. 'And I'm to tell all of that to Miranda without General Wilkinson's men noticing? Ha! Somebody must have hit you on the head as well, and a damn sight harder than I was.'

Jones brushed aside the objection. 'As you said, Macleod, you're no intriguer, but I am and so is Bentley. Just let Miranda make contact and leave the rest to us.'

'Do I have any choice?'

'Oh yes. You can go back to your cell any time you choose and wait for General Wilkinson to decide what to do with you.'

'Which is no choice at all.'

'It's all there is, Macleod, and I need an answer now.'

'Very well, but remember, this sort of thing is your business, not mine. I'll do as you ask but don't expect me to play the part as you or Bentley might.'

'Just do as I say and all will be well.'

'And if it isn't?'

'Oh, that needn't bother either of us.'

'Why?'

'Because in that case both you and I will be dead.'

Chapter Fifty-seven

Lord Melford sat at the table with Miranda. Gregory was out on the streets trying to find some new safe lodging before the soldiers arrived. But time was running out. Already, only two streets away, the soldiers were searching every establishment and searching thoroughly. When they came, as they soon must, Miranda would be taken but, with the soldiers so close, they also knew that to move in daylight without a safe place to go would be madness, so they waited.

'Tell me, Lord Melford, what do you know of General Wilkinson?'

'A soldier, served with honour in their war. Became aide to General Horatio Gates in '76 and got himself involved in the Conway Cabal to replace Washington with Gates as Commander-in-Chief. Gates kicked him out for his trouble. After that he served himself and left honour for others. Got made Clothier General to the Army but had to resign when he was caught with his fingers in the cash-box. Went into politics, tried to take Kentucky for himself, failed and went back into the army. Somehow, God only knows how, he's always managed to have powerful political friends who have helped him up the ladder or welcomed him back into the fold. Jefferson himself gave him his present post but that hasn't stopped him hooking up with Burr.'

Miranda was impressed. 'You seem well informed.'

'Trent is, not I. When Trent gets involved he's thorough. If you know him at all, you'll know that.'

'Yes, from the acquaintance I had with him in London I got the impression that Mr Trent is nothing if not a thorough man. And would you say he was a good judge of character?'

'As good as any, but character is always a difficult thing to gauge with certainty. And with corkscrews like Wilkinson it's doubly difficult.'

'And your own judgement of the General?'

'Proud, venal, self-serving, and ambitious.'

'And intelligent?'

'Oh yes, clever as be-damned. Keeps on the right side of the right people whatever else he gets up to.'

'Yet what do we find? Here he is, Governor of the Louisiana Territories, General of the New Orleans Army, probably the most senior post a man like him could aspire to, all dropped into his lap by his close friend President Thomas Jefferson. He has achieved all that any man might reasonably want and his prospects are of the brightest, would you not say?'

'Hmm. I see where you're going? Why, with all that to lose, would he risk getting involved with Burr in some treasonous plot that, at best, has a dubious chance of success?'

'Exactly. When Blennerhasset told me of his involvement, my suspicions were at once aroused. Wilkinson is an experienced soldier, not some wealthy fantasist living on a private island dreaming of new kingdoms. He would know, as Aaron Burr does, that if this kingdom they both pretend to desire was taken, it would be threatened by both the Americans and the Spanish and even the British from Canada. How could it be held? It couldn't. And as for using the New Orleans Army, how could he be sure of his officers? And if sure of enough, how could they in turn be sure that the soldiers under them would respond if called on to fire on men who marched under their own American flag?'

'Aye, with British ships at their backs flying the flag of King George?'

'So, Lord Melford, what is it that General Wilkinson is really up to?'

'Not taking a kingdom with Burr?'

'No, I do not think Aaron Burr, for all his undoubted skills of persuasion, ever took in our clever and experienced General Wilkinson.'

Melford stood up and walked up and down the room a

couple of times thinking, then returned to the table and sat down. 'Well I'm damned if I can see it.'

'But it stares you in the face does it not?'

'No, it does not. Spell it out for me.'

'Wilkinson intends to hand Aaron Burr over to Jefferson all neatly tied up in his conspiracy. A present for past and, hopefully, future favours. Wilkinson has too much to lose to be part of any plot and certainly any plot doomed to failure.'

'But Burr believes he'll join him. We spoke at length about Wilkinson and he seemed sure of him.'

'Of course he is. But look at your own assessment so carefully compiled by the thorough Mr Trent. Aide to General Gates and trusted, but Gates was wrong. Given Clothier General to the Army and trusted, but again wrong. Made representative of Kentucky by none other than George Washington himself, but even the wise Mr Washington was wrong. Now given Louisiana by President Jefferson. So, Lord Melford, is it Mr Jefferson who is wrong to trust General Wilkinson or is it Mr Aaron Burr? Which man, do you think, will he betray and which will he faithfully serve? Will it be President Jefferson or ex-Vice President Aaron Burr?'

'Yes, I see. Jefferson is certain, Burr is mere speculation and what sane man bets on a doubt against a certainty?'

'Wilkinson could go along with Burr without any danger to himself because he would have known that Burr only wanted the army here to blockade the Mississippi. The way Burr planned it there would almost certainly be no actual fighting. Your navy ships would anchor here. A show of naval power would be enough. No actual engagement would be necessary if those in Washington were sensible and agreed to Burr's terms.'

'Which they might if the only alternative seemed a small civil war.'

'Perhaps not so small. There are those in the North ready to reject slavery, but the South depends upon it. If a conflict broke out here in New Orleans for any reason at all, it could quickly resolve itself into a full-blown war to decide the slavery issue. It would be North against South.'

Melford saw the force of the argument.

'It's not likely but I give you that it's possible. That particular kettle is simmering nicely already. It would take only a little more to make it boil over.'

'Once Burr was dropped by Jefferson, his fortune was gone and his political career finished. This clever, almost brilliant charade, was the last desperate throw of a desperate man. But Wilkinson is a man of wide experience in intrigue and deceit. He would have seen the flaw as soon as I did. No, as soon as Burr gives Wilkinson the order to begin, Wilkinson will hand him over to the authorities and await the reward of a grateful President.'

Melford thought about it. It made some sort of sense, but the whole damn thing was getting like some Gordian Knot, so confoundedly tangled that he could be sure of none of it. Trust Burr's version? Trust Miranda's version? Wilkinson was self-serving and dishonest and had proved himself inveterately false. But was Miranda any better? He had served half the countries in Europe at one time or another as agent and spy and never stayed loyal to any one of them.

The door burst open and Gregory rushed in. 'They're gone. The soldiers are off the streets and gone back to barracks.'

Melford was so surprised he forgot to remonstrate with Gregory for speaking without removing his tall hat or closing the door. 'Gone? What do you mean gone?'

'What I said, gone off the streets and marched back to barracks.'

Lord Melford looked at Miranda amazed. 'Good God.'

Miranda, although equally surprised was more calm. 'Quite so, Lord Melford, a good and most merciful God indeed, and truly unpredictable.'

Chapter Fifty-eight

Order had been restored, the door was closed and Gregory stood with his arms by his side, his good eye fixed on the middle distance, his roving eye still roving and his tall hat clutched in his hand.

'The soldiers are off the streets but not gone from the docks you say?'

'No, m'lord, the docks is still well picketed. But they're changing how they do it. The uniforms are being pulled off and plain clothes being put in.'

'Are you sure?'

'Quite sure. Soldiers is soldiers whether in uniform or not. Not that you could mistake them for anything else seeing as how none of them's a blackamoor like those as works on the docks here. What anyone can see if they care to look, which most don't, is a powerful number of white men trying to appear inconspicuous while keeping an eye on any passengers going aboard, so I'd say there's still no chance of our Señor slipping out that way.' Gregory turned his good eye on Miranda, 'unless you would consider dressing as a woman, sir?' Miranda gave Gregory a look. Wasted of course, but he gave it. 'No, sir. I thought not. I've heard Spanish gentlemen are a bit touchy in that direction. But I ask you to consider it, sir. If his nibs in the barracks turns out the troops again, you'll be taken. I can't see that there's a safer place for you than we have here and we'd have been done for today for sure if the troops hadn't been pulled off.'

Miranda shook his head.

'No. Out of the question.'

'As you wish, sir. Then I'd say the docks is closed to you.'

'And the roads still well guarded?'

354

'The soldiers who've been pulled off kicking in doors are free to be added to the guards and patrols so I doubt even dressed as a woman that you'd make it. No, sir. We're proper bottled-up now. It was bad before but, by my calculation, even with the bullies off the streets, it's got worse.'

Melford joined in. 'But we're safe here?'

'Safe as long as the soldier-boys don't come back on to the streets. But there's a considerable effort still going into this search, considerable. That General wants you, Señor Miranda, sir, and he means to have you. It's my opinion that he'll give it a few days in this quiet fashion hoping that you might be gulled into thinking it's safer, make a run for it and be taken. If that gets no result, he'll put his bullies and their boots to work again and, when he does, we're crunched.'

Gregory, having pronounced his opinion, held his arms straight at his side, his tall hat in one hand, and stood in silence.

'Well, Miranda, I warned you that staying on to help your friend, Macleod, was unwise. Now it seems your gallantry to a friend will cost you your freedom. Do you have anything to suggest?'

But, before Miranda could reply, Gregory suddenly spoke, 'As to *that* gentleman, Mr Macleod,' both looked at him, 'I've seen him.'

Gregory's simple statement caused both men some astonishment but it was Miranda who spoke first, 'Seen him where?'

'Walking, large as life in the street, sir.'

'Free?'

'Free as air.'

'No guard, no one with him?'

'None as I saw, but that don't signify as I wasn't told to look for him nor follow if I came upon him.'

Melford gave him an angry look. 'Damn you, Gregory, I thought you had some brains. You may not have been instructed ...'

'*Wasn't* instructed, my lord.'

'No, but surely basic common sense would tell you –'

355

'To follow?'

'Yes, dammit.'

'Ah, well, if you're saying that acting by my own judgement, *not* having been instructed, was the right thing to do?'

'Of course you should have used your damn judgement.'

'Then I left Mr Macleod in a tavern not far from the docks. A higher class of drinking house favoured, from what I could see, by merchants and tradesmen in a decent way of business. He ordered ale and I left him sitting on his own.'

'Bravo, Gregory.'

Melford reluctantly added his words to Miranda's, 'Yes, well done, Gregory. He was on his own you say?'

'No company too close. But there was another in the tavern that I recognised. Kept himself out of Mr Macleod's sight but was watching all the same.'

'Another?'

'Gent we came across in Boston, my Lord. Man with a limp, uses a stick. Friend and close companion of another gent we met in Boston, a Mr Bentley, man who visited other people's houses by night with a dark lantern and a pistol if you remember.'

'By God I do.'

'There's more, sir.'

'Go on.'

'All the ways in and out of the tavern were covered, well covered. Not clever men at their work, visible enough to anyone who knew how to look, but plenty to take or follow anyone who might make any contact with Mr Macleod.'

'Lord Melford, I congratulate you on your choice of assistants.' Miranda turned to Gregory. 'Well done, my most excellent friend.

'Thank you, sir.'

'So, Jean Marie has the appearance of a free man.'

'And you think that signifies?'

'Oh yes, Lord Melford, it signifies considerably. General Wilkinson stirs up New Orleans but finds he also stirs up trouble for himself. He decides that for a time a gentler approach is necessary. He has my friend Jean Marie so he decides to use him. He assumes that those who shelter me will be watching the docks, hoping for an opportunity, so he arranges for Macleod to walk near there. He is seen, of course. The question now is, what do we do?'

'A good question, Señor. I hope you have an equally good answer.'

Miranda smiled confidently. 'Yes, Lord Melford, I think I have an excellent answer.'

Chapter Fifty-nine

'I've had a message from the guard room, General. There's a foreign gentleman asking to see you, says he has information as to the whereabouts of the man Miranda.'

'Does he indeed? Bring him up.' The General was sitting at his desk and Jeremiah Jones was standing, leaning on his stick, by the window. 'Well, Jones, perhaps your methods have proved successful.'

'An interesting development, I agree.'

Both men waited in silence until the door opened and the aide re-entered followed by Miranda.

Jeremiah Jones, on seeing him, almost let his stick fall from his hand.

The aide stood to one side. 'Señor Rodríguez , General.'

General Wilkinson nodded to the aide who left the office closing the door.

'Well. You say you have information as to the whereabouts of the man Miranda.'

'I do, sir. In fact I can tell you where he is at this very minute. He is standing in this office addressing General James Wilkinson and one other gentleman whose name he unfortunately does not know.' Miranda gave a small bow. 'Allow me to introduce myself, General. I am Sebastián Francisco de Miranda Rodríguez. I understand from friends that you were looking for me. Naturally, once I was aware of this, I decided to save you any trouble. Tell me, General, what is it you wish to talk to me about?' Miranda's manner of asking, so casual, so friendly, so very unafraid, left the General momentarily speechless and Jeremiah Jones, though thinking hard, found he also had nothing to put into actual words, so Miranda continued. 'Ah, I understand. The matter is confidential. You have a natural delicacy and do not wish to ask your friend here to leave the room. Admirable. However, I think you are correct. Our conversation is, of necessity, of a private nature. If you will permit me.' Miranda turned to Jones. 'My dear sir, please take no offence, but the General and I must speak together and speak alone. Would you do me the infinite courtesy of withdrawing?'

General Wilkinson finally found words. 'Damn you, sir. If you are Miranda I'll have you in a cell this instant.'

'Oh I can assure you, General, that I am who I say I am and it surprises me that that you still doubt it, considering the description which you have so widely circulated. However, no matter, if you will give me a moment of your private time,' and Miranda gave a meaningful look to Jones, 'I will not only prove this to you, but satisfy your undoubted curiosity as to why I am here.' In answer General Wilkinson rang his bell. 'Before your aide takes me away, may I ask if you still correspond regularly with Señor Miró, Señor Esteban Rodríguez Miró?'

The door opened and the aide entered. He stood for a moment but General Wilkinson said nothing.

'You rang, General?'

'I did. Mr Rodríguez here and I have private business to discuss. Most private. Take Mr Jones somewhere and make him comfortable. I'll send for him when I'm ready.' The General turned to Jones. 'I will, of course, keep you fully informed, Mr Jones, of any developments or information which might impinge on our mutual interests.'

Jones paused for a moment but, realising he had no choice, followed the aide who led him from the room. Once the door was closed Miranda, uninvited, sat down.

'Well, General, I think you have made a wise choice.' He pulled a chair closer to the desk. 'I will sit and we will talk. We will not be overheard, I hope?'

'You mentioned a Señor Miró, sir. What do you know of him?'

'Ah, you require assurances that I can back up what I so airily throw out? Very well. The Señor Miró whom I mentioned was Spanish Governor of the Louisiana Territories.'

'Which is well known to everyone.'

'True. What is not so well known is that eight years ago he met with a senior American politician who represented a faction in Kentucky interested in the idea of creating a new republic independent of both the United States of America and Spain. You, General, were that politician were you not?'

'I was, and I have never made any secret of that meeting, but it had nothing to do with any new republic. I negotiated a Kentucky trade monopoly on the Mississippi, no more. If that's all you know of Miró, sir, you know no more than everyone else.'

'But it is not all. I also know that you agreed to promote the Spanish interests.'

'As no more than part of the monopoly agreement.'

'A little more than that, I think. Tell me, General, would you say the number thirteen is a lucky or an unlucky number in your opinion?'

Wilkinson's eyes narrowed slightly and he seemed to stiffen.

'What has that to do with anything?'

'Number thirteen is a Spanish-English cipher. I have been pursued for some time by the Spanish, as you are surely aware. I have a wide knowledge of their codes and ciphers. I have come across this particular cipher very rarely. It is used only for their most secret agents. In fact I know that their most secret agent is code-named for it, agent thirteen.'

Miranda stopped and the two men looked at each other in silence. Finally Wilkinson spoke 'If this agent is an American, it is your duty to inform the United States Government of all you know.'

'My duty, General, is to my cause, South American liberty, nothing else. I have no wish to reveal what I know to anyone unless it furthers my cause. Will you, as Governor of Louisiana and Commander of the United States Army here force from me what I know?'

'You are a foreign national, sir, who has to my knowledge committed no crime or violation of American laws. As things stand I have no sound reason for taking you into custody. But that is only as things stand now. They may change.'

'Good. We understand each other, I think, so let us begin. I know exactly why you want me, General. You would like to hand me to the Spanish.' Miranda made a dismissive gesture. 'Well, that is of no matter. The Spanish want me. I am a thorn in their side. I seek liberty for my country.'

'Leave the speeches for another time, Miranda. Why have you come here?'

'To save you.'

'Save me? And who are you saving me from?'

'Yourself. You are playing games, but they are dangerous games and the time has come to put an end to them. You pretend to Aaron Burr that you will support him. But you will not. You are a soldier and have not been taken in by his fantasy of a new kingdom. You give him rope, yes? You give him rope to hang himself and you will be the hangman. You wait until he is compromised beyond any shadow of a doubt and then you will hand him over to your good and close friend, President Thomas Jefferson. Very well, why not? But others are aware of Aaron Burr's plan, others give him rope. But they do not intend to hang him. They wait, and for whom do they wait? You. Mr Aaron Burr holds in his head too many secrets, too many things which, if he spoke them in open court, would do great harm to some great men. Who can tell? They might even bring down these great men and leave them in the dust. This cannot be allowed to happen of course, so some way must be found to stop Aaron Burr, but without putting him in the dock. The way is to put you in the dock instead, General. Plans are already laid to ensure that it is you who will become the arch plotter. You will be cast as the villain who ensnared Aaron Burr. You will be the traitor and Burr will become your dupe.'

Miranda waited. What he was saying was so close to the truth that it might well have been the whole truth and nothing but the truth.

'You're lying.'

'No, and you know that I am not. Why did you try to arrest

361

me? You were asked, were you not? What story were you told? No matter, whatever you were told was no more than a story. When you arrested me, the fuse would have been lit. I came here at the personal request of Secretary of State James Madison. To arrest me would have given your enemies in Washington the opportunity to ask questions, to mount an enquiry. What would be the outcome? The plot, that most treasonous plot would have been discovered.' Miranda assumed a look of mock horror. 'Madre de Dios! Treason. Treachery most foul, and from one so high, so trusted and so heaped with honours. Horror upon horror.' The look of mock horror dropped away. 'You are already caught, my friend, the net is already around you. As for me? Give me to the Spanish if you wish. It will be but one more knot in the noose that is already about your neck. To die in shame for a treason that was not of your own making would be a tragedy. But you and I know, do we not, that in reality it would be not be tragedy, but farce? Treason there is already and treachery enough to your name, but not with Aaron Burr.' Miranda stood. 'Now, General, I have said my say. Do with me as you wish. Throw me into a cell and then hand me over to Señor Rodríguez Miró, with whom I know you are still very much in contact, or let me go and I will return at once to New York where I have urgent business. I find that there is nothing here that either interests or concerns me. You, Aaron Burr, Secretary Madison and President Jefferson may all go your own merry ways to hell or heaven as you wish. Come, General, a decision if you please.'

But General Wilkinson said and did nothing. He was thinking hard. Suddenly things made more sense. That he was being ensnared to save Burr explained Bentley's involvement, and Bentley's arrival was obviously timed so that he could find some excuse to institute an enquiry, the outcome of which had already been decided. No doubt the taking of Miranda was to have been that excuse which in turn made the connection between Jones and Bentley. Unfortunately he had made their job easier by using his troops to find Miranda. He almost smiled with admiration. It was a neat piece of work.

'Señor Miranda, you are, from all I've heard, an old hand at treachery and deceit. I know from personal experience that you are a capable and resourceful man. From your action in coming here I see that you are a man confident in his own abilities. Very well, I salute all those accomplishments. But I am not without my own accomplishments. For instance I know the value of words, and that value is nil if not backed up by something that can be tested as hard fact. I have your words, and fine words they are. But can you now back them up with any facts?'

Miranda put his hand inside his coat, pulled out a letter and threw it on the table.

'Read that, General. Its twin is now in the hands of the man who took me from the dock under the nose of your soldiers. He will copy it and will see that it is in the hands of ten more men, all men of power and influence, within the week. Read the letter, General, it is a concise but complete account of your relationship with Governor Esteban Rodríguez Miró and through him, the Spanish government. You will know better than I how long it would take to confirm beyond any shadow of a doubt the truth of what it claims.'

General Wilkinson read the letter. It was indeed concise, complete and, sadly, all too true. 'You were able to stop me leaving New Orleans because you had my name and my description,' Miranda continued, 'could you stop my friend? You do not have his name nor his description. And if you wrung them from me, how would you know that it was he and not some assistant who carried the letter or how many copies were carried? No, General, if there is any truth at all in that letter, and I think it all true, you must leave me to go about my work. Come, General, enough of these games. A decision. A cell or freedom.'

Chapter Sixty

Macleod, in well-cut clothes, his head tidied up and a fashionable hat on the bed beside him, sat once more in the same cell. The only difference being that the bucket in the corner was empty. He had done what had been asked of him, he had paraded himself by the docks. He had sat in a busy tavern and drunk ale. And he had waited. All exactly as he had been told to do by Jones. And it had, exactly as he had anticipated, produced no results. Nor was it, in his opinion, ever likely to. That being so, he fully anticipated that before many more days he would renew a more permanent association with his cell and the bucket would begin to refill.

His thoughts were interrupted by the key turning in the lock. The door swung open. It was Miranda.

'Ah, my old friend, how surprised you look. Are you not glad to see me?'

Macleod stood up from the slats of the bed. 'Great heavens. They've taken you, have they? Are you to be thrown in here with me?'

'No, no. I am no prisoner and no longer are you. Come, take up your hat and let us be on our way.'

'On our way? You mean, walk out of here?'

'What else? We are free men. We can walk wherever we choose in this great, free country, can we not? Come, Jean, let us be gone.'

Macleod picked up his hat and followed Miranda from the cell. The soldier on guard waited until they were both out then closed the door and left them.

Miranda walked in the opposite direction to the soldier and Macleod quickly followed. Neither spoke as they walked through the corridors, left the cell block and crossed the parade square. Miranda didn't look up, he didn't need to. He knew General Wilkinson would be watching from his window.

Once across the square they arrived at the guard house which stood inside one of the two massive towers that guarded the main gates of the barracks. Here they were waved through a small open doorway set into the great wooden gates by the General's aide who was waiting for them. The door was pulled closed behind them and a few steps took them into the street where life was going on as normal. The two armed sentries, one on either side of the main gates, ignored them and looked straight ahead at nothing in particular. The pedestrians who passed them as they stood also ignored them. They were of no interest whatever to anyone at all.

Macleod put on his hat and looked around him. 'Is that it? Are we indeed free?'

'Free and finished with all this sorry business. Tomorrow I arrange for you and I to go to Baton Rouge to collect your wife, then we head back to New York. Me to take up again my great task, you and Marie to go home to Boston and resume your lives together. Come, we must find accommodation for the night.'

'But how did you do it? I thought General Wilkinson wanted you? Jones told me only Bentley could get you out.'

'No, no, my friend. Forget General Wilkinson, forget Mr Jones and Mr Bentley. Forget Aaron Burr and Blennerhasset. Forget them all. Look,' and Miranda held up his hand with the palm upwards and blew on it, 'poof, they are gone. Just like that. For you they never existed, they were a dream, a nasty dream, but now you are awake.'

'I wish it was so easy. Much as I would love to forget the whole damn shameful, shabby business, I can't, can I?'

'But why not?'

'Because I was part of it, I'm still part of it.'

'No, there you are wrong. For you and your wife it is over, believe me. Come, we will find lodgings, arrange for horses to be made ready for the morning, then we will eat.'

They walked on in silence for a while and Macleod tried to

365

think things through. He failed. 'Look here, Miranda, I don't understand. One minute all hell is breaking loose and they're trying to find you. Next minute you stroll into my cell and we walk out as free as air. It can't be as simple as that. It can't just end because you say so.'

'Why not? You were put by my side by Bentley to spy and report on me. You told me so yourself.'

'Yes, but I explained that. I had no choice. He had a warrant with mine and Marie's name on it.'

'I know, I know. I kept you by me because I could trust you. And I was right to trust you. In all of this shameful, shabby business, as you rightly call it, which has been nothing but lies, deceit and treachery, only you have been loyal and honest. In all this baseness only you have been pure. I now know what all the plotting has been about and I know that it is of no consequence. It has no bearing on my great cause. It is children playing games for which they will be scolded when they are discovered. But to confirm what I already suspected I needed you by my side and you were there for me through all of it. That is why I could not leave you here. That is why I brought you out of your slavery and why I am sending you out of Egypt and back to Boston, your Promised Land.' Miranda laughed at his own little joke.

'But how did you do it?'

'I gave my word.'

'Just that?'

Miranda gave Macleod a sad look. 'Ah, do you lump me with all this other trash? Do you think my word has no value? You wound me, old friend.'

'No, no, of course not. You would no more break your word than, than –'

Miranda laughed. 'Than you would, Jean. I bought your freedom with my word to a man who, though a general in your Union Army, is a cheap, treacherous, nobody of a man. I swore to him that I would keep his loathsome little secret.'

'And he believed you?'

'He had no choice. If there was any way he could have

silenced me, any way at all, he would have taken it. But, thank God, he had no way, so he took the honourable course and accepted my word and gave his that you would be free. And he was right to take my word, Jean. I *will* keep his secret.'

'Of course, you gave your word.'

'True, because I gave my word.' He paused then leaned his head slightly to Macleod, lowered his voice and spoke in a conspiratorial manner. 'But also because it may come in very useful on another day.'

Then he burst out laughing and, to his surprise and without quite knowing why, Macleod found himself joining in.

In the barracks which Miranda and Macleod had just left General Wilkinson finally left the window. He had watched Miranda and Macleod leave the cell block, walk across the parade ground and enter the guard house. He had stood for many minutes wondering if there was anything further he could do either to make sure he was not made the scapegoat for Burr's plotting or somehow still take Miranda. Unfortunately he decided that, in both cases, all that could be done was done. Except perhaps one thing. He went back to his desk and rang his bell. His aide entered.

'Get Jones in here.'

'Yes, General.'

A few moments later Jeremiah Jones limped in. Miranda was gone and Jones saw at once that Wilkinson was in a foul mood. 'Where is he, in a cell?'

Wilkinson's tone was icy. 'No, no cell. He is gone, free as a bird.'

'I see.'

'Do you, Mr Jones? Do you indeed?'

'What I mean, General –'

'And I don't give a damn in hell what you mean. Get out, Jones. Get out of my sight and go running back to Bentley and, when you get there, tell him his little game is finished and done, and that if you aren't both out of New Orleans by tomorrow by God I swear I'll have you both shot and the Devil can take care of the consequences. Now get out as fast as that crippled leg of yours will carry you.'

Jones had not the slightest doubt that the threat was not an idle one. Something cataclysmic had happened, what it was he could not even make a guess at, but it was abundantly clear that Wilkinson knew him to be working with Bentley and somehow Bentley's plans had been discovered, but, he decided, this was no time to ask questions. He was grateful that he was being allowed to leave upright instead of in a pine box. He limped past the aide and left to do exactly what he had been told to do, run straight back to Bentley as fast as his crippled leg would carry him.

The aide waited by the door.

'Is there anything else, General?'

'Yes there is. Cancel all check points and patrols and have all men withdrawn from the docks. They are no longer needed. And when you've issued that order choose two good men to accompany you.'

'Accompany me where, General?'

'I will be sending a message direct to President Jefferson. It will be for his eyes only marked most secret and most urgent. You're to take ship to Washington and all three of you will go armed. Now do as I say and then come back here and wait until I ring.'

The aide left and General Wilkinson picked up his quill and began carefully to compose his impeachment for treason of ex-Vice President Aaron Burr.

Chapter Sixty-one

Not much more than a few hours after leaving the barracks, Jones arrived at Burrell's plantation and made his report.

'When I was brought back to his office Miranda was gone and Wilkinson was in a murderous mood. He threw me out and not only that, he told me to come running back to you.'

'Me?'

'Back to Bentley as fast as that crippled leg will carry you. His very words. He knew we were working together and he told me to tell you your little game was finished and done. Somehow Miranda has sunk us, but God knows how.'

'And what about Miranda?'

'Gone, Wilkinson let him walk away, free as you like. I asked at the guard-house as I left. They'd seen me come and go and knew I visited the General. They couldn't yet have known I'd been declared *persona non grata*, so they told me that Miranda had left accompanied by another man name of Macleod, both of them free as you like and flown away to God knows where.'

'Anything else?'

'Oh yes.'

'What?'

'Wilkinson said that if we hung about in New Orleans he'd have us both shot and damn the consequences and I think he actually meant it, such was the mood Miranda had put him in. God knows what he said or did but it must have been something pretty spectacular. Wilkinson's not the sort to be rattled by threats even from a man like Miranda. I'd dearly have loved to get even an inkling of what went on but it was hopeless to try and speak with him any more, so I left and came here.'

'Well, however Miranda's done it, it's done and we must

make the best of it.'

'What do you think will happen now?'

'Oh that much is clear. Burr's plot is somehow blown wide open. Wilkinson will save himself by denouncing Burr to Jefferson.'

'And Miranda?'

'All he'll want to do will be to get back to New York and his Venezuelan project. I doubt if he'll even bother to go back to Washington to report to Madison. Jefferson will do all the reporting that will be necessary as soon as he receives Wilkinson's dispatch charging Burr with treason.'

'And Blennerhasset?'

'What can he say? If he says anything at all, he involves himself in a treason trial. No, Blennerhasset will be no problem.'

'So what do we do?'

'If I know Jefferson, when he receives Wilkinson's denouncement of Burr, he'll sit on it. The last thing he wants is to be dragged into the courts, so he'll be in no hurry to get any arrest warrant issued. He's set his sights on being remembered as the great statesman but, if he gets dragged into this mess and faces a lawyer in court briefed by Burr, he'll be damned lucky to walk away only looking like a bungling ninny. Burr was his choice as Vice President, Wilkinson was his personal choice to be Governor of Louisiana and Army chief at the same time even though that appointment was not without considerable opposition. That's all bad enough, especially considering Wilkinson's past record, but God knows what else Burr has tucked away that he could bring out and use. No, Jefferson will play for time and he will expect us to use that time well. Our job now will be to muddy the waters and confuse the issues, to make sure that any evidence that might come to light will prove at best to be inconclusive. Most important of all we must make sure that General Wilkinson can do no real harm to Jefferson in the evidence he might give personally. In fact we must try and ensure that whatever he says in court will tell against him rather than the President or even Burr.'

370

'And how would we do that?'

'That's tomorrow's problem. Today's is to make sure that if Burr *is* charged with treason, he can go into court and be pretty certain of an acquittal. If he can be sure of that then we can bargain with him and maybe keep the whole thing so confused and unsatisfactory that it goes nowhere and, please God, will be soon forgotten.'

'So where do we begin?'

'That much at least is clear. There's only one truly weak link in all this. Macleod.'

'Macleod?'

'He knows it all and, damn him, he's not a politician nor a schemer but a loyal and honest American. If he decides to say anything, he'll tell the truth, and not only the truth but the whole truth and nothing but the truth. Wilkinson I'm sure I can control. He's as crooked as a spiral staircase and now he'll be worried. He's had his hand forced by Miranda somehow and he'll be quick to save his own skin. But he knows he's vulnerable. He has too many enemies and too much in his past that could easily come back and bite him.'

'And Burr?'

'Burr should be no problem. He'll know he's beaten and he'll take the defeat like the soldier he was. He'll parley and make terms. He'll not harm America if he isn't forced to, so we won't force him. I can even persuade Jefferson to be accommodating. It's him, after all, that we'll be doing it all for. I'll make sure that everything from now on goes in slow motion and gives us time to do whatever is necessary. But Macleod, he's our one loose cannon. There's no telling where he might go with his story if he's allowed to brood on it. You say he left the barracks with Miranda?'

'Yes, but I have no idea where they went and I can hardly return to New Orleans and start snooping about looking for them. Wilkinson made that much quite clear.'

'That's no problem. He never wanted to be in this in the first place and now I rather wish I'd listened to him. He's a homing bird but, before he can fly away back to Boston, he has a collection to make. If we're quick I think I know exactly where I can lay my hands on our Lawyer Macleod. Come, Jones, we must travel. We must be ready to meet with Lawyer Macleod and see to it that he fulfils his duty to the President as we must fulfil ours.'

Chapter Sixty-two

Miranda and Macleod had taken a room at a rather grand hotel in the Vieux Carré or French Quarter. Miranda had chosen it because, even though they would only be there for one night, he intended to eat well and sleep at last in a soft bed. And he was proved wise in his choice, for their evening meal was nothing less than sumptuous. Miranda insisted on starting with oysters and champagne, "to the memory of our meeting in New York". Macleod agreed but was careful that this time he treated the wine with the respect and caution it deserved. There followed boiled crawfish and other dishes which, though distinctive in flavour and delicious, Macleod had never tasted before. Their room was well-furnished and the beds comfortable enough to satisfy even the most fastidious, and both slept soundly, partly because their travails were finally over, partly because they had eaten well and partly because they had both celebrated their freedom with perhaps a little more wine than was strictly judicious.

The following morning, neither having any great appetite, they breakfasted lightly on chicory-flavoured coffee accompanied by deep-fried French choux pastries, known as beignets.

'Tell me, Miranda, who was it who sent that man to the docks to save us from the soldiers?'

'Do you want to know?'

Macleod thought about it. 'No, you're right, I don't. I don't want any more to do with all of this damnable business.' Macleod paused. There was something he wanted to say, but hesitated to say it. 'You know, Miranda, this whole thing started because I doubted Marie.'

'What? Doubted she was faithful to you?'

'Good God, no, not that. I doubted she was happy, I thought she had become bored with me. I'm not exactly a dashing fellow, and I'm not young.'

'But, my friend, what foolishness. Doubt the sun will rise, doubt the grass will grow, doubt whatever you like but never doubt Marie loves you with all her heart.'

'Oh I know that now. But I didn't then. You see, we have no child and a woman ought to, well, a woman needs ...'

But the words failed him as the doubts about his own manhood returned. Miranda reached across the table and held his arm.

'A child will come if it is God's will. But, child or no, Marie loves you and will always love you. Let that be enough and rejoice in what you have and do not let yourself dwell on what you have not.'

'Yes, of course you're right and I know it. We have each other and, for any sane man, Marie should be enough.'

'And you, Jean, in a mad world, are most pre-eminently a sane man. Go back to Boston and be happy yourself by making your lovely wife happy.'

'Yes. All I want now is to go and get Marie and then head on back to Boston and make up for my stupidity. But you know, Miranda, we seem to have been involved in this madness for so long that I still find it difficult to think of it as all over.'

'That is because it is not all over.'

'But you said it was.'

'And for you it is, but simply because you are free of it, it does not end. Others go on. I go on because I must free my country. Your Mr Bentley will go on because he must serve America by doing all the many unpleasant things with which politicians choose not to dirty their own hands. Aaron Burr will go on doing whatever he can to return to power and prominence. Our friend Harmon Blennerhasset will go on dreaming. General Wilkinson will go on scheming. Oh yes, my friend, it will all go on. But it will go on without you and Madame Macleod, that is all. You will be part of the great, everyday public who are never to know what is done in their

374

name by the agents of their oh so respectable governments. It is a secret world with secret servitors like Bentley and, yes, like me. Now, my friend, we are rested and resourced for our journey. I have arranged horses and enquired of the route. I am assured that there is a good river road, well marked and well supplied with places to rest and refresh oneself.'

'How far is it to Baton Rouge?'

'About eighty miles. With good horses we should make forty miles a day comfortably. In two days, three at the very most, you will be reunited with your lovely wife. Then we will all return to New Orleans.'

The idea of returning alarmed Macleod who thought himself well-rid of the place. 'Back here?'

'Why not? We are not pursued, we are not fugitives. No one is interested in us any more. We are travellers on our way to New York, nothing more. General Wilkinson will have dismantled all his oh so strenuous efforts to take me. Why not? He is no longer looking for anyone. We will pass in complete safety, believe me. From New Orleans we will take ship north and after a restful sea journey we will arrive safe and sound. Once there we will make our farewells and you and your wife will return to Boston. You see, I have mapped out your future for you. Is it not as you would wish it?'

'Very much so. I only hope it all turns out as you say it will.'

'Have I been wrong yet? Have I yet failed you?'

'Well, no. No, I suppose not.'

'Then trust me. It will all be as I say. Come now. We must go and collect our horses and be on our way.'

Miranda paid the hotel bill and went to the stables where the horses were waiting and ready. There they took directions from the stableman, mounted, walked their horses out of the cobbled hotel yard into the dust of the busy street and set off for the river and the river road.

Back at the stables a man had walked in and began talking to the ostler who had dealt with them, a man in a tall hat with a roving eye. Money changed hands and the man in the tall hat left at a brisk walk.

'They're taking the river road, me lord. They're off to Baton Rouge.'

'Yes, there is still Madame Macleod to collect.' Gregory nodded. 'Well, all is finished for us here in New Orleans so we can take our leave of this interesting city.'

'I doubt Mr Trent will be overjoyed at what we'll be telling him when we get back to London, me Lord.'

'Do you think so, Gregory? Not happy with what we have to report?'

'Well, sir, we haven't exactly covered ourselves with glory, have we?'

'No. But that was not the aim of our mission. Our mission was to find out if Mr Burr was a sound proposition and advance the British position in South America through giving whatever assistance we could to Señor Miranda.'

'And have we done that?'

'We have had some small part in doing that.'

'How's that, sir?'

'Señor Miranda leaves New Orleans free and in safety, helped by ourselves who act for King George. We have selflessly served him, unlike the Americans who tried to use him. We have saved him from Wilkinson who would have taken him and handed him over to the Spanish. Miranda will not forget and, what's more, he will persuade others where their best interests lie. When freedom comes to South America, as it must, then Miranda, Bolívar, O'Higgins and all the other liberators will look on our American cousins with doubt and suspicion as at best a devious and unreliable ally and at worst an aggressive and expansionist neighbour who covets their land. And as for Mr Aaron Burr, we find that he is not all he presented himself to be, and His Majesty's Government will not, after all, be able to support whatever ambitions he entertains.'

'And did we do all that, sir?'

'No, Gregory. Mr Trent did most of it. He sees the whole board.'

'Board?'

'Chess board. That's how he looks at it. As a great game played between secret armies and fought by invisible soldiers. We were involved in a small skirmish with the Americans, a few pawns moved hither and thither, but we won. That is what we did, Gregory, that and nothing more.'

'So now we go back to London?'

'Almost, Gregory, but not quite. Just one more small task remains to us. Señor Miranda does not like loose ends. He wants us to make sure that this small skirmish will end neatly with all the pawns accounted for and dealt with. You've arranged horses?'

'Ready and waiting, m'lord.'

'Weapons?'

'All ready in the saddle bags.'

'Then let us be on our way, Gregory, and complete this last move of our game.'

Chapter Sixty-three

The river road passed by many plantations which were similar to that of Bentley's accommodating friend, Burrell. Over its whole length it was a well-used social and commercial highway, running alongside that other great highway, the Mississippi. Macleod had taken no real notice of the view when travelling downriver in their flat-bottomed boat but now, riding alongside the plantations, he could not but admire the owners' great white houses built in the classical Greek style with massive colonnades and wide front porches redolent of wealth, ease and culture. Macleod was impressed.

'They're damn fine, these planters' houses.'

Miranda answered abstractedly, 'Yes, I suppose so.'

'They're a marvel of beauty and magnificence, but all built on slavery.'

Miranda made an obvious effort to enter into conversation as Macleod seemed to wish it. 'You object?'

'Slavery never bothered me much in Boston. It was a political topic talked about at the Gallows Tree Club, but politics was not something I took any interest in. But here, once you see it up close, men, women, and children owned and worked like cattle, well, it sort of forces its attention on you.'

'And you find yourself in opposition?'

'Slavery's done with and finished in the North, but here in the South I don't see how they can go on without it. To my way of thinking, you can't have a united country if one half has something as illegal that the other half has as a way of life. Either we make it legal or illegal and make that the law for the whole nation. Anything else simply won't work.'

'But if your country were to choose to make slavery legal, would you be against it?'

378

'No, I'm not saying that. I don't see how the South could function if you took away their slaves. I'm against having a situation that can't continue. It needs resolving.'

But Miranda seemed to tire of the topic. 'Well, no doubt it will be resolved, and I hope it will be done peacefully.'

Macleod pressed on. 'Of course it will. This is America. We'll not go the European way and tear each other apart.'

However, Miranda cared no more for the topic of the American Way than he did for slavery, so Macleod gave up and the two men rode on in silence, each busy with their own thoughts.

Macleod was puzzled. Usually Miranda liked to talk yet, almost as soon as they had left the outskirts of New Orleans, he had become silent. In fact he seemed to become preoccupied and Macleod had noticed another thing, Miranda seemed to cast about on occasion, as if looking for something or someone.

'Is all well, Miranda?'

Miranda turned and gave Macleod a smile. 'How could it be otherwise, we are going to see your beautiful wife and reunite two loving hearts.' He drove his spurs into his horse. 'Come, let us gallop for a while, this journey is becoming tedious.'

Galloping made further conversation impossible, but Miranda kept it up until they came to a wooded area which went back from the road for some way. Here Miranda finally slowed his horse to a trot and then stopped.

'We must halt, Jean, I have been in the saddle for far too long, my backside aches and also I need to relieve myself.'

Macleod was surprised at this sudden halt. 'Come, Miranda, this whole road is well provided. Why stop in this lonely spot?'

'My friend I cannot go on. I must stop and ease my poor buttocks. Also I must give some consideration to my bladder. I am not as young as I was.'

Macleod reined in his horse. 'Very well. Get down and do what you must. Here, hand me the reins and I'll hold your mount.'

'No, let us both dismount and tie up the horses.' Without waiting for a reply Miranda dismounted and led his horse off the road on to the grass by the edge of the trees. He tied his horse on a long rein and it immediately lowered its head and began to graze. Miranda turned back to Macleod who sat on his horse watching. 'Come, Jean, a few minutes rest and then we will go on and find lodgings. We have made excellent time and we need not hurry. Come.' Reluctantly Macleod dismounted, led his horse on to the grass, tied it on a loose rein where it at once imitated its fellow and began to graze. 'You know, Jean, things do not always turn out as we might wish. We plan, we dream, but alas sometimes our plans and our dreams go awry.'

'I know. I didn't intend to get involved in any of this. I only went to New York to consult a medical friend. But then we met and my life changed. Fate, destiny, luck, call it what you will. But now I intend to get things back to where they were.' Suddenly Macleod realised that they were standing talking. Why were they standing talking? 'I thought you wanted to relieve yourself?'

'Ah, yes. Strange, the feeling has passed.'

'Then for God's sake let's get on.' Macleod moved to untie his horse.

'No, Jean. I regret we cannot as yet continue our journey. We must wait here.'

'Why?'

'I fear I have not been entirely frank with you. There is still some unfinished business.'

'What unfinished business?'

'You.'

'Me?'

'Yes. As you said yourself, you never wanted to be any part of this, but you were nevertheless drawn in and, once in, it is not always possible to be allowed to walk away. You know too much. You are a part of this side-show, this farce, this ridiculous comedy dreamed up by Aaron Burr which, even though it is ridiculous, is still dangerous. Powerful people have become involved, reputations and careers have been threatened. I cannot help that. It is the way of these things. Honour, friendship and loyalty become too expensive. Necessity drives

380

all.'

'What the hell are you rambling about, Miranda? You make no sense and you're wasting time.'

'Yes, wasting time. Waiting for ...' he turned on hearing a movement among the trees, 'ah, the wait is over, those who have followed us have at last arrived.'

Two men walked out from the trees, Bentley and Jeremiah Jones. Macleod looked at them.

'Bentley, Jones? What the hell are you two doing here?'

Bentley pulled back his cloak and raised a cocked pistol. 'Sorry, Macleod but I'm afraid it's necessary.'

A shot rang out and Bentley pitched forward dropping the weapon as he fell. Macleod looked down at the body.

'My God, what's happened?'

Lord Melford stepped from the trees, his pistol still raised and smoking.

'Damn close thing, too damn close but all's well that ends –'

Suddenly Jones pulled at the end of his stick, stepped forward and thrust the short stick-dagger he'd drawn into Macleod's chest. Macleod, a look of bewilderment on his face, held his hand to the dagger handle sticking from his chest.

'I don't understand –'

But the words died away. Macleod looked down at the blood running through his fingers and gently, almost with grace, fell onto the grass.

For a second no one moved, then Jones stooped down and picked up Bentley's loaded pistol and pointed it at Miranda. Gregory came out of the trees and looked at the bodies. Melford looked angrily at him.

'Damn you, man, have you no weapon?'

Gregory shook his head. 'Wouldn't know how to use it even if I had, sir.'

Jones looked at Melford. The important thing was not to panic. He spoke slowly and calmly, 'Well, gentlemen, I have the loaded pistol, but I have only one shot and there are three of you so, a parley I think is necessary.' He paused. If they were to rush him, it would happen now, but no one moved. Slowly he

381

lowered his weapon. 'What's done is done, no need for any more to die. You have a man down and I have a man down and if anyone moves, my pistol will point at you, Señor Miranda. I think I will get a shot off and, at this distance, I cannot fail to hit my mark.' Jones paused to let the situation sink in. 'Come, gentlemen, let's say we're all losers and leave it at that. Bentley's business is done. Macleod is dead.' Miranda looked down at his dead friend then back at Jones. 'I dare say you're sorry, Señor, but you know it was necessary, as much so for you, I think, as for us.' Miranda bowed his head and Jones knew that his words had struck home. 'If this business comes out in full, your Venezuelan project is finished.' He turned again to Lord Melford, uncocked and lowered his pistol. If he was to die it would happen now. But nothing happened, all the men stood still. 'I can cover Bentley's death and I can see to our side of the matter. Come, Lord Melford, what do you say, bury them both here and go our separate ways,' he threw the pistol onto the grass by Macleod's body, 'or do I die? I freely admit the choice lies with you.'

Lord Melford looked at Miranda who stepped forward and stood looking down at Macleod's body.

'Sorry, old friend, I hoped to save you from this, but how could I do anything else?' He looked up to Lord Melford. 'It is as this man says, what is done is done. Now I must consider my cause. Let us leave those who have fallen, for them it is finished. We must go our separate ways.'

Lord Melford stepped forward, stooped down and pulled the stick-dagger from Macleod's chest and threw it at Jones's feet. Jones bent down awkwardly, picked it up and returned it to his stick and raised his hat.

'Good day, gentlemen, and goodbye.'

They watched as Jeremiah Jones, stick in hand, limped off into the trees and was gone.

Melford turned to Miranda. 'So, it's all finally finished.'

'But not as I had wanted, nor as I had planned.'

'You did your best. You knew Bentley would make a try for Macleod and made sure we'd be on hand. It was a risk, and it

382

should have worked but for Mr Jones. He showed admirable resource and was damnably quick for a cripple. I didn't expect that, nor the knife in his stick.'

'No, nor I. Well, as you say, it is over, finished.'

'Gregory will see to the bodies.' Lord Melford turned to Gregory who was standing with his arms by his side. 'Take them well into the trees, search them both and strip them of any identification, then bury them as best you can.'

Gregory stepped forward, took up Bentley's legs by the boots and began to drag him off into the trees. Melford put his hand inside his coat and drew out a folded letter and held it out.

'Here, Miranda, I suppose you might as well have this. I sent a man to Baton Rouge to warn Madame Macleod that her husband would soon be coming and she should make ready to travel. He brought this back. It was to be given to her husband.'

Miranda took the letter and opened it.

Dearest Jean,
How I have missed you and how slowly time passes without you. I was born in Baton Rouge and grew up here and have always thought of it as my home. But now I know that my home is with you, only with you. I write this in the hope that it may reach you by the hand of the one who brought me the news that you are coming. I do not know when you will read my poor words but God will help me. I know this for certain because God is good and has blessed me. Oh, Jean, how I wish I could say this to you myself, but I must say it even if only as words on paper. God has blessed me, Jean, he has blessed us both. I am with child. Our union has at last been blessed.
Your loving and devoted wife,
Marie.

Miranda re-folded the letter, stooped down on one knee and slipped it into Macleod's coat.

'Take it with you, old friend, and if there is a God and a heaven to reward honour and loyalty I know you will be there.'

Melford untied and mounted Macleod's horse. 'Come,

Miranda, we must be on our way.'

But instead of rising Miranda put his other knee to the ground, folded his hands and closed his eyes. Melford looked on impatiently as Miranda's lips moved silently. After a few moments he crossed himself and stood up, looking down at the body of his friend. 'Say a prayer for me wherever you are, Jean Marie, for I must go on. So long as I live, the cause never stops, deceit, lies nor even death can stand in the way of freedom.'

He went to his horse and mounted as Gregory came from the trees. Melford nodded to the body. 'See to it, Gregory and, when you've done, bring my horse with you.'

'Bring it where, m'lord?'

Melford turned to Miranda. 'Where? Do we head for Baton Rouge or New Orleans?'

'New Orleans. I must return to New York. There is work to be done.' Miranda turned his horse's head back the way they had come.

'And Macleod's wife?'

'Send her a message. Tell her that her husband died.'

'No more?'

'What more is there?'

'What more indeed?'

Vice-President Aaron Burr

General Wilkinson did indeed denounce Aaron Burr to Thomas Jefferson for plotting treason. President Jefferson, however, for reasons that historians have never been fully able to explain, did not have an arrest warrant issued for a full year. Burr learned of the warrant's existence in January 1807 by reading about it in a newspaper. He was arrested in February 1807 in Macintosh, Washington County, Alabama, and taken to Fort Stoddert. On August 3 Burr's trial began in Richmond, Virginia, presided over by Chief Justice of the United States John Marshall even though, when arraigned before a Grand Jury, the only physical evidence submitted against him had been a letter submitted by General Wilkinson and purported to have been written by Burr proposing to him the illegal and treasonous seizing of American lands in the Louisiana Territories. However, the letter was not in Burr's handwriting and, when questioned, Wilkinson claimed it was a copy which he had made himself from the original, which had been in cipher, having since been lost!

President Jefferson appeared to use all his considerable influence to gain a conviction against Burr yet strangely no credible witnesses came forward and the jury found Burr not guilty. He was discharged a free man. However, his career was finished and Burr left America. He was made welcome by the Government in England and lived in a house on Craven Street in London from 1808-12. After much travelling Burr returned to America and settled in the village of Port Richmond on Staten Island. He suffered a severe stroke in 1836 and died two years later, a forgotten man. He was buried near his father in Princeton, New Jersey.

Sebastián Francisco de Miranda Rodríguez

Miranda returned to New York and in 1806 set sail with Steuben Smith on Samuel Ogden's ship which Miranda had renamed the *Leander* in honour of his eldest son. In Haiti at

Jacmel he was joined by two more ships, the *Bee* and the *Bacchus* and raised on the *Leander*, for the first time, the Venezuelan flag which he himself had designed. However, the Spanish had received forewarning of the invasion and Miranda's small fleet was intercepted by Spanish warships. The *Bee* and the *Bacchus* were taken and with them Steuben Smith, but the *Leander* escaped. Miranda, ever the optimist, pressed on with his adventure. He landed his small force at the port of La Vela de Coro with what appeared to be the sole purpose of raising his new Venezuelan flag on Venezuelan soil for the first time. The force then moved inland and took possession of the town of Santa Anna de Coro itself. But such a small force had no possible chance of holding the town and Miranda withdrew and sailed to the British Caribbean to await reinforcements. They never came.

Miranda then returned to Britain where he was promised military support for a re-invasion of Venezuela. Unfortunately for him, Napoleon invaded Spain in 1808 and, from being Britain's enemy, Spain suddenly became an ally and the force assembled for the Venezuelan invasion under General Arthur Wellesley, the Duke of Wellington, was sent to fight in what became the Peninsula War. This sudden development of Spain becoming an ally rather than an enemy also put an end to Britain's Maitland Plan. Miranda's subsequent career was, to say the very least, spectacular but chequered. He was persuaded to return to Venezuela by, among others, Simón Bolívar and immersed himself in the political and military struggle for freedom both as a soldier and as a political writer. In the end he was handed over to the Royal Spanish Army by none other than Bolívar himself and died in prison at the Arsenal de La Carraca near Cadiz while awaiting trial. He was buried in a mass grave and no identification of his remains was ever possible. His legacy, however, remains. His name is engraved on the Arc de Triomphe in Paris and he is known throughout South America as one of the great leaders; the Liberators, whose efforts gained independence for the countries of that continent.

386

General James Wilkinson

Wilkinson was indeed removed from his positions as Governor of the Louisiana Territories and Commander-in-Chief of the New Orleans Army after complaints to the Government in Washington of his heavy-handed abuse of power. His almost comic performance at the arraignment of Aaron Burr caused various accusations to be brought against him and two Congressional enquiries were undertaken into his past activities. These enquiries led the United States President, by then James Madison, to order his court martial in 1811. Like everyone else in the tangled and muddied aftermath of the Aaron Burr conspiracy he was found not guilty. Wilkinson, however, had no intention of retiring into private life. He was nothing if not persistent and apparently still did not lack friends in high places who ensured him preferment. He was commissioned Major General in the British-American War of 1812 and led the American force which took Mobile but after two further disastrous campaigns he was relieved from active service and forced to face a military enquiry. Naturally he was cleared. In 1816 he published a book, *Memoirs of My Own Times*, his account of the various machinations which he said his enemies had deployed against him throughout his career. Sadly, his efforts to be remembered as a true American were frustrated by the Louisiana historian Charles Gayarré who found and published Wilkinson's correspondence with Esteban Rodríguez Miró who had been the Spanish Governor of Louisiana and had recruited Wilkinson as a Spanish spy. Known as Agent 13, after the Spanish cipher so named, Wilkinson had in 1778 sworn allegiance to the Spanish Crown, solely it seems, for personal gain. Wilkinson remained as an agent in the pay of Spain up until his death. No less a person that Theodore "Teddy" Roosevelt, who would become 26th President of the United States in 1901, wrote of him, *"in all our history, there has been no more despicable character."*

Colonel William Smith and Samuel Ogden

Both stood trial for violating the <u>Neutrality Act of 1794</u>. In his defence, Smith claimed he was acting with the support of President Jefferson and <u>Secretary of State</u> Madison. Both of these men refused to appear in court. In this trial Judge <u>William Patterson</u> made a landmark ruling that the President *"... cannot authorise any person to do what the law forbids ..."* which supposedly enshrined in US legislation that even the President is not above the law. Both Colonel Smith and Samuel Ogden were, needless to say, found not guilty and Smith went on to become a Federalist member of Congress.

Harman Blennerhasset

Blennerhasset and his niece/wife abandoned their island kingdom after it had been thoroughly ransacked and plundered by Virginia militiamen looking for weapons and other incriminating evidence of their involvement in the Burr Conspiracy. All that was found was a landing stage and empty warehousing. No charges were ever preferred. Blennerhasset tried his hand as a planter in Mississippi and as a lawyer in Montreal before returning temporarily to Ireland. He died in the Channel Island of Guernsey in 1831. His wife, during this time, displayed a hitherto undisclosed literary talent and published two successful books, *The Deserted Isle*, in 1822 and *The Widow of the Rock and Other Poems* in 1824.

Steuben Smith

This very fortunate young man escaped from his Spanish jail and somehow managed to return to New York. Such an amazing feat of derring-do was never explained, least of all by Steuben himself who, after the conclusion of his adventures with Miranda, retired into a private life of anonymity and obscurity.

Lord Melford

Lord Melford succeeded his brother Hector, who died childless one year after assuming the title, and became Fifth Earl. He retired from any active Government service and married the youngest daughter of the Earl of Harrowby. Though never holding any political office he was, through his father-in-law, an active promoter of electoral reform and the emancipation of slaves.

Jeremiah Jones

Jeremiah Jones returned to Washington and assumed temporary control of the Administrative Office of the Contingent Fund. He carried out to the letter Bentley's plan to minimise the damage arising from the Burr Conspiracy. No one involved was ever found guilty of anything, although almost all were charged and tried with something. So successful was Jones that today little is known, even in America, about the Burr conspiracy and the name of Vice President Aaron Burr, although numbered among the Founding Fathers of the United States, is all but forgotten.

Molly O'Hara

Also known as, Madame de Metz, Dolly Bawtry and Fanny Dashwood.
In her incarnation as Fanny Dashwood she lived on at Hocking's Landing. Being an educated woman, able to read, write, calculate and speak French and having a knowledge of science, philosophy and politics, all picked up in her youth in a Paris brothel from her aristocratic clients, she opened a school for young ladies. She was a determined woman and directed her considerable energies and efforts into seeing that the young girls of Hocking's Landing would not be regarded as second-

class citizens only fit for domesticity and motherhood. She became a tireless champion of women's equality of opportunity. Hocking's Landing was a growing place with social aspirations and their taking the radical step of allowing a quality education to some of their young womenfolk placed them firmly in the avant-garde of new radicalism. After three years she changed her name once more and for the last time when she married and became Mrs Thomas Dallyset. Mr Dallyset was a lawyer and had a prosperous practice up the Hocking River in Athens, the main city of Athens County. There she tirelessly worked to promote education and was considered to be one of the moving forces behind the development of the fledgling Ohio University. It is believed by many that she was, in fact, the person who first framed the words:

Religion, morality and knowledge being necessary to good government and the happiness of mankind, schools and the means of education shall forever be encouraged

which are now enshrined on the main college gateway. She died, four years after her husband, in 1865, aged eighty-two, admired and respected and considered by all who had known her to have been an outstanding example of true American womanhood.

Marie Macleod (widow)

Marie Macleod stayed on in Baton Rouge where she gave birth to a baby girl whom she had baptised Jeanne Marie Macleod. She sold up her husband's property in Boston and bought a comfortable house and two slaves, a young woman and her baby. The young woman became her maid-housekeeper and the baby her daughter's companion. She never, despite several proposals, re-married.

Secretary of State James Madison

Madison used the Contingent Fund for Foreign Intercourse widely during his term as Secretary of State to finance secret agents in the same manner as he had used Miranda and Macleod. In 1809 he succeeded Thomas Jefferson and became the fourth President of the United States.

President Thomas Jefferson

Jefferson saw himself in many ways as a father of the nation and was determined to ensure his place in history. Up to the present historians have generally subscribed to his own view of his abilities, achievements and stature as a statesman. What the future holds for his reputation remains to be seen. Perhaps it is as well to leave him with the words of his epitaph engraved on his tombstone which, of course, he wrote himself:

Here   Was   Buried   Thomas   Jefferson Author Of The Declaration Of American Independence Of The Statute Of Virginia For Religious Freedom And Father Of The University Of Virginia.

… as for the historical truth or otherwise of the version of events related in this work I can only offer the view of others who have shown themselves more worldly-wise in such matters than myself …

A great part of information obtained in war is contradictory, a still greater part is false, and by far the greatest part is of doubtful character. Clausewitz

One should not as a rule reveal one's secrets, since one does not know if and when one may need them again. Joséph Goebbels

"The only history that is worth a tinker's damn is the history we made today." Henry Ford

The Eagle Turns

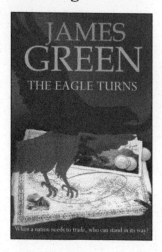

It is 1850 and America is deeply divided on the issue of slavery. When President Zachary Taylor dies suddenly it is left to his Vice President Millard Fillmore, a weaker man, to find ways to keep the North and the South apart.

In New York Irish immigrant Matthew O'Hanlon is fired from his job as a newspaperman on the Herald and finds work as Foreign Correspondent for the Associated Press in Panama City. There he is given accommodation with a Dr Couperin, his wife and beautiful daughter, Edith, but soon finds out that he has been living in a house of cards when it crashes down around him.

Set against the Gold Rush and the opening up of California and the Oregon Territories, at a time when America walked a fine and dangerous line, *The Eagle Turns* charts the course of history as America's Secret Services. And Matthew finds himself caught up with the secret agents protecting the country's commercial interests during the struggle for control of Panama's trade routes.

Never An Empire

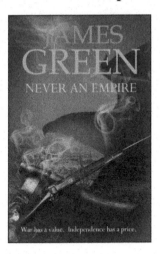

War has a value. Independence has a price.

1896. The Peace Treaty ending the Spanish-American War ceded Cuba, Porto Rico and the archipelago known as the Philippine Islands to the United States. America had become a colonial power! But the Philippines were already in a state of revolution against Spain and wish its defeat the insurgents declared independence.

America had to fight or withdraw. She chose to fight. The American forces were victorious but at a cost beyond human life. They met with force a subject people's aspiration for freedom and independence.

America finds itself at the beginning a new century as a colonial power and its Intelligence Services have to cope with a different kind of conflict …

For more information about
Accent Press titles
Please visit

www.accentpress.co.uk